DEADLY CATCH

The dead sailor floated toward the western shore of the bay and the beach of sharp stones and driftwood. Brine shrimp waited in the coastal shoals to feast.

The fisherman on the small boat dried in minutes under the high sun in a purple sky. His two companions stood around him and they examined the blue rag cut away from the body. Though badly faded, "THURSTON" was still clearly stencilled above the left breast pocket. Just above the boldface name was a stylized rendition of two small dolphins poised upon a wave. The fish faced each other like aviator's wings. The fishermen recognized the dolphin ensign instantly.

The blue shirt and the corpse floating toward shore were from a United States submarine.

INCIDENT IN MONA PASSAGE

DOUGLAS SAVAGE

AVON BOOKS ◆ NEW YORK

AVON BOOKS
A division of
The Hearst Corporation
1350 Avenue of the Americas
New York, New York 10019

Copyright © 1994 by Douglas Savage
Map by Lizbeth Nauta
Published by arrangement with Combined Books
Library of Congress Catalog Card Number: 93-46328
ISBN: 0-380-72485-5

First Avon Books Printing: April 1995

AVON TRADEMARK REG. U.S. PAT. OFF. AND IN OTHER COUNTRIES, MARCA REGISTRADA, HECHO EN U.S.A.

Printed in the U.S.A.

RA 10 9 8 7 6 5 4 3 2 1

For Joseph Anthony Vazzo,
who permits me to write
on company time

ACKNOWLEDGMENTS

The author gratefully acknowledges permission from the following manufacturers for their generous permission to use registered trade names, trade marks, or brand names:

Carl Zeiss, Inc., Thornwood, NY, by Irv Toplin; Gilson Medical Electronics, Inc., Middleton, WI, by Robert Gilson, President; Scanalytics/CSPI, Billerica, MA, by Joan Nicoll; Ambis Image Acquisition and Analysis, San Diego, CA, by John D. Cambon, President; Bio-Rad Laboratories, Inc., Hercules, CA, by Dr. Burton A. Zabin, Vice President; Meridian Instruments, Inc., Okemos, MI, by Carol L. Genee; and Rainin Instrument Company, Inc., Emeryville, CA, by Kenneth Rainin, President.

The Synthecell Corporation of Columbia, Maryland, provided valuable monographs and brochures on the latest techniques in genetic engineering.

Although the biological equipment from some of these companies was not pirated for this story, their technical brochures and abstracts did provide valuable insight for the author into genetic engineering science.

None of these manufacturers nor their products have been involved in the fictional events portrayed in this novel.

I gratefully acknowledge the generous patience and encouragement of Mr. Paul Dinas, Executive Editor, Pinnacle Books, New York.

This is a work of fiction. The author assumes full responsibility for offense taken by persons or microbes who might resemble the fictional characters in this novel. Certain public figures in the former Soviet Union and in the government of Cuba are mentioned by name.

Each state party to this Convention undertakes never in any circumstances to develop, produce, stockpile, or otherwise acquire or retain:

(1) Microbial or other biological agents, or toxins whatever their origin or method of production, of types and in quantities that have no justification for prophylactic, protective, or other peaceful purposes;

(2) Weapons, equipment or means of delivery designed to use such agents or toxins for hostile purposes or in armed conflict.

Convention on the Prohibition of the Development, Production and Stockpiling of Bacteriological (Biological) and Toxin Weapons and on their Destruction
Signed, Washington and Moscow, 10 April 1972
Ratified, United States Senate, 16 December 1974
Entered in force, 26 March 1975

———

Pursuant to Section 152 of the National Defense Authorization Act for Fiscal Year 1987, Public Law 99-661, I hereby certify with respect to the Bigeye Binary Chemical Bomb that:

(1) Production of the Bigeye Binary Chemical Bomb is in the national security interests of the United States; and,

(2) [T]he design, planning, and environmental requirements for production facilities have been satisfied.

I also certify that this Bigeye program is, in my considered judgment, vital to our national defense . . . [T]his and other actions to modernize our limited chemical retaliatory capability serve to deter the use of chemical weapons by our potential adversaries . . .

Ronald Reagan, President
19 January 1988
Presidential Determination 88-7
53 Federal Register 3845

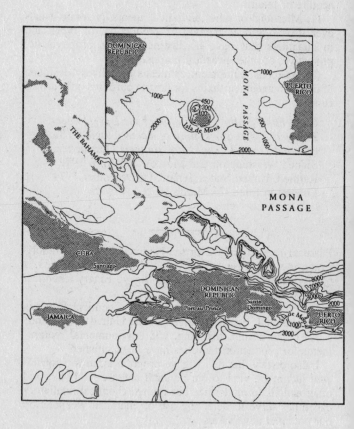

ONE

---

14 MARCH; 0200 UTC

BUDDY THURSTON'S head crushed like an eggshell filled with red foam.

When his skull collapsed in the black water, the air trapped inside his chest was forced from his body by the unspeakable pressure of the cool sea 800 feet beneath the surface. His small body was pressed from all sides by 360 pounds of force on each square inch of his shrinking cadaver. Sea water shot into his mouth, eye sockets, and rectum with a force three times greater than that of a standard fire-hose. The pressure compressed him like a garbage compactor.

But there were no bubbles in the puddle of red body juices. The intense water pressure instantly dissolved the globules of air before they could rise more than twenty feet above the hull of the black submarine.

With every molecule of gas inside Buddy Thurston absorbed by the dark sea, his twisted body slowly rolled end over end, hovering above the black hole of the Puerto Rico Trench: the deepest pit in the Atlantic Ocean, 100 miles northwest of Aguadilla, Puerto Rico. The trench extends the length of the island, running east and west. The seaman was suspended in the murky water 27,000 feet above the ocean floor and its dunes of talcum-fine silt off the island's northwest corner.

If permitted by the natural buoyancy of what little body fat he carried, he would settle to the bottom in an hour. The sea

1

at the bottom of the trench would press every inch of his body with six tons of water pressure. At that depth, pitch black and freezing cold, the microscopic sea organisms would not graze long on what was left of Buddy Thurston, Torpedoman First Class.

The old submarine *Sam Houston* had not even twitched when Buddy Thurston had spit himself out of the 21-inch wide torpedo tube. Since the retired missile boat had been refitted with substantial automatic systems at her last dry dock, torpedoman Thurston had stepped into the amidships torpedo room when it was momentarily deserted during a crew watch change. He had set the newly automated fire control system to secure the torpedo tube's compartment door and to open the outer door to the ocean fifteen seconds later.

It had been a tight fit even for a sailor as small as Benjamin Thurston. Buddy lay in the darkly moist, 21-foot long pipe where he waited for the tube to automatically flood before the outer door opened. By the time the door slid back and the compressed air pushed him into the black ocean, he was already dead with a strange and terrifying smile frozen onto his pale face.

Everyone loved Buddy Thurston. Since he had been selected for the Navy's submarine basic training after high school six years earlier, he had been the kind of young man whom other grown men could love without shame. Although his enlistment contract had read "Benjamin Waldon Thurston," he had been called Buddy since boyhood when it had become clear that he would never grow taller than five feet and two inches. "You're not long enough to be a Benjamin," his older sister had warmly teased him. So Buddy it became and Buddy it stayed through basic, through nuclear power school, and during his special posting on the highly secret mission of the old boat, *Sam Houston*.

"Oh, God!" the Command Chief Petty Officer groaned as if wounded deeply. "Not Buddy, too." The noncommissioned officer served as Chief of the Boat, COB.

"I'm sorry, Chief," Executive Officer Phillip Perlmutter sighed.

"The last man I would have expected," Chief Robert Wilcox said with his face in his hard hands. American submarines are the only fleet vessels which carry on the tradition of posting a Chief of the Boat. The COB is essentially "captain" of a sub's enlisted men. He serves as the real captain's liaison between the officers and the seamen. The administrative provisions of the thick manual, *Submarine Standard Organization and Regulations of the Navy* (SSORN for short), officially ranks the ship's executive officer as the captain's go-between with the men. But a skillful and experienced XO knows to trust the instincts of his COB.

"The old man wants us in the wardroom immediately, Chief." The XO sounded as pained as Chief Wilcox.

"Aye aye, Sir."

Chief Wilcox led the way through the old sub's narrow passageways. Where clumps of seamen whispered about Buddy's suicide, the chief shouted "Gang way!" to carve a path for the officer. The XO followed the chief. No one saluted the executive officer, a lieutenant commander, as he passed. Certain formalities are dispensed with when under way. "Evening, Sir," was the only deference he heard.

The two men squeezed through the spaces of *Sam Houston*, United States submarine number SSN-609. Around them the vessel was the sterile quiet of a nuclear submarine on war patrol.

Well behind the executive officer and his chief, the Westinghouse S5W pressurized-water nuclear reactor powered the ship without a sound. Only the coolant water pumps of the reactor hummed softly, well insulated from listening posts on board an oceanful of Russian (formerly Soviet) submarines on their own permanent war patrol.

Sam Houston had been born an *Ethan Allen* class, nuclear ballistic missile submarine in February 1961. The class had been composed of five ships, each weighing 7,000 tons when running on the surface. Submerged, they carried another 880 tons of water in their ballast tanks.

Four hundred feet long and 33 feet thick, *Sam Houston* cruised silently and slowly in lazy circles over the 200-mile long canyon in the Atlantic Ocean called the Puerto Rico Trench. She cruised the length of the gorge for two days, then turned back across its ten-mile width to retrace her path along the opposite rim. During the first half of her 70-day cruise, the submarine had circled the trench eight times.

Although her 15,000 shaft horsepower, steam turbine could drive the sub through the deep water at 30 knots, she plied the trench's upper limits making only 4 knots: the speed of a normal walk. That was all the speed required to keep enough water flowing over her tail planes and over the stubby, diving plane "wings" which jutted from her black sail—called the conning tower in the old days. These control surfaces were steered by the planesman and the helmsman to keep the ship on an even keel.

The *Ethan Allen* boats were the country's first submarines specifically designed from scratch to carry intercontinental ballistic missiles. *Sam Houston's* Polaris A-3 missiles had been removed forever in 1980 when the *Ethan Allens* were all converted to hunter-killer subs deployed to rout out Soviet missile submarines. Of the five boats converted, four were already on the scrap heap: *Ethan Allen* decommissioned in 1982, *Thomas Edison* decommissioned in 1984, *Thomas Jefferson* removed from service in 1985, and *John Marshall* decommissioned in July 1992. *Sam Houston* was placed on the Navy's "reserve, in commission" list in March 1991: the first step toward the Bremerton, Washington, scrap heap.

When the naval architects had pulled *Sam Houston's* missiles, they poured concrete down the empty silos to provide enough weight to make up for the sixteen missing rockets.

Now the three-deck-high missile tubes were dark and empty. Tense and youthful sailors once clustered at launch control consoles amid the thick missile tubes known as the "tree farm" among submariners (never pronounced "submare*eeners*"). In the black water 100 miles north of Puerto Rico, 800 feet beneath the warm tropical air, *Sam Houston's* tree farm was now surrounded by three decks of laboratory work stations. Electron microscopes and protein-growing stills had replaced nuclear-tipped missiles in the old boat's midsection. Her normal complement of 142 officers and men were replaced by highly automated systems which could be managed by a skeleton crew of one-third the usual company.

Sam Houston was a floating laboratory, invisible under 800 feet of brine. To the United States Naval Biosciences Research Laboratory at Oakland, California, and to the Army's Medical Research Institute of Infectious Diseases at Fort Detrick, Maryland, *Sam Houston* was known in top secret documents as the Dugway Wet Project—referring to the Army's Dugway Proving Ground test site for chemical and biological weapons in the Utah desert.

But to the 55 officers and men huddled inside the black hull of HY-80 steel, *Sam Houston* had been "The Bug Boat" since the night she had slipped silently out of her last out-fitting at the Newport News Shipyard. The crewmen were all handpicked and specially trained to live and work with biological toxins. Their submarine incentive pay reflected the added risk which goes with every cruise beneath the sea.

Chief Wilcox and the executive officer were not thinking about their secret mission when they climbed the companion-way leading through the mid-deck ceiling (the "overhead" to seamen) into the upper deck's control room. Their friend was floating outside where no sunshine had ever penetrated and where one-celled sea protozoa were already swimming into the dead man's nostrils to feed. As they walked grimly through the ship's nerve center forward to the wardroom, they thought of Buddy Thurston, lost at sea.

In the wardroom, usually off limits to all but officers, XO Perlmutter, Chief Wilcox, Quartermaster Bill Rogers, and Lieutenant Stan Shaffer helped themselves to black, government-issue coffee. The lieutenant was a physician and served *Sam Houston* as GMO: General Medical Officer. The four men rose silently when Captain Kurt Milhaus stepped into the wardroom. On the captain's khaki, open-necked collar was the silver oak leaf of a commander.

"Be seated, gentlemen," Commander Milhaus said softly as he filled his own coffee mug. He closed the door to the passageway so the five men could speak privately at the ward-room's single, long table. Half a dozen chairs were empty.

"Well, Chief?" the captain asked without wasting time with small talk.

"I know what you know, Captain. Torpedoman Thurston went out the tube during the two minutes when the com-partment was empty. Our preliminary search of his things has turned up nothing. No note left behind, so far. I spoke to the two men who had breakfast with him this morning. They confirm that Thurston was showing no sign of stress or depression. Everyone liked the boy. You know that, Sir."

"Yes, Chief. I liked him too. But this is the second death in ten days. Washington is likely to call us in after this one. At least it's the first suicide."

The first fatality had been an accidental electrocution in the engineering compartment.

The captain seemed as distraught by the prospect of going home as he did about Buddy Thurston decomposing on his way to the icy bottom.

"Doc?"

The bearded physician shook his head.

"Nothing, Captain. His file is clean. I saw him for his weekly blood work four days ago. There was simply nothing."

The hazardous chemicals and biological toxins on board the submarine required weekly consultations for the crew in Dr. Shaffer's examination room.

"Damn it anyway!" Commander Milhaus sighed. He fumbled with a thick manual on the formica tabletop. "I wrote this battle bill myself. Every man on this boat was screened and rescreened for his billet. Buddy was as sane as any member of this crew."

Every ship of the line carries a battle bill which sets out job descriptions and assignments for the vessel. The battle bill contents for each class of warship in the Navy is dictated by NWIP (Naval Warfare Information Publication) 50-1, *Battle Control*.

"Sorry, Captain. But the medical file is incomplete for the moment. Unlike the accident last week, I have no body for an autopsy. I can only guess right now." The GMO appeared uncomfortable. Commander Milhaus liked answers.

"What about noise, Pappy?"

Executive Officer Phillip Abraham Perlmutter's initials had made him Pappy since the academy.

"I spoke briefly with sonar on the way up here. The towed array heard nothing when the outer door opened."

Sam Houston's underwater sound detection system carried the latest, towed array listening device refitted to the old boat before she had sailed. The BQQ-5 passive towed array dragged a 2,624-foot long cable behind the submarine when submerged. The cable trailed out of a 350-foot long tubular housing mounted on the outside of the ship's starboard side. Thirty-two hydrophones strung along the length of the cable listened to the sea far enough behind the ship to be free from background noise generated by *Sam Houston*. The BQQ-5 could pick up the telltale drumming of Russian submarines' propellers from 50 miles. The passive sonar listened for very low frequency, unnatural noises in the 1 kilohertz spectrum.

"The blue room says no one heard Buddy leave the boat, Captain."

Sonar compartments are bathed in blue lights to soften the glare from radar-like screens where sonar men hunch at consoles during ten-hour duty days.

"Well," Commander Milhaus said dryly, "let's talk about security. What about it, QMC?"

The Chief Quartermaster unrolled a large chart onto the tabletop.

"Captain," Quartermaster Rogers said as he leaned over his chart, "Torpedoman Thurston went out at 800 feet. I doubt if he would float all the way to the surface, but the doc can answer that one. Looking here at the currents, this time of year the current runs westward across Mona Passage. The March current runs northwestward, north of the Dominican Republic at only 7/10 knot. We're 360 nautical miles east of Cuba out here. I hesitate to state the sadly obvious, but Buddy would hardly be recognizable after some 400 hours in that water. What is that? Sixteen, seventeen days?"

"Doc?"

"I think the body will sink, Captain. He was small and light. Not very much reserve buoyancy. The initial pressure pulse down here would certainly force any residual air from the body in a hurry." The little company grimaced. The medical officer struggled to maintain his clinical detachment.

"All right. Phil? Send the damn message to Washington. We have no choice." The captain looked at his watch which read 2:30 in the morning, Coordinated Universal Time (UTC), formerly called Greenwich Mean Time. That put the sea above in evening darkness at 10:30 pm, local Atlantic Time. "Our feather should be secure this time of night. We'll bring her to periscope depth for a burst when crypto is ready. After you send, take her down to 400 feet in case anyone calls us with an answer."

Submarines communicate by high frequency radio signals broadcast from an antenna secured to the attack periscope on the sail. The antenna must poke through the surface to transmit and receive complex or voice signals. The metal tube cutting through the nighttime sea generates a "feather" of white foam.

"Very good, Sir," the XO nodded.

Commander Milhaus looked at the physician.

"Doc, let me know instantly if you find anything. Wake me if you need to."

"Aye, Sir."

The meeting adjourned and the empty coffee cups were left in the sink for the mess management detail.

From the wardroom, Executive Officer Perlmutter walked back through the dimly lighted control room, climbed down the companionway in the deck hole, called a hatchway, and then walked back forward toward the mid-deck sleeping compartments. The XO entered the space known as the rackroom where he stopped beside one of the triple-decker bunks. He touched a sleeping man on the shoulder. The sailor opened one sleepy eye without a start. Beneath the sea, no one sleeps too soundly.

"Mister Perlmutter," the sailor said softly with a dry mouth.

"Sorry, Steve. I need you in the radio room."

"Okay, Sir."

Steven Bently, Master Chief Cryptologic Technician (CTACM), jumped down from his middle bunk. He slept in his denim trousers and blue shirt. The XO handed the sleepy man a cup of coffee brought down from the wardroom.

"Thanks, Sir."

As the two men walked rearward toward the ship's midsection, the deck angle tilted very slightly down toward the stern as the ship's single propeller pushed the sub upward so the periscope could break the surface in the dark. Compressed air blew small amounts of water from the ship's small trim tanks. Her main ballast tanks remained flooded with nearly 800 tons of sea water. Unlike World War II fleet submarines which carried their water ballast along the outside of the inner pressure hull, modern boats have ballast tanks inside the ship's rounded nose and in the rearmost compartment just ahead of the propeller. The old subs had double hulls with the ballast in between; modern boats have but one hull with the men on one side and the black ocean on the other.

In the radio compartment, the XO and Chief Bently were met by the ship's CMS, Communications Material Security Custodian, and the Top Secret Control Officer. The CMS man and the control officer are never permitted to be the same seaman.

"Radio room," a loudspeaker crackled, "periscope depth."

"Very good," the XO responded. He scratched out a message in plain English. The ship's cryptographer hunched over his code books to translate the words into unintelligible gibberish.

On the radio room bookshelf was the manual *Department of the Navy Security Manual for Classified Information*, (OPNAVINST 5510.16). The code books were kept in a safe for which the Communications Material Security Custodian held the key.

Before the antenna broke the nighttime surf, the ship's surface search radar mast poked through to scan for nosy ships in the area. The sea was deserted between the sleeping islands of the Dominican Republic to the southwest and Puerto Rico to the southeast.

When the dispatch was drafted in code, the radioman punched the message into the radio room's computer. The computer squeezed the words into a series of computer codes. Then the "compressed" message was fired through the antenna on the attack periscope in a burst of energy beamed upward into a starlit, Caribbean sky. The beam was sucked into a military communications satellite hovering 23,000 miles above the Equator. The satellite then relayed the news of a sailor's death down to the Navy's Communication Area Master Station, Special Communications Division, Atlantic. From there, the encrypted message went through channels until it landed on another cryptographer's desk at the Naval Intelligence Command. There, the dispatch was translated back into the military jargon understood only by men with stripes on their blue sleeves and ribbons on their chests.

The decoded message required fifteen minutes to transit 46,000 miles up and back from space, be transcribed, be wrapped in a confidential file folder and be hand-delivered to the crypto officer of the watch at the Office of Naval Operations, the Pentagon. The folder was handed to a captain at 10:00 pm, Eastern Time. The captain relayed the file to a door marked "N-89." He took the file inside to the office of the Vice Chief of Naval Operations, Special Programs.

The officer on the night watch studied the cryptic, freshly translated message. His eyes read:

CD. CD. SSN-609. 0314/0245. CASREP. TM1 THURSTON
KNA/SIW. WLRMNSN UFN. ADV NDVECC. AI. EOM.

The officer doing time at his Pentagon shore billet mentally reduced the navyspeak cable into English: "Confidential document. Confidential document. From Submarine SSN-609, *Sam Houston*. March 14th; time, 2:45 am, Greenwich (UTC). Casualty report: Torpedoman's Mate, 1st class, Thurston killed, not by enemy action but by self-inflicted wound. Will remain on station until further notice. Advise Naval Disease, Vector, Ecology, and Control Center. Awaiting instructions. End of message."

Both officers endorsed the message logbook.

"Thank you, Sir," the watch officer said as he rose. He did not salute as he stood at attention. The lieutenant commander on watch could not salute without his hat on. "I think I had better alert the DCNO."

The captain nodded. As the senior officer went through the door, the watch officer was already on the telephone to the Deputy Chief of Naval Operations.

"Good evening, Sir. Hope I didn't wake you . . . Message from six-oh-nine, Sir."

The officers knew that the phone line was scrambled and secure between the DC's home in Alexandria, Virginia, and the Pentagon.

"Better come down, Sir . . . Yes, Admiral. I believe so."

Buddy Thurston had now been in the water for an hour.

Seamen had crawled on their hands and knees in the torpedo compartment for two hours. They all knew that Buddy Thurston had killed himself there not quite three hours earlier. They were told to look for anything.

Unlike prior generations of submarines, the forward torpedo room of all current United States boats is not actually in the ship's foremost bow. The massive sonar dome now takes up the entire front end of American subs. Just behind the sonar sphere is the 30-foot high, forward ballast tank. The manned compartments are then further aft of the forward water tanks.

The single torpedo room on *Sam Houston*, like all American submarines, is actually amidships: in the first third of the ship but well behind the bow area. The torpedo tubes are canted outward such that the 21-foot long, Mark 48 torpedos are fired slightly sideways rather than straight ahead. Once in the water, the "fish" steer past the bow and speed toward their targets: not surface ships, but other submarines.

Four seamen examined every inch of the torpedo compartment. They did not know what they were searching for. They only knew that they would know it if they found it.

"Shit!" a youthful seaman rasped. His excited voice was subdued in the space filled with torpedoes and harsh, fluorescent lighting. No one shouts in the undersea world where the enemy is always listening. "Call the doc!"

A call over the intercom brought the physician from his upper deck, forward berth in the officers' quarters. He had nearly broken his ankle when he careened through the upper deck control room down through the hatchway carved in the deck and down through another hole in the mid-deck. The torpedo compartment is on the lowest deck, Deck Three.

"Well done," the breathless lieutenant said to the seaman. "Good head not to touch it."

Dr. Shaffer took a clear plastic bag and tweezers from his pocket. Kneeling, he steered the tweezers toward their small target. Working quickly, the physician picked up two purple lumps which he stuffed into the plastic bag.

"BL-2," the lieutenant ordered, handing the find to a seaman.

"Aye, Sir," the sailor said as he crouched through the compartment's watertight doorway. He headed aft and up two decks to the first deck, behind the control center. He hurried to the old, cemented-up missile room. He was trained to stop at the missile compartment's doorway and to call inside through the intercom. The closed hatch had a sign posted which read "BL-2: Biological Containment Facility."

A technician in white coat opened the hatchway and took the plastic envelope from the breathless seaman. The man in white wore rubber gloves when he held the plastic up to the light fixture in the overhead.

The technician and the seaman stared silently at two swollen fingertips inside a glassine packet.

"Damn Navy!" Paul Knuteson mumbled as he climbed out of his warm bed beside his warmly round and pregnant wife. The air was filled with the squeal of pigs and the cackle of roosters. "Damn Navy!" He threw a robe over his long woolies.

Standing on his front porch, Paul Knuteson looked up into a brilliantly star-filled sky. The barnyard was alive in the middle of the night. The farmer looked northward to the distant Upper Peninsula of Michigan. The mid-March air was still bitter. Paul Knuteson satisfied himself that coyotes were not in the henhouse. He had been right from the first: his animals had felt the U.S. Navy's top secret radio beacon making a midnight broadcast around the world.

The naval beacon at Sawyer Air Force Base in Upper Michigan contains a buried antenna at least 125 miles long. Through it, the Navy sent out radio messages over the extremely low frequency radio band to American submarines. The ELF broadcast is the only nonlaser beacon which can penetrate the sea down to 400 feet. Since the ELF beacon is horribly slow, it takes 12 minutes to beep out a single letter of the alphabet. At this low frequency, the powerful radio waves are well over 2,000 miles long from electromagnetic crest to crest. The long waves can wrap around the Earth for 10,000 miles. Painfully slow at data transmission, all it does is alert submerged subs to come up to receive their real, electronic mail. The submariners call the beam a bell ringer.

"Sorry, Captain," the junior officer said softly when he entered the captain's darkened cabin.

The captain slept at 2:00 in the morning, local time, 150 miles northwest of San Juan, Puerto Rico, and 400 feet under water.

"They've rung the doorbell, Sir."

"Thank you, Mister. I'll be on the bridge in five. Have the XO take her up to periscope depth."

"Aye aye, Sir."

Captain Milhaus quickly dressed and arrived in the radio compartment within four minutes. The ship was already on the way up. She stopped just beneath the moonlit Caribbean.

The men waited impatiently until the control room called to confirm periscope depth. Instantly, the radioman sent a burst message of compressed code up to the military satellite far overhead. Minute bursts of radio energy at super-high frequencies criss-crossed the starlit sky. The radioman's computer translated the incoming message which came out in hardcopy on a teleprinter. He handed the fresh dispatch to his captain.

"Whatchagot?" the CO inquired over steaming coffee. His weary mind read the military acronyms and shorthand.

CONF. CONF. DCNO. 0314/0555. SSN-609. CARBASORD.
CHNAVRSCH ASGG SSN-609 NRLREP. TTI 10. NRLREP
SUNO. ADSTADIS. EOM.

"Message, Captain?" the executive office asked as he entered the compartment. Captain Milhaus handed the dispatch to Lt. Commander Perlmutter.

"Seems we can stay put, Pappy. At least for a while."

The XO turned the dispatch over in his sleepy mind. "Confidential. Confidential. Deputy Chief of Naval Operations, 5:55 am, Greenwich time (55 minutes past midnight, Washington time) March 14. To *Sam Houston*: Carry out remainder of basic orders. Chief of Naval Research is assigning to *Sam Houston* a Naval Research Laboratory representative. Time to intercept, ten hours. NRL representative is not submarine qualified. Advise your status or disposition. End of message."

"Just what we need, Captain. A skimmer!"

To submariners, a real seaman lives under the dark ocean. Lesser men are condemned to spend their miserable days on the surface as lowly "skimmers."

"Better than having to go home with the mission unfinished, Pappy."

"Suppose so, Captain."

"Captain Milhaus?" the intercom crackled in the radio compartment.

"Here," the captain replied, pressing the transmitter button.

"Doctor Shaffer in BL-2, Sir. Could you come back here, please?"

"On my way," the captain acknowledged.

From the after section of the upper deck control room, Commander Milhaus stooped through the bulkhead opening toward the upper deck's top third of the abandoned missile silos. Lieutenant Shaffer waited for the captain outside the missile room.

"Come on in, Sir."

The captain followed the physician into the laboratory which had once been a missile launch pad.

The upper deck contained the first of three levels of laboratories. The BL-2 lab was the least stringent level of biological containment. The middle deck held the BL-3 lab, and the lower deck was BL-4 with the maximum biological protection from the ship's secret cargo.

"Here, Sir."

"Did he lose his fingers when the torpedo inner door closed, Doc?"

"Don't think so, Captain."

Dr. Shaffer pointed toward a bank of microscopes of all sizes and shapes. Ten technicians were hunched over the instruments around the clock.

The physician guided Commander Milhaus' darkly lined eyes to the twin eyepieces of a Unitron LWZ-UNI-39 stereo microscope. On the base of the instrument was a pickled fingertip smelling of formalin.

"Sorry, Captain. Can't help the smell. We just fixed it in preservative. Better take a look."

Kurt Milhaus blinked into the scope. His right hand found the focusing knob and he zoomed up and down the tip of bone fragment which protruded from the shrinking tissue of Buddy Thurston's fingertip.

"Do you see it, Sir?"

The captain squinted.

"All I see are stripes or grooves of some kind running through the bone. The torpedo tube hatch didn't slice that?"

"No, Captain. Those are tooth marks. I cross-checked the impressions with Buddy's dental records." The physician sounded gravely subdued. "The other fingertip is identical."

Captain Milhaus straightened his back at the laboratory table. He whispered with the physician out of earshot of the other technicians.

"Buddy chewed his own fingers off, Captain. I won't have the quantitative analysis on the blood finished until morning. But from what I see on the bones . . ."

The captain frowned and waited for the tired physician to finish his thought.

"Buddy was infected, Captain."

TWO

RUIS ESTOBAN Vicente loved the game. The Cuban airmen called it "running the banks" when they flew low from eastern Cuba toward Puerto Rico. They flew 50 miles north of the large island called Hispaniola with Haiti on the western half and the Dominican Republic on the east side. The channel is 90 miles wide between the great island and its northern neighbors, the Caicos Islands claimed by the United States.

Playing the game of running the banks required help from Cuba's neighbors and its enemies. The pilots of the patrol aircraft and occasional helicopters would navigate by the radio beacons in the Dominican Republic and the Caicos. In daylight, the pilots would try to spot the changing patterns of the ocean waves where deep water washed onto the shallow sand bars of the great banks in the sea. Thirty miles southeast of Grand Turk Island just east of the Caicos was the Mouchoir Bank where the mile-deep water lapped up to sand plateaus only 90 feet deep. When the sky was just right, the brilliant blue of deep water turned gray over the sand bar as if a dirty line had been drawn across the face of the sea.

Twenty-five miles further east, the deep water shallowed out again above the Silver Bank where the sand was only 30 feet beneath the surface along the northeastern coastline

16

of the Dominican Republic. Then the ocean floor plunged down 2 1/2 miles before rising steeply to the last sand bar, the Navidad Bank 30 miles east of Silver Bank. The water over Navidad was only 40 feet deep. From there, the sea bottom plummetted out of sight 28,000 feet down into the Puerto Rico Trench. From the air, the banks looked like dirty blotches on the blue sea.

The game appealed to Captain Estoban (he dropped his mother's maiden name, Vicente, in formal communications according to the Spanish custom). The scout plane had left the Cuban air base at Moa on the island's northeastern tip just over an hour ago. The 5,900-foot concrete runway was also used by civilian aircraft. The runway ended at the coral shoals of Punta Cabanas. The five-year-old Harbin SH-5 made 300 knots only 1,000 feet above the nighttime sea. Outside the copilot's window on the right of the cockpit and facing south, the airmen could just make out the flashing maritime beacon at Viejo Frances on the northern coastline of the Dominican Republic near the town of Abreu. They looked southeast but could not yet see the flasher on the island's easternmost tip at Cabo Engano near the large civilian airport at Punta Cana.

The four Harbin WJ-5A-1 turboprop engines droned loudly in the headphones of the eight Cubans who manned the patrol plane. A 1988 gift to Cuba from the People's Republic of China, the propjet was on antisubmarine patrol in the middle of a Caribbean night. The four engines, each cranking out 3,000 horsepower, dragged 5 tons of airplane eastward. She could land either on land or in the water with her boatlike hull.

From the tail of the graceful amphibian, a 10-foot long stinger extended into the salty night. The long boom housed the MAD, magnetic anomaly detector. The MAD sensors scanned the ocean surface for the magnetic signature of submarines. The heat of welding and the hammering of rivets during sub construction magnetize the metal being worked. All boats must undergo periodic degaussing to neutralize this built-in, permanent, magnetic field. A submarine also creates a magnetic disturbance called its induced field. When the dense metal hulks of steel boats cross the Earth's lines of magnetic field, the submarine acts like a submerged iron nail passing between the prongs of a toy horseshoe magnet. The MAD probe can sense the weak electrical pulse given off as the planet's magnetic field is tickled by the sub disturbing the Earth's natural magnetism.

The Chinese Harbin with her Cuban crew navigated off the omnidirectional radio beacons, the VOR, broadcasting into the night from Grand Turk International Airport to the northwest and the VOR at Puerto Plata International due south on the Dominican Republic coastline. The copilot's omni was tuned to 110.6 megahertz, listening for the Morse code identifier of the VOR at Mayaguez, Puerto Rico. But he heard only static from 150 miles away from the island's western point.

"Anything yet?" Estoban asked sleepily at 2:00 in the morning, local Atlantic time, 0600 UTC.

The copilot fiddled with his squelch button to tune out the static. The game of running the banks was simply not complete without using the Americans' own radio beacon on Puerto Rico.

"Not yet, Comrade Capitan. Shouldn't be long."

"Keep trying, Guillermo."

The Harbin could approach Puerto Rico no closer than the island's circular FIR which surrounded the island to a 90-nautical-mile radius from the center. Entering the island's Flight Information Region would violate United States airspace, something The Game discouraged.

"ESM to the captain," the intercom headphones crackled.

"Go ahead, Electronic Support Measures," Captain Estoban radioed to the airmen behind the cockpit bulkhead.

"Sir, I had something painting on the MAD, just for a second."

"Did you lose it?"

"Yes, Capitan. The contact was firm, but only for maybe ten seconds."

"Okay, Roberto. We'll do one sweep before we go home. Let me know."

"Yes, Sir."

Ruis Estoban banked the Chinese aircraft into a gentle turn. The Harbin executed a two-minute, standard-rate turn 1,000 feet above the black water of Mona Passage, the 75-mile stretch of sea between Puerto Rico and the Dominican Republic. At that altitude, the starlit horizon was 42 statute miles away in all directions. The Cubans circled 35 miles northeast of the civil Punta Cana Airport. The copilot tuned in 118.8

on the communications radio to listen for the Punta Cana, Dominican Republic, control tower. The silence on the frequency at 2:10 in the morning local time confirmed that the airport did not know that a Cuban aircraft was making a wide circuit of the sky near the horizon. The Cubans knew that Punta Cana Airport did not have radar facilities, so the aircraft was safe from observation.

"Anything yet on the MAD?" Captain Estoban asked anxiously. Although the Dominican airport was blind in the dark, the pilot knew that the civilian field at San Juan, Puerto Rico, had powerful radar searching for aircraft traffic throughout the island's airspace. The Harbin so low over the water was still 30 miles too far out at sea to paint on the American air traffic control radar. But being so close made Estoban impatient. On Puerto Rico's eastern coast, the American naval air station at Roosevelt Roads was 175 miles away. The Americans could launch fighter planes only ten flying minutes away at 1 1/2 times the speed of sound.

"There it is again, Capitan! And gone again. Probably just a sunken wreck, Sir." Mona Passage was treacherous water, full of sunken ships going back to 16th century Spanish galleons filled with Montezuma's gold.

"Okay. We can look at the hardcopy when we get back."

"Bingo!" the copilot interrupted. He flipped a switch which put one of the three navigation radios into the command pilot's headphones. The headset filled with Morse Code, "dash-dot-dotdot/dash-dash-dot-dash/dash-dot." The code was the identifier for the VOR beacon out of the Borinquen VORTAC navigation transmitter at Aguadilla, Puerto Rico.

"Now you're happy, eh Guillermo?" Captain Estoban laughed. "Now we can go home. A good game tonight."

The copilot adjusted the navigation receiver until the vertical needle was centered on the VOR dial. He would use the American radio to steer the Harbin northwestward, up over the Dominican Republic, back over the nighttime sand banks, and back to Cuba an hour away.

The patrol plane left Mona Passage behind at 2:30 local Atlantic time.

Five minutes after the tired Cuban pilots disappeared homeward bound over the eastern horizon, the surface-search radar antenna of *Sam Houston* erupted from the pitch black sea.

Within five minutes, the sub had received its message from the Pentagon by way of a buried antenna in the Michigan wilderness.

An hour later, at 7:30 in the morning UTC (3:30 on *Sam Houston* and 2:30 in Cuba), the Harbin subchaser touched down at the Moa airport which civilians shared with the People's Air Force.

By 4:00 in the morning, *Sam Houston* time, Buddy Thurston had been soaking up sea water for six hours. The Caribbean sun was still an hour further east when the drowned seaman bobbed heavily to the surface. The bacteria inside his decomposing intestines had been busy generating microscopic gas bubbles as they did their silent work.

Wearing its United States Air Force colors as a T-39, the Sabreliner-40 cruised at 35,000 feet making 400 knots over the sparkling Atlantic. The small, corporate class jet had been over open water for nearly two hours. Seven miles high, the Sabre-40 had been in broad daylight between Jacksonville Naval Air Station, Florida, and Puerto Rico for twenty minutes before the sun had touched the sea below.

For most of the 780 nautical miles between Florida and the island, Lt. Commander Jessica Dugan had dozed. The Navy physician had been wakened from a sound sleep shortly after midnight with instructions to report to Naval Operations, the Pentagon. She had combed her hair in the rearview mirror from the back seat of the car sent over by the Deputy Chief. In her late thirties, the unmarried officer's tired face was rapidly closing in on middle age. Now fine lines around her eyes and mouth tended to be permanent.

Half asleep, she remembered her brief meeting at the midnight Pentagon.

"A sub?" Dr. Dugan gasped at 1:00 in the morning, Washington time. "You can't be serious."

"We wanted Christopher Kostiuk," the Deputy Chief of Naval Operations confessed. "But Captain Kostiuk is stuck in Oakland growing something nasty in his test tubes, I'm sure. You were lucky enough to be in D.C. for the Agent Orange conference. So you're nominated," the admiral had smiled.

The DCNO liked Jessie Dugan. She was respected, as regular Navy as any woman could be, a Navy brat by birth, and a brilliant physician. And she was not hopelessly unattractive. The Chief tried not to smile in the middle of a damp Washington night when he noticed that Dr. Dugan did not have a mustache. Most female physicians have whiskers, he thought.

"I can only tell you that *Sam Houston* is a research boat. You will be briefed on the island. It is up your alley. I can't say more. As for the billet, Commander, you are an officer and virtually every man on board 609 is an officer or noncom. The boat is mostly automated now with one-third of her normal complement. The crew will accept you as an officer. I have every confidence, Jessie."

"Well, Admiral, were it not for my fear of water and my claustrophobia, I would thank you for locking me up on a ship with 55 men who have been underwater for six weeks." The medic had known the DCNO since her billet at Bethesda Naval Hospital three years earlier.

"Thank me later, Jessie." The Deputy Chief was not smiling.

"I just wish you would tell me why a secret research submarine should suddenly need a predictive ecologist. I haven't seen a real patient in ten years, you know."

"I can only repeat that we have a potential, although highly unlikely, infectious disease situation in *Sam Houston*. We need to rule that out. Your credentials are perfect."

Not until the admiral had escorted Dr. Dugan to the door did she summon the nerve to look him in the eye with one final question.

"Is 609 The Bug Boat, Admiral? I've heard rumors for a year."

"Six-oh-nine is your next billet, Commander. Smooth sailing to you, Doctor."

The physician smiled wearily into the small, triangular window of the Sabre-40. The sunrise was spectacular over open water northwest of Puerto Rico. She wore a flightsuit instead of her work uniform. The brilliantly orange sunshine on her cheeks and pale eyes washed out some of the hardness in her face.

The Sabre-40 crossed the island's northeastern coastline three miles high over San Juan. Thirty miles and ten minutes later, the T-39 banked left over the small civilian airport at Humacao. Descending toward the northeast over Puerto Rico's east coast, the military jet set up a long final approach under a purple dawn sky for runway seven at the Roosevelt Roads Naval Air Station. The wheels squeaked onto the 11,000 feet of concrete too gently for Lt. Commander Dugan to feel the ground. Navy pilots may be aviators, she thought, but the old boys in blue in the Air Force still did it best.

Dr. Dugan was not quite awake in a dazzling Caribbean daybreak when she shuffled from the T-39 toward the operations center at the naval base. Her watch still set to Eastern Time was an hour slow at 6:00 in the morning, Atlantic Time. By the time she had washed her face and poured her first cup of coffee 30 minutes later, Buddy Thurston had been in the water for over eight hours.

Commander Dugan closed her blue eyes and inhaled deeply of the strong vapors from the warm mug. On the table next to the saucer was a crumpled telex cable with her orders.

CRD ESI. DCNO 0314/0530. PROWDELREP DCNO OP-098.
DISUB ICSP ADDPLA. FMEA. NOPHYSRET. 10 BAGAIR. EOM.

Lt. Commander Jessica Dugan had read the cable enough times to have it memorized: "Confidential, restricted data. Extremely sensitive information. From the Deputy Chief of Naval Operations, 5:30 am, UTC (12:30 in the morning, Washington Time), March 14th. Proceed without delay and report to the Deputy Chief of Naval Operations, Research and Development. Duty in submarine; vessel status: in commission, special; and such additional places as necessary. Failure mode and effects analysis. No new physical examination is required unless there has been a material change in health since last physical. Ten pounds of baggage permitted for air transportation. End of message."

The warmth on the back of her neck was putting her to sleep after 30 hours awake. She had to put the coffee mug down and close her eyes. It felt too good to have the new sun burning through the window onto her shoulders.

The same low sun twinkled on the saltwater swells which swept over the back of Buddy Thurston's head after his gas-filled corpse broke the surface.

*   *   *

The facsimile machine buzzed out a sheet of wavy lines like a row of parallel electrocardiograms at the sprawling Cuban navy base at Cienfuegos. The great bay is nearly ten miles wide on the southern coastline of central Cuba. The next major inlet was 25 miles further west: the Bay of Pigs where John Kennedy had learned his first bitter lesson about being President in the spring of 1961.

At 5:00 in the morning Eastern Standard Time, a Cuban naval officer snapped the document from the fax machine at the Antisubmarine Warfare Command. The sheet was three feet long and had been sent over military telephone lines from the air base at Moa.

In the operations center of the antisubmarine warfare division of the People's Navy, few Cuban officers were on duty two hours before the daylight shift assumed their positions.

The night watch's senior ASW officer scanned the impression left five hours earlier on the magnetic sensors on board the Harbin patrol plane.

"I agree, Lieutenant, with Capitan Estoban. Looks like a wreck to me."

"Begging the capitan's pardon, Sir, but look at the tracing. The contact moved during the MAD survey."

The senior officer was impatient and tired. He harrumphed as he bent closely over the long sheet of shiny, thin paper.

"Humm. Maybe." The peaks on the squiggly tracing were a millimeter apart, suggesting movement of a metallic target—or natural phenomena. "What time of night was this, Lieutenant?"

"0100 local, Sir."

"Hum. Deep water. What's the magnetic variation out there, north of Puerto Rico?"

"Eight degrees West, Sir. And the isogonic lines are stable throughout the region."

"Well done, Mister." The senior officer did not suppress his smile. Promising youngsters were Cuba's military future and he welcomed them. "But there are at least two underwater communications cables out there between Hispaniola and Puerto Rico. Our Harbin may have picked up their electromagnetic radiation."

The young lieutenant frowned. It was too early in the morning and too late in his eight-hour watch to argue.

"On the other hand, Lieutenant," the officer nodded, "let's send out a helicopter anyway. The Americans like to do their torpedo practice in that area." The ASW watch commander looked the junior officer squarely in his dark Spanish eyes. "I wouldn't want you to have an uneasy sleep when you are off watch."

"Thank you, Sir." The lieutenant felt better. He would rest well.

"Detail a chopper out there when the watch changes. Carry on, Lieutenant."

By 7:30 in the morning Atlantic Time near San Juan, Puerto Rico, Jessica Dugan, USN, was sound asleep with her head on her crossed arms upon the tabletop. The morning sunshine low in the window brought out the graying highlights in her thick brown hair which hung to her shoulders.

Lt. Commander Dugan awoke startled by a light hand upon her shoulder. She still wore her sweaty orange flightsuit.

"Sorry, Commander," a tall officer smiled.

The exhausted woman started to rise as she blinked in the bright daylight.

"Don't get up, Doctor. I hated to wake you, but we do have business."

"Yes, Admiral," she stammered dryly. She glanced at the empty coffee mug beside her elbow.

"Orderly," the senior officer called to the closed door of the narrow briefing room.

"Sir!" a young seaman said firmly as he entered.

"May we have a fresh coffee for the commander? . . . How do you take it, Doctor?"

"Black, thank you, Sir."

"Two black, please."

"Aye, aye, Sir," the seaman nodded as he left the room.

"How was the flight down, Commander?"

"Dark, Sir," Dr. Dugan smiled. She fumbled to pull her hair back up into a regulation twist above her collar.

"Don't worry about your hair, Commander. We can dispense with the formality this early."

"Thank you, Sir." It was not easy for the sleepy physician to be informal with flag rank.

Her senior wore the single star of a rear admiral "lower half." The rank equivalent to a brigadier general had once carried the title of commodore. But when the commodore rank was discontinued, one-star rear admirals became "lower half" and two-stars represented rear admiral "upper half." (Vice admirals wear three stars like a lieutenant general and full admirals wear the four stars of a full general in the other services. A Fleet Admiral, like a General of the Army, wears five stars—a breed and rank extinct since 1945.)

"Sir. Ma'am," the young sailor said softly when he came back through the door. He laid two cups on the table. "Will that be all, Admiral?"

"Yes. Thank you very much." The officer nodded.

"Good morning, Sir. Ma'am." The seaman left and closed the door behind him.

Jessica Dugan lifted the steaming cup and she gently blew into the black liquid before taking a tentative sip. She closed her eyes for an instant.

"Thank you, Sir. Guess I needed that."

"I know. You have been on the go for something like a day and a half."

"Yes."

"And a long day still to come, I'm afraid."

The woman's dark eyebrows raised into the creases on her smooth forehead.

"Your credentials are impeccable, Commander. Your first and second fiche were forwarded ahead of you."

"Oh."

Every Navy officer's records are reduced to a set of five microfiche kept by the Navy Military Personnel Command. Fiche One details the officer's fitness reports and commendations. Fiche Two contains professional history, education, and special qualifications. The third fiche notes personal and family information with Fiche Four containing the officer's orders. Any confidential or privileged information, such as disciplinary sanctions, live forever on the fifth microfiche.

"You are perfect for this detachment, Commander: Yale BS in biochemistry, your MD from Johns Hopkins, and post-graduate work at MIT's Whitehead Institute for Biomedical Research prior to medical school." The admiral spoke from memory. "Your lack of submarine qualification is more than compensated for by your posting with DSB-CWB." She had never attended Nuclear Power School.

Jessica Dugan stopped the coffee mug bound for her pale lips. She had indeed spent six months with the Defense Science Board on Chemical Warfare and Biological Defense. But that was well over ten years earlier. She had done little more than sort and categorize reports. But she had just been told all she needed to know.

There was a Bug Boat after all.

"Very impressive, Commander."

"Thank you, Sir."

"May I ask what brought you to the Navy?"

"I was born Navy, I guess. My father was a petty officer. Grandfather, too. I was born at Subic Bay, you know."

The admiral looked surprised. But then he had not received her personals on Fiche Three.

"Excellent, indeed, Doctor. What were you told in Washington?"

"Only that there might be some kind of infectious incident on board one of our submarines. I really do not know anything more than that." She labored not to sound frustrated.

"Sorry to give you so little. But this operation is utterly need-to-know only. Washington may have told you all they really knew. I can only add a few details, I'm afraid."

Dr. Dugan sat up and took a stiff swig of the cooling coffee. She wanted to be as alert as her exhaustion would permit.

"There was a suicide last night on *Sam Houston* 100 miles northwest of here. There was also another death of a seaman ten days ago—ostensibly an accident and unrelated. The 609 is a highly classified, floating research laboratory for biological defense."

The admiral paused so the last words could sink into the drowsy woman who was momentarily wide awake. The physician silently nodded: The Bug Boat.

"Can you tell me, Admiral, what toxins or agents they're working on down there."

"Several. Routine and exotic. That's all I know. I suspect that only AMRIID knows the whole story. It's Dugway's baby, as I understand it. Intelligence is kept quite fragmented so that perhaps no one really has the big picture . . . Except for the technical part of the crew on 609. And I can't swear that all of them really know."

Dr. Dugan had to shake her head. She hated the secrecy game. Any project bearing the fingerprints of the Army Medical Research Institute on Infectious Disease made her uneasy. AMRIID directs most American military research into biological and chemical warfare. The admiral's casual reference to Dugway Proving Ground where the nastiest government bugs are kept told her the scope of the project going on under water. In 1943, an anthrax weapon was tested at Dugway near Salt Lake City. In March 1968, some 6,000 sheep owned by local farmers were killed in Rush Valley when a Dugway nerve gas experiment got out of hand.

"You will find *Sam Houston* to be the most complete—for its size—biological laboratory you could imagine. She contains three biological containment labs with the latest equipment, including transmission and scanning electron microscopes. I do know that much of their work is on genetic engineering. Really spooky stuff. And rather over my head, I must confess. I am kept relatively up to date on 609 since it is on station here in my department."

"On that element, Admiral, why would they put the ship here in particular? Why not closer to home? Or even in the Pacific to be closer to Dugway?"

"I suppose it might have something to do with sanitizing any accidents: *Sam Houston* cruises continuously on the lip of the Puerto Rico Trench, the deepest part of the Atlantic Ocean with 28,000 feet of water."

She grimaced at the thought of five miles of water.

"Well, Doctor, the sea makes everything clean." The admiral did not strain to sound cheerful. His middle-aged face hardened, but only for an instant. "Likewise, this side of the continent puts the laboratory closer to Fort Detrick." Fort Detrick in Frederick, Maryland, is the headquarters of AMRIID and Army research into chemical, biological, and toxic weapons.

She nodded and sagged deeper into her painful chair.

"While you were flying down here, DCNO coordinated your transfer to *Sam Houston*."

"I wondered about that, Sir. Aren't we going to wait until after dark to get me out there?"

"No need to worry, really. In the field, there is no such

thing as dark. The other side can see us and we can see him in the dark, or under water once we know about where to look. But we shall take every precaution not to compromise 609's position or her mission, of course."

The woman nodded stupidly from her fatigue.

"During the night, we put together quite a little demonstration in ship-handling for you." The admiral sounded cheery and proud. "We intend to keep the personal risk to you as minimal as possible. So we ruled out either an air-drop to 609 or an underwater transfer exercise. We shall put you off in a boat to *Sam Houston* which will be completely screened by coming up right in the middle of an underway replenishment-at-sea exercise, an RAS. We just got lucky on our ship manifests."

Without thinking, the physician shook her head. It already sounded like she should have retired from the Navy yesterday.

"Don't worry, Jessica." The admiral had not used her first name before. "This area is criss-crossed with undersea communications cables. Two of them run from San Juan straight up to West Palm Beach, Florida. One of them crosses the western corner of the Puerto Rico Trench, 180 miles northwest of here. *Sam Houston* has been ordered to station-keep there for the transfer.

"We were lucky enough to have a fleet oiler and a marine cable-layer within six hours steaming from that position. The oiler *Savannah* is making flank speed at 20 knots toward the rendezvous point. The cable repair ship *Zeus* was on her way down here from working on the SOSUS link near Andros. They will perform a mid-ocean, underway replenishment maneuver. *Savannah* will make an approach alongside *Zeus*. When they are 1,000 meters abeam, *Sam Houston* will surface between them. We'll helicopter you out to *Savannah* which has a helideck for Sea Knight choppers. A launch from *Savannah* will take you over to 609. The submarine will lie between the larger vessels and will be all but invisible. The rendezvous time will be 1600."

Jessica Dugan looked tired and befuddled. Her weary mind did not know whether to subtract an hour to go from Atlantic to Eastern Time, or add four to convert from Puerto Rico, Atlantic Time, to UTC (Greenwich), or to just carry the ten and forget the whole damn thing. The admiral saw her distress.

He looked at his wristwatch which read 8:00 in the morning, San Juan time.

"That's four hours from now. Your helicopter leaves here in two hours."

Lt. Commander Dugan struggled to make sense of the operation.

"But broad daylight for a secret submarine, Sir? What about sonar?"

It was the admiral's turn to look surprised.

"I may only sail test tubes and urine samples, Sir, but I did pass basic."

"Indeed you did, Doctor. With honors all the way through, as I recall." The senior smiled. The woman seemed to make him smile. "You are quite right, of course. But we're not worried about being heard if any Russian subs are prowling around this afternoon. First, the pick-up will be just east of the Navidad Bank, a sand bar formation which will block any passive sonar listening from the west side between Cuba and the Dominican Republic. The water north of the Dominican Republic is shallow enough that any ships out there with sonar should have quite a bit of bottom reverberation to scatter their sonar. Secondly, the rendezvous is only 60 miles from the Dominican coastline. That's only 40 miles from a really nice shrimp bed.

"The snapping shrimp click their one large, front claw incessantly. A million or so of them make a sound like a forest fire to sonar. The water may also have warmed up enough for the deep scatter layer of plankton to come up enough to ruin the sonar of anyone listening from underneath you. Six-oh-nine will also have the advantage of the so-called 'afternoon affect.' By noon local time when she comes up, the sun's heating of the upper layer of ocean changes the wave propagation properties of the surface just enough to bend sound waves or active sonar down toward the bottom and away from the submarine.

"And finally, *Zeus* and *Savannah* each have two propellers. Between their four screws and 609's propeller, there will be enough blade-tip cavitation noise to make anyone listening think you're an aircraft carrier at flank bell.

"I hate to jinx you, Commander, but all of the sonar variables could not possibly be any more favorable."

"Okay, Sir." The physician was fading fast.

"So we'll just hustle you out to *Savannah* and transfer you by MWB over to your ride in 609."

An MWB is a motorized whaleboat.

"Enjoy your stay in 609, Commander."

Dr. Dugan nodded. Her cheer had been pushed aside by numbing fatigue.

"Just don't let any of the boys on *Sam Houston* send you off to search for relative bearing grease." The admiral sounded chipper as he rose.

"I won't even go hunting for a bucket of steam, Sir," the physician smiled as she stood up.

The admiral raised an eyebrow at the woman's knowledge of the pranks played on new seamen during their first cruise.

"I've been a Navy man for almost forty years, Sir." She grinned with her eyes too heavy to open. The admiral had to notice that she was almost beautiful.

"Well said, Doctor. We have a BOQ upstairs where you can sack out for two hours. I'll have an orderly secure your privacy."

"Oh, that sounds wonderful," she slurred.

"No wonder Capitan Estoban had a MAD contact! Look at that silhouette."

The pilot of the Mi-14PL patrol helicopter was more conscious of his chopper's fuel gauges than of his own pulse and breath. The Russian helicopter with the Cuban paint scheme was 350 nautical miles east of Cuba. The chopper could remain on station just north of the eastern coastline of the Dominican Republic for no more than 15 minutes. That would give barely 20 minutes of reserve fuel when the helicopter returned home to Moa.

"Watch our position," the chopper captain called to his flight engineer. Normally carrying a five-man crew, the Mi-14PL was stripped to only three crewmen to extend its range. The engineer-navigator was charged with carefully maintaining their position over international waters north of Hispaniola. He monitored the VOR radio navigation beacon out of Puerto Plata and backed that up with the VOR just south of Puerto Plata at Santiago, both in the Dominican Republic.

At 9:00 in the morning, local Atlantic Time, the sun was well up. Five-foot seas broke whitely over the shoals of Navidad

Bank behind the Mi-14. The deep water between the bank and the Dominican coastline was much bluer with no whitecaps.

The chopper wearing Cuban colors was one of fourteen in Cuban service. Twin Isotov TV3-117MT turbines generated nearly 4,000 horsepower through the single set of rotors. The 15-ton bird carried magnetic anomaly detection gear in her tail and surface-search radar mounted in a small dome under the forward cockpit.

"Pretty sight," the Cuban pilot called over the intercom.

Two thousand feet below the chopper, *Zeus* steamed toward the Puerto Rico Trench 50 miles further southeast.

"She's in a hurry," the Cuban copilot responded. *Zeus* left a half-mile wake of churning white water as she made 15 knots at maximum speed. Commissioned in March 1984, the cable-repair vessel still looked clean. Little smoke percolated from her two white funnels standing side by side in front of her aft quarterdeck.

The helicopter made a slow circle over *Zeus*. Morning sunshine highlighted her bow number, RC-7.

Operated by the Military Sealift Command, *Zeus* was not armed. The United States Navy rented her but she was crewed by eight civilian officers and 80 civilian seamen.

"We'll have to wake up Ruis when we get home to show him his submarine!" the chopper pilot laughed. "You taking a MAD trace back there?"

"I have it, Sir," the flight engineer in the back radioed. "Excellent trace for Capitan Estoban. Too bad it's not a submarine."

"Okay," the pilot called, turning west. "Let's go home. The wind is with us this way at least." He had 400 miles of fuel left in the standard and auxiliary long-range tanks, and 360 nautical miles of blue sea lay between the Mi-14 and home.

The Cuban helicopter chugged homeward, 1,500 feet directly above the floating and swollen body of Buddy Thurston. After eleven hours in the water, Torpedoman's Mate Thurston was bloated to half again his small stature. The buttons on his blue cotton shirt had popped open at his distended midsection. His shirt tails floated beneath him like soft fins on a faded blue fish.

THREE

14 MARCH; 1500 UTC

CAPTAIN MILHAUS paced the wardroom. He pounded his right fist into his left palm. *Sam Houston*'s sole physician sat alone at the long table. The door was closed to the passageway. Lieutenant Shaffer looked very much the prisoner waiting for the call from the governor.

"Just tell me how you could have missed it, Doctor."

Commander Milhaus was seething in his private meeting with the ship's doctor. On both of his prior commands at sea, the career officer had been dubbed "Captain Zem" by his crews who caught on quickly. "ZEM" is Navy for Zero-error Mentality.

"The toxicology tests required in an autopsy are for toxins and drugs, Captain. When Electrician's Mate Hendrix tested clean for poisons and drugs, there was no protocol for testing his blood for natural and normal substances. I stayed up most of the night working on the new toxicology tests. I had to wait for the blood samples from his first autopsy to thaw to redo his blood work. After eleven days in the freezer, the blood had to thaw slowly. I couldn't microwave it without destroying it. I only completed the work an hour ago."

"Yes, Doctor. Forgive me. I know you're doing all you can do. But now you're telling me that two men were infected and both of them are dead. And you're telling me that Hendrix' death was probably a suicide, too."

The captain had appeared struck by a thunderbolt when Dr. Shaffer had reported that new blood tests on the electrocuted seaman had revealed massive concentrations of uric acid. Early kidney failure and incipient arthritis had also been found during the pre-dawn autopsy. His death had originally been declared an accidental electrocution in the sub's generator room. This was the second post-mortem on the seaman whose body had been badly charred by the accident. His hands had been burned to a crisp. Nearly two weeks in the ship's deepfreeze (and standard, temporary morgue) had not helped the tired physician redo his earlier work. But Buddy Thurston's death dictated a second look at *Sam Houston*'s other casualty and the physician had not waited for orders or for permission.

"All right, Stan. Just do what you can do." Commander Milhaus stopped walking in circles. He was calm but deeply troubled. "We rendezvous with *Savannah* in less than an hour. The XO managed to get the RAS evolution into the POD. Engineering is satisfied they can execute the negative-pressure emergency protocols when we surface. You comfortable with all that?"

Kurt Milhaus looked hard at the medic.

"Yes, Sir. As comfortable as it gets, I suppose."

"Okay. Then carry on and keep me informed. I'll be in CIC."

"Yes, Captain."

When Dr. Shaffer made good his escape into the passageway, the narrow hallway smelled somehow as sweet as a Caribbean beach although he still inhaled the submarine's bottled air. He descended the companionway two levels to the ship's BL-4, maximum containment laboratory where pieces of an electrocuted seaman were still defrosting for further examination.

As the lieutenant went below decks, Commander Milhaus retired aft on the upper deck to the control room, the CIC— combat information center.

Lt. Commander Pappy Perlmutter was already at the conn supervising the presurfacing evolution for the rendezvous in the Caribbean with *Savannah* and *Zeus*. There had been no underwater communication with the Pentagon since none is possible at the submarine's operational depth. The orders to proceed with the RAS, replenishment-at-sea ruse, were beamed by ultra-high frequency, coded instructions over six hours earlier. The extremely low frequency "bell ringer" beacon had alerted *Sam Houston* to punch her UHF antenna through the water for the detailed, encoded transmission.

The executive officer had taken command of the control room in his captain's absence. The XO worked with the officer of the deck. The OOD had already briefed the necessary crewmen on the RAS operation. Although coming up is always a complicated exercise when steering 7,880 tons of nuclear submarine, special care must be taken when surfacing blindly between two ships running close together on the surface. The captain and his XO had worked in the pre-dawn hours to formulate the detailed POD—the plan of the day. The crew and their newly automated submarine were ready in the control room, in the engine room, and the reactor compartment.

The submarine had been zeroing in on its targets' propeller and engine noise for two hours. *Sam Houston* had turned the westernmost corner of the trench at a depth of 400 feet. Coming about from west to east, the sub would surface with all three ships steering eastward into the wind. This would put the vessels running three abreast and perpendicular to the wave fronts. Six-foot seas breaking over each ship's bow would induce pitching motions. But this was more stable than the rolling movement caused by taking the waves broadside.

"CIC to Sonar," the XO called by intercom.

"Sonar aye," the squawkbox crackled.

"What's the B-scope say, Sonar?"

A sonar man forward of the control room examined his television screen. The clatter of engines above the submarine generated distance and relative bearing readouts. Four propellers close to the surface chugged away and tiny air bubbles on the propeller blades hissed loudly through the sea as the props cavitated at slow speeds.

"Ten miles dead ahead, Sir," the sonar man radioed aft to the CIC.

"Thank you," the XO replied. "Diving officer, take her up to periscope depth. Ahead one-third."

*   *   *

The thwack-thwack-thwack of the helicopter's four blades pounded inside Jessica Dugan's skull like some bad memory. The high-pitched whine of twin, 1,690-horsepower GE T700-401 jet engines leaked through her protective headphones. Making 120 knots 2,000 feet above open water, the Sikorsky SH-60B Seahawk chopper was built for function, not for comfort. The physician's two-hour nap at Roosevelt Roads had revived her only enough to feel the jet turbines to the marrow of her bones.

Dr. Dugan could feel her cheekbones hurt from the chopper's vibrations after 90 minutes in the air. She flew with her bloodshot eyes closed until her earphones crackled with the voice of the helicopter's commander.

"Outside your starboard hatch, Ma'am," a youthful lieutenant called from the flight deck.

Dr. Dugan forgot her painful brain when she leaned toward the plexiglass window in the side hatch of the helicopter. Down below she saw three white wakes behind three ships which glistened in the bright sunshine of local noon at sea.

The chopper from Puerto Rico had flown northwestward to the rendezvous point 60 miles north of the Dominican Republic's northeast coastline. Coming around through half a circle, the U.S. Navy chopper had slowly changed course from northwest to southeast. This put the helicopter into the wind as it approached the three ships from behind.

The brilliantly white *Zeus* sailed 100 yards from the supply ship *Savannah*. Between them was the black and narrow shape of *Sam Houston*. The submarine ran low in the light surf with white water breaking over her rounded bow all the way back to the base of the towering black sail, formerly called a conning tower. Half a dozen tubes jutted from the top of the sail for antennae, twin periscopes, narrow radar dishes, and a fat snorkel for sucking air into the emergency diesel generator while shallowly submerged. Between the two surface ships of the line, the long and narrow submarine looked small indeed—and very frightening to an exhausted test-tube jockey.

"Pretty," she mumbled into the microphones touching her perspiring lips inside a hard flight helmet.

The sudden secret orders from Washington required the two vessels to actually execute the delicate replenishment-at-sea operation while screening *Sam Houston*. There could always be foreign or unfriendly ships steaming over the horizon. Such ships had to see the true evolution of the RAS, so both *Savannah* and *Zeus* flew their "Romeo" pennant from their rigging. The yellow cross on a red background is the signal flag for Romeo, representing the letter "R" for "ready." The pennants are left flying when the cargo to be transferred is either fuel or munitions. The Romeo flag would be removed before transfer of less dangerous supplies.

"We're cleared to land, Commander. Please check your lap belt," the copilot radioed from up front. He looked over his left shoulder to see the woman flash a thumbs-up from the rear cabin.

The supply ship *Savannah* sports a helipad on her stern just behind a raised hangar which berths two UH-46 Sea Knight helicopters. One of the Sea Knights hovered 500 feet above the formation to spot for the Seahawk pilots approaching the floating landing pad.

Lt. Commander Dugan squinted into the noontime glare. She could just make out the white-on-gray letters on *Savannah*'s bow: OR 4. Steaming at 12 knots, the white cable-layer *Zeus* had RC-7 on her bow. On *Savannah*, the overhead sun made no shadows between the four sets of crane towers, called kingposts, which handle the winches and fueling hoses. The 41,000-ton, *Wichita* class oiler can carry 160,000 barrels of fuel, 600 tons of ammunition, and 300 tons of supplies for underway replenishment. Her main weather deck was covered with equipment crammed onto her 659-foot length.

The sparkling white *Zeus* was 150 feet shorter and carried only 14,000 tons of steel on the far side of the submarine.

The three ships steamed at 12 knots into the wind blowing from the east. Their speed was dictated by the underway replenishment guidelines in Naval Weapons Publication number fourteen. NWP14 notes that speeds less than 8 knots can lessen the steering effectiveness of ships' rudders and speeds faster than 15 knots can create a suction venturi effect in the sea between ships which could suck one vessel into the other.

When the Seahawk helicopter turned southeastward for final approach to *Savannah*'s helipad, the chopper turned her back on the Navidad sand bar 30 miles behind. Underneath the three ships, two underwater cables lay on the bottom under two miles of blue water. Two miles further east, the sea bottom dropped away into the Puerto Rico Trench, nearly six miles deep.

"Roosevelt Roads arriving," *Savannah*'s boatswain's mate of the watch called over his ship's IMC public address system as the Seahawk bounced gently onto the helipad.

Not until the chopper's four rotor blades were completely stopped did Dr. Dugan jump down from the white helicopter. Feeling gritty in the orange flightsuit in which she had sweated for 15 hours, she came to attention on the oiler's aft flight deck and smartly saluted the stars and stripes (the "steaming ensign" when underway) snapping atop a spar secured to a communications mast. (The national flag only flies from the flagpole on the stern when a Navy ship is in port.) Two seamen greeted her. She tossed her flight helmet back into the Seahawk cabin.

"Welcome aboard, Ma'am," they saluted. Lt. Commander Dugan returned the courtesy.

"This way, Ma'am."

Lt. Commander Dugan followed the seamen into the shadows of the aft superstructure which towered two decks above the stern's helipad. Within the gray passageways she was led down two deck levels. Emerging into blinding sunshine, Dr. Dugan followed her guides across the main, weather deck to the ship's middle. Amidships, she was greeted by *Savannah*'s commanding officer, Commander Richard Rice, USN, detailed to the Military Sealift Command.

"Lt. Commander Jessica Dugan reporting, Sir," the physician saluted the CO.

"Welcome aboard, Doctor." Navy physicians and chaplains may be addressed by their professional pedigree instead of their ranks if their rank is below that of full commander or lieutenant colonel.

"Thank you, Sir."

"Your launch is ready when you are, Commander." The CO had no time to waste on small talk. His ship was station-keeping dangerously close to a nuclear submarine which was close aboard the cable ship *Zeus*.

"I'm ready, Sir."

"Very well, then. I wish you well in *Sam Houston*. I'm going to lay forward to monitor the RAS. My exec, Mister Sanders, will assist you here."

The ship's executive officer shook hands with the physician of equal rank.

"Thank you, Captain Rice. I really appreciate everyone's trouble here." The tired woman smiled weakly, squinting into the noontime sun. Sweat beaded on her lined forehead.

"Sounds to me, Commander, that my troubles will be less than yours." The CO glanced over the rail to the black hull of the submarine. "Good luck, Doctor."

As the CO walked forward toward the bridge, Lt. Commander Sanders steered the only woman among 450 sailors toward one of the ship's motorboats suspended from *Savannah*'s davit on the main deck. The four rows of kingposts towered overhead.

Dr. Dugan was uncomfortable from her fatigue, from the glaring sun, and from the sudden sensation of being pushed faster than she cared to move.

The XO handed her an orange helmet.

"Don't fasten the chin strap. And don't forget your vest, Doctor."

The woman glanced down at her life jacket which she had neglected to cinch across her chest. She secured her vest after donning her safety helmet which is left unfastened at the chin in small boats.

"Mister Sanders, I request permission to leave the ship."

"Granted, Doctor. Good luck."

Before stepping into the launch, she turned, looked up at the radio mast, and saluted the steaming ensign.

"Watch your fingers on the falls," the XO added as Dr. Dugan grabbed the steel cable secured to the bow and stern of the motor launch. The boat had already been lowered slightly until the open launch was level with the weather deck's railing. The gangway was open so she could step into the launch. The little boat's coxswain in the stern extended his hand to steady her.

"Ma'am," the seaman smiled.

Dr. Dugan sat down unsteadily upon one of the motorboat's thwarts—the wooden boards which run across the open hull. She rested her elbow upon the gunwale.

"Ready?" the XO asked.

"Ready, Sir," the young coxswain replied.

"Hoist out!" the executive officer ordered. A motor then slowly lowered the boat down to the water, 40 feet beneath the weather deck. When Jessica Dugan realized that there were only two sailors in the 26-foot launch, she got another uneasy feeling about the risks she had assumed at the midnight Pentagon some fourteen hours earlier: no need to expose more crewmen than necessary to whatever evil lurked within the submarine. *Savannah*'s bell clanged a pair of two short rings to signal the debarking of a lieutenant commander.

The launch rubbed against *Savannah*'s side when it contacted the water. In an instant, the coxswain steered the little boat toward the submarine. In the swells between the two ships, Jessica Dugan felt progressively worse from the boat's sudden heaving, the stifling sun, and an acute case of gripping fear. The boat quickly closed the short distance to the low silhouette of the submarine.

Jessica Dugan did not allow herself the luxury of losing her breakfast. She was too taken by the looming side of *Sam Houston*, SSN-609—The Bug Boat.

Approaching the ship, she first noticed that the hull was not smooth, black steel at all. Instead, the sub was completely blanketed with brick-size chunks of a black, rubber-looking material. She had noticed the ship's anechoic tiles: rubbery bricks designed to absorb nosy sonar beams from enemy subs. Soviet (now Russian) missile submarines had carried them for years, especially the behemoth Typhoon class ships where the tiles are called Cluster Guard.

The motor launch came alongside the submarine. Four submariners in life jackets received a line thrown over by the sailor in the launch's bow. They took another line thrown by the coxswain in the stern. When the engine in the launch sputtered to silence, the seamen pulled the boat against the submarine's side.

In sudden quiet, Jessica Dugan heard nothing but the sea lapping against *Sam Houston* and the distant and muted chugging of engines on the three large ships.

"Good luck, Ma'am," the launch's coxswain at the tiller smiled as Dr. Dugan reached over the gunwale for the portable Jacob's ladder slung limply over the sub's side. After handing her safety helmet to the coxswain, she clambered clumsily up the rope ladder to the black back of the sub. There were only four feet of freeboard between the frothy ocean and the damp deck of *Sam Houston*.

Lt. Commander Dugan, suddenly pale, stiffened and saluted the sub's ensign which hung wet and heavy on the backside of the towering black sail. Naval courtesy allows saluting the flag on the quarterdeck even though she was uncovered and her hair blew in the salty breeze. Salt water still dripped off the winglike planes jutting from the sail's sides.

"Lt. Commander Jessica Dugan reporting," she stammered. "Permission to come aboard?"

"Welcome, Doctor," a lieutenant saluted. "If you would follow me, Ma'am."

As she tried to keep her footing on the slick deck of wet rubber, she heard one of the submariners behind her call to rig in the Jacob's ladder to carry it below.

Dr. Dugan was unsteady as she negotiated the twelve-foot long ladder from the 26-inch hatch in the deck, down into the bowels of the black submarine. She worked to retain the large envelope wedged into her moist, right armpit. She felt a blast of warm air which fell in upon her from the open hatch above. The current of humid air smelled salty and wet. The wind nearly blew her down the ladder.

She blinked in the dim light of the sub's large, central control room which she entered at the compartment's rear. Commander Milhaus and Lt. Commander Perlmutter met her at the foot of the ladder.

Captain Milhaus returned the woman's salute.

"Lt. Commander Dugan, Sir," she sighed. Instinctively, she handed the sweat-stained envelope containing her orders and her officers' qualification jacket to her new commanding officer.

"Thank you, Doctor. Welcome to 609."

Jessica Dugan realized that she had to speak up to be heard over the strange wind which still blew at her from above and behind. She looked puzzled.

"The air is negative pressure, Doctor. I'm Lt. Commander Phil Perlmutter, XO. Welcome." Pappy Perlmutter extended his large hand. "Our septic control protocol calls for negative pressure when we crack the hatch under the circumstances."

Sam Houston's engineering division had reversed the ship's atmospheric controls such that outside air was sucked downward into the ship. This prevented any of the known and unknown contaminants in the laboratories from escaping to the outside. One such contaminant had driven Buddy Thurston to a watery suicide fourteen hours earlier. Before the outside air was vented back outside through the snorkel atop the sail, the air would pass through a series of filters in the maximum containment BL-4 lab two decks below.

Dr. Dugan was startled when she heard four men drop to the control room deck behind her. The last man down pulled a lanyard which jerked down the hatch which was secured quickly. Her ears popped from the sudden pressure change.

"Hatch secured, Sir," one of the seaman called above the sound of rushing air.

"Very well," Captain Milhaus replied firmly. "Secure from negative pressure."

"Aye aye, Sir. Secure from negative pressure." The seaman pushed a button on the CIC bulkhead and activated the intercom. He advised engineering to stop the blowers which sucked air out of the combat information center and out of Jessica Dugan's lungs. It felt like her eyeballs were about to explode from her head.

In a moment the rush of air stopped, the noise stopped, and the woman's tired blue-gray eyes retired to the rear of their sockets.

"Mister Perlmutter will escort you forward, Doctor," the captain said with as much cheer as he could muster. "Just as soon as you get squared away in your stateroom, we'll brief you with our own physician in the wardroom." He paused and looked into her perspiring and anxious face. "Have you ever been in a submarine?"

"No, Sir." Jessica Dugan's best voice was hoarse.

"Okay, Commander. I have complete confidence that you'll adapt just fine. Your credentials and DCNO's recommendation precede you. It won't take long." The captain smiled as if he meant it.

"Thank you, Sir. I'll do my best not to get in anyone's way."

Captain Milhaus nodded.

"The crew has been briefed that you are not exactly one of the boys," the CO had to grin. "You'll be welcome here, I can assure you."

The woman shrugged. To her moist nose, she certainly smelled to herself like one of the boys.

"Lieutenant Baker," the CO said over Jessica Dugan's sweat-stained shoulder. "Trim to dive and alert *Savannah* and *Zeus*."

"Aye aye, Sir."

"This way, Commander," the executive officer pointed forward. He led her out of the control room.

"Captain," Dr. Dugan said as she left the CIC to follow the XO.

"Twelve o'clock, Sir," the OOD said to the commanding officer.

"Make it so, Lieutenant."

It cannot be local noon aboard any U.S. Navy vessel until the captain officially accepts the noon report and declares it to be noon.

Dr. Dugan blinked in the dim red glow of the passageway's standing lights which burned around the clock. Her eyes were bloodshot from lack of sleep and still accustomed to the blinding sunlight outside.

"You might as well call me Pappy," the XO smiled over his shoulder. "I think everyone else does by now."

"Okay, Pappy," Jessica Dugan said wearily.

On the far side of a bulkhead, the XO opened a stateroom door and pointed inside.

"Two of our officers will double up next door so you can have the stateroom down here in boys' town."

"Boys' town, Pappy?"

"Yep. What we call the junior officers' spaces."

"Oh."

"I'll send your ditty bag forward while you get squared here. I'll give you a few minutes before I come back."

"Thanks."

She entered the stateroom. The compartment was not more than ten feet wide, with most of it taken up by a double bunk. The mattresses were only 36 inches wide. Hardly room to turn over. Her tired eyes were wide at the sight of her cell.

"Just like home in Washington, huh?"

"My walk-in closet maybe." She felt suddenly uncomfortable about insulting the XO who was being a gracious host. "Sorry."

"Don't be," Pappy Perlmutter smiled. "My kid's Saint Bernard has a bigger house. See you shortly."

Lt. Commander Dugan closed the door and found her way to the even narrower bathroom—the "head"—in the stateroom. When she unzipped the flightsuit and sat down heavily, her elbows touched the stall's coldly metal sides.

She startled when the public address speakers on the passageway walls crackled.

"Prepare to dive. Diving stations, report."

Not until the radioman confirmed that *Savannah* had completed recovery of her motor launch did Captain Milhaus execute 609's descent and give the order to haul out from the formation.

Within one minute, Jessie Dugan astride the stainless steel pot could feel her stall tip very slightly sideways. When the hull creaked, her empty stomach knotted and her palms erupted in chilly sweat. She was going down into the darkness aboard The Bug Boat.

With her small trim tanks adjusted to keep *Sam Houston* level, the submarine popped the vent valves on the top of her black bow and stern. Atomized air and water vapor exploded into the humid air. Since the free-flooding holes in the sub's belly are always open, sea water rushed into the ship's main ballast tanks with explosive force when the upper vents opened. Air was forced out of the upper vents with such force that the explosive roar could have been heard one mile away. Men stopped working on the outside decks of *Savannah* and *Zeus* when the sea breeze suddenly sounded like a train wreck as 609 blew tanks and pulled out ahead of the two surface ships.

Nearly 900 tons of sea water flooded the submarine's fore and aft main tanks. Trimmed with smaller, internal water tanks to maintain a horizontal attitude, SSN-609 slipped slowly beneath the warm surface. White water rose in towering geysers as water mixed with the air spout surging out of the fore and aft vents in the ballast tanks. The roar of the vented air became a peculiar gurgling sound as the black hull slowly swamped. Gray waves rolled over the tubular body of *Sam*

Houston until only the black sail cut through the turbulent surface.

With a final explosive cloud of mist and water, the winglike dive planes on each side of the sail smacked into the rolling seas generated by the submarine moving out and down at 15 knots.

A frothy wake of churning water swirled over the top of the sail. All of her radio masts and periscopes had been fully retracted for the dive and the crest of the black sail was smooth as it disappeared beneath the Caribbean.

Only a white wake of furious ocean blemished the surface where SSN-609 had vanished. Within minutes, the sea calmed herself. The last eddies of disturbance were absorbed by a tranquil ocean between the two vessels left astern of the submarine.

Sam Houston was gone.

With 609 submerged and underway eastward toward her station within the canyon walls of the trench, Captain Rice passed the word on *Savannah* to commence the RAS evolution.

Although no stores and no fuel would actually be transferred during the mock, underway replenishment, the moves at least were real. Seamen in red helmets fired bolo lines, messenger lines, and a heavy Osborne shackle across the green water between *Zeus* and *Savannah*.

For half an hour, sunburned seamen on both vessels milled about as nothing flowed through the steward elbow and Elokomin rig suspended between the heaving ships steaming 90 feet apart. Each ship's Romeo pennant snapped in the sunshine.

By 12:30 Atlantic Time, 1630 UTC, *Sam Houston* had leveled off at her operational depth of 800 feet. Her compensating tanks were carefully trimmed for neutral buoyancy perfectly matched to the density, temperature, and salinity of the midnight-black ocean around her. While leveling off, she blew a little water out of these trim tanks to slightly increase her buoyancy. The outside water pressure as heavy as 24 atmospheres had compressed the ship's steel hull. When the ship literally shrank in all dimensions, she displaced less ocean and became less buoyant. Air had to be pumped from the high-pressure air bottles into the trim tanks to make up for the gradual loss of flotation.

The submarine carried reserve buoyancy by carefully remaining slightly lighter than the amount of sea water pushed aside by her hull. Only her normal, forward cruising speed of just 4 knots kept her locked into her assigned depth. That speed sent enough water flowing over her forward dive planes on the sail and her stern planes to force her bow down. She "flew" through the water. With a small downward deflection of her dive planes, SSN-609 overcame the ship's desire to float upward.

The long cable of the sub's towed passive sonar array had played out from the fairing on the ship's starboard side. Sonar men carefully listened to the sea around them in the underwater darkness. They heard clearly the engines and hissing propellers of *Savannah* and *Zeus* four miles behind them.

Jessica Dugan had thanked Pappy Perlmutter for bringing her ditty bag forward. While he waited in the passageway, she gratefully climbed out of her flightsuit which smelled of female sweat and oily jet fuel. She bathed standing up at the steel sink in her private head. The shower was communal and down the passageway of "boys' town." She ran a wet cloth under her arms. The physician wished that she could use deodorant. But aerosols and aromatic toiletries are forbidden in submarines where the atmosphere can carry wisps of explosive hydrogen gas emitted from the boat's huge backup batteries. A blast of spray deodorant could blow up the ship. Seventeen hours of perspiration had broken a rash in her armpits. Although she pulled her hair into a tight knot to keep it regulation and off her collar, she did not bother to put on a face. Nothing could fix the dark circles under her eyes anyway.

After her quick freshening up, she climbed into officers' khaki trousers and open-collar workshirt. Her collar carried a gold oak leaf of rank on one point and the larger oak leaf with tiny acorn of the medical corps on the other point.

"Thanks for waiting, Pappy," the physician smiled at the open door.

"No problem. These are for you, Doctor."

"Please call me Jessica, if you don't mind," she said cheerfully.

The executive officer seemed troubled by that informality on his part. The doctor understood.

"You're not my patient, you know."

"Not yet, anyway," the XO said softly. "Here."

He handed her a yellow object the size of a cigarette pack.

"Your dosimeter. And this is the film badge. Engineering will develop the film pack daily." Each device would record cumulative radiation exposure from the ship's Westinghouse pressurized-water nuclear reactor. In United States submarines, radiation exposure levels are minimal. There never has been a public confirmation of any serious radiation leak. Everyone on every nuclear ship wears similar monitors, usually dangling from belts.

"We passed the wardroom on the way down here." The XO waited to escort the ship's guest. "After you."

They walked a short distance aft and entered the rather spacious wardroom.

Captain Milhaus was already there in the company of Dr. Shaffer and Lieutenant (junior grade) Peter Gentry. Also present was the ship's one Army officer, Lt. Colonel (and PhD in biochemistry) Don Epson. Colonel Epson was the designated Principal Investigator for the biological project underway in *Sam Houston*.

As is the Navy way, steaming coffee was poured first. The wardroom clock on the wall indicated 1700, UTC. Eight hundred feet above them, the light seas were warmed by the dazzling Caribbean sun one hour past local noon.

Pappy Perlmutter and Dr. Dugan both saluted Captain Milhaus. Aboard ship, junior officers salute their superiors only upon their first contact of the day. The CO is always saluted by his juniors.

"Dr. Dugan," the captain said firmly, "may I present Colonel Epson detached from the Army, and Lieutenant Peter Gentry, head of our weapons division." The woman shook hands with the officers.

"Good afternoon, Sir," a new man said softly in the doorway. He looked uncomfortable. The wardroom is known as "officers' country."

"Come in, Chief," Captain Milhaus smiled after returning the man's salute. "Help yourself to coffee please."

"Thank you, Captain. Mister Perlmutter, Colonel, Dr. Shaffer, Mister Gentry."

"Chief, this is Lt. Commander Dugan, the medical officer who joined us this afternoon. Doctor, this is Master Chief Foster from the engineering division."

"Commander." The chief did not salute his superiors since he was not wearing a hat.

The executive officer pulled the wardroom door closed and the company was seated at the long table.

"Dr. Dugan," the captain began quickly, "I want to get you oriented immediately. Once you're briefed on our little situation, Pappy will give you a tour of the ship and will introduce you to our damage control bill and emergency procedures." The woman suddenly broke a sweat on her forehead. For just a moment, she had forgotten that she was already "sunk."

"What did they tell you in Washington? Knowing that will save us all some time."

"Well, Captain, I was told only that 609 was a biological laboratory, quite secret, and that there may have been a containment compromise. I wasn't told much more than that about the particulars."

"That's all?" Colonel Epson interrupted.

"That's it, Sir." The woman was junior to a full bird colonel.

"You have no idea what projects we're working on out here?"

"No, Sir. Only that 609 was refitted for BW investigations about a year ago and that this cruise has been out for about six weeks. That's all I really know."

"Well, Doctor," the colonel continued, "the biological warfare applications of our research are quite attenuated at best. We're still basically involved in pure research. Field applications are years away." The Army biochemist paused and faced the ship's captain. "Shall I go into details, Captain?"

"Please."

"Okay. Our principal project here is researching the field applications of Lesch-Nyhan Syndrome."

The officer let the words register in Jessie Dugan's weary brain. Her blue eyes squinted at the thought.

"Lesch-Nyhan! My God, Colonel!" She seemed appalled, or perhaps repulsed.

"That's our little bug, Dr. Dugan. Are you familiar with it?"

"Only slightly. There is so little literature on it. It's also rather outside of my general research concentration. As a predictive ecologist, my work is mainly analysis of airborne and waterborne biological weapons."

"Indeed, Doctor. In a nutshell, Lesch-Nyhan wasn't even named until 1962. It is a genetic defect on the human X chromosome. It's one of the sixteen or so genetic diseases mapped so far on the X. It is also one of the few hereditary diseases traceable to just one gene location. The actual gene was isolated at the University of California, San Diego, in '82. The defect is carried by the mother only and it affects maybe one in 100,000 children—all boys."

The woman shivered slightly before she spoke.

"I am familiar with the effect: total absence of HPRT enzyme required for the body to purge uric acid. The primary symptom is self-mutilation, with secondary symptoms of arthritis, kidney failure, and mild to severe retardation. Oh, it's just horrible. Patients will chew their own fingers off! The only known treatment is to strap them down and pull their teeth so they don't bite their own lips off and eat themselves alive!"

"A bit dramatic, Commander," the colonel said coldly. "But quite true. We've been working on the gene here for nine months during two cruises. The potential military applications are too obvious: infect an enemy army and the other side simply eat themselves! After all, it only affects males."

"No one told me!" She sounded somehow offended.

"Well, I don't really know who knows at the Pentagon," the colonel said, this time with a measure of sympathy in his voice.

"Aren't you under NIH supervision? Isn't NIH and RAC approval for genetic research required?" Now she sounded anxious.

"No," Dr. Shaffer interrupted. "National Institutes of Health standards for gene research in human test subjects do not require prior approval by the Recombinant DNA Advisory Committee in two situations: first, if the research is conducted outside the United States; and second, if some other Federal agency has approved the experiments. The first criterion is why we're out here at sea beyond the territorial limits. And, all of our work has been approved by the Navy's biosciences laboratory and the Army's infectious disease research people. We are quite legal."

"I hasten to add," Colonel Epson cut in, "that we do observe every single requirement of NIH guidelines on biological containment and personnel requirements. That's why I'm here

...as Principal Investigator. We have separate men serving as Biosafety Officers and Biohazards Control Officers for the BL-4 laboratory. We are exceedingly careful to follow the NIH procedures for hazard control."

"Then why was I sent down here?" Dr. Dugan was overcome with fatigue and a sudden sense of anger which she did not understand.

"Well, Commander," the colonel said with a detached and clinical voice, "tests done overnight confirmed that Torpedoman Thurston was infected with Lesch-Nyhan and that he had self-amputated. He bit off his fingertips, to be specific. And Dr. Shaffer's second post-mortem this morning on Electrician's Mate Richard Hendrix confirmed that he was also infected—even more advanced than Buddy, judging by his kidney damage. We had thought that his electrocution two weeks ago was a tragic accident. Now, we tend to think it was another suicide induced by the mental deterioration of the disease."

Dr. Dugan lowered her face. She fought sleep.

"I'm sorry, Commander, I know you're exhausted." Captain Milhaus was subdued and courteous.

"Sorry, Sir. I'm trying to follow. I've been up for like two days, I think."

"I know, Doctor. We'll try to move quickly here. Colonel?"

"Captain. Commander Dugan, you also need to know the mechanics of our experiments here."

"Yes, yes. Of course. What about the vector mechanism?"

"We are doing gene splicing research to determine a way to clone a gene which would induce Lesch-Nyhan by inhibiting the normal gene activity on the X chromosome which causes production of the HPRT enzyme, hypoxanthine guanine phosphoribosyl transferase. We think we have isolated the required gene. We are working on implanting or splicing this gene into either LaCrosse or dengue fever viruses."

"Dengue?" Dr. Dugan interrupted. Her blue-gray eyes were cold.

"Yes. We hadn't planned on either virus as the host. But the vector for delivering the gene dictated the virus." The colonel paused and glanced around the table. "We are testing the Asian

Tiger Mosquito as the delivery vector. It has already migrated to the southern United States, appearing first near Houston, Texas, in '85. Texas soon recorded its first dengue case in 35 years. Since the mosquito is so hardy and voracious, it's the perfect vector for delivery of a biological toxin. It prefers to carry dengue and LaCrosse, so that's where we are concentrating our research."

Jessica Dugan could only shake her head.

"And the bottom line is rather obvious: somehow two crewmen have been infected. We can only presume their inoculation occurred by mosquito." Captain Milhaus tried to keep the discussion moving quickly. "You're here to confirm that possibility and to advise on correcting the breach in containment, if any."

"I can do that," the woman said as if talking in her sleep.

"Good. Lieutenant Gentry and Chief Foster are here since they had such close contact with Hendrix and Thurston. Mister Gentry was officer of the watch in the weapons department when Thurston went out the torpedo tube last night. And Chief Foster was engineering officer of the watch when Hendrix was killed in the generator room ten days ago."

Both men suddenly looked guilty.

"All right," the woman sighed. "What kind of documentation do we have?" She spoke into her third cup of black coffee within 30 minutes.

"Lieutenant Gentry and the chief have brought for you the evaluation sheets on both men and their division notebooks. Maybe you can find something in there concerning the personalities or medical histories of Thurston and Hendrix."

"I'll study the records, Captain."

In the Navy, enlisted men are evaluated on their performance and promotion prospects by evaluation sheets. Officers are graded by fitness reports. Each Naval vessel must be divided into administrative departments. The departments are divided into divisions. Each department is supervised by its own department head. Division leaders must maintain a division notebook containing personal data on the division's men as well as training records and qualifications of the crewmen.

"And these documents are the Watch, Quarter, and Station bills for those two departments. Maybe you'll find something in there as to the men's traffic patterns through the ship as they circulated from watch to watch. This may have some value in tracing the containment breach."

"Excellent, Captain. The WQS bills will help me get started."

Each department has its own "Watch, Quarter, and Station Bill." It is a document indicating each crewman's sleeping berth and locker assignment, watch positions, emergency stations, and battle stations. The ship's executive officer maintains the warship's master bill listing everyone's assignments. At the lower end of the administration of a ship of the line, each division head maintains his division's edition of the bill. There can be no personnel changes or assignment changes at the division level without the XO's approval.

"Good. Do you have any questions, Doctor?"

"Questions, Captain? Thousands," she smiled wearily. "But I'll first ask the chief and Lieutenant Gentry if either Hendrix or Thurston had any psychiatric quirks at all?"

"None as to Hendrix," the master chief said sadly. "He was a good man. He was recommended for our engineering department by his last CO on an attack submarine." On Chief Foster's right sleeve was the Navy's "E" award, an embroidered "E" symbolizing the service's battle efficiency award. The award is worn for one year before it must be won again. The chiefs "E" was gold, attesting to five annual citations in a row. Jessica Dugan took the chief's word for it.

"Lieutenant Gentry?"

"Same as to Thurston, Doctor. He was the best of the best from seaman recruit up to his first class rating. He should have been a chief petty officer."

"I would add, Commander," the captain interrupted, "that *Sam Houston* is a special ship in terms of personnel. We have few enlisted men aboard at all. Most of the crew are at least petty officers since the ship was largely automated at our last refit for this assignment. Everyone here is qualified as a minimum, and over-qualified as the rule. We have no strikers at all on this ship. This is a very special command, indeed."

Strikers are seaman apprentices, the Navy's second lowest rating, above seaman recruits.

"Yes, Sir," the doctor said respectfully. "DCNO made that very clear to me last night." She lifted her tired face to look

squarely at her captain. "I *shall* find the containment compro
mise and fix it, Sir."

"Good. Anything else by way of preliminaries?" The CO
looked around the wardroom.

"Very well. Commander Dugan, I want you to see the ship.
Then I take the liberty of ordering you to put an even strain on
all parts." The CO smiled.

An "even strain, all parts" is Navy for a nap.

"Aye aye, Sir," the tired doctor nodded.

"Very well." The captain rose and everyone followed. "You
may carry on."

Superior officers may say "very well" to their juniors, but
never the other way around. The Navy has its traditions.

The company followed the CO into the passageway. Pappy
Perlmutter led Jessica Dugan aft through the control room.
Beyond the control room was the BL-2, lowest level, biologi-
cal containment facility in the submarine.

"Four-oh" a submariner said softly as Dr. Dugan passed
in to the cluttered CIC. No one speaks loudly in a cruising submarine. The seaman spoke to a seaman at his side.
"Four-oh" is Navy for 4.0, standing for perfection, which
described the sailor's review of the only woman on their
man-of-war.

"Like to find her in my lucky bag," the second man whispered when Jessica Dugan had passed. Every Navy ship has a
lost-and-found box, called the lucky bag.

"Sir. Ma'am," the petty officers said to the XO and the
physician at the aft control room bulkhead.

"Men," the executive officer nodded, "this is Commander
Dugan."

The seamen saluted, not quite knowing what courtesy to
extend a woman at the bottom of the sea.

"That's no seagull!" the first man smiled when the officers
had passed. A seagull is Navy for the kind of woman a submariner would most like to meet after a 70-day, submerged
patrol.

"She's a doc, after all," the other man said very softly.
"Maybe she'll do the short-arm inspections!"

"Wouldn't mind!"

Seamen also have their own way of describing a venereal
disease examination.

The XO and Dr. Dugan stopped at the rear of the control room compartment. Ahead of them was the bulkhead leading into the upper deck of the old missile compartment.

"This is the BL-2 facility. Minimum containment. We'll just run through this lab and the BL-3 down below. We won't do the BL-4 right now since you're tired and BL-4 would require changing into smocks and the disinfectant shower. At least it's better than a Navy shower down there." The XO smiled.

"Even a Navy shower would be welcome right now," Jessie Dugan laughed softly. She had picked up on the general quietude of a submarine cruising at Condition IV readiness: peacetime alert. A Navy shower conserves precious fresh water: wet down; soap up, with water off; rinse off, with water on—quickly.

Lt. Commander Dugan stumbled as she passed through the bulkhead hatchway. She was now almost staggering from exhaustion.

"Think I'm about at half-switch," she nodded sleepily.

"Where did you learn submarine?" the XO asked, surprised at her knowledge of sub lingo. Half-switch referred to old, diesel-electric boats running at reduced speed with the batteries connected in parallel to conserve energy.

"Used to date a sub jock."

The executive officer nodded.

They entered the BL-2 minimum containment laboratory behind the control room and CIC. Dr. Dugan blinked at banks of equipment and technicians in long, white coats.

"Here, Jessica," the XO pointed. "Look."

She stared at a short, green tobacco plant standing in a clay pot. The leaves glowed with brilliant and pulsating yellow.

"It looks like a damn lightning bug!" Jessica Dugan felt as if she were walking in her sleep.

"It *is* a lightning bug, sort of."

She could only blink at the winking tobacco plant.

"It's from UC, San Diego," Pappy said gravely. "In 1986, they were able to splice the luciferase glow enzyme into tobacco plants . . . That's what we do here."

It was Jessica Dugan's turn to sound grim.

"I guess that's why they call this The Bug Boat."

"I didn't know they did."

FOUR

14 MARCH; 1800 UTC

THE SPRING tropical depression had been building columns of cumulus clouds over the Dominican Republic since dawn. After nine hours of heating by the white sun, the cloud deck lingered over the 10,000-foot high Cordiller Central mountain range on Hispaniola's southern coast.

Blowing against the eastern face of the mountains, the wind turned skyward and drove the clouds ever higher. The mountain peaks were lost in the base of the clouds. On the cooler, leeward side of the ridge, a sudden tropical shower drenched the valley between the Cordiller Central range and the Los Botaos range further south. The lush valley, 10 miles wide and 125 miles long, ran southeastward from Haiti, across the Dominican border, and down to the sea at the Bay of Ocoa. A foggy mist closed the civilian airport at Barahona, Dominican Republic, on the great island's southern coast. Three parallel mountain ranges—the Cordiller Central, the Los Bataos, and the Sierra De Baoruco—held the sudden rains in a swirling wind storm of standing mountain waves and tropical updrafts.

As is the case in the tropics, the clouds built for half a day, but the violent and localized downpour lasted only 30 minutes before the brilliant sun popped through a dazzling clean sky.

The barometric depression and the rising air currents over the mountains had sucked hard at the atmosphere over the blue sea between Hispaniola and Puerto Rico. The showers were not even seen from Mona Passage between the two islands where the sky stayed clear with only a sudden, tell-tale wind blowing from east to west.

The wind drove the sea before it and the normally docile current sped from 1 knot up to 6 knots for ten hours.

The low pressure over central Hispaniola had sucked the wind and the ocean below into the Dominican Republic's eastern coastline. Surf rose along the coastal estuaries and tidal basins.

After sixteen hours in the water, Buddy Thurston bobbed face down in the Bay of Samana just north of the Dominican Republic's easternmost point.

Only 6 miles wide and 30 miles long, the bay ended in marshes and swamps. The only civilization was the hamlet of Los Robalos on the northern rim of the bay. The little runway of the Arroyo Barril airport ended at the water's edge.

Buddy Thurston's bloated body had silently ridden the sea westward across 90 nautical miles of ocean.

Even in early spring, the tropical heat of the afternoon had driven a dozen small fishing boats to anchor in the bay. The heat of the day would force the good fish into deeper, cooler water. So the wind-burned fishermen paused to nap or to smoke or to speak saltily of women waiting at home.

In the balmy bay at 2:00 in the afternoon, the air smelled of distant rain and nearby fish. Of the one- and two-man crews on the little boats with peeling paint, half of the fishermen spoke their Spanish with a Cuban accent.

Buddy Thurston's body floated between two of the boats which had genuine Dominican crews. All of the fishermen at anchor who were not sleeping stood to watch the sudden activity on the boat closest to the object in the water.

Fishermen stood on their musty decks where they kept their balance by holding on to the lines securing their nets to short masts of rotting wood. It took two stout and barefoot boatmen to haul the drowned man's body to the gunwale. The body was too waterlogged to be lifted by the shepherd's hook which the two men worked over the side. So they swung their net out, pushed Buddy Thurston's corpse into the seine, and cranked

the net onto the deck with a muscle-powered winch. Brown
arms strained to swing the body to the deck.

After sixteen hours in the water, the seaman's body was
barely recognizable as human. He would have done better in
cold, northern waters. The tropical ocean had caused rapid
deterioration.

Thurston's crushed skull was dark and swollen. The gas of
decomposition had so blown up his face that his cheeks had
expanded until his eyes and nose were lost in a gelatinous blob
of flesh. His blue cotton shirt had ruptured along the button line
and the upper arm sleeves had been ripped open by his biceps
swollen like thighs. The body had dropped from the net face
up. Skin was already hanging in clumps from the white chest
and distended abdomen. A small rip in the belly fat was already
home to tiny, shrimplike creatures which had ridden their meal
into De Samana Bay. The same surge of gas which had filled
Buddy Thurston's belly enough to float him to the surface had
also pushed the contents of his bowels into his denim trousers.

The two bronzed fishermen were nauseated by the sight and
the stench. Rotting human meat smelled worse than rotting fish
which has less fat to render into festering suet. Overcome in
the hot sun, the men pushed the body back into the net, cranked
the winch furiously, and dumped the dead sailor back into the
calm sea.

Too superstitious to remain at their anchor, the fishermen lit
the little boat's ratty old diesel and chugged a full mile closer
to the 4,200 feet of blacktop at the Arroyo Barril airfield.
They reset their anchor and agreed never to speak again of
their ghastly catch. Then they blessed their vessel, crossed
themselves, and resumed their afternoon nap.

Another of the boats puttered over to the scene of the first
boat's fit of hauling and winching, winching and dumping.

Three fishermen in the second boat again hooked Buddy
Thurston with a long pole under his armpit. One of the men
jumped into the water where he rolled the cadaver over onto
its back. The dead man's knees were flexed in rigor mortis
and the knees broke the surface. Tiny whitecaps swirled at the
tight, dark blue cloth.

The swimmer pulled a fishing knife from his belt. He quickly cut both of Buddy Thurston's ripped sleeves at the shoulder
seams and sliced the material on each side of the grossly

wrinkled neck. Then he jerked the blue, sleeveless shirt over the swollen head. Already open in the front, the shirt slipped over Buddy's head like an open vest.

Before climbing over the low gunwale into the boat, the swimmer rolled the body over so it floated bare backed and face down.

"To the sea, your mother," the wet fisherman said as if in benediction. For a nameless but brother seaman, he mourned in Spanish with a Cuban accent.

The dead sailor floated toward the western shore of the bay and the beach of sharp stones and driftwood. Brine shrimp waited in the coastal shoals to feast on Buddy Thurston, USN.

The fisherman on the small boat dried in minutes under the high sun in a purple sky. His two companions stood around him and they examined the blue rag cut away from the body. Though badly faded, "THURSTON" was still clearly stencilled above the left breast pocket.

The dark hands of the fishermen carefully fingered another stencil just above the boldface name. This was a stylized rendition of two small dolphins poised upon a wave. The fish faced each other like aviators' wings.

The fishermen agreed that the body had not been afloat more than two days and they recognized the dolphin ensign instantly.

The blue shirt and the corpse floating toward shore were from a United States submarine.

Lt. Commander Jessica Dugan did not remember going to sleep on the floor.

She knew only that she could not open her eyes and that her face hurt and that, somehow, she was on her hands and knees.

With all her might, she forced her eyes to open. Her heart skipped a beat in her throat because she was either blind or in the dark.

Her ears pounded full of heart and then pain, a stabbing pain. When she clasped her hands to her ears, she fell down hard upon her elbows.

She had to scream in the dark. She wanted to scream. She needed to scream.

But something deep inside her stopped the scream. As if she knew that screaming would violate her training and her instinct.

So instead of screaming down there on the deck where she knelt like a terrified animal, she whispered the name of her dead grandfather. When Jessica had been Jessie in pigtails, she would cry for her grandfather when the night demons came for her. The spirit of her grandfather never failed to drive the terrors away.

Jessica Dugan never knew her grandfather. Her father's father had spent a lifetime in the United States Navy. Before she was born, her sailor grandfather had ridden the aircraft carrier *Yorktown* to the bottom of the Pacific in 1942. Her father had made the dead man a living presence in her childhood. She never knew how to pray to the sky; but she had always called to her grandfather to save her from peril and from fear. She called to him now where she trembled down upon her bruised elbows.

Through the sound of her heart which filled her ears, she heard her grandfather's voice inside her head. The terror subsided. The pain inside her ears did not. She heard a pop behind each of her temples as her ear drums strained to accommodate a terrible pressure.

When her grandfather came to her in the dark, she caught her breath and she forced her eyes to focus.

The stateroom was not completely dark. A red, standing light in the overhead illuminated the tiny cabin. Slowly, she gathered her wits as the darkness retreated when her eyes adapted to the dim red gloom.

Through the fog of deep sleep, she remembered the submarine and her narrow mattress on the lower level of a bunk bed. She thanked her grandfather for not allowing her to scream on a ship where silence and stealth are the rules.

Before Jessica Dugan could reach out for the corner of her boxlike bunk, more a drawer than a bed, she was forced off balance.

The deck close to her sweating face lurched and she rolled hard against the frame of her bunk. She hit her head as hard as she had hit the floor when she was thrown out of bed.

The drowned grandfather allowed the woman to moan softly.

First the deck pitched upward. Then it rolled sideways away from her.

Groping in the half dark, she found her soft-soled shoes—every submariner's uniform of every day. Street shoes would make noise against the deck and noise is the enemy where submariners live far from the sun and from real air.

Still on her hands and knees, Jessica Dugan lowered her face toward the rolling deck. When her nostrils were filled with the scent of rubber and of socks, she held the shoe to her mouth. She vomited into her shoe.

When her left shoe was full, she threw up into her right shoe. She heaved up black coffee and a slurry of doughnuts. The spasms of muscle contractions made the small of her back hurt as much as the side of her head.

When the second shoe was full, the deck stopped pitching. The stateroom was again level.

Trembling and sweating, Jessica Dugan climbed to her feet. Her legs shook as she held tightly to the corner of the bunk. With her free hand, she flicked on the cabin lights. She blinked in the glare.

Her ditty bag had hit the floor when she did. The deck was littered with pens, pads of paper, toiletries, and a broken coffee cup.

It took her two minutes to make it to her small bathroom. In the metallic head, she rinsed her mouth and combed her hair. In the mirror she could see that the left side of her forehead had been bruised by her fall from bed. She had no idea if she had fallen five minutes or an hour earlier. Were it not for her battered face and her shoes brimming with barf, she would have thought it all a terrible dream.

In her stateroom proper, she almost gagged when she lifted her shoes. She carried them to the head and flushed her wardroom lunch.

She stood wrapping a rubber band around a plastic laundry bag in which she had stuffed her wet shoes. The bag went into a fake wood drawer made out of formica.

"Commander!"

The woman turned to the open door to her stateroom.

"Lieutenant Shaffer?"

"Are you all right?" The ship's physician seemed breathless as he entered and looked at the mess on the stateroom floor. Small items were strewn everywhere.

"I think so."

"Your face looks terrible!" The medic laid his hand gently upon her cheek.

"I think I was thrown out of bed. Did we hit something?" She had remembered where she was.

"No. You better go back to the CIC."

"Why do my ears hurt?" The woman realized that her ears were so full of air that she could hardly hear him. Her ears felt like she had just landed too quickly after a bad airplane ride.

"Does yawning help?"

She had forgotten to try that. Her ears popped when she forced a yawn. That helped some, but not completely.

"A little better, Lieutenant."

"Please, call me Stan. Try again?"

This time, she held her nostrils while she tried to blow through her nose. Her ears popped again.

"I heard that!" Dr. Shaffer said. "That should have done it."

She heard him clearly this time.

"What the hell happened?" Jessica Dugan was recovering quickly.

"I'm afraid you are needed. I just came from sick bay. The planesman tried to get us all killed!"

"My God!" The woman was more confused than frightened.

"Almost, Commander. You better go."

Jessica Dugan pulled her hair up and straightened her shoulders. She took a step toward the passageway.

"Doctor Dugan, your shoes?"

The woman looked down at her feet. She was in socks only.

"The shoes the XO gave me were too big. Where can I get another pair?"

"I'll take care of it. Please hurry."

Before she closed the door behind her, Jessie Dugan paused and looked back over her shoulder. "Thanks, Grandpa," she whispered.

"Did you say something?"

"No."

The physician walked quickly aft toward the control room. She was greeted in the combat information center by Pappy Perlmutter and the captain standing side by side.

"Jessica," Pappy said without a smile. "Are you all right, Jessica?" He frowned at her face which was turning purple. Her left eye socket was rapidly darkening. "I think you actually have a black eye."

The doctor touched her eye.

"What happened?"

"I don't know, Jessica," the executive officer shrugged. "The planesman simply came unglued. He took us down to 1,300 feet before the diving officer could jerk him out of the chair. He was either hallucinating—or worse. It all happened within 45 seconds. . . ."

"We could have crushed," the captain continued. "Twenty years in the sub service, and I never saw anyone lose it at the helm. When the diving officer grabbed him, the planesman bit half his ear off. Lieutenant Shaffer has both of them below. Pappy will take you down, Commander."

Jessica Dugan visibly shuddered in her stocking feet. "Crushed?"

Before either officer could answer the shaken woman, a first class petty officer approached the captain.

"Sir, maneuvering room on the horn. Sounds serious."

"Thanks."

Dr. Dugan and the XO followed Captain Milhaus to the rear of the control room and the radio consoles. The captain energized the 1JV, two-way intercom which connects the CIC with the maneuvering room well aft, behind the nuclear reactor compartment. The reactor is behind the far bulkhead of the missile compartments which were now laboratories in *Sam Houston*. Unlike the ship's general intercom circuit, IMC, which is only a one-way public address system, the 1JV is one of the submarine's several two-way telephones.

"Captain here," the officer said in a submariner's constantly subdued voice. The CO listened intently.

"Crawford here, Sir. We're running a casualty protocol down here, Captain. We had a condenser vacuum loss on train alpha when we went to full power on main steam. Chief thinks we took some thermal shock to main feedwater on the SG when we crashed through 1200 feet. We're checking the steam seals now on main turbine and the feedpump turbines."

"Understood, Mister Crawford. Keep the XO advised. You didn't trip did you?"

"Negative, Sir. Neither the EFIC nor the AFW kicked in. Everything is still on line—for the moment."

"Okay. Thanks. Advise on the feedwater and reset the EFIC and AFW."

"Yes, Sir."

"Feedwater, Captain?" Dr. Dugan felt herself overwhelmed and very deep in the black ocean indeed. She had heard only the captain's half of the conversation.

"You explain it, Pappy."

"Yes, Captain."

Captain Milhaus left the CIC and went down the companionway to the mid-deck below.

Lt. Commander Perlmutter took Jessica Dugan aside to the rear corner of the control room.

"Did you spend any time at nuclear power school, Jessica?"

"Are you kidding?"

The expression of stubborn determination on the XO's tired face answered the question.

"Sorry, Pappy. No, never."

The seamen who manage a floating nuclear reactor in the United States Navy have spent a minimum of 20 months in intensive training. Nuclear power school at Orlando, Florida, begins with two months of basic electronics class followed by six months of advanced electronics. Then comes another half year of nuclear power theory and then six more months of hands-on experience at a land-based nuclear power station.

"The reactor simply heats steam into superheated, high pressure steam which runs our main turbine. It's like a jet engine that uses steam for power from the reactor circuit instead of air. The turbine drives our propeller. When the steam exhaust comes out of the turbine, it goes through condensers which turn the steam back into water. The coolant water for the condensers is just sea water brought in from outside. The water from the condensers then passes through pre-heaters which turn the cooled water into hot water for recycling through the steam generator. That's the SG.

"When we dove to 1300 feet, the water from outside was colder than up here at our cruise depth. The colder water must have over-cooled the condenser or something. That's what maneuvering was talking about. The condensed feedwater pumped back to the steam generator might have been too cold for the pre-heaters. EFIC is the emergency feedwater initiation control and the AFW is the auxiliary feedwater system."

Back in the maneuvering room, highly trained technicians manage the reactor. The reactor operator controls the nuclear fission and coolant pumps. The throttleman operates the high-pressure turbine which drives the propeller and the low-pressure turbine which runs the generators for producing electricity. The generators are managed by an electrician. The engineering officer of the watch supervises everyone else.

"Oh. How dangerous was the dive, Pappy?" The physician whispered. Perspiration beaded on her upper lip.

"Dangerous enough to go into the permanent logbook of this boat, Doctor. Now, let's go see what we have in sick bay."

"What about my shoes?" The doctor was disoriented by her controlled terror, although *Sam Houston* was safely back to cruise depth and on her even keel.

"We'll stop at the commissary."

Submarines have three depth ranges. Test depth is an easy ride for all ship's systems and is the normal operating depth—600 to 800 feet for *Ethan Allen* class missile boats. Safe excursion depth, also called maximum permitted depth, is the deepest dive allowed only occasionally. Each such dive must be recorded in the ship's permanent logbook for maintenance purposes and for keeping track of depth-limited parts. Somewhere below maximum permitted depth, but before crush depth, is a water pressure level which is greater than the watertight integrity of fittings.

There are many holes in a sub's hull. The propeller shaft passes through to the outside ocean as do periscopes, antenna and radar masts, torpedo tube doors, and electrical lines to the hydrophone passive sonar. All these outlets are sealed to the sea pressure by fittings called glands. Below a certain depth, the glands cannot keep the water out. Below the depth where the fittings begin to leak, there is crush depth where the pressure would smash *Sam Houston* like an eggshell. In the United States Navy, crush depth is 1.5 times deeper than safe excursion depth.

The helmsman steers a submarine left or right like an airline pilot. American subs also have a planesman who controls the dive planes on the sub's sail tower and on the pointed tail end. The diving officer sits immediately behind them. The dive planes are like the elevators on an aircraft: they deflect the stern upward or downward. Since the main ballast tanks are either fully flooded or dry, it is only the ship's forward speed which controls depth. If the ship is awash at all with ballast tanks filled, she would sink straight to the bottom without forward speed over the planes. Submarines are truly "driven" up or down.

When the planesman lost his grip on reality, the diving officer grabbed him by the shoulders, jerked him from the seat, and threw him to the deck in the forward control room. When the officer bent over the convulsing seaman, the man on the deck reached for the officer and bit half an ear off. He swallowed it while he cried like a paddled child.

As she stepped into the well of the companionway hole in the aft control room, Jessica Dugan glanced over her shoulder at the clock on the bulkhead. It read 1945. Somewhere above, it was 3:45 in a Caribbean afternoon. She must have slept for only two hours in over thirty.

In sick bay on Two Deck, the middle of three decks, the second-class petty officer was barely conscious. He laughed and whimpered simultaneously.

"Dr. Shaffer?" Dr. Dugan stood close to the GMO.

"All I can say for the moment is that there is joint tenderness. His kidney output seems normal. I won't know if it's Lesch-Nyhan until I can do a serum scan for HPRT. That'll take two hours, minimum."

"Doctor?"

Stan Shaffer turned to see Captain Milhaus enter the four-bed infirmary.

"Sir."

"What do you have here?"

"I won't know for certain for maybe two hours, Captain."

"Then speculate," the impatient CO demanded softly.

"I would rather not, Sir."

"I would rather you did, Doctor."

Jessica Dugan studied the other physician.

"I think maybe. There is no other logical explanation at the moment. This man has been in the sub service for eight years. Not a blemish on his record. Not a twitch on the psychological tests before this cruise. He is—was—as sane as anyone else on this ship, Captain."

"So," was all the captain had to say. He turned his back on doctors Shaffer and Dugan and his executive officer. He took ten steps toward the man dozing in another bed: the diving officer of the afternoon watch. Captain Milhaus laid his hand upon the man's shoulder. The seaman did not open his eyes. His left ear was lost in a baseball-sized bandage which oozed brown blood.

"So," the CO repeated as he turned to face his officers. "We seem to be between wind and water."

The expression is used by old sailors to refer to the place on a ship's hull where the waves rise and fall, covering and uncovering a vessel's waterline. Since the days of iron men in wooden ships, 'tween wind and water was the worst possible place to take a hit. It became synonymous with anything terribly vulnerable.

"Thank you, Stan." The CO looked down into Jessica Dugan's eyes, the color of a New England sea after the rain. "Commander Dugan, you cannot sleep until you find out what's happening to my ship."

Captain Kurt Milhaus left the compartment for the passageway before anyone could breathe or answer.

" . . . to *my* ship" was the way he had said it.

"I am not surprised that it should have been Ruis Estoban," the admiral said warmly. Vice Admiral Perez was Chief of Naval Troops, Revolutionary Armed Forces.

It was 3:00 in the afternoon in Nicaro, Cuba, on the beautiful Bay of Nipe. The 4,000-foot-high peak towering over the Sierra de Micaro mountains could be seen 10 miles to the south from the window of the headquarters of the Eastern Naval Flotilla on Cuba's northeast coast.

"I knew his father in the Revolution, you know." The old admiral smiled as he remembered better times. "Capitan Estoban said he found an American submarine last night. And now our people in the Dominican Republic would seem to confirm that with the body they found this afternoon."

"The body could have been from one of the ships in the refueling formation, too, Admiral. Submarines don't just leave a man behind who fell overboard."

"Indeed, Porfirio. But the body had submarine insignia. And more important, American naval vessels always post a special lookout on the stern of their ships during replenishments at sea. That lookout's sole duty is to watch for men who fall in. No, Capitan, that man was from an American submarine. Somewhere north of Mona Passage."

"North of the Passage, Sir?"

"Yes. The current in March could have carried a body south, through the passage if that's where he went into the water. But he was found well north. And he was only in the water for maybe two days. So he had to go in before the passage."

The seaman walked to a large chart on the wall.

"Maybe here."

Vice Admiral Perez pointed to the deepest hole in the Atlantic Ocean.

"What can we get underway from Cienfuegos?"

"You want one of our submarines, Sir?"

The great bay and harbor at Cienfuegos on Cuba's southern shore is the country's submarine base.

"Yes. I don't want to send out a Koni. If the Americans do have a sub out there, a Koni is no match."

The Cuban Navy operates three ex-Soviet Koni class frigates.

"What do we have ready to deploy?"

"Nothing in less than three weeks, Admiral. Except for *El Tiburon*."

"*El Tiburon*? Good."

"It's deployed now on a training mission. It left Cienfuegos twenty-four hours ago. But the captain has never had operational orders in a sub, Sir. And the crew is mostly right from the service academies."

"Who is in command?"

"Capitan Barcena."

Vice Admiral Perez nodded with a faint smile.

The former Soviet Union has given three Foxtrot class, diesel-electric submarines to the Cuban Navy. The first one arrived at the island in February 1979, the second in January 1980, and the third vessel in February 1984. Foxtrots are 300 feet long and 26 feet wide with two decks inside. Non-nuclear, their three diesels turn three propellers to drive the old boats 16,000 miles while running at 16 knots on the surface and 13 knots submerged.

The admiral stepped away from the chart to gaze out the window. He spoke to the ocean.

"The Party was crippled at the recent Fourth Communist Party Congress. We must restore the confidence of our armed forces. It will do them good to learn that we sent a vessel to sea for the purpose of harassing an American submarine. If we find her, that will be enough. The Americans will not be anxious to engage us after their painful experience in Somalia. And we will not engage them. To find them will be enough. The risk of an actual engagement is small indeed, Porfirio."

The admiral turned to face his junior officer.

"Shall I brief the president, Admiral?"

"No need, I shall be back in La Habana tomorrow. I shall brief El Commandante. Fidel will be pleased that we have challenged the Americans to their ocean."

"All right, Admiral." The junior officer did not sound convinced.

"How soon can you alert *El Tiburon*, Porfirio?"

"Now, Admiral. Right now." The officer's black eyes were troubled eyes.

Vice Admiral Perez looked out the window toward the sea, his sea.

"Inform *El Tiburon* that her training cruise is terminated. If there is a Yanqui boat off the Dominican Republic, I want her found."

"Yes, Admiral."

FIVE

14 MARCH; 2000 UTC

FROM *SAM Houston*'s sick bay, the ship's physician led Lt. Commander Dugan aft. Behind the submarine's infirmary on Deck Two was the BL-3 research laboratory. The boat's middle deck contained the second of three labs, each built around the old nuclear missile bays.

The BL-2 lab on the top deck contained the least toxic chemicals and cultures. The BL-4 on the lowest deck, Deck Three, required maximum protection and rigorous containment of contamination. The animal test subjects lived in BL-4.

Lt. Shaffer led Dr. Dugan toward the sealed bulkhead. Although far from shore, the National Institutes of Health protocols for gene laboratories were carefully observed 800 feet under water on board SSN-609.

"Shaffer and Dugan," the ship's general medical officer said softly into a wall mounted intercom.

"Yes, Sir," a voice answered from the wall speaker. "Coming, Lieutenant."

The two physicians stood before the watertight hatch in the passageway. The round steel wheel on the door spun without a sound and the hatch opened inward toward the laboratory.

"Sir. Ma'am," a young petty officer nodded. He wore denim duty fatigues. "Sorry, I had to change before I could come out, you know."

"No problem," Lt. Shaffer smiled.

"The LD says you may come in, Sir," the sailor said softly as he stepped aside to permit his superior officers to enter. All three had to step over the bottom of the hatchway and crouch down to avoid hitting their faces on the top rim of the watertight door.

Each laboratory has its own Laboratory Director per NIH guidelines. Although each of 609's Laboratory Directors was a chief petty officer outranked by both physicians, the LD commanded his lab and answered to no one but the ship's captain. The LD has absolute authority to limit access to a lab when recombinant DNA work is in progress. It is his duty to confirm that everyone seeking entry has been properly warned of the risks and has received any required immunizations. In the BL-3 lab, only persons essential to the experiments may be allowed access. All BL-3 work on DNA must be conducted in biological safety cabinets. Open beakers or vials on work benches are forbidden by the NIH rules.

The noncommissioned officer sealed the door behind them. The two officers and their guide stood in a compartment 10 feet long and 30 feet wide. It looked like a very clean locker room.

"BL-3 requires gowns, Jessica," Dr. Shaffer said. He opened one of the metal lockers on the port side and pulled out white coveralls which he handed to Dr. Dugan. He gave a second pair to the young technician and kept the third for himself. The seaman had discarded his protective clothing before he went into the outside passageway. "On our way out, we'll dump these in the contamination bins." NIH guidelines require that the gowns and smocks must be decontaminated before they can go to the laundry.

When the officer closed the metal locker, Jessica Dugan noted that the metal on metal made no sound: the door's edges were all covered with rubber bumpers. The Silent Service worked hard to justify its name.

The seaman and his guests pulled fresh coveralls over their service clothing. The long-sleeved jumpsuits buttoned to their chins.

"Don't forget your booties, Sir," the seaman said firmly when the three converged on the center of the compartment. He handed the two physicians a pair of white, rubberized overshoes which fit over their soft-soled, submariners' shoes. "Now we're ready."

The petty officer flicked a switch on another squawkbox.

"Three to enter," he said to the wall.

"Approved," a voice crackled. When the seaman pushed a pneumatic lever, another watertight door swung open to reveal a brightly lighted compartment. A blast of cool air swept over the visitors from behind. NIH rules require that BL-3 and -4 labs must have directional airflow sucking air into the lab so that no air blows from the lab out into the outside areas. The seaman waited for his superiors to crouch through the hatchway before he followed them. In all BL-3 laboratories the inner door closes automatically and it slammed closed when an electric eye sensed that the hatchway was not occupied.

"Hatch secured," the seaman said softly toward the Laboratory Director whose white smock showed the insignia of a senior chief petty officer: one stripe above three stripes. Above the upper stripe sat a blue eagle and above the eagle, a single blue star.

The guide lingered beside the closed hatch.

"Lt. Commander Dugan, this is the Biosafety Manual. There's another one in the ship's library." The seaman's gaze stopped for an instant at the woman's blackened left eye injured 90 minutes earlier when the submarine dove toward the bottom five miles below.

The physician nodded.

"If you would be kind enough to sign in please," the sailor said as he pointed to the lab's log. Both the BL-3 lab and the maximum containment BL-4, one deck below, required sign-in records of the crew's coming and going. Dr. Dugan signed the log, followed by Dr. Shaffer.

Dr. Shaffer pointed to a cabinet secured with glass doors. The cabinet contained rows of test tubes filled with yellowish liquid.

"Baseline serum samples," he said toward Jessica Dugan. "The NIH guidelines require blood work-ups on crewmen exposed to hazardous biologicals. Down in BL-4, we draw it weekly."

Lt. Commander Dugan looked up and her black eye squinted against the harsh glare of the lab's lights. The black silos of the sub's empty missile bay rose from the deck and continued up through the overhead. Technicians in white moved among the lab tables sandwiched between the sixteen silos.

The forward end of the lab where the physicians stood contained work stations for processing DNA and RNA proteins. These heavy chains of proteins direct cell reproduction in all living organisms. DNA—deoxyribonucleic acid—is the blueprint of all living things. In every human cell, the DNA dictates the individual traits by some 100,000 separate genes arranged in a string of 3 billion subunits of organic material called nucleotide bases. One such gene may even create poets.

"We start the process in earnest right here," Dr. Shaffer gestured toward a bench of tiny vials. The weary woman with the bruised face stared at the technicians' white coveralls and latex gloves. "We generally use Invitrogen reagents to build our DNA libraries." Hundreds of small, thumb-size vials of genetic raw material had found their way from San Diego to the outskirts of the Puerto Rico Trench. "We have modified the Invitrogen reagents for application in higher life forms. These cloning agents off the shelf are limited to bacteria cells. We use a modified Invitrogen Copy Kit to build our library of complementary DNA.

"When we need to use the polymerase chain reaction to build large fragments of DNA, we start at this station with the Fast Track Kit which isolates messenger RNA. We can do that in as little as 90 minutes. Seventy-five micrograms of messenger RNA can be harvested from a single gram of tissue culture.

"And you'll notice that the NIH rules also require that all BL-3 lab sinks must be elbow or foot operated, or automatic. No one can touch the sink fixtures with his hand. You'll also see that all of the vacuum lines on the equipment are equipped with HEPA filters. That's high-efficiency, particulate air filters. The HEPA filters all have disinfectant traps, too."

Lt. Commander Dugan suddenly felt unclean. The NIH safety standards certainly made a contamination leak very unlikely. On the other hand, the rules underlined in red the toxic environment which she had agreed to visit. She hoped that the bearded physician did not sense her shiver.

"Creepy, huh?" Dr. Shaffer said softly.

"A little. All this equipment under water, for God's sake! I feel like I went to school a hundred years ago. This is all over my head."

The woman labored to absorb the science surrounding her. Perspiration beaded on her forehead from fatigue, her nausea hardly an hour earlier, and her ever present and suffocating awareness of hovering nearly 1,000 feet under water.

At Johns Hopkins medical school thirteen years earlier, routinely constructing designer DNA in test tubes was science fiction. Now she was sunk in a DNA factory. The befuddled expression around her gray eyes within dark circles of fatigue spoke to her physician guide.

"Guess predictive ecologists don't spend much time toying with molecules," Lt. Shaffer smiled.

"No, not much. I'm a little rusty, I'm afraid. The eleven hours between the DCNO's telex and coming on board didn't give me much time to bone up on molecular biology. Sorry."

"Not to worry, Commander. I'll lead you through it. I speak the language of all this mad science."

"I'm glad, Stan. But I hate to burden you."

"My pleasure, really. Besides, I could be shot for discussing this anywhere else. I enjoy talking about our work out here."

"Well, then. Lead on." She smiled weakly. Her face throbbed with increasing pain. Her ears still rang from the pressure pulse during her nap when 609 dived in the grip of the crazed planesman.

"We have to start by building libraries of complementary DNA. We call it c-DNA. First we isolate the messenger RNA— m-RNA for short—from the target cell's nucleus. Then we use the Invitrogen kits to make c-DNA fragments from the m-RNA. The c-DNA is a copy of the m-RNA, only it's exactly opposite. Each nucleotide on the m-RNA binds to its complementary, opposite nucleotide on the c-DNA. Remember your Biology 101: DNA and RNA are strands of nucleotide bases which always bind in the same pair matches. Adenine will bind to thymine only, and guanine will only bind with cytosine. In DNA-RNA hybrids, uracil replaces thyrosine in the bond with adenine."

"Yes, yes. I remember the basics." The exhausted woman hated to sound impatient. But her head pounded too hard to be coy.

"Good. Well, the original m-RNA from our specimen tissue attaches itself—hybridizes—to the newly made c-DNA. One more bit of magic at this point turns the RNA-DNA duplex into two attached strands of c-DNA. This new, double-stranded, complementary DNA is then ready for cloning into some host cell or bacteria. We have a dozen work stations here in BL-3 where we build these c-DNA libraries for research applications down below in BL-4. Step over here.

"We can progressively shorten the DNA fragments until we isolate the on-off molecular switch for a single specific gene. We use traditional Northern Blots to study RNA and Southern Blots to analyze DNA."

Blotting refers to the techniques used to identify tiny pieces of the double-helix "spiral staircase" strands of DNA. Every human cell—like all animals and plants—has a DNA strand in its nucleus: a cell's reproductive Mission Control. A single human DNA strand in a single microscopic cell would stretch out six feet in length. There is enough DNA in a human being to form a nucleotide thread from Earth to the planet Pluto at the end of the solar system.

Southern Blotting is named for E. M. Southern who perfected DNA gel electrophoresis. The similar technique for targeting and identifying the building blocks along an RNA strand has been dubbed Northern Blotting. For the sake of alliteration, molecular biologists also perform Eastern and Western Blotting.

"Here at this station, we use electrophoresis and denaturing agarose gel to sort the various RNA fragments. The fragments are then transferred to nylon membranes so irradiated DNA probes can zero in on specific parts of the RNA. Our blots are done with Oncor reagents and membranes. We use Oncor Extract-A-Gene kits for isolating and purifying messenger RNA. The RNA takes about five hours and we can run the DNA in about a day.

"With Oncor kits, we can locate specific genes on specific chromosomes. We use fluorescence microscopes after we fix the chromosome specimens with fluorescein-labeled avidin."

The little kits from Oncor Molecular Cytogenetics came from Gaithersburg, Maryland.

DNA normally carries a negative (-) electrical charge. When DNA in a gel is exposed to a positive (+) charge, the negatively charged DNA is attracted to the positive end. This electrical trick is electrophoresis. Smaller fragments travel faster than larger bits. When the gel is then stained with ethidium bromide, ultraviolet light illuminates neat rows of traveling DNA fragments. How far a fragment advances can identify the chemistry of the broken bit of the genetic staircase.

"Do you build your DNA with the polymerase chain reaction?" the doctor asked sleepily.

"Generally, yes. But just about everything here is automated as much as possible. We're operational with test and analytical procedures down here that won't be routine State-side for another two or three years."

She nodded with her eyes half open.

"And these are my favorite toys."

The physician pointed proudly to several computer arrays.

"This baby is the ACAS-70 interactive laser cytometer from Meridian Instruments in Michigan. Five hundred fifty pounds of amazing."

Lt. Shaffer sat down at the desk-like console. At his left elbow was a large microscope built into the quarter-ton machine. Mounted on the desktop to his right were two television monitors.

"We can do cellular microsurgery with this. The ACAS-70 can isolate individual cells on a tissue culture growing on a film-lined dish. Inside here is an argon ion laser which can carve out one cell at a time. They call it a 'photon scalpel.' We can use fluorescence redistribution after photo-bleaching procedures—we call it FRAP—to scan parts of individual cells with a laser beam pulse.

"The system is especially useful since we can use this machine to monitor how molecules diffuse across the cell membrane. Fluorescence analysis lets us see DNA damage within the cell itself. The 80386 computer inside the ACAS-70 generates color images of cells on these TV screens. It can sort cells electronically according to specific characteristics which we feed the computer. That way, we can determine if and where our little bugs are being absorbed by the cell. We have five of Meridian's Dasy-9000 work stations for raw data analysis. Two of them are below in BL-4."

Dr. Shaffer rose and walked further aft.

"Is that the same equipment?" Jessica Dugan asked.

"No. This is a Scanalytics Masterscan interpretive densitometer. We have three: two here and one down below."

The two physicians walked over to another modular console with a desklike work station, computer screen, and large hooded attachment.

"The Masterscan is a computer which analyzes high-resolution, digital pictures of cells. We run our gel images through it to clean them up electronically. It filters out the garbage.

"With Masterscan, we can examine our blots and electronically evaluate them. This hood contains the high-resolution camera which can image cells or cell parts as small as one millionth of an inch. Masterscan can automatically identify the DNA or RNA band patterns. Otherwise, we would have to do it with X-Ray photographs and our own eyeballs. And down here, we have neither enough time nor enough eyeballs."

The Scanalytics equipment came from Billerica, Massachusetts, to the Puerto Rico Trench.

"It does look like NASA's basement in here, Stan, with all this high-tech razzle dazzle." Dr. Dugan was waking up as her weary brain was slowly inspired by the sight of wall-to-wall 21st century biology.

"Nowhere else in the world has this much hardware," the ship's doctor said with pride. He glanced around the work stations anchored to sixteen empty missile silos. "And this is just the heavy, glamorous stuff. The lighter equipment is aft."

He pointed toward two parallel rows of tables which ran along *Sam Houston*'s steel pressure hull from the lab's center to the rearmost watertight hatchway.

"Those are the HPLC systems. Some are manual but most are automatic. We use the equipment from several manufacturers to cross-check accuracy."

High-performance, liquid chromatography (HPLC) equipment sorts complex protein molecules by size or weight in liquid solution. The heart of the devices are stainless steel columns. The columns of varying size are densely packed with microfine, sand-like granules which essentially strain the solutions. Fluid is forced through the HPLC columns under pressure as high as three tons per square inch. How fast a protein molecule is strained out of the column depends upon the molecule's unique size and weight. Every molecule has its own straining time as unique as a fingerprint. Monitors record graphic peaks as each group of similar molecules is squirted out of the column at its proper time.

As the sorted molecules squirt out of the columns, they must be identified. Ultraviolet detectors do this delicate job.

Both sides of the BL-3 missile compartment's rear third were lined with banks of HPLC machines for breaking down proteins. Five Series 9000 Gradient Auto-analytical HPLC machines sat beside five Series 8000 Isocratic Auto-analytical devices, all from Gilson Medical Electronics, Middleton, Wisconsin. The automated separators ran off IBM PS/2 computers for sorting proteins or their individual amino acid molecules.

"The other side of the lab uses HPLC equipment from Rainin Instruments of California. Their Autoprep HPLC system can pump solutions through the columns at 9,000 pounds per square inch pressure. Some of our people prefer the Rainin equipment because their Method Manager software runs off a Macintosh computer. We also have two of their model RF3 protein fractionators for separating proteins."

Jessica Dugan stumbled against Dr. Shaffer. *Sam Houston* was rock solid in her 4-knot cruise. The doctor was too tired to stand.

Lt. Shaffer grabbed her shaking shoulders.

"Are you all right, Jessica?"

She opened her mouth but said nothing. Cold sweat beaded on her upper lip. She breathed in short, rapid pants.

"I . . . I . . . What time is it?" Her eyes were closed and the lids were moist.

"Sit down, Commander."

A technician shoved a chair behind her knees and the medical officer gently eased her backward.

"Just sit down, Jessica. You're hyperventilating. Try to hold your breath. Please, Jessie."

Her ashen cheeks bulged for fifteen seconds. When she took a breath, the color rose on the side of her face which was not bruised. She opened her good right eye.

"What time is it, Stan?"

"Ah, 2100 . . . 5:00 in the evening, local time, Jessica." She had only taken two brief naps in the last 40 hours.

"Stanley . . . I have to sleep . . . I have to barf." She almost cried. "Oh, God." Her pale forehead dropped against Lt. Shaffer's chest. His right hand reached for the back of

her clammy neck and he rubbed the base of her hairline.

"You'll be okay. You'll be okay."

She only mumbled.

"Someone help me, please!" the physician called out in a
submariner's hoarse whisper.

Two technicians grabbed each side of the fainting physician
under her soaking-wet armpits. With Dr. Shaffer holding her
head up, they nearly dragged her forward to the hatchway and
the outer containment area.

In the compartment between the watertight doors, Lt. Shaffer
held her up while the two seamen peeled her overalls from her
officers' brown uniform underneath. Then they held her up until
the lieutenant could remove his own protective suit and toss
both garments into the decontamination bin.

"Thanks, I can take her outside."

"Yes, Sir," a seaman said quietly as he opened the outer
door. The inner hatch to the laboratory had closed automatically after they had dragged the stumbling doctor through
it.

The two physicians staggered down the passageway toward
sick bay.

"I wouldn't mind tucking her in," one seaman smiled to the
other before they returned to the lab.

In the ship's small hospital 15 yards down the passageway
from the sterile missile compartment, Lt. Shaffer heaved his
limp burden upon a 36-inch wide mattress. He had to lift her
legs onto the cot. After he had removed her soft-soled shoes,
he pulled a blanket over her clothes up to her chin. She was
already drooling from the side of her mouth. As the physician
stepped back, Jessica Dugan sucked in a snore worthy of a
lumberjack.

"Good night, Commander," Lt. Shaffer gently smiled. "We'll
make a sailor out of you yet."

The wasted woman looked pale and gray. But with her hair
falling upon the small pillow in the soft light, she looked nearly
beautiful to the silent medical officer.

The physician turned and walked past the sedated planesman
who two hours earlier had tried to kill them all. He slept fitfully
with his arms restrained to the side of his bunk by leather
straps.

At the fake wood door to sick bay, Dr. Shaffer heard Jessica Dugan let out another gurgling snore. He smiled.

"Hope Brother Ivan doesn't have his ears on tonight," he whispered to the empty passageway.

El Tiburon had stood out of Cienfuegos harbor proudly with her Cuban steaming ensign snapping smartly in a warm, afternoon breeze. She had left port 26 hours ago. Half her crew in dress whites had manned the rail when she rode light surf toward open water.

El Tiburon had been everyone's training boat. Her complement of 75 officers and men were the cream of the People's Navy. The officers under Captain Martinez Barcena were graduates of the Punta Santa Ana Naval Academy to the last man. All of her enlisted men and petty officers were in the top of their classes at the naval school at Playa Del Salado.

El Tiburon was an elite billet with a crew representing Cuba's finest seamen.

Although thirty years old, the ship's machinery hummed with clean oil and fresh polish. She was the first of the three Foxtrot class diesel submarines given to Cuba by the Soviet Union and the first to be given a Spanish name. Three propellers pushed her 1,950 tons of steel at flank bell, 15 knots. She pitched in light swells where she rode ten meters beneath the surface.

At 2200 UTC, 5:00 in the afternoon Cuban time, water pounded over *El Tiburon*'s rather stubby bow with its protruding Fenik sonar dome. The bow had to be square enough to house her six forward torpedo tubes. The aft torpedo room in the stern contained four more tubes for 21-inch diameter Type 53, Russian homing torpedos.

Captain Barcena knew that his men and officers called him El Viejo behind his back: The Old Man. But he did not mind.

Captain Barcena was indeed old by the reckoning of his youthful crew. At 60, he was one of the seasoned veterans of the People's Navy. In the permanent financial disaster of the Revolution, he stood out among the crusty old hands of the Cuban military. Martinez Barcena was a patrician among pot-bellied revolutionaries who prided themselves in feigning austerity.

The Barcenas were old Spanish and old money. The officer's father had enjoyed taking drinks in La Habana at the Florida Bar long ago at the sunny table of Ernest Hemingway. As a boy, the sailor sat between his father and the bearded and rounded Yankee whom he had learned to call Papa. Father and son came to the revolution by accident.

The son had managed to fall in love with a beautiful student activist when they both attended university in Havana in the mid-1950s. When the girl followed El Commandante Fidel into the mountains, Martinez Barcena followed the girl. Between firefights with Fulgencio Batista's regulars, the pair made love in the shade of the mangrove trees. Only one day before Batista fell from power on New Year's Day 1959, the girl was killed by a sniper beside a dirt road. After Fidel Castro Ruz took over the government, Captain Barcena's father took the family jewels and silver with him to Argentina. The grieving and abandoned son stayed on.

Martinez Barcena had not thought so warmly of his dead Amalia for years. But now there was something in the air which covered the white-haired sailor in moist memories of secret moments stolen on mountain sides in the Sierra Maestra among a thousand soldiers. *El Tiburon* cruised just beneath the choppy surface eastward along Cuba's southern coastline. At shallow periscope depth, the submarine made way only 25 nautical miles southeast of the United States Naval Base at Guantanamo Bay, Cuba. *El Tiburon's* snorkel broke the surface to suck in warm sea air. The island's scent seemed to linger in the humid control room 30 feet below the surface. El Viejo knew that he must be imagining the smell on the wind since the sea breeze blew toward shore and not out to sea. But he could not shake the feeling.

El Tiburon, like all Soviet-built submarines, diesel or nuclear powered, was double-hulled with all of her main ballast tanks on the outside of the internal, pressure hull. With her external tanks on the sub's flanks and the main tank in her bow and stern flooded, she rode with her weather deck thirty feet beneath the green surf. Not flooding her many trim tanks and compensating tanks kept her light enough that her forward speed and the water flowing over her dive planes maintained level cruise close to the surface. Her sail superstructure supported the snorkel mast, periscope mast, and the radar mast which scanned the horizon for American planes out of Guantanamo. Captain Barcena stood at the periscope and looked northward through the tube for the great lighthouse at Morro de Cuba just west of Guantanamo. But it was too far and too bright topside to be seen.

Three propellers ran off her three 6,000-horsepower diesels and the blades made turns for 15 knots through green water 12,000 feet deep. Although her old hull contained two decks, the crew lived and worked mainly on the top deck. The lower deck was crammed with 175 tons of batteries for submerged propulsion and several tanks filled with diesel fuel, lubricating oil, and fresh water.

Captain Barcena had announced to his youthful crew an hour earlier that their first operational orders had been decoded in the radio room. Seamen quickly buzzed with anticipation and the giddy chatter which drives fear from young warriors' hearts.

In another two hours, El Tiburon would alter course from due east to northeast. Steering northeastward would drive her past Cuba's southeastern point and into the Windward Passage. The passage separates Cuba from Haiti on the island of Hispaniola.

El Tiburon's captain welcomed his assignment on board a submarine. Most of his career had been in the island's little surface navy. He had served for one year as a senior watch officer in Cuba's second Foxtrot class submarine when it had arrived at Cienfuegos in January 1980. Then he had been transferred back to the surface to apply what he had learned under the sea. His first command from 1984 through 1988 had been on board the second of three ex-Russian, Koni class frigates.

The 2,000-ton Koni arrived in Cuba in February 1984 and its specialty is antisubmarine warfare. From August 1990 through November 1991, he had skippered a 580-ton, Pauk class fast attack craft. This retired Soviet ship had arrived in July 1990 and its forte was also antisubmarine warfare. The People's Navy had reasoned that anyone with so much training at finding and fighting subs on the surface should have his own submarine. So after several months behind a desk, Martinez Barcena had been given command of El Tiburon two months ago. During one cruise since then, his crew came to know him and to admire him greatly.

The Russian Foxtrot subs had been built from 1958 to 1972. The Russians still sail at least 60 of the old boats and other client states operate 13 more. She might be old—like me—El Viejo thought, but she is also tried and true, like me.

If the drowned American sailor were indeed from an American submarine, then Captain Barcena would hunt it down for a good round of cat-and-mouse. Then he would sail home in glory. He felt as spry as his anxious crew.

With two miles of Caribbean Sea under his keel, Captain Barcena hailed the engine room spaces through the control room's intercom. He inquired about the submarine's massive batteries. A charge had been put on them in port at Cienfuegos. Running the diesel engines attached to generators earlier in the day had warmed up the batteries which lined most of *El Tiburon*'s lower deck level. The engineering officer of the watch radioed back that the batteries were healthy.

The noisy diesels suck air through the snorkel mast. But the diesels were shut down to cruise on quieter, electric power as the boat sailed past the Guantanamo base. The Americans there could hear the diesels chugging through their listening post on the coast.

Captain Barcena was always concerned about his batteries. Unlike nuclear boats which can stay down until the crew starves to death or goes insane, diesel-electric submarines must surface at least every two days to recharge their precious batteries.

The boyish crew monitored their systems in eerie red light. Red lights illuminate the control room during darkness above so the captain's and officers' eyes will remain dark-adapted for nighttime periscope use.

The white-haired captain began to relax as the Yankee base at Guantanamo receded astern. He walked from crewman to crewman in the control room to keep tab on their stations. At last, Martinez Barcena had a ship and a real command.

It had been a good day, El Viejo thought. Too bad that Amalia had not lived to see it.

SIX

15 MARCH; 0100 UTC

CAPTAIN KURT Milhaus showed the strain. The Eight O'clock Report had not gone well. Executive Officer Phillip Perlmutter had commenced the formality nearly an hour ago at midnight UTC. By the time Lt. Commander Perlmutter had come to the wardroom to sit with his captain, Buddy Thurston had been in the water for 22 hours.

The Eight O'clock Report is a protocol which carries the weight of ritual on every United States Navy ship.

The XO formally reports to the ship's captain at 8:00 (0800) in the morning, noon (1200), and 8:00 (2000) in the evening. Generally, surface ships time their daily affairs to actual local time: the Zone Time wherever the vessel happens to be steaming. Routine housekeeping events such as meals and changes of the watch follow the real sun. Only official entries into the ship's various logbooks will carry a standardized UTC ("Greenwich") time. Submarines, however, are different.

Fleet submarines—attack boats ("hunter/killers") or missile subs ("boomers")—have no sun to exert its immutable influence on a crew's natural body clocks. Outside the pressure hull, local noon is as freezing black as local midnight. So submarines set their daily routines to the local time of their home ports. American submarines based at Holy Loch, Scotland, keep time to British clocks which happen to be UTC anyway. Subs out of Seattle keep Pacific Time just as subs out of Newport News keep Eastern Time, except for the logbook entries which are always UTC.

Sam Houston had opted to observe the Atlantic Standard Time Zone of the Puerto Rico Trench as its clock time for meals, watch changes, and reports. Normally, she would have kept Eastern Standard Time since she had sailed from Virginia after her secret refitting into a submerged laboratory. But little on SSN-609 was regarded as normal by the few officers of flag rank who knew of her post-retirement mission.

So the formal reports to Captain Milhaus were Atlantic Time, an hour ahead of Eastern Standard and four hours behind UTC time.

Executive Officer Pappy Perlmutter brought Captain Milhaus his evening Eight O'clock Report at midnight, UTC.

On all Navy ships at sea, the department heads bring their thrice-daily reports to the XO advising on the status of equipment and crewmen in the five departments required by U.S. Naval Weapons Publications 50 (A): Operations, Navigation, Weapons, Engineering, and Supply. Nuclear-powered ships have a sixth Reactor Department reporting. The three daily reports coincide with changes of the watch.

All days on board U.S. Navy ships have seven watches. The day begins with the Midwatch at midnight which ends at 4:00 in the morning. The next 4-hour watch is the Morning Watch from 0400 till 0800. Then comes the Forenoon Watch from 8:00 in the morning until noon. The Afternoon Watch runs from noon to 4:00 in the afternoon (1600). At the end of the Afternoon Watch, the next 4-hour period is broken down into two "dog watches," each of two hours. This split of the First Dog Watch (4:00 to 6:00 pm) and the Second Dog Watch (6:00 to 8:00 pm) allows the men standing watch to take a normal dinner time. After the dog watches, the normal 4-hour watch standing resumes with the First Watch from 8:00 pm till midnight (2000-2400).

The evening Eight O'clock Report comes at the beginning of the first watch. Although the executive officer brings his reviewed department reports to the CO, the ship's Officer of the Deck (OOD) is charged with officially announcing the time of day (actual, local time) before each such report. The OOD announces 0800, noon, and 2000 to the captain who responds, "Make it so."

Each department head delivers his report to the XO who delivers it to the captain with the department head's respects. Among the Navy's two centuries of tradition is the protocol that when juniors send messages to a superior through an intermediary, they must do so "with respects." When the flow of reports or messages is reversed, a senior will send a message through an intermediary to a junior "with the compliments" of the superior officer.

Pappy Perlmutter brought the Eight O'clock Report to his captain in the wardroom where the two officers held a private conference over black Navy-issue coffee.

Captain Milhaus looked and sounded tired. The two officers reviewed 609's official Deck Log which catalogs the entire history of a U.S. man-of-war. The first Deck Log entry was the day her builders released her with commissioning pennant and all flags flying to the Navy Department. The last entry would mark the day she was stripped naked and towed to the scrap heap. Only six months' worth of Deck Log entries are actually aboard ship. The bulk of the entries are sent to the Department of the Navy.

A vessel's Deck Log is her life history. Rigid protocols mandate that each daily entry shall begin at midnight as the midwatch begins. The first entry is always a reference to the previous day's last entry.

Captain Milhaus scanned the first line of the March 14th Deck Log: "Underway as before." Navy canon law requires no more.

The next entry detailed *Sam Houston*'s speed, course, readiness condition, powerplant status and tactical status. If applicable, this midnight entry like all first entries for a new watch would have noted weather and sea state, and distances and bearings to friendly ships steaming in formation. Enemy or unidentified contacts are only recorded when their CPA—closest point of approach—is three nautical miles or less. The entire record was written in longhand by the Quartermaster of the Watch for each watch.

The logbook entries are supervised by the ship's navigator. The Officer of the Deck signs the Deck Log at the end of each 4-hour watch. The log must be in ink and no blank lines are permitted except one blank line between a change of watch. All proper names must be printed.

The handwritten log is referred to as a rough log. Errors may be crossed out and fixed, but erasures are forbidden. Later, the rough log will be typewritten. The ship's commanding officer only signs the log at the end of each month. Once each month, surface ships forward their Deck Log to the Chief of Naval Operations for permanent storage at the Naval Personnel Bureau. Nuclear subs which generally do not surface during their standard 70-day patrols keep the monthly logs until their return to port. The month's worth of rough logs can be destroyed on board ship after six months.

The Deck Log must record all casualties. Captain Milhaus' finger gently touched the entry detailing the death of Buddy Thurston at 2:00 in the morning UTC, March 14th. Not until ten hours later did Captain Milhaus permit an entry confirming the possibility that Torpedoman Thurston might have been infected with Lesch-Nyhan Syndrome. The replenishment-at-sea ruse and Lt. Commander Jessica Dugan's mid-ocean arrival were duly logged at noon, Atlantic Time (1600 UTC), at the end of the forenoon watch.

Studying the day's entries physically wearied the captain as he read on to the planesman who had nearly killed them all four hours after the Caribbean rendezvous—not quite five hours before the Eight O'clock Report in the wardroom. The planesman's dog-bite of the diving officer was also recorded. The CO winced.

"Two men dead within two weeks; one petty officer gone berserk; and the diving officer and Dr. Dugan both on the binnacle list." The CO shook his head as he looked down into his coffee mug. A ship's sicklist has been called the binnacle list since the days of sail when a roster of out-of-commission sailors was posted on the binnacle, the short wooden stand which held the magnetic compass.

Captain Milhaus finally looked up with exhausted eyes.

"How is Commander Dugan?"

"Dr. Shaffer advised that she virtually collapsed in BL-3 three hours ago. She caulked-off in sick bay, Captain."

Kurt Milhaus only nodded.

"Been up like two days straight, I guess, Sir."

"Yes, I know. I just wish she would get to work here. She'll have to maintain the pace once she comes to—shortly, I hope—if we are to contain this damn thing."

"I know, Captain. Stan is still collecting the records for her and he's still redoing all of the autopsy tests on Hendrix just to be sure."

"Good. Good. They just didn't quite prepare me for days like this at knife and fork school, Pappy." The CO labored to sound cheerful. "Knife and Fork School" is the street name for the Navy's Officer Indoctrination School where career officers learn how to properly fold their napkins and how to eat soup without slurping at table with foreign dignitaries. (Enlisted men do not acquire table manners unless they are recommended for Officer Candidate School.)

The CO fumbled through more documents.

"Engineering is still trouble-shooting the condenser?"

"Yes," the XO said with his captain's contagious fatigue. "They still don't have a handle on the problem."

"Okay, Pappy, what about the N-O-B?"

"Here, Commander."

Lt. Commander Perlmutter pushed the Night Order Book across the shiny tabletop. In it are the captain's "night orders" which on all Navy ships underway spell out the procedures for conducting ship business as the CO sleeps. Part I of all Night Order Books are the standing orders which detail standard procedures for routine or predictable events. Most can be executed while the CO sleeps. The rest will list incidents or changes in conditions which warrant waking the captain. Part II lists tactical changes issued nightly depending upon a vessel's condition of readiness. The Night Order Book is the Bible for the Officer of the Deck who assumes command in the CO's absence and for the Engineering Officer of the Watch who oversees the powerplant and, in a submarine, the delicate life-support equipment.

The CO scanned Part II and jotted down the orders for the night watches.

"We'll maintain readiness Condition IV and material condition circle-William for the time being. I know circle-William is hard on engineering, but I just don't see any choice until Dr. Dugan advises otherwise."

"Agreed, Captain."

"Very well."

Captain Milhaus signed one of three signature lines. The

nightwatch navigator would sign the Night Order Book as would the night's OOD.

All warships must maintain one of four conditions of readiness: Condition I is general quarters and battle stations; Condition III is wartime cruising with at least one-third of the crew manning their watch stations; Condition IV is peacetime cruising with watches manned as needed; and, Condition IAS is battle stations with alerts for hostile submarines. Captain Milhaus ordered a peacetime watch for the make-believe night on board a submerged submarine.

Likewise, all warships must maintain one of several degrees of watertight integrity or material condition.

All doors, hatches, hatch covers, vents, and plumbing fixtures on every Navy vessel are conspicuously labelled with at least one of the letters X, Y, Z, or a circled X or Y, or Z inside a larger D, or plain W, or W with a circle around it.

X and Y openings are referred to as conditions x-ray and yoke, respectively. The fittings marked with x-ray are those closed for the barest minimum of watertight security. Material condition x-ray would be ordered when anchored in a friendly port. Condition yoke would close all fittings and watertight doors labelled with both x-ray and yoke markings. This condition would be routine for minimum, peacetime cruising at sea. During material condition zebra, all openings marked with X, Y, or Z, are sealed for maximum protection during muster to battle stations. Openings on a surface warship with a Z inside a capital D are referred to as dog-zebra and are closed during nighttime, darken-ship conditions.

Fittings which are a circled X ("circle x-ray") or a circled Y ("circle yoke") opening may be opened without the CO's permission and then closed again, as necessary by the crew. But in condition zebra, none of the X, Y, or Z fittings may be opened without permission of the commanding officer relayed through the ship's DCC—Damage Control Central department—with these exceptions: x-ray and yoke fittings may be opened briefly to transfer crewmen or ammunition and zebra hatches may be opened during general quarters to distribute food or to allow access to lavatories ("heads" on board ship). But whenever a zebra fitting is opened, a guard must be posted to assure its prompt closure ("dogging").

Fittings marked with a W ("William" fittings) or a circled W ("circle-William") are plumbing fixtures and valves essential to ship operation. Plain W fixtures are never closed. But circle-William valves, vents, and fixtures are ordered closed during a CBW alert—chemical-biological warfare alert.

Captain Milhaus had ordered material condition circle-William the moment Dr. Shaffer had suggested that Buddy Thurston might have been infected with one of 609's lethal viruses. Since that time, all but absolutely essential vents and air ducts had been either closed or re-routed through special biological filters built into *Sam Houston*'s duct work during her refit.

"Well," the CO sighed as he stood up, followed by his exec. "Think I'll lay aft before I sack out for a few hours. I want to talk to engineering myself about the condenser. You're welcome to join me, Pappy. Then you better rack out yourself. It's been a long day."

"Thank you, Captain."

The two officers opened the non-watertight "joiner" door of the wardroom. The passageway aft was bathed in the eerie red light of the ship's standing lights.

From the spacious wardroom, the two officers walked aft along the passageway. Another protocol: Executive Officer Perlmutter walked to the left of Captain Milhaus as they walked shoulder to shoulder. A superior officer always walks on the right when walking abreast.

"Captain in CIC," a voice said softly when the two men entered the reddish gloom of 609's control room. Near the center of the upper deck, the combat information center is the ship's cockpit. All nerves run to the CIC's electronic and human brains. The CO paused at the forward end of the control room.

Three men sat side by side facing forward. Two second-class petty officers held airplane-style control wheels. The seaman sitting on the starboard side of the threesome was the helmsman whose control yoke steered only the tail's vertical rudder for turning the ship left or right. The sailor in the center seat drove the stern planes and winglike planes on the fairwater (also known as the sail) which control the up or down angle (the "bubble") of the bow. The third seaman close to the portside rounded hull was the chief of the watch: a seasoned, first class petty officer.

Seated just behind the middle man was the diving officer

of the watch who monitored both the planesman and the helmsman. The DOW on the afternoon watch had had his ear bitten off 5 1/2 hours earlier.

Standing behind the sitting DOW was the senior officer in CIC: the Officer of the Deck. The OOD was a senior lieutenant. To his far left stood a third-class petty officer who manned the CIC's telephone for communicating with other compartments, especially the engineering spaces.

"Evening, Captain," the OOD said in muted tones. "Steering 0-9-0, making turns for 5 knots at 800 feet, Sir."

"Very well," the weary CO replied. "Pappy and I'll be in engineering."

"Aye, Sir."

"Carry on," the CO nodded.

The OOD is third in the chain of command on every Navy vessel. Even with the captain and his executive officer on hand, the OOD has the watch in CIC or on the bridge of a surface combatant. During some evolutions, a Command Duty Officer will supervise the OOD. The OOD comes on duty not less than thirty minutes before his watch begins. He uses this time to confer with the standing OOD to bring himself up to speed on all ship's systems and any evolutions in progress. He must know every detail of ship status and conditions of readiness. The ship's safety is in his able hands.

Commander Milhaus led his XO aft, through the CIC.

"Captain off the bridge," a voice said quietly in the CIC's red lights as the CO walked toward 609's rear compartments.

Behind the CIC, the CO and his exec reached the sealed hatch outside the upper deck's first level of the old missile compartment, now the BL-2 laboratory.

"The captain and XO," Pappy Perlmutter said into a wall intercom.

"On my way, Sir," a voice crackled from inside BL-2.

With the Deck One, BL-2 Laboratory Director's authorization, a petty officer opened the watertight door of the former missile compartment.

"Sir. Commander Perlmutter," the seaman greeted the CO and his exec.

Ordinarily in the Navy, all ranks of lieutenant commander and below may be addressed as Mister. But a ship's executive officer is always addressed as Commander, whatever his or her rank.

"Just passing through to engineering," the captain smiled with fatigue in his eyes.

"Yes, Sir."

The second-class petty officer stood aside as the two officers entered the outer compartment. He pulled the heavy door behind them and dogged the hatch tightly closed. Then he quickly handed both men a clean white coat as required by NIH guidelines for the second level of biological containment. SSN-609 had dispensed with a BL-1 lab. Since *Ethan Allen* class missile boats have only three main decks, the lowest degree of containment on 609 was BL-2 where levels one and two research and preparation were conducted. The modern *Ohio* class missile boats do have four decks inside their huge hulls, but all of them carry Trident nuclear missiles in their 24-silo bays instead of an ultra-secret genetics laboratory.

Once all three men had donned fresh coats, the seaman opened the anteroom's inner door so they could pass through the BL-2 facility. Captain Milhaus exchanged quick pleasantries with the LD, a chief petty officer with four stripes on his khaki sleeves. The CO walked through the 100-foot long compartment past sixteen silos half full of concrete where the Polaris missiles once rode.

"Thanks, Chief. Carry on," the CO smiled at the lab's aft hatchway.

Commander Milhaus led Pappy Perlmutter through the hatch which sealed behind them. In the small gowning compartment at the lab's rearmost end, the two officers peeled off their lab coats and dumped them in the decontamination bin before they cranked open the after watertight door. They dogged the heavy door behind them.

The captain and exec stood in another narrow passageway running down the rounded hull. The corridor bathed in red standing lights was on the outer edge of the deck. On the far side of the inboard bulkhead was *Sam Houston*'s S5W, pressurized-water reactor. After thirty years, the old reactor quietly boiled water by the ton. The S5W can power the ship for 4,000 hours through 140,000 miles of ocean on one load of nuclear fuel. Within the passageway, the two men could hear no sound at all from the nuclear powerplant on the other side of the lead-lined containment vessel. Past the shielded reactor, they opened another watertight door and entered the brightly lighted, engineering spaces.

"Good evening, Sir. Commander Perlmutter." A cheerful Engineering Officer of the Watch greeted his two superiors at the hatchway.

Lt. Richard Stone had the night shift in engineering. He commanded the submarine's powerplant, as compact and complex an array of machinery as ever put to sea.

Fully one-third of every nuclear missile submarine (and just less than half of the shorter attack boats) is the engineering space where four separate, watertight compartments contain all machinery for electrical, environmental, and propulsion systems—all plumbed to a nuclear reactor powerful enough to light and heat a small city. The first (forward) compartment contains the reactor within its three-deck high containment vessel. The next space aft within the circular hull contains the maneuvering room on the upper deck above the diesel generator room on the middle deck and the condenser spaces on the bottom deck. The next compartment houses tons of auxiliary machinery. And the aftmost compartment contains the engine room space where high- and low-pressure turbines drive the ship's single propeller shaft.

All of the reactor controls are in the maneuvering room. The Reactor Officer supervises the reactor department and his reactor control assistants, reactor mechanical assistants, and assorted electricians. Each is a highly trained specialist in nuclear power. Each could make a handsome living manning a civilian, ground-based nuclear powerplant. And not one would trade his submariner's claustrophobic world of bottled air, artificial light, perpetual "silent running," and the best hot food in the entire U.S. military for a sprawling plant in the sunshine. The Engineering Officer of the Watch commands them all and reports directly to the Officer of the Deck.

"What do we have, Rick?" the CO asked quietly.

"Still not quite sure, Sir. It's definitely a condenser glitch. Saw it right after the unplanned dive this afternoon." Lt. Stone glanced at his watch. "We've been running the casualty protocols for six hours. We ran through the EOCC three times."

The CO only frowned.

The EOCC is the manual of equipment failure checklists known as the *Engineering Operational Casualty Control*. It makes up half of the department's thick EOSS text. The *Engineering Operational Sequencing System* is a two-part, master manual for all normal and emergency situations which might occur in the engineering department. Every ship of the line has its own EOSS. The other half of the EOSS guidebook is the EOP: *Engineering Operational Procedures* which details all normal operations of the ship's heavy equipment.

"Speculate," the CO said impatiently.

"Might be a condensate depression. We have logged some water hammer in Main Steam's hot leg. It is not a crisis yet, Sir."

The captain nodded grimly.

"Could it become one?" XO Perlmutter asked.

"Unlikely, Commander. But a possibility."

A land-based or floating nuclear powerplant runs on water. Lethally radioactive water circulates through the reactor's nuclear core where it is heated to three times the normal boiling point of water. A ton of pressure within the water pipes keeps the 600°F water from turning into steam and exploding the reactor. That hot water circulates through a steam generator where a second loop of non-radioactive water flows.

The flows of radioactive reactor water and the steam generator's non-radioactive water never touch. The steam generator water is allowed to boil into steam and that steam then drives the ship's steam turbines like jet engines. Steam lines passing through the propulsion equipment are never radioactive. The main turbines turn the propeller shaft and the smaller turbines drive the electrical generators.

Temperatures must be rigidly regulated in the tightly packed, steam-powered machinery. Fluctuations from normal ranges can turn benign pipelines and turbines into infernos of twisted metal and radioactive shrapnel.

Captain Milhaus enjoyed faith absolute in his reactor people and the engineering divisions. Their training and quality control are rigorous in the American Navy. Powerplant crews are subjected to comprehensive PEB inspections by the Propulsion Examination Board. When a reactor has been refueled with nuclear pellets, it cannot be powered up until the unit and its crew have passed the PCRSE: pre-critical, reactor safeguards examination. An overhauled reactor must pass a stringent PORSE test: post-overhaul, reactor safeguards examination. Reactors on-line are subject to ORSE drills: operational reactor safeguards examination. And every nuclear-powered ship in the fleet is carefully honed to exacting safety standards by periodic RCPE inspections: radiological control-practice evaluations.

There has never been a published radiation accident in the U.S. nuclear Navy.

Failure to manage the temperatures of the system would spell disaster. Steam exhausted from the turbines after doing its work must be condensed back into pure water. Condensers cooled by outside sea water brought into the system cool the steam so it condenses back into a liquid state so it can return to the steam generator to be boiled again. One potential failure mode of the condensing system is a condensate depression when precise temperature control is lost.

Even though steam enters the condenser at 600° Fahrenheit at the exhaust steam inlet from the engine room's low-pressure turbine, there must be a 2 to 5 degree difference between that steam and the condensate dripping into the condenser's "hot well" water trap. A temperature differential less than 2° Fahrenheit can cause the main condensate pump to cavitate and fail. This temperature spread is carefully regulated by the amount of sea water let into the coolant loops.

"We still have the theory, Captain, that we shock-cooled the condenser heat exchanger when we dove so fast and so deep. The heat exchanger automatically reduced the sea water induction to prevent over-cooling. At that moment, we probably got insufficient cooling of the exhaust steam which would have allowed the exhaust and the hot well condensate to drop below the two-degree differential. We're running the casualty protocols on the condensate pumps. Still can't say for sure, though."

"Okay, Rick. You said you had some water hammer?"

"Not much, Captain. But enough to investigate."

When the steam line pressures and temperatures are not perfectly regulated, water droplets can condense with the flow of pure steam. All pressurized-water reactors require perfectly "dry" steam with no traces of solid water. When the steam lines are pressurized to their normal 900 pounds per square inch, suspended water droplets would slam into bends in the pipe lines so fast that they would create a hammer effect powerful enough to rupture pipe elbows.

"No sign of pipe damage?"

"None," the engineer nodded to Lt. Commander Perlmutter. "We're still running vibration analysis tests just to be sure."

"Well done, Rick," the CO said with strained authority. "Keep the OOD advised while the exec and I rack out. It's been a long day."

"Will do, Captain. Sir," the lieutenant in brown officers' khakis hesitated. "Any word yet on what happened to Buddy— Torpedoman Thurston?"

Everyone loved Buddy Thurston.

"Not yet, Rick. Commander Dugan and Doc Shaffer are on it though."

"Good." The engineer looked down at the deck. "Thurston was a good man."

"That he was," the executive officer said sadly.

"Pappy and I will just walk through before we get some sack time forward." The CO tried to sound cheerful. The XO beside him smiled. There was little point in pretending that the entire crew did not refer to the exec as Pappy. The confines of any submarine, no matter how large, make complete observance of formalities very difficult.

"Glad to have you back here, Sir," Lt. Stone nodded.

"Thank you, Mister Stone. We'll just help ourselves and you can run herd on your condensers."

The Engineering Officer of the Watch smiled and returned to his banks of consoles. The reactor and its massive plumbing maze were controlled from the maneuvering room. Wall to wall and floor to ceiling arrays of instruments were required to sandwich a nuclear reactor control room into the narrow compartment. Only massive computerization permitted half a dozen men in a space the size of a three-car garage to duplicate the efforts of the two dozen engineers who would run a ground-based reactor from a control room two stories high with the volume of a small house.

Still on Deck One, the CO and his executive officer passed through another watertight door into the next compartment further aft. They entered the two-deck high main machinery compartment. Here, the ship's high- and low-pressure steam turbines hummed softly, driven by the high-pressure steam from the reactor compartment's steam generator.

The turbines drive the propeller shaft for 609's single screw. Although the turbines hummed at high speed, everything was carefully insulated for quiet running. Vibration dampers were everywhere to prevent engine noise from passing through the steel hull into the sea beyond. Escaping noise meant discovery by enemy submarines and discovery could mean death by drowning for all.

Captain Milhaus and Lt. Commander Perlmutter stood on the upper platform deck that was more like a balcony overlooking the powerplants on the main deck below. From their position they could see that the main deck did not actually touch the ship's hull. Instead, the turbines and electric motors were bolted to a "raft" rather than to a deck anchored to the ship's sides. The steel raft floated atop massive springs and shock-absorbing struts. Since the deck did not touch the hull, a dropped wrench or balky turbine would not transmit sound further than the deck. The vibration would stop at the shock absorbers and would not vibrate into the hull and into the sea where an enemy's finely tuned sonar could hear it.

Kurt Milhaus loved the feel and the smell of the machinery spaces on his ship. The feeling of power radiated into his soft-soled shoes through the fidley deck overlooking the machinery. Vertical beams—"stanchions" aboard ship—supported the raised deck. The space was crammed with large and small pipes which carried the vessel's lifeblood.

Pipes ran everywhere: horizontally along the hull and across the overhead. The large, main steam lines were painted white with "MS" stenciled every few feet. The smaller auxiliary steam pipes were also white but were stenciled "AS." The low-pressure, auxiliary steam lines carried steam at 150 pounds per square inch. White paint also covered the steam exhaust piping. Pipes carrying lubricating oil were painted yellow with "LOS" stenciling. Navy lube oil is regulation 2190 TEP oil which is used and reused throughout the voyage. Centrifugal purifiers cleaned the lube oil between each circuit through the turbines and machinery. Lube oil pipes on the purification line were painted black with yellow stripes stenciled "LO."

The deck beneath the machinery raft contained more condensers, the steam-powered air conditioning unit, and various pumps for sea water induction. Rising through the deck, lines carrying high-pressure air at 5,000 pounds per square inch for blowing the aft, main ballast tank were gray with "AHP" stenciled on the side. Medium pressure air lines at 1,000 pounds per square inch were used to start the ship's diesel generators. These thin pipes were tan with "AMP" stenciling. Fresh drinking water pipes were dark blue with "PW" (for potable water) lettering.

Light blue pipes carried feedwater for the reactor compartment. Sea water pipes attached to the ship's dozens of fire hoses were dark green and labeled "FM" for fire main. The submarine's toilets flushed with sea water through gold colored pipes with "CHT" stenciled on the plumbing. And high-pressure, hydraulic fluid surged through orange pipes labeled "VH." Waterbury pumps rated at 3,000 psi drove the hydraulic fluid.

Kurt Milhaus loved the pipes, the humming turbines, and the smell of sweat and lube oil.

The turbines driving the electrical generators kept the lights burning and the bottled air circulating. The standard electrical load in the U.S. Navy is 3-phase, 450 volt lines with 60-cycle AC juice. All electrical conduits are routed through the sub's SSDS: Ship's Service Distribution System.

"That's a 'joyful noise,' Pappy," the CO nodded.

"Yep."

The captain turned toward his exhausted exec.

"Let's hit the rack for a few hours. Doc Dugan should be up by then, I hope."

"Sounds good to me." Pappy Perlmutter's dark eyes blinked heavily.

Captain Milhaus looked at his watch as they left the engineering department. It was 2:00 in the morning, UTC—10:00 in a balmy Caribbean night 800 feet above. As he walked forward to his cabin, he mentally noted that Buddy Thurston had now been in the water for exactly 24 hours.

Vasily Fyodorovich Golitsyn did not start off as a nobody in the Soviet Ministry of Defense. His political star had risen with breathtaking speed. Mikhail Gorbachev had personally brought

Golitsyn along when the former became General Secretary of the party in 1985. The young Golitsyn had been one of the promising new faces within the inner councils of Prime Minister Nikolai Ryzhkov who had taken office in September of 1985, six months after Gorbachev's election.

Only 35, Vasily Fyodorovich had been a military advisor within the Kremlin since he had graduated from Lomonosov University in Moscow. He had started out as somebody and he knew the very day and the very hour when he had descended overnight into a nobody. He had not even seen it coming; it had happened so quickly.

Golitsyn fell from grace on Sunday morning, January 6th, 1991. New snow was on the ground, cold and dry, and it crunched under foot. The River Moskva was frozen throughout Moscow like cement. The air that morning was so hard that Golitsyn imagined that he could hear the grinding sound of the ice skaters' blades gliding atop the great river as his limousine crossed Kammenyi Bridge along Polanka Boulevard toward the main gate in the Kremlin's western walls.

On that morning, the inner circle had debated sending Soviet troops into the country's dissident republics under the pretext of rounding up draft dodgers.

Golitsyn had vigorously opposed the plan. The older and wiser hands favored the action. But Golitsyn had just met and had been captivated by Lithuania's liberal president, Vytautas Landsbergis. And he had been moved by the will of Lithuania's female Prime Minister, Kazimiera Prunskiene.

"Your age is showing, Vasily Fyodorovich," was all that Marshal Sergey Akhromeyev had said.

The next day, January 7th, Soviet paratroops were sent into Lithuania as well as Latvia, Armenia, Georgia, Moldavia, and the Ukraine.

One day after that, Golitsyn's weekly essay column on military policy in the official military newspaper *Krasnaya Zvezda* was cancelled forever. Within two days, his limousine was reassigned elsewhere and he was told that henceforth he could ride the Metro.

So at 6:00 in the morning Moscow time (0300 UTC), Vasily Golitsyn trudged through foot-high snow to cross in front of the Kalinin Museum just outside the main gate in the Kremlin's west side. Although sorely discouraged, he con-

tinued to work in the Defense Ministry until that day when he
might hitch his future to some other rising star. It had worked
before.

The Russian winter lingers well into April and the morning
was cold and damp. The sky was still black and full of icy clear
stars. The Russian technocrat was miserable and tired. He had
been working late, but he suspected other motives behind his
orders to make a diplomatic call at daybreak. He presumed
that a low-level assignment was meant to remind him of his
present place in the pecking order.

The Russian people have a popular name for the current crisis in the body politic. They call their disintegrating Union and
their crumbling economy *smutnoye vremya*: "troubled times."
Vasily Golitsyn thought of his own troubled times when he
stepped out of the nighttime cold into the subterranean cold
of the Moscow subway, the Metro.

He descended into the ground at the Kalininskaja station at
the corner of Marx Boulevard and Kalinin. The Metro begins
running through Moscow's 125 miles of subway tunnels at
6:00 in the morning. Golitsyn walked from the buried platform
into the first train of the day on the red line. (Other trains run
on their own color-coded routes every two minutes.) The fare,
a single 5-copeck coin, was good for going anywhere in the
capital, regardless of the distance.

Golitsyn took his seat and swayed with the clean car's
motion as it sped through the depths of Moscow toward the
southwest. The train ran parallel to the River Moscow (*Reka
Moskva*) which still had large ice floes on its freezing surface.
In minutes, the train lurched to a stop at the Kropotkinskaja
station. Golitsyn did not look up as a load of commuters
pushed into his car before the train jerked away from the
platform. It stopped in succession at the depots of Park Kultury,
Frunzenskaja and Sportivnaja. The sleepy passengers could feel
the tunnel go deeper into the frozen ground as it approached the
river to cross underneath the frigid water at the old Olympic
Stadium complex of the 1980 summer games. The train then
rose slightly on the south side.

From the river, the train rumbled southwestward parallel to
Wernadski Boulevard. As the cars slowed, Golitsyn rose to exit
at the platform in Universitet station at the corner of Wernadski
and Lomonosov streets. When the Russian climbed into the

dark morning, the March wind felt like a razor on his face. He had not been on the train for more than ten minutes, but that was long enough to forget how bitter the morning wind had become.

With his gloved hands stuffed into his coat pockets, Golitsyn walked another two blocks south on Wernadski before turning left to walk another block down Kravcenko. It was a long block to the corner of Kravcenko and the wide Leninskij Boulevard of southwest Moscow. He did not linger at the corner in the dark and he quickly entered the warmth of the Havana Restaurant.

The Havana was still closed but the door opened before the cold Russian could touch the knob.

"Good morning," a voice said in Russian with a Spanish accent.

"Yes," was all the Russian could say cheerlessly.

"This way, Mr. Golitsyn." The old man at the door led the Russian though the deserted dining room to a secluded corner away from the Havana's front windows facing Leninskij Prospekt.

At the table, another man stood up to take Golitsyn's hand.

"Thank you for coming, Vasily. They opened especially for us, you know. The Havana doesn't open until 11:00."

"Well," the Russian said coldly, "guess I should be grateful."

"Indeed," the comfortable man said to his shivering guest. "I already have your tea poured for you."

"That is very nice." The Russian could not hide his appreciation. He threw his coat over a chair before he wrapped his cold hands around the hot glass of Russian tea. "Ah, much better. Thanks."

The two men settled behind the table. Around them, the cafe was mostly dark, like the Moscow dawn outside the windows.

The Havana is one of Moscow's handful of restaurants specializing in international menus. Here, the featured selections were Cuban meals.

"The Ministry said only that you needed to see me immediately," the Russian said over his glass of tea. He had no patience for small talk when the morning sky was not yet pink in the east.

"Indeed, Vasily," the older man nodded. "I wish to review Cuban military matters with you."

Senior Enrique Hernandez looked older than his 45 years. His black hair was thinning and the temples were graying. He had been an attaché with the Cuban Embassy in Moscow for seven years. He knew the Russians and he knew the town. It was customary for him to hold court at the Havana, although not usually at 6:00 in the morning.

"Aside from this ridiculous hour, Enrique, we have been through all of this a thousand times already. My government simply cannot afford to bankroll your revolution forever."

"Yes, yes, Vasily Fyodorovich," Sr. Hernandez smiled with exaggerated warmth. "I know the speech: 25 billion dollars in aid since 1960; 4 billion annually. Too, too much for the new and bankrupt Commonwealth of Independent States in the midst of political turmoil." Not far from their table, the Russian Parliament building remained charred from Boris Yeltsin's October 1993 suppression of his own Vice President's little rebellion.

"That's right," the impatient Russian frowned. He looked down into his empty glass.

The Cuban diplomat snapped his fingers. The sleepy owner of the Havana appeared quickly out of the shadows. He carried a tray with a single steaming glass of black tea which he silently placed in front of the Russian.

"Thank you," the Russian said in Spanish. Then he turned toward the Cuban and continued in Russian. "You surely didn't summon me here at this hour to rehash old business. President Gorbachev assured President Bush at the August 1991 summit in Moscow that we would curtail aid to Cuba. The Americans made an offer we could not decline."

The Cuban had to laugh out loud.

"Offer, my friend? Your government traded the principles of the Revolution for blue jeans and McDonald's." Hernandez sounded as coldly brittle as the morning wind blowing outside the window.

The Russian had warmed to the second glass of hot tea. He had not warmed to his host.

"You did not invite me here to discuss foreign aid, did you Enrique?"

"Of course not."

"Well?"

"All right, Vasily." The Cuban smiled his chilly little smile. He was in no particular hurry. "Your career seems—shall we say—standing still. For the moment anyway."

The Russian could say nothing. He looked into the second empty glass. His host did not snap his fingers this time.

Vasily Golitsyn knew very well that Enrique Hernandez' life in Cuban politics had been much like his own: the ability to know a rising star when he saw it. The only thing he had in common with the Cuban was his ability—his former ability— to master political astronomy.

When the Russian was walking two steps behind Nikolai Ivanovich Ryzhkov before the latter's ascent to the post of Prime Minister in 1985, the Cuban was walking two steps behind Raul Castro. Raul is the most powerful man in the Cuban government after his brother. He serves Fidel as both Vice President and Defense Minister. Hernandez made certain that he also caught the eye of Cuba's next generation of leaders and their principal spokesman, Carlos Aldana.

Also in his mid-40s like Hernandez, Carlos Aldana is as outwardly refined as Fidel and Raul are loud and, to some, crude. Aldana is a seasoned and respected diplomat. He had negotiated Cuba's 1988 withdrawal from Havana's African military adventure in Angola. His skill and international credibility had propelled the mild-mannered Cuban into a seat as one of the island's nine Party Secretaries. When Enrique Hernandez was not carrying the briefcase of Raul Castro, he was offering quietly sensible counsel to Carlos Aldana. Hernandez' reward was a posting to Cuba's Moscow embassy, Cuba's very umbilical cord.

Sr. Hernandez was clearly on the way up. Vasily Golitsyn was somewhere near the bottom of a long and rapid descent. The Cuban knew it.

"How was the Metro ride, Vasily?"

The Russian winced visibly.

"Cold, Enrique."

"Yes, it would be this time of day." He glanced over the Russian's shoulder toward the front window. The sky was just turning pink in the hard chill of mid-March in Moscow.

"What do you want?" The Russian sighed. He was done playing.

"I need you to relay a message to your people in Defense. My government believes that an American submarine is operating near our waters. We received that intelligence only yesterday." He paused too long to sound casual. "We have dispatched one of your Foxtrot class submarines, *El Tiburon*, to hunt it down."

The Russian was appalled.

"Why, for God's sake?"

"Because we can, Vasily. Your government cannot. But we can. Your government has no Caribbean ports at all . . . without Cuba. We can. So we will."

The Cuban's Russian was flawless. He allowed his words to sink into Vasily Golitsyn's head.

"You can't sink one of those ships even if you wanted to."

"We have no desire and no need to sink it. We have only to prove that we can find it and harass it. And we need only demonstrate that without Havana, the Western Hemisphere is abandoned."

The Russian looked puzzled and a little angry.

"Why not send your message through normal channels? Why use me?"

"I know that you have been demoted for your opposition to the use of force to restrain the Baltic states. I know, Vasily Fyodorovich, that you need an opportunity to prove that you have the stones to return to your old position of authority. I am giving you that opportunity now. You can—if you wish, of course—convince your Ministry that our success at sea justifies renewing our military aid. That is, if the Kremlin has any hope at all of projecting its influence into the West. With or without Russian assistance, we shall be the Revolution's foothold in that part of the world. Now, and forever."

The Cuban sounded resolute. He gave a firm speech to an audience of one.

"Wouldn't Cuba be better off joining Boris Yeltsin's efforts to open doors to the Americans? Your economy is no better than ours after Washington's economic embargo for over three decades. We both know that Cuba wants to open channels to Washington. And what little communication you had ended when the Czechs slammed the door on Havana."

In March 1991, the embassy of Czechoslovakia stopped being Cuba's indirect emissary in Washington. With that action, Cuba lost its only direct line of communication to the Americans.

"We won't need a mission in Washington once we convince the United States that the Caribbean is not their private lake. If the Kremlin cuts off our aid, we will go forward without you. Your western frontier will become Lithuania. My people tell me that we can confront the American submarine in about three days."

The Cuban paused again. His black eyes drilled into the Russian's pale face.

"You decide, Vasily. You can be our advocate. I am giving you the chance—perhaps your last—to side with your Ministry's conservatives who advocate pressing the Americans in my hemisphere. I am giving you the chance to climb back up to where you were, my friend."

The way the Cuban said "friend" made it quite clear to the Russian that he was anything but.

"How do you know, Enrique, that I won't vigorously oppose this foolishness which could easily set back our *rapprochement* with the Americans?"

The Cuban smiled a smile which made Vasily Golitsyn feel suddenly ill. For an instant, he regretted taking the Cuban's tea. He nervously glanced at his wrist watch to ease the tension. It was almost 7:00.

Enrique Hernandez said nothing. Instead, with much theater he slowly reached deeply into his pocket. The young Russian could hear loose change jingling in the Cuban's fingers. The Russian diplomat who had once been a somebody could not stand the suspense.

"How do you know?" he repeated.

Without a word, the Cuban pulled his hand from his pocket. He laid at least ten 5-copeck coins on the table top. Then with the palm of his hand, he pushed them across the table toward the uncomfortable Russian.

"For the Metro, Vasily Fyodorovich."

SEVEN

---

15 MARCH; 0400 UTC

WHEN JESSICA Dugan opened her eyes, she needed five minutes to awaken. She had slept without dreams for seven full hours. Her left eye and cheek were so sore that she touched her face. Her fingers could feel the heat radiating from her bruised face and her black eye. At least she knew immediately where she was this time.

Swinging her legs to the deck, she sat on the bedside for another five minutes as she gathered her wits. Taking a breath, she could smell her own stale sweat. In the subdued lights of *Sam Houston*'s sick bay, she could open her sleepy eyes wide to the compartment. The planesman bound to his berth moaned softly and his semi-conscious body twitched against his restraint straps. Close to a bulkhead, the diving officer who had lost half an ear nearly nine hours earlier slept soundly from the drugs which trickled into his forearm.

"Jesus," she whispered as she stood up and stepped into her soft-soled shoes. She glanced at herself in a mirror. Her summer khaki shirt and men's trousers were totally rumpled and her brown hair had exploded around her swollen face. Her left eye was black and swollen almost shut. The left side of her face was black and blue from her eyebrow to her jaw.

I don't think black coffee will fix this face, she thought and smiled silently. She did the best she could to pull her wild hair back and to secure it with the barrettes she found inside the tangled mess. The Navy dress code allows two barrettes for women, as long as they match hair color.

Other than her painful face, she felt completely restored after her first full night's sleep in three days. She was anxious to get to work and to find the cause of the epidemic which made SSN-609's sick bay look like a battlefield triage station.

She found her own way down the passageway bathed in the red standing lights, up the companionway, and into the aft end of the red-lit control room. The submarine's CIC was hushed where quiet seamen manned their positions. She wished that she could sneak through to her stateroom without being noticed or sniffed. No man alive had ever seen her look so mangy. Now she would give a dozen sailors the pleasure.

A tall and youthful officer stood behind the seated diving officer of the watch at the fore end of the CIC. The standing man turned when he heard Lt. Commander Dugan slip through the compartment.

"Good morning, Dr. Dugan." Jessica Dugan recognized Lieutenant Pete Gentry, weapons officer, whom she had met when coming aboard. "We changed watches fifteen minutes ago and I have the bubble as OOD."

The officer of the deck did not salute his superior officer since he was "uncovered" without a hat.

"Lieutenant," she nodded. Her one good eye studied the officer who wore a single silver bar on each brown collar: a lieutenant, junior grade, and unrestricted line officer. The boy would command his own ship someday. The intense, young OOD looked like he had escaped from a high school debate team.

She glanced up at a round clock on the forward bulkhead above the chief of the watch, a first class petty officer who was the leftmost of three seated sailors who manned the propulsion and steering consoles. The clock read twenty minutes past midnight, local Atlantic Time in the Caribbean, a quarter hour into the four-hour midwatch.

"Where are the captain, Pappy—I mean Commander Perlmutter—and Dr. Shaffer?" Her hand still covered her sour mouth.

"The skipper, the XO, and Lt. Shaffer went forward three hours ago for some rack time. The captain's night orders authorize me to wake him if you want me to." The OOD regarded the disheveled woman closely. She looked like she had been in a saloon brawl on shore leave.

"No, no. I'll just stop by my stateroom for a few minutes before I get down to work. What are the mess hours, Mister Gentry?" Jessica Dugan suddenly realized that she was starving. Her last meal had wound up in her first pair of shoes nine hours earlier.

"We're a sub, Ma'am. The three messes never close."

A ship the size of an *Ethan Allen* class submarine was large enough to have a mess compartment for the junior ratings of enlisted men, another for the senior noncommissioned officers (chief, senior chief, and master chief petty officers), and the officers' wardroom. All three dining rooms were serviced from the sub's single galley. Food services are run by the mess management specialists.

"Great. Thanks, Lieutenant. I can find my way forward."

"Yes, Ma'am," the OOD said formally. "Dr. Shaffer wanted me to send the ship's secretary up to you whenever you woke up."

"Okay. I'll be in the wardroom in fifteen minutes."

"Yes, Ma'am."

Dr. Dugan was grateful to leave the CIC where twelve pairs of eyes had been glued to the round backside of her wrinkled trousers. These men had been off duty or sleeping when she had come on board twelve hours earlier.

Walking through the passageway in the ship's forward spaces of Deck One, she made her way past boys'town: the tiny staterooms where the junior officers slept. She could hear ten men snoring on the far sides of the flimsy joiner doors. She had to smile at the collective sound of a moose rut. So much for silent running, she thought.

Jessica Dugan braced herself before she opened the door to her stateroom. She expected to see the deck still cluttered with the debris from the small desk and her overturned ditty bag. Everything had gone flying when the planesman drove *Sam Houston* toward the bottom of the Puerto Rico Trench. She had not picked up anything except her soggy shoes when Dr. Shaffer summoned her to sick bay after the incident, so she expected to see what seamen call a "mare's nest": a first-degree pig pen.

She was surprised when she opened the joiner door. Her stateroom was tidy. The ditty bag was open but rightside-up on the compartment's single metal chair. Her toiletries were aligned on the tiny writing desk. And on the 36-inch wide double bunk were two neatly folded sets of khaki shirts and trousers, the duty uniform of submarine officers and chief petty officers.

"Pappy," she whispered to herself. For some reason, no one else's name popped into her mind.

She quickly brushed her teeth in the private latrine, not much more than shoulder wide. Although she tucked her hair up to regulation standards, she did not bother to put on a face over her bruised cheek and blackened eye. When she sat on the cold, stainless steel head, she closed her eyes and she listened to SSN-609.

The nuclear reactor and the ship's turbines nearly 400 feet further aft made no sound at all. Only the slightest vibration could be felt through her bare feet on the cold deck. She could hear the soft wind blowing through the stateroom's ventilation ducts. In the present state of material condition circle-William, the air vents still functioned, but each array of compartments between the three-deck high, watertight bulkheads was isolated from all of the other compartments. At least half a dozen bulkheads separated *Sam Houston* into a series of watertight cells. Each bulkhead has but one watertight door. This means that two of the three decks had no opening through the bulkheads at all. Crewmen on Deck Three on the ship's lowest level must climb two decks to Deck One just to cross over to the next compartment if it's on the other side of a bulkhead. The doors were being kept closed now to keep the spread of the Lesch-Nyhan infected mosquitos under control—if they were the source of the contamination.

Standing at the small metal sink, she ran a soapy wash cloth under her arms and between her thighs.

She felt refreshed by the time she stood in her civilian-issue underwear beside her bunk. Her one life-long rebellion at military life was her refusal to wear GI underwear. She stepped into fresh trousers and buttoned up her pressed, khaki shirt. Everything fit. Whoever had left the clothes on her bunk had a good eye, she thought. From her dirty shirt, she removed her collar insignia and pinned them on her new shirt: a lieutenant commander's gold maple leaf on her right collar and the acorn on top of an oak leaf of the Medical Corps on the left. Not wearing her rank on both collars marked her as a restricted line officer: staff corps, but no command in her future. (Her dress blues also lacked the five-pointed star of an unrestricted officer above the thin gold stripe between two thicker stripes on the forearms. Restricted line officers wear their staff corps insignia in place of the star.)

With a final swish of mouthwash, she left her stateroom for the officers' mess.

Sitting alone in the Deck One wardroom, she used one of the J-circuit telephones to call below to the galley. She asked the "stew-burner" for pancakes and coffee. Within ten minutes, a seaman delivered a tray to the wardroom door. Her midnight breakfast disappeared almost without chewing. She found herself wondering why coffee always tastes best at sea or in the woods on a cold, fall day. She sucked up three cups of Navy black coffee: the best in the service.

As she finished her last cup of coffee, she heard a soft knock at the thin door. She was met by a two-stripe, second class petty officer who did not look much older than a teenager. Since she had not been to sea in over three years, she had almost forgotten how truly young the military is. He carried a stack of books and folders.

"Ma'am," the uncomfortable boy stammered. Dr. Dugan did not remember him. He must have been off duty when she came on board. The look on his pimpled face made it clear that he had not seen a woman in months. He forgot to close his mouth when he was not speaking softly. "I'm Tom Foster, rate A-two D-two, and I'm the ship's secretary, Commander."

"Mister Foster. Nice to meet you. What's A-two D-two, if I may ask?"

"Sorry, Ma'am. I forgot you don't do this. My position is AADD—we call it A-two D-two. That stands for auxiliary active digital display. It's part of sonar." He shrugged in discomfort. In the narrow passageway outside the wardroom, he thought that he could smell her soap or makeup. His ears were becoming redder by the moment.

Jessica Dugan had to smile at the boy. His eyes were the oldest part of his face. Were it not for his brow's furrowed intensity of a submariner, the face belonged in the back seat of an old convertible at a Midwestern drive-in.

"That sounds too complex for me, Mister Foster."

"Yes, Ma'am," he mumbled as he shifted his weight for the tenth time.

"Lieutenant Shaffer wanted me to show you some records."

"Good. Let's go in." She went into the wardroom first as protocol dictates.

The sailor hesitated before entering "officers' country." Then he nervously crossed the threshold and laid his paperwork on the large, barren table.

"I'm to show you these." He wanted to smile. But he could not.

All Navy men-of-war have a ship's secretary billet. The secretary rides herd on the vessel's administrative paper flow and the ship's library. Every ship from a tiny patrol boat to a nuclear-powered aircraft carrier maintains some form of library for storing maintenance manuals, safety publications, and technical handbooks.

"If I may show you the manuals over here first?" the seaman said softly. He led his superior officer to a wall cabinet with metal doors. The doors had wire trusses in them instead of glass. It was a bookshelf which Dr. Dugan had not noticed during her prior visits to the wardroom. "This is the ship's basic library. Every manual required for the ship's departments and divisions has a copy here. Even the laboratory, safety and contamination control handbooks are here. Copies of everything are in their proper space throughout the ship."

Dr. Dugan quickly scanned the book jackets through the wire doors. The thickest, black manual was six inches wide and was entitled *Maintenance Requirements for Continued, Unrestricted Submarine Operations to Design Test Depth.* She felt the hair rise on the back of her neck for an instant. Next was the smaller text, *Standard Submarine Operations and Regulations Manual.* Beside these was the *Ship's Organization and Regulations Manual.* Every Navy vessel has a regulations manual unique for its class. Various technical and maintenance manuals finished the three-foot long shelf. The next to the last title was *Nuclear, Biological, and Chemical Defense.* The last manual was thin but had some kind of band running around the jacket. Her eyes stopped on the volume which had no title stenciled on the spine.

The seaman felt her eyes linger on the lone title. He stood close to her elbow and he struggled not to smell her hair.

"That's the bridge folder, Commander. It's quite classified. Every ship has one. It details a vessel's unique handling characteristics. CIC has the master copy. It contains tables and graphs for turn-rate diagrams, surge tables, acceleration tables, and the like."

"Oh." When she looked squarely into the boy's face, he took a step backward. "It's been fifteen years since I studied shiphandling, Mister Foster."

The underwater handling of a submarine is so secret that all of its maneuvering characteristics are classified by the U.S. Code of Federal Regulations. Turn rate diagrams detail how wide a circle a submarine would make during a change of course; surge tables plot how far forward on its old heading a sub would travel after the rudder is thrown over for a turn to a new heading; and acceleration tables tabulate how much time a submarine would require to change speed. If an enemy submarine or surface vessel had the bridge folder, it could more accurately guess a hiding sub's position from its last known position.

"Good morning, Ma'am," the seaman blushed as he excused himself and escaped from the officer's blue-gray eyes. The thought of morning made her look upward. All she saw was the wardroom overhead with criss-crossing pipes and wire conduits. Glancing at her wrist watch, she thought of a dark tropical sky beyond 800 feet of water where it was thirty minutes past midnight, local time.

She returned to the table where she sat down in front of a coffee mug and the stack of books and folders.

Dr. Dugan spread the documents across the tabletop and she organized them in order of importance. This finished, she rose and fumbled through two drawers until she found a steno pad and ballpoint pen.

Making notes as she went through the papers, she started with the evaluation sheets of *Sam Houston*'s two weeks worth of sudden casualties: Buddy Thurston who was rotting somewhere outside, Electrician's Mate Hendrix who was as hard as Lot's Wife down below in the meat freezer, and the planesman bound and gagged in sick bay whose last solid food had been the diving officer's ear.

As was the case with everyone serving in SSN-609, the records of all three men were exemplary. The only trends revealed by their evaluation sheets were superior aptitudes and high intelligence. Their Navy service school records were no different. Each had excelled in his Class "A" school at basic technical training and in his Class "C" advanced training. The three men were singled out as outstanding even back at Class "R" basic recruit training. If their sudden deaths or suicides (or suicide attempt in the planesman's case) was the product of some deep-seated, psychological imbalance, the shrinks had certainly missed it.

From the evaluation sheets, the physician went on to the submarine's complex tables of division bills. She drew tables on her steno pad to correlate the three subjects' common assignments in the ship. Her work was slowed by the detail recorded in the Watch, Quarter, and Station Bill which lists every crewman's assigned position for administrative duties, operational posts, watch station, emergency position, and individual battle station. The master WQS Bill is maintained on all Navy ships of the line by the executive officer. Each division head has a similar log for his own department.

All Navy ships are divided into departments for administration. Each department is subdivided into divisions. At the division level, there can be further administrative units called sections. The chain of command begins with the section leader who reports to his division leading petty officer whose superior is the junior division officer under the command of the division officer. The division officer maintains a "division notebook" containing personal information on each of his men such as training records and qualifications.

Dr. Dugan paid close attention to the division notebooks for the weapons department where Torpedoman Thurston had served, the engineering department where Electrician's Mate Hendrix had served, and navigation where the planesman had been billetted with distinction until the moment when he had lost his mind. The notes she scribbled all said the same thing: the best of the best doing what they loved.

From the submarine's Battle Bill, Jessica Dugan plotted the battle stations assignments of the three casualties. SSN-609's personnel assignments were all dictated by the Unit Bill issued by the Department of the Navy for *Ethan Allen* class attack submarines (formerly, missile boats). There is a unique Unit Bill for each class of warship in the fleet.

Ten pages of Lt. Commander Dugan's longhand tables of billets and duty-time presented only one conclusion: The paths of the three men would have crossed often in the confines of a submarine. During their last two months at sea, their duty times and off-times overlapped daily. They could bump into each other at mess, during video or movie breaks, and during changes of watch. If *Sam Houston* did indeed have a containment breach, it was probably ship wide.

Jessica frowned and pushed the stack of records away. When she rose with her coffee cup in hand, she realized that her lower back hurt. Looking at her wrist, she was surprised that she had been hunched over her work for two hours. Her knees felt stiff when she walked the five steps to the ever hot pot of coffee. She poured another dose and worried that she was becoming a real sailor: a human caffeine sewer.

After stretching her legs beside the drip percolator for five minutes, the physician returned to the table. She looked over her shoulder when the joiner door opened. Even the doorknob latch sounded muted.

"Good morning, Captain," she said as she rose at her place.

"And to you, Doctor. Please sit down."

As she woman resumed her seat, Commander Milhaus filled a coffee mug. He sat down opposite Jessica Dugan. The door opened again and Executive Office Perlmutter entered.

"Captain. Jessica."

"Coffee's hot, Pappy," the captain smiled.

"Thank you, Sir."

The XO took a seat beside his captain. The two men faced Dr. Dugan. Except for her battered left cheek and completely blackened eye, she looked remarkably fit and rested. To Jessica's one good eye, both men appeared tired after their five- or six-hour sleep.

The captain glanced at the stack of ship's records.

"What did you learn?"

"Only that I now believe, Sir, that the containment breach must be throughout the ship." She referred to her detailed

notes. "If you look here at the billets and duty times of the three
casualties, you can see that their watches would have taken
them through just about all ship's spaces except the reactor
compartment. While most of Thurston's and the planesman's
time was spent forward of the laboratories, Electrician's Mate
Hendrix spent all of his duty time aft of the missile bays
in the engineering and propulsion spaces." She spread both
hands upon her pile of log books and duty rosters as if she
were absorbing information through her palms. "It must be
everywhere, Captain." She sounded depressed; saddened even.
"Assuming, of course, that Lesch-Nyhan is the fundamental
agent."

"So," Kurt Milhaus sighed. "Colonel Epson's bugs are buzz-
ing everywhere?"

"It would seem so, Sir," she said firmly. "If a mosquito
escaped from BL-4, it could be anywhere by now. Also, there
may be more than one, of course."

Pappy Perlmutter's face twitched. He imagined himself suddenly itchy.

"What do you mean 'assuming it's the disease?' " the XO
asked with fatigue in his voice.

"Well, Dr. Shaffer's findings are preliminary at best on
Hendrix and the planesman. And there will never be a post
mortem on Thurston."

"Did you find any suggestion of psychological dysfunction
among the casualties, Commander?" The CO's voice was
strange to Dr. Dugan's ears. The captain sounded vaguely
angry; angry that she might entertain the notion that his hand-
picked crew had any unstable men; angry that he secretly
hoped that the men had simply cracked instead of being poi-
soned down to their very chromosomes.

"I mean no disrespect, Sir," Lt. Commander Dugan said.

"Yes, yes, Doctor. I know. Please continue." Kurt Milhaus
smiled as if he meant it.

"Captain, I found absolutely no evidence of anything within
either of the three men which would suggest that they lost
their mental balance. These men don't even have a single
captain's mast in their histories. Their records and medical
evaluations confirm their stability, even the planesman who
lost it yesterday, or last night—whenever." She was frustrated by the submarine's peculiar lack of calendar reference

points. Without the sun, she was becoming disoriented in time.

Masts are audiences by enlisted personnel with a ship's commanding officer. A captain's mast is a disciplinary hearing before the CO for minor infractions of rules or Navy regulations.

"I understand, Jessica," the CO said soothingly. "The planesman suffered his breakdown eleven hours ago—yesterday afternoon, by the real world."

"Thank you, Captain. I'm trying to adjust." She blinked her good eye.

"You are doing quite well, Jessica," Pappy Perlmutter smiled warmly. "It takes weeks really. You haven't been on board 24 hours yet. It'll come."

"Hope so," she nodded. "And thanks for fixing my stateroom."

"The least I could do. We don't get much company."

"I suppose not," she smiled back.

"Now what do you do?" the CO asked impatiently.

"Now, Sir, I continue to work closely with Dr. Shaffer. I'll start with an inspection of the BL-4 lab. I sort of didn't make it down there last evening." She had to look down at her pile of papers.

"All right. Stan was up and about when we came through."

Dr. Dugan rested her hand on Buddy Thurston's personnel file folder.

"He really thrived here," she said softly. "Poor sandblower."

She felt the sudden coldness in Pappy Perlmutter's eyes when she looked at him.

"We all liked him, Doctor. He was the kind of man who gave this ship its character and its spirit. He was no sandblower to his shipmates."

"Sandblower" is Navy for a short person. Buddy Thurston's file noted his small stature: hardly more than five feet tall.

"Pappy, I'm sorry. Truly." Her subdued voice was almost pleading.

"Okay, me too," Pappy said gently. "We all have a job to do here."

"Yes, Commander, and I intend to do mine."

"I know you will," the captain interrupted. "This is a special boat, Jessica. She has her own character. Every ship is different. Buddy was one of the men we rather depended on to keep us in good cheer."

The CO was still quietly grieving.

"Different ships; different long splices," Jessica Dugan nodded.

"You *are* regular Navy!" Pappy chuckled. The old expression from square-rigger days referred to the fact that every warship assumes her own unique personality from her crew.

"Born and bred," she said softly.

The two junior officers rose when Commander Milhaus stood at his place.

"I'm counting on you, Jessica."

"I know that, Sir."

"Very well," the CO sighed. "Looks like you've eaten. The mess detail will take care of your tray. You can meet Dr. Shaffer below."

"Aye, Sir." The standing woman aligned the piles of ship's bills, muster rolls, and personnel files. "What about these?"

"The librarian will pick 'em up." The CO gestured toward the door of the wardroom.

The captain and the physician entered the passageway together. The XO followed them. Captain Milhaus sidestepped to Jessica Dugan's left. Military courtesy requires a junior officer to walk on the left of a superior, but junior women are invited to assume the superior's right. Kurt Milhaus dutifully walked aft on the Dr. Dugan's left.

"Captain on the bridge," a seaman said softly when the three officers entered the spacious control room. The standing officer of the deck saluted the captain as did the diving officer of the watch who rose from his seat behind the helmsman and planesman. They saluted their CO since it was their first meeting of a new day.

Several petty officers milled about the CIC. In ten minutes, at 0800 UTC (4:00 in the morning Atlantic Time outside), the mid-watch crew would yield their places to the morning watch-standers. The morning watch will last from 0400 until 0800 in the morning, local time. At the end of the morning watch, the officer of the deck will change, the captain will take his first Eight O'clock Report of the day from his XO, and the ship's department heads and division leaders will execute the 0730 muster-to-quarters throughout *Sam Houston*.

"Good morning, Captain," the OOD nodded.

"Morning, Mister Gentry," the CO said to his youthful lieutenant. The captain returned the OOD's brisk salute.

"Steering 0-9-0, Sir, 4 knots, and we've come up to 400 feet per the night orders."

"Very well, Lieutenant. Anything on the horn, yet?"

"Not yet, Sir. Radio room is standing by."

"Then carry on, Mister Gentry. Commander Perlmutter will take the conn. I want to stop by sick bay to look in on the casualties. Is Dr. Shaffer below?"

"Yes, Sir. He's in BL-4."

"All right. Call me if the doorbell rings."

"Aye, Sir."

All fleet submarines come within 400 feet of the surface at predetermined times to listen for the extremely low frequency, ELF, "bellringer" beacon.

Jessica Dugan stood quietly out of the way.

"Doctor, if you want to come with me as far as sick bay, I'll point you in the right direction for Deck Three."

"Thank you, Sir," she said softly.

The CO led her out of the red-lit CIC. They passed the maneuvering table of the navigator's position. The quartermaster of the watch stood beside the table where the deck log lay open awaiting the OOD's signature at the end of the midwatch. The QMOW maintains the deck log for the OOD to sign. The quartermaster is the middleman between the OOD and the navigator underway.

"Captain off the bridge," a seaman announced as the officer led Dr. Dugan down the companionway in the rear of the control room.

Lt. Commander Perlmutter picked up the hand-held microphone of the sub's all-ship IMC public address circuit.

"This is the XO," Pappy Perlmutter announced. "I have the bubble."

Protocol requires that the ship be informed of who is in charge in CIC.

El Tiburon ran at flank bell just beneath the surface in the calm darkness two hours before a tropical sunrise. Three air-breathing diesels made turns on three propellers for 15 knots. At full speed, the throbbing engines each put out 6,000 horsepower.

Captain Barcena entered the narrow control room at 0730, UTC. The submarine's clock mounted on the forward bulkhead was set to its home port in the Eastern Time Zone. The clock read 2:30 in the morning. On the surface, it was 3:30 in the morning, Atlantic Standard Time.

"Good morning, Capitan," the Cuban officer of the deck saluted.

The captain returned the courtesy. He was still tired, both from his long day and from the excitement of having received tactical orders ten hours earlier. But he felt much better after a four-hour nap in his tiny cabin.

"You are rested, Capitan?" the young officer asked his CO.

"Much better, thank you."

"Good, Sir. We're steering 0-9-0 True, making 15 knots, depth 15 meters. Engineering reports the snorkel induction is normal."

"Very well, Lieutenant."

El Tiburon ran submerged with her keel 45 feet beneath the surface. Her thick snorkel mast had been run up to full extension out the top of the conning tower sail. The rounded head of the snorkel cut through the surface with a long white feather of turbulent water.

"How's the sea state," the captain inquired of his OOD.

"Looks like two-meter waves, Sir, and the QM says the pressure seems to have fallen some."

"Very well."

The white-haired skipper walked forward a few steps to his navigator's position. The navigator was sleeping so the quartermaster manned the maneuvering table.

"Any problem, Chief, with the weather?" the captain asked his quartermaster. "The sea seems smooth right now."

The submarine so close to the surface was susceptible to the rise and fall of rough surf. But the sea remained unremarkable, although the waves were twice as high as normal at six-foot seas.

"Well, Capitan, the barometer is down to 1012 millibars. But the snorkel has remained clear for two hours. Sea is up,

Sir, but the diesels have stayed on line. I'm not worried. The weather people did report that brief storm over the Dominican Republic yesterday afternoon. Nothing serious and it dissipated quickly."

While the captain had napped, his Night Order Book had authorized returning to diesel power at local midnight.

"Very well, QM. Keep an eye on the barometer. At least our ride remains smooth, even so close to the swells."

"Yes, Sir." The quartermaster had to stifle a smile. The Old Man was worried about a gentle ride for his crew. "El Viejo" the quartermaster smiled to himself.

Normal sea level, atmospheric pressure is standardized at 29.92 inches of mercury as measured within a barometric tube. The metric equivalent is in millibars with 1013 millibars equal to standard sea level pressure. *El Tiburon*'s snorkel mast protruding through the surface in the darkness sensed 1012 millibars or 29.88 inches of mercury. The slight decrease from normal meant that a storm was brewing somewhere to the east.

El Tiburon's thick snorkel stuck three feet out of the water. Since the boat rose and fell with the surface swells, the mast remained in the air.

The snorkel had two hollow tubes: the induction tube sucked salty air down into the diesel engines. The exhaust tube blew hot gases out of the three diesels.

Modern snorkels, also carried aboard U.S. nuclear submarines, have water sensors which automatically seal the tube should a wave break over the open valve. This prevents sea water from being sucked into the diesels and snuffing them out and causing grave corrosion damage from the salt water which attacks all metal, even aluminum.

The snorkel also is wired to the diesels. When the snorkel's ring float-controlled head valve senses water and slams shut, the diesels are automatically shut down. Otherwise, the interruption of snorkel air would cause the diesels to violently suck air from inside the submarine's living spaces. World War II submariners learned to hate this ear-popping effect. They called it "pumping."

Diesel-electric subs depend upon old-fashioned, lead-acid batteries, very much like automobile batteries. Tons of them drive the boat's three 5200-horsepower electric motors.

Precious battery reserves are conserved by running at periscope depth whenever possible so the snorkel can poke through the surface. Air drawn down from outside is breathed by the diesels which also run generators for charging the batteries.

The prospect of a falling barometer and its associated worsening weather might mean that El Tiburon would have to retract its snorkel and run on batteries alone. This would limit her underwater endurance to hardly two days.

El Viejo stopped at his radioman in the control room. A young seaman wore headphones where he slouched over his communication consoles.

El Tiburon ran eastward on a magnetic course of 097, 20 nautical miles north of Haiti. Due south was the hamlet of St. Louis du Nord on the mainland. Between El Tiburon and the coast was the Ile de la Tortue.

She skirted and ran parallel to Hispaniola's northern coastline. The sea bottom had shallowed to 6,000 feet of water beneath the keel since she pulled out of the Windward Passage during the midnight watch.

"Can you raise the VOR for a fix?" the captain asked his studious radioman.

El Tiburon's narrow antenna mast also broke the surface behind the thick snorkel.

"Just barely, Capitan. But I have a fix which I've passed to the quartermaster. The NDB was better than the VOR due to the atmospherics."

The boy was gratified that El Viejo had such a clear picture of their probable position even though he had been sleeping for the last four hours. The seaman was listening hard through crackling static to hear the airport navigation beacons broadcasting across the water from the little field at Cap Haitien. Intended for aircraft, the NDB broadcast in the AM radio band which tends to follow the Earth's curvature. FM signals climb out over the horizon. Cap Haitien's FM radio would not hug the sea close enough to be monitored clearly by El Tiburon's antenna only four feet above the choppy sea.

The submarine drew an electromagnetic bead on the AM-band, Non-Directional Beacon broadcasting from northern Haiti's coastline 40 nautical miles southeast of El Tiburon's position. The radioman had dialed in 288 kilohertz and strained his ears to pick up the NDB signal's Morse Code identifier: dot-dot-dot-dot, dash, dash-dot, or "H-T-N." He tried to get an FM radio fix off the tandem, aircraft VOR on 113.9 megahertz, but there was too much static.

The radio beacon fix cross-checked with the navigator's star sight shot through the midnight periscope. It reduced to a most probable position solution of 20° north latitude by 72.5° west longitude.

"Very well," El Viejo nodded. "Keep the QM updated."

"I have been, Sir."

"I know," the captain smiled as he gently laid his hand upon the boy's hunched shoulder.

El Viejo looked up at the submarine's overhead where massive pipes and wire bundles crossed the cluttered ceiling of gray steel bathed in red light. He imagined forty feet of sea water and an overcast Caribbean night above the water.

"I'll be in the wardroom," the captain said to his OOD. "You have the conn."

"Yes, Sir."

"Steady as you go, Lieutenant."

"Yes, Sir," the young officer nodded.

"El Capitan off the bridge," a sailor said when the CO left the control room to get some breakfast at 4:00 in the morning, local Atlantic time.

The tall captain had to stoop through a series of low, water-tight hatches which separated his ship's compartments. The smell of fresh coffee near the wardroom stopped him in the red-lit passageway.

"Smells good, Rafael."

"Capitan." The off-watch electrician handed his cup to the captain. The CO smiled, gestured for the petty officer to drink up, and poured his own cup.

When the captain sat down, the seaman stood awkwardly. The Revolution had done away with most military formality, but the captain was still the captain.

"Please, Rafael." The sailor sat down opposite the weary CO. The lines and care on the older man's face made the electrician look like the captain's grandson.

"Can we find the American boat, Capitan?" The boy did not look up from his coffee mug.

"I have every confidence in this crew." The CO's face cracked into a smile with deep lines carved into the thin face. "Is this your first operational cruise?"

"Yes, Sir. I hope to learn much." His voice was strained.

When the petty officer glanced up, he was surprised to see the CO's eyes looking hard at him. The young seaman blinked when he sensed the older man's face reading his mind as intensely as *El Tiburon*'s passive hydrophones were scouring the black ocean. El Viejo's stubbled face softened behind the steam rising from his coffee. He leaned back in his chair.

"I remember my first time when it was all real, Rafael. It was on the beach at Manzanillo in "56." The CO waited patiently for his words to sink in.

"My God, Sir!"

"I was there, Rafael. One of the original twelve who made it into the Sierra Maestra with El Caballo, Che, and the rest. I was afraid, too. Terrified. But it did get easier with time."

The Cuban Revolution began July 26th, 1953, when Fidel Castro led 167 rebels in an attack against the Moncada Barracks near Santiago, Cuba. The 27-year-old lawyer's revolt was crushed. Fidel was sentenced to fifteen years in prison. His brother, Raul, got thirteen years. They were released two years later when the Cuban dictator, Batista, declared an amnesty. The brothers fled to Mexico to train their army. "July 26th" became the rebellion's rallying cry.

Fidel landed again on Cuban soil at Manzanillo in December 1956. His 81 rebels were cut to ribbons on the beach. Only twelve escaped into the mountains. Argentine physician and rebel Che Guevara was one of Fidel's primary lieutenants. Castro marched so hard without rest that his men called him El Caballo-The Horse. A beautiful student radical from Havana had wanted to wade ashore with her long black hair tied back with the red and black armband of the July 26 Movement. A 19-year-old Martinez Barcena took her place in the little invasion to keep her safe. Amalia met them in the Sierra Maestra mountains two weeks later.

"It will be all right, Rafael. I have been a soldier a long time. The closer we get to our enemies, the less you will feel the fear."

The young sailor did not look convinced. He could not take his eyes from the strange expression on El Viejo's face. In the old man's memory, the CO saw a young woman. Her hair was bound in the colors of the Revolution.

"It will be so, Rafael." The older seaman smiled.

When Captain Barcena stood up, the electrician also stood.

"You must rest when you are off-watch," the CO said firmly. "We may have a long day tomorrow. I'll be in my cabin."

"Yes, Capitan."

The petty officer stood quietly looking at the open door when El Viejo walked into the passageway. The electrician noticed the determination in his captain's step.

As the midwatch crew rotated with the morning watchstanders throughout *Sam Houston* at 0400 Atlantic Time (0800 UTC), Jessica Dugan and Dr. Shaffer were gowning in the outer decontamination space of the maximum containment, BL-4 laboratory on SSN-609's lowest deck. Forward of the lab and old missile bay, Deck Three was mainly storage compartments, equipment lockers, reserve batteries, and air bottles used to blow the forward ballast tank.

The two physicians were already dressed in clean white jumpsuits, sterile booties over their deck shoes, cotton surgical caps, and rubber gloves. The National Institutes of Health guidelines for BL-4 facilities are rigid. No vials or containers may leave BL-4 until they are roasted in autoclaves or bathed in disinfectant for sterilization.

This anteroom was larger than the outer compartments in the BL-3 and BL-2 labs on the upper decks. This compartment was large enough to hold small privacy stalls with doors. No deck clothing of any kind is allowed inside BL-4. Each crewman entering the lab proper must first remove all clothing and then don a jumpsuit. Even lab underwear is provided. Past the watertight hatch leading into the lab is another small compartment containing two complete showers. That inner compartment has another electric door leading into the lab itself. No one may leave the lab for the outer ship without showering first. The floor drains in the shower contain disinfectant traps and HEPA filters.

Equipment and glassware must enter the BL-4 lab through a small double-door airlock which bakes or fumigates everything before the inside door is opened to pull the materials into the lab.

The officers stood beside a first class petty officer who had come out to greet them. They had to wait for him for ten minutes since he could not leave the inner lab until he had showered and changed. He had to change again before leading them through the locked double-doors into the laboratory.

"Spooky, huh?" Dr. Shaffer smiled.

"Yeh," Jessica nodded.

"Wait till you see the space suits inside."

"Space suits?"

"Yes. The technicians working with animal subjects must wear positive-pressure suits when they work with the animals housed in Class III containment cabinets. There's a shower inside to scrub the suits after contact with the animals."

"Oh," Jessica Dugan shrugged.

"I guess we're ready," the petty officer said firmly.

The young noncom was the assistant Biohazards Safety Officer for BL-4. He alone was authorized to unlock the double doors.

"You'll need to clear your ears when we go in," he said calmly. "The pressure out here is substantially higher than inside to maintain positive airflow inward for contamination control."

"Okay," Lt. Shaffer answered before Dr. Dugan could comment.

The instant the seaman laid his latex gloved hand on the speaker switch, the loudspeaker on the bulkhead crackled.

"Fire alert! Fire alert! This is not a drill! . . . Fire party and Repair Three party report auxiliary machinery. Fire class charlie or bravo. Lieutenant Shaffer and Lt. Commander Dugan report to aft BDS immediately . . . This is not a drill!"

Stan Shaffer was half out of his jumpsuit as he stepped into the changing stall. He looked over his naked shoulder toward the wide-eyed woman who stood frozen in the center of the compartment.

"Move out, Jessica!"

EIGHT

15 MARCH; 0900 UTC

"THIS IS the captain. Secure from material condition zebra. Rig for conditions yoke and circle-William."

In the forward end of *Sam Houston*'s control room, the instrument panel in front of the chief of the watch was full of blinking lights. The leftmost of the three seated sailors, the first class petty officer watched a row of lights blink off as half a dozen watertight doors were opened throughout the ship. With the fire alarm, all such hatches had been tightly dogged to avert flooding from either fire hoses or a hull rupture. Having stood down from condition zebra and general quarters, only the most critical hatches remained sealed. Such doors were marked with a large "Y" for condition yoke and peacetime cruising.

"DCC says we are watertight, Sir."

"Thank you," Kurt Milhaus said wearily to his telephone-talker in touch by the sub's intercom with the Damage Control Center.

"Pumping continuing, Captain," the third class petty officer added as he pressed his earphone closer to his cheek. "Partial flooding at worst, Sir. Should be drained within fifteen minutes. No hull leaks reported."

"Thank you."

The captain stepped over to the maneuvering table at the navigator's position in CIC. The quartermaster of the watch stood beside a large plotboard laid upon a chart of the sea bottom of the Puerto Rico Trench and the adjacent Caribbean.

"Lucky we were at 400 feet, Captain."

"Maybe," the grim CO nodded. He knew very well that dumb luck had ignited the fire after SSN-609 had ascended to 400 feet to await the ELF beacon. Had she been down at her 800-foot cruise depth, the added pressure of the sea-24 atmospheres at the greater depth—might have buckled the hull plates where intense heat weakened the HY-80 steel shell of the ship. "Guess we'll have to stay up here until engineering can look it over. I'd surely rather be deeper, QM."

"Yes, Sir," the quartermaster agreed.

To a submarine, depth means security: deeper water means more opportunity to take advantage of the sea's various layers of salinity and water temperature to hide behind. Such layers scatter enemy sonar and increase a submarine's stealth qualities.

"Wish the compartment were green, though," the CO added softly, looking down at the large space colored pink on the diagram of his ship.

"Well, it'll be dry in another ten minutes."

The CO said nothing. He simply tapped the board atop the maneuvering table. His index finger rose and fell on a series of cut-away diagrams of *Sam Houston*'s deck plan. Each compartment and space was colored pink, green, or yellow. The captain tapped the upper deck space in the center of the aft, engineering and propulsion spaces where the fire had erupted.

Captain Milhaus concentrated on the Flooding Effect Diagram issued for every ship in the fleet. When any vessel takes on water, there is a danger other than sinking. Flooding means radical shifts in a ship's center of buoyancy and its center of mass or gravity. The weight of water taken on can render a stable ship highly unstable.

Water is heavy. A single cubic foot of water weighs nearly 65 pounds. Even a small space ten feet square and eight feet high would hold 26 *tons* of water if completely flooded.

There are two kinds of flooding: solid and partial. Complete flooding of a space is referred to as solid; partial flooding is less than solid. In many ways, partial flooding is the more dangerous from the standpoint of ship stability.

Partial flooding causes "free surface." A partially flooded

compartment allows the water to slosh. This movement of the water's "free surface" causes sudden changes in the compartment's center of mass. Enough free surface sloshing in a partly flooded space can roll a ship over as tons of free water slam out of balance into the hull.

The Flooding Effect Diagram is a stability chart. Compartments colored pink are spaces where flooding causes instability. These spaces are usually high in a ship where massive additions of weight above the center of gravity (buoyancy) could make the vessel dangerously top-heavy. Flooding of compartments colored green on the diagram would actually increase stability. Such spaces are usually low in the ship and would stabilize it by making the vessel ride deeper in the water. Yellow compartments are those in which solid flooding helps stability while partial flooding and free surface would lessen stability. Some of the spaces on the diagram were not colored at all: Flooding of these does not affect stability one way or the other.

Commander Milhaus tapped the diagram of the burned compartment in the aft engineering spaces. The compartment was dyed pink: flooding is dangerous for stability.

The pink compartment was dead center in the engineering spaces behind the reactor compartment. On the upper Deck One, the large compartment contained sensitive equipment needed to monitor the ship's vibration. Any vibration radiating from a submerged submarine is transferred to the sea in the form of waves of pressure. That pressure is "heard" by the passive sonar which is ever listening on enemy submarines. A good sonar man, known affectionately as the ping jockey, can identify the class and type of an unseen ship by its pressure and sound wave signatures. The very best sonar man can actually name a noisy boat whose sounds are as unique as a finger print.

Carbon dioxide had been used to smother the fire. Then to cool the burned area to prevent reflash, tons of high-pressure salt water from SSN-609's fire main had dumped three feet of water into the watertight compartment which had blazed for only seven intense minutes. The fire was hot enough to buckle part of the watertight bulkhead and to melt a low-pressure steam pipeline which crossed the overhead.

High in the ship's aft third, partial flooding of the compartment made the submarine's tail top-heavy. The helmsman up front in the control room could feel his 410-foot long ship heel from side to side as the tail wobbled from the sloshing, free surface which was being slowly pumped out of the space. The water went down into sump tanks where high-pressure bilge pumps would dump it overboard.

The first fire-fighting team to reach the compartment quickly identified the flames as a class charlie, electrical fire. A circuit breaker box was engulfed in white-hot flames.

The Navy trains its service personnel to recognize and fight four kinds of fires: Class alfa fires are ordinary, dry matter; class bravo fires are burning liquids; class charlie fires are electrical in origin; and class delta fires are super-hot fires from burning metals such as aluminum, magnesium, zinc or sodium.

Ordinary class alfa and delta fires are fought with high-pressure water hoses shooting sea water. Class bravo fires are doused with fire-suppression foam, fogs, wet steam, or potassium bicarbonate powder called "purple K powder." Class charlie fires are fought with carbon dioxide extinguishers.

Each ship's Watch, Quarter and Station Bill assigns every crewman to various casualty parties. Repair parties officially represent the ship's Damage Control Assistant, DCA, at the site of any emergency. Each party is led by a first class petty officer or a chief petty officer.

Generally, the parties are numbered with permanent assignments: Repair Two handles emergencies in forward compartments; Repair Three is assigned aft; middle (amidships) areas are managed by Repair Four; disasters in the propulsion plant are the billet of the Repair Three party; Repair Six has the most dangerous job of dealing with casualties to the weapons and ordnance spaces; and, electronics failures or casualties are the assignment of Repair Eight.

The DCA is junior to the supervising engineering officer. Repair parties and division damage control petty officers all report to the DCA. The ship's damage control library is maintained in the Damage Control Center.

The highly trained men of SSN-609's Repair Three party reached the burning engineering compartment moments behind the fire party.

Each fire party has at least half a dozen seamen: the hose man (or men), the fireplug man, the compartment access man, the foam-generator man, the foam-supply man, the carbon dioxide extinguisher man, the ventilation detail man, an electrician, and an emergency air man.

Ten men were on the scene in *Sam Houston*'s aft spaces within half a minute of the alarm in CIC. Communications with the Damage Control Center were instantly opened over the 4MC two-way intercom circuit as is routine for Navy casualties underway.

The access man with huge gloves opened the smoke-filled compartment. The carbon-dioxide man wearing an air pack on his back then entered the compartment where he discharged a cloud of fire-smothering snow. The gas in his extinguisher instantly expanded 450 times when the nozzle opened. The carbon dioxide cloud shot from the extinguisher was 110°F below zero. The burning electrical box was quickly covered with snow and the fire suffocated.

With the circuit breaker box extinguished, the fire hose men wearing air tanks on their backs and masks on their faces entered to finish the job of cooling down the box. A cloth hose 1 1/2 inches in diameter was carried into the compartment from the passageway. Throughout the ship, as in all U.S. Navy vessels, were double racks of 50-foot lengths of the hose suspended on bulkheads on either side of fireplugs. Only one length of hose can attach to the plug, but the two hoses can be spliced together for distant fires.

A fireman worked the three-position fire hose nozzle. The smoking box was first blasted with high-pressure streams of water at 100 pounds per square inch pressure with the T-handle of the nozzle in the back position. Then, the handle was placed in the middle position for a water fog. After twenty minutes, the nozzle was closed when the fireman pushed the T-handle full forward.

The box was still steaming when the repair party entered the space to evaluate the damaged steam pipe melted by the heat. They quickly rigged a "jubilee patch" to the sagging pipe. The patch and clamp affair returned the steam pipe to service in the ship's auxiliary steam circulation.

Sam Houston cruised the trench at a depth of 400 feet. Ship's physicians Lt. Shaffer and Lt. Commander Jessica Dugan paced an aft section compartment set aside for emergency triage and first aid. From their post in the after BDS area, they waited for further instructions from CIC. Emergency battle dressing stations, BDS, were spread throughout the ship.

"Captain, the compartment is secured now. DCA would like a word, Sir."

The control room telephone-talker handed his headset to his CO.

"Damage Control, Captain," the CO said into the microphone.

"DCA, Sir," the damage control assistant responded over the telephone 4MC circuit. "Compartment secured, Captain. Pumping completed. It's pretty well dry now." The chief petty officer hesitated. "We have a body here, Sir. Maybe the doc ought to come back. The air is fine, Sir."

"Very well," the CO replied. "Thank you, Chief."

The high-pressure carbon dioxide sucks all oxygen out of an area when the gas is used to suppress fires. Men not wearing air tanks would smother along with the fire—hence the air packs and masks on the fire party.

"Captain to after BDS."

"CIC, after BDS. Go ahead, Sir," Dr. Shaffer radioed forward.

"You can go back, Lieutenant. Is Commander Dugan with you?"

"Yes, Sir, she's back here."

"Very good. Take Dr. Dugan with you. DCA advises they have a casualty."

"Yes, Sir. On our way."

The two officers made their way aft to the upper deck's vibration monitoring compartment. As they approached, the acrid stench of burned insulation became more pungent. But as reported, the air in the passageway was breathable. Seamen continued to fold the long firehose so they could hang it back on the bulkhead racks. Fire fighters call it "faking" the hose.

"In here, Lieutenant," the leader of the repair party gestured. The two medics crouched through the watertight door in the bulkhead.

Dr. Dugan followed close behind. In a corner of the long compartment they found a motionless figure slumped against the hull. The body was soaked in foam and salt water from the hose. The physicians stood over the unconscious sailor,

The chief petty officer of the fire party sloshed through the standing water to join them.

"Lieutenant," the CPO nodded grimly.

"Chief. Anyone else?"

"No, Doc. Just Brad."

"Who is he?" Dr. Dugan asked gently.

"Radioman second class Brad Frazier. This is where we found him."

"Radioman?" the physician asked. "Are there radiomen in this space?"

"No, Ma'am. I already asked engineering. Frazier was off duty when the fire broke out. The compartment was supposed to be empty for this watch."

"He didn't call in the fire, Chief?"

"No, Lieutenant. It was an auto alarm direct to CIC and DCC."

"Oh."

"No other injuries?" Dr. Dugan asked as she stepped forward, closer to the radioman who appeared to sleep wedged into a corner.

"None, Commander. Frazier must have tried to open the box, though."

"What makes you say that, Chief?"

"He burned his fingers." The CPO pointed down toward the dead man's left hand.

Dr. Shaffer could see that the dead man's left hand was blackened to the wrist. Grotesque blisters had ruptured on the palm. The physician nodded up toward the chief.

"His right hand, too, Lieutenant," the CPO pointed.

The hand was resting next to the dead seaman's denim knee. The fingers were behind the leg, but the wrist area was clearly visible in two inches of water. The skin was white and normal along the top of Frazier's right hand.

"Doesn't looked burned to me," Lt. Shaffer said as he reached down. He grabbed the man's blue cotton shirt at the wrist cuff and he pulled the hand out from behind the dead leg.

"See, Lieutenant?" the chief nodded toward the deck-wide puddle of sea water which was still being pumped into the sump tanks below deck.

Dr. Shaffer held up the limp arm. He moved the lifeless arm closer to Dr. Dugan who stood close by. The dead man's index, middle, and ring fingertips were all gone back to the third knuckles by the palm. The pool of salt water had washed any blood away. The small stumps were cut with tiny grooves through the bone.

"Musta been burned clean off," the CPO said dryly. He had seen fire casualties before.

"Seems so," Dr. Shaffer said. He lowered the arm gently beside the body. When he looked over at Jessica Dugan, she was frowning.

"Maybe you should tell the CO?" Lieutenant Shaffer smiled grimly.

"Thanks. But no thanks." She did not smile at all.

Rising, the bearded physician led the doctor out of the compartment. Only when they returned to the passageway running parallel to the sealed reactor compartment did they realize how hot the smoky space had been. The passageway was cool and extremely comfortable. They elbowed their way past the men of the fire party and repair team who waited their turns to enter.

"I'll brief the captain if you want to get ready down below," the lieutenant said softly in the reddish light.

"All right. Set up in the cooler?" she asked.

"Yep. Just like with Hendrix yesterday. Dress warm."

"Sure."

They stopped at the massive bulkhead separating the aft passageway from the top deck of the missile compartment. Lieutenant Shaffer would have to observe the BL-2 containment procedures when he cut through the laboratory toward the control room on the lab's far side toward the ship's bow.

"I'll head below from here," Jessica said. Although she was wide awake, her voice betrayed new depression. Her colleague felt it too.

"Frazier certainly didn't burn those fingers off, did he?" Dr. Shaffer's voice was hoping for the answer he did not hear.

"Not hardly. Micro analysis will show only tooth marks, I'm quite certain." Dr. Dugan was grim.

"See you below."

"Enjoy," she said with half a smile on her bruised face. It hurt to chuckle but she had to anyway.

Lt. Shaffer only shrugged as he pushed the intercom button to request entry permission from the BL-2 laboratory director.

With the outer, sterilization compartment at both ends of the lab, signing in and out at both ends, and donning a lab coat before he could pass through, the physician wasted ten minutes making his way forward into the CIC control room.

Commander Milhaus required only one brief look at his medical officer's face to know that their conversation should be private. So he led his GMO forward of the CIC into the wardroom. Pappy Perlmutter stayed in the combat information center to conn the ship.

"Straight talk, Stan," the CO said firmly behind the closed door of the wardroom.

"Okay, Captain. I won't waste time reminding you what we don't know for sure yet. We do know that Frazier's right hand was severely damaged. Three fingertips missing. Didn't look like burn damage to either of us. I guess that speaks for itself."

The CO lowered his face. His sigh sent a ripple across the surface of his coffee.

"When can you do the post mortem?"

"Commander Dugan is waiting for Frazier's body now. She'll be set up by the time I get down there."

"Not much doubt then?"

"I think not, Sir. Sorry."

"Yes. Me too, Stan."

The weary captain glanced at his wristwatch: 0930 UTC; 5:30 in the morning, local time 400 feet above. The clear sky northwest of Puerto Rico would just be turning tropical pink in the east over the island.

"It's just about twilight topside. Can't pop the antenna up now. Comm did not get a call 90 minutes ago on ELF when we came up here to listen. I hate to do it, damn it anyway, Stan, but I have to get a report off. We'll use a buoy in daylight. Whatya want me to say?"

"Till we have confirmation, Sir, all we can say is that all indications suggest another case of Lesch-Nyhan. I think it's also time to propose appropriate inoculation of the crew."

"Prophylaxis, Stan? What do you have?"

"Well, due to the nature of the bug they sent us out here with, we are well stocked with medication for at least the gouty symptoms of the disease. We can treat the crew for uric acid build-up. Treat it like gout for the moment. I don't know what else to do until we know more."

"Gout?"

"Yes, Captain. Lesch-Nyhan occurs in the complete absence of HPRT enzyme. But only partial absence or abnormally low levels of HPRT causes gout. Without sufficient HPRT in the brain, blood levels of hypoxanthine rise. When the hypoxanthine is converted by xanthine oxidase enzyme into uric acid, that acid collects in the joints as gout."

The physician paused when he noticed the CO's eyes glazing over, then he continued more slowly.

"We can treat the uric acid build up with allopurinol. There is also some evidence from around the world that Lesch-Nyhan also arises from or causes lower than normal levels of dopamine, a neural transmitter. We would also monitor the crew's dopamine levels and supplement it where necessary with eldopamine."

The captain's eyebrows rose into the lines crossing his forehead.

"Eldopamine? You mean I can choose between an insane crew or a crew with Parkinson's type symptoms?"

The physician said nothing but looked down at his own coffee mug.

"But no cure, Stan?"

"Not yet, Sir. We're really close and British scientists are really close to perfecting an HPRT deficiency treatment. It involves using retrovirus vectors—like we use in BL-4 here—to introduce human, HPRT complementary-DNA into patients. That DNA would actually turn on the disabled HPRT producing gene. Bone marrow injections into mice have also proven promising for implanting viruses which produce HPRT protein. But we remain years away from a useable, mass-produced treatment. The best we can do is manage the symptoms until Dr. Dugan can isolate the containment leak and then go home to better facilities for treatment."

"Very well. We'll brief DCNO and ask for inoculation permission."

"When can you broadcast, Captain?"

"Just as soon as we encrypt the message. Within thirty minutes. By that time, engineering should have a feeling on whether we can take her back down. I get real antsy up here. I really want to go below the thermocline ASAP. Maybe meet the deep scatter layer on its way toward the surface by this afternoon."

Captain Milhaus was anxious to dive deep enough to take refuge in the sea's layers of temperature variations and marine microorganisms all of which would disguise *Sam Houston*'s acoustic signature from listening ears aboard Russian nuclear attack submarines which routinely cruise North American waters.

"Will you be kind enough to let me know when we can begin inoculations, Captain? I'll be below with Dr. Dugan."

"Okay, Stan. Just light a fire under Commander Dugan."

Commander Milhaus winced at his own metaphor.

"I know what you mean, Sir."

The captain rose slowly as if in deep pain.

"Very well, Doctor. Let me know."

"Will do, Captain. Thanks."

Jessica Dugan wore a furry parka in the ship's deep freeze located amidships on Two Deck forward of the sealed BL-3 laboratory. When Dr. Shaffer entered the roomy meat locker, he too was dressed for arctic conditions: parka and latex surgical gloves.

Bradley Frazier, radioman second class, lay stark naked and markedly pale on a metal table bolted to the deck.

The rock-hard body of electrician's mate Hendrix lay in a black plastic body bag secured with straps to clips in the deck off to the side. The rest of the large, refrigerated compartment was brimming with frozen beef, chicken, fish, and vegetables. The ship's pantry was her morgue.

Frazier's body was still supple. Rigor mortis was hours from contracting his dead muscles into grotesque rigidity. His well muscled and youthful body was quite white when contrasted to the bluer folds of skin along his back and the backs of his legs and arms. His blood was already seeping into the lowest portions of his body. Reposing on his back, a gallon of blue, oxygen-deprived blood would soon form blue pools along his spine, buttocks, and the backs of his thighs. If not frozen in the large freezer, the lower quadrants of the dead seaman would take on a black and blue bruised appearance from the pooling of stagnant blood.

"We are examining the body of seaman Bradley Eric Frazier, radioman second class, USN. Time is 0945 UTC, 15 March. Decedent is 20 years old and a well developed, white male. Extremities show no sign of trauma with the exception of his right hand where three fingers were recently amputated at the third phalanger of the first, second, and third fingers. Micrographs of the damaged tissue will be performed later."

Dr. Shaffer spoke into a portable tape recorder which had been laid on a small metal table beside the dead man. The small stand was covered with stainless steel instruments between the two fur-clad physicians. Among the cutting tools was a large power tool resembling a cordless power drill. This was the bone saw.

"Which end you want, Jessica?"

"Doesn't matter. You do the cutting. I haven't done this since Gross Anatomy 103. I do test tubes, remember?"

"Okay. You gonna be all right?" The GMO looked closely at the woman's distressed face. His breath came in clouds of steam in the chilly freezer. His white breath mingled with the woman's.

"I'm a physician, thanks." Her voice was as cold as the meat locker.

"Sorry, Jessica. I just didn't want to make you uncomfortable. That's all."

She linked her large, blue-gray eyes—the left one blackened and swollen.

"That's okay, Stan. Didn't mean to snap at you. I'll do my job, don't worry." She sighed deeply with a large cloud of steam. "Just didn't think I'd be hacking up teenagers on this assignment."

"Me neither, Jessica. Ready?"

The woman nodded without a word.

Stanley Shaffer picked up a scalpel. With a single smooth reach, he cut an incision from the body's right ear to the left ear along the forehead hair line then behind the ears to the nape of Frazier's neck. After laying the bloodless scalpel down on the tray, he gently pulled the scalp all the way back until it lay above the dead boy like a wig still attached to the skin on the back of the body's neck. The lights in the overhead reflected off moistly pink skull bone.

Dr. Shaffer snapped on the power tool. A small, circular blade spun with the painful whine of a dental drill. He laid the drill upon the bone to carve a notch through the skull completely around the head so he could lift the skull away from the top of Frazier's brain. The physician did not look sideways at Lt. Commander Dugan as he laid the tool down and pulled off the upper skull like a pink poptop.

Jessica Dugan's gray eyes were tightly closed.

"Cranial cavity is now exposed," the GMO spoke into his recorder. His fingers probed the gray surface of the dead brain where two years of Navy training and the telephone numbers of schoolgirls had resided with equal weight.

"Meninges appear normal with normal vascularization. I see no sign of trauma to the dura. No sign of subdural hematoma nor CVA of any kind. I am now removing the brain."

When the physician pulled the brain back like a bloody sponge with one hand and slit the medula oblongata at the top of Frazier's spinal cord, Dr. Dugan stepped backward. Lieutenant Shaffer looked over his shoulder to her. He held Bradley Frazier's brain in his left hand.

She had taken three giant steps into a metallic corner. Her shoulders touched sacks of potatoes on both sides. She buried her face into the corner.

"Jessica?"

"Just leave me alone! I'll be okay."

She swallowed over and over, trying to get the taste of shiny copper pennies out of her mouth.

"Jessie, please! Just go outside. I can handle this." The physician did not leave the body although he laid the clump of gray tissue into a steel scale like a butcher shop's. He did flip off the tape recorder.

"Leave me alone, damn you! I'm a goddamned scientist! I don't do autopsies. I don't do subfuckingmarines! Just let me be a minute!" She was crying and shouting with the same choking breath.

She sniffed hard and wiped her nose on the furry back of her arm.

"Lt. Commander Dugan," the man said softly through clenched teeth. His voice was icy and furious. "Be quiet!"

Jessica Dugan was visibly stung by the physician's voice. There was not a shred of kindness in it.

When she turned to face him, Dr. Shaffer nearly burst into tears himself.

The woman's badly bruised face was soaked with tears. Her black left eye was swollen shut and her nose ran freely down the corners of her mouth and off her chin. He walked over to her quickly.

With Jessica pinned in the corner and her face scourged with pain, the man wrapped his fur-clad arms around her trembling shoulders. He took care to keep his bloody gloves away from her head.

"Jessie, Jessie," he whispered. "You're on a submarine. I just meant that we cannot raise our voices down her. Never, never. Not even when the water comes rushing in. Please." Dr. Shaffer pleaded with his own hoarse voice choked with emotion. He was suddenly seized by an overwhelming and suffocating urge to put his mouth on hers, snot and all.

Lt. Shaffer stepped back from his superior officer.

"Doctor Jessica, you'll be okay. I have faith in you. The captain and Pappy have faith in you." He spoke calmly and warmly. He worked to sound resolute, but his knees felt strangely weak. "The sooner we finish, the sooner we can put this boy back together and let him sleep. His mother is waiting for him and we must hurry."

The GMO's sudden poetry forced her to look up into his sadly dark eyes. He had to blink at her blue-gray right eye. Her blackened left eye was only half open.

"I'm sorry, Stan. I won't let you down again. Not you," she sniffed hard, "not the captain. And not Pappy." Somehow, she whimpered Pappy's name differently from the rest. Lieutenant Shaffer felt the difference in tone. He stepped back from her.

"All right, Jessica. Please do me a favor."

"Yes?"

"You just wait here until I open him. Then we'll weigh the vitals together and finish up. I'll cover his face before you come back in. Okay?"

"Please. Please. Thanks."

The GMO turned quickly and sniffed twice, from the cold perhaps, and returned to the brainless boy who had come from the cornfields of Kansas to die in the black water of the Puerto Rico Trench.

Lt. Commander Dugan stood in the cold corner like a scolded child where she collected her composure.

The GMO first weighed the brain and then swiftly excised the basal ganglia region from the underside of the grapefruit-sized meat. The gray matter was still comfortably warm from the last of the dead man's body heat. The basal ganglia normally has the body's highest concentrations of HPRT enzyme. If the seaman were suffering from HPRT deficiency, it would show up during chemical analysis of the thumb-size chunk of brain.

Then Lt. Shaffer slipped the tissue back into the empty skull. Two optic nerves dangled like half-inch lengths of yellow kite string from the back of the cadaver's eye sockets. He pulled the flap of scalp back over the bisected forehead like a hairy ski mask. From a metal drawer in the portable instrument stand, the physician pulled a pillowcase size bolt of green surgical drape. He laid the cloth over Bradley Frazier's pale face.

It took the physician less than a minute to buzz through the dead man's breastbone with the hand drill.

"Jessica?"

"Here," she said with new firmness in her voice.

"You up to handling the rib spreaders?"

"Sure."

She shuffled in her bulky parka to the makeshift autopsy table. She stood on one side and the GMO stood on the other beside the little stand. A twenty-inch gash ruined the dead man's chest, still pink with the life it held not half an hour earlier. A stainless steel tool resembling barbed wire cutters sat across the incision. The metal rib spreader would crank the chest open to allow examination of the lungs and heart sac. If the lungs were seared, the sailor died from the fire when he inhaled hot gases. If the lungs were still pink, then he had died of electrocution.

Dr. Dugan stood on the body's left side. With her gloved hands, she turned Radioman Frazier's left hand over, palmside up. The fingers were badly charred.

"Can you tell from the burns if they are electrical or thermal?"

"Not really, Jessica. But the liver will probably tell us. Its color will confirm or rule out sudden death from electrical shock. Otherwise, he probably died from heat or smoke inhalation."

"Hum." She gently laid the dead hand beside the naked corpse. "I hate electrocutions."

Stanley Shaffer had to look up across the open chest toward

the woman. Her submariner-soft voice carried a strange disquiet.

"Oh? They're never pretty, Jessica."

"I know." She paused and visibly shuddered. "When I was in med school at Johns Hopkins, I rotated through a special course in public health at the University of Virginia. We circulated through the charity hospitals in Richmond." She looked down, not at the dead boy, but at the deck. She closed her eyes: the clear, blue-gray one and the blackened one. "They sent me for a week down the interstate to Jarratt, to the Greensville Correctional Center: the penitentiary." She looked up with her one good eye squinting with anguish.

"They sent me as a joke, I think. The only woman in the class—the only woman at a prison." Her gaze returned to the floor. "I was there for one of the state's first executions after they started again. I had to pronounce the prisoner dead and sign the certificate. I didn't see them kill him. I wouldn't go. Wanted me to; but I wouldn't go. They used 1,800 volts for ten seconds and 240 volts for a minute and a half. I understand they double the dose now in Virginia. Some guy didn't go after just one shot in '91."

Lt. Shaffer regarded her closely. She was lost in her own quiet monologue.

"So I had to pronounce this kid. Seems like yesterday right now." She looked down at the burned hand of Bradley Frazier. "His head was charred black where he took the juice. His eyeballs actually exploded. Vitreous was running down his face when they took me in." She touched the corner of her good eye with the back of her furry sleeve. "His testicles ruptured too." A shudder went through her entire body. Even under the parka, Dr. Shaffer could see her quake for an instant. "God, I hate electrocutions."

"You still with me, Jessica?" The GMO did not want to lose her again.

"Let's crack this chest, Stan." She struggled to sound cheerful on a burned submarine 400 feet under water.

Captain Milhaus waited impatiently in SSN-609's torpedo room. The captain was not amidships on Deck Two in the weapons compartment for a torpedo launch. Instead, he was waiting for the ejection of a small radio canister.

"Ready, Captain," a young torpedoman said softly.

"Very well, Mister Crowell. Let her go."

"Aye, Sir."

With the push of a large button, a SLOT messenger buoy was shot from a three-inch ECM tube. From the electronic countermeasures tube, the SLOT canister rode a trail of air bubbles toward the surface 400 feet overhead. The ECM tube's plumbing automatically sucked the bubbles back into *Sam Houston*; otherwise, enemy sonar would hear the bubbles gurgling upward.

From this depth, only a one-way messenger buoy with a tape-recorded message could be used for communications. SLOT was not connected to the submarine once it left the boat. Were *Sam Houston* closer to the surface, a SLATE two-way buoy could have been used. SLATE buoys stay attached to the sub by a cable which relays two-way voice signals from SLATE's antenna down the wire into the submarine. But 609 could not ascend until engineering inspectors had completely assessed the fire damage.

The torpedoman studied his stopwatch. He monitored the seconds until the predicted time the buoy would bob to the surface.

The compartment was quiet for 110 seconds.

"She's there, Sir," the seaman said.

"Thank you, Mister Crowell. Carry on."

"Aye, aye, Sir."

The CO left the mid-deck compartment for the climb up the companionway to CIC. He would wait there for the preliminary report of his medical department working below to carve up Bradley Frazier.

The black SLOT buoy twisted in four-foot waves. The swells were widely separated as a distant storm front brewing east of Puerto Rico stirred up the Caribbean at daybreak.

At 0600 local Atlantic Time, the sun was still sitting on the eastern horizon which was unusually red from building clouds over the Atlantic's middle latitudes. Spring storms are very rare in the Caribbean. But the swells which lifted and dropped the SLOT buoy were topped with whitecaps. Foam from the crest of the wave fronts spilled down the wave troughs on their leeward side.

After stabilizing on the choppy surface for two minutes,

the SLOT began to transmit its encoded, compressed burst of communications. The beacon transmitted to the U.S. Navy's Tactical Data System, NTDS, over the HF-band, Tactical Digital Link alfa, TADL-A. High frequency was used since it can broadcast over the horizon unlike UHF which is limited to line-of-sight ranges. The TADL-A, also known as Link Eleven, electronically connected the SLOT transmitter to Navy airborne listening posts.

A U.S. Navy aircraft plying lazing circles in the sky over the Roosevelt Roads naval base, Puerto Rico, sucked in the high-speed signals from the SLOT. The message was repeated by the buoy five times within two minutes. From the aircraft, the coded signal was beamed 23,000 miles into the sky where a communications satellite digested the burst of radiation and broadcast it down to the Department of Defense antennae in Virginia where the sky was still pink with morning twilight. From the land-based antenna, the coded message leap-frogged across the Navy's microwave network of Tactical Digital Link bravo, TADL-B. The end of the communications links was the Pentagon and a walk down the hall to the Deputy Chief of Naval Operations, DCNO.

After its last automatic transmission, the SLOT buoy shut down. Vents in the three-foot long buoy opened and the canister flooded. Within ten seconds, it had slipped beneath the white waves to begin a 45-minute descent through five miles of green water. By the time it had passed *Sam Houston* 400 feet deep, it was already deeper than daylight had ever penetrated.

In SSN-609's CIC, the captain seemed preoccupied as he bothered several seamen who hunched at their stations. The CO nosed from man to man as if killing time. Commander Milhaus imagined his coded message bouncing from aircraft to satellite to the desk of the DCNO.

The distracted CO looked at his wristwatch. It was just past 6:00 in a new morning above, 1000 UTC. And already his ship had burned and another man had died, perhaps by his own feverish, uric acid flooded hand.

NINE

---

15 MARCH; 1200 UTC

BY 7:00 in the morning, the Pentagon's acres of parking lots were already two-thirds full. The sun of early spring was at treetop level between the branches heavy with cherry blossoms ready to erupt with dazzling white.

"From Dugway Wet, Admiral," the night shift Cryptographic Officer of the Watch said wearily. The commander should have been halfway home to Fairfax by now. But his signing out had been aborted by the coded telex from the Puerto Rico Trench. The Navy Department's computers needed only a moment to decode the dispatch from *Sam Houston* and to translate it into military shorthand.

The vice admiral with three stars on his collars (unrestricted line) was impatient to read the message which had come first to N-87 (formerly OP-02): Deputy Chief of Naval Operations, Submarine Warfare. The DCNO sat at a small conference table with the Chief of Naval Research, an unrestricted, two-star rear admiral (upper half), the two-star Deputy Chief of the Navy's Bureau of Medicine and Surgery (BUMED), and the two-star Deputy Commander for Ship Design and Engineering, Naval Sea Systems Command. The latter two, rear admirals (upper half), wore their stars on only one collar since they were restricted line officers from staff corps (medical and engineering).

142

Over their morning coffee, the four officers passed from hand to hand the decoded cable from SSN-609:

CRD. CRD. SSN-609. 0315/1000.
MOVREP: 19/55N. 65/50W. 090-04. CASCOR: R HENDRIX
LKLY INFTD. B FRAZIER RM2 KNA. MEDOFCMD SUSP
INFTD. ADALCON. RECM TRT. AAHA NAVMEDNPRSCHU.
SPOTREP: CAS RPFW. ERT UK. AI. EOM.

Each officer silently translated the dispatch from the Caribbean:

Classified, restricted data from SSN-609, *Sam Houston*. March 15th, 1000 UTC (5:00 in the morning, Washington Time). Submarine movement report: position 19 degrees, 55 minutes north latitude; 65 degrees, 50 minutes west longitude; course made good, 090 degrees, true; making 4 knots speed. R[ichard] Hendrix likely infected. B[radley] Frazier, radioman second class, killed not by enemy action. Medical officer in command suspects infected also. Advise all concerned. Recommend treatment. Awaiting action and higher authority from the Naval Medical Neuropsychiatric Research Unit. Significant occurrence report: casualty to reactor plant fresh water. Estimated repair time unknown. Awaiting instructions. End of message.

The movement report confirmed that 609 was steaming slowly eastbound toward the trench's eastern corner. In another 60 nautical miles, she would have to reverse course to stay within the trench spanning 180 nautical miles. The sub ran almost parallel to Puerto Rico's northern coastline which was 70 nautical miles south of *Sam Houston*.

"Well?" the vice admiral inquired. "The condition would appear to be deteriorating."

"Not necessarily so," the scientist from the Navy research laboratories responded. "Another case of Lesch-Nyhan does not have to mean that infection is somehow spreading or that a containment breach is shipwide."

"Explain," the three-star officer urged.

"Torpedoman Thurston only went out some 34 hours ago. True, Hendrix the electrician's mate was infected at least two weeks ago, and now Frazier sounds infected. But keep in mind, Admiral, these men may all have been infected weeks ago. Only the neurological symptoms are appearing now. It is entirely likely that only a handful of the crew were affected and that they were all affected at the same time. No one else may show the effects."

". . . Or," the BUMED physician interrupted, "the whole ship may be infected and likely to go mad one by one."

"How do you vote?" the vice admiral asked the one physician in their company of four officers. "A single outbreak of Lesch-Nyhan among select crewmen, or an epidemic throughout the boat?"

"I'm sorry, Sir, but I am inclined to expect a shipwide exposure with continuing contamination."

"And you?" the senior officer asked the rear admiral from Navy research.

"I believe that an isolated leak is possible. But I must reluctantly agree with BUMED analysis. I'm glad Lt. Commander Dugan is now out there."

"So far," the chairman frowned, "she has not done too much to contain this thing whatever it is."

"She will, Sir. Jessica Dugan is very good," the BUMED man nodded.

"I hope so. In the meantime," the vice admiral said impatiently, "quarantine and inoculation seem to be a good idea until Commander Dugan gets a handle on all of this."

"Agreed, Sir," BUMED nodded. "But keep in mind that 609 has medication on board only to arrest the gouty, inflammatory symptoms of HPRT enzyme deficiency. She carries enough allopurinol to keep 60 or so crewmen free from excessive uric acid production for perhaps three weeks: enough time to get them to a sub tender for an emergency evacuation. Captain Milhaus was briefed before the mission on such an evolution. DCNO has maintained a tender within 500 miles of *Sam Houston* since she left Newport News."

"Are you advising a rendezvous and evac now, Doctor?" the DCNO for Undersea Warfare asked warily. "We have managed to keep the lid on this problem and on the entire project thus far. I hate to compromise it unless we absolutely must."

"I don't think we need to rush into a rescue just yet, Admiral."

"Do you concur?" the DCNO asked the rear admiral from Research.

"I do, Sir," the research man shrugged.

"Very well then, gentlemen, if there are no objections, I'll have our permission to medicate sent back out to 609."

"Fine with me, Sir."

"Me too, Admiral."

"All right. On the reactor situation, does engineering have a recommendation?" the DCNO addressed the rear admiral from Sea Systems.

"Nothing yet, Admiral. We don't have anything to go on, based upon Commander Milhaus' sparse communication this morning. A problem in his reactor's cold leg or fresh water condenser may be minor which would explain the lack of detail in his report. Even though he is out there with a half complement of crew, his engineering and propulsion personnel are the best we have. When 609 was decommissioned and refitted for their research assignment, we kept on the very best of the boat's blue and gold teams. If the problem can be managed, it will be managed. I would anticipate that they may need a day or two to really assess their situation."

All U.S. nuclear submarines have two separate crews identified as the blue or gold crews. When one crew is at sea, the other crew enjoys 70 days of liberty and shore-based retraining.

"Okay," the DCNO said into the bottom of his coffee mug. "We'll just have to wait for an update on the reactor casualty and give the go-ahead for quarantine and inoculation if necessary. Anything else?"

The weary vice admiral glanced at the clock on the wall which read 0730, Eastern Standard Time. It was barely breakfast time in the world outside the sterile walls of the Department of the Navy.

Three rear admirals shook their heads.

"Very well. Then let's wrap it up here and I'll brief the Secretary when he checks in. I'll get Crypto on our reply immediately."

All four officers of flag rank filed into the hallway. They left four empty coffee cups on the massive mahogany table.

Vasily Golitsyn was exhausted. He had slept in his Defense Ministry office only fitfully the night before and he had left his office before dawn for his meeting with the Cuban emissary at the Havana cafe ten hours ago. The young Russian was tired to the bone.

At least he did not have to ride the Metro for another discussion with the Cuban. Golitsyn looked over his shoulder at the three clocks on the wall which told him it was 1300 UTC, 8:00 in the morning Washington time, and 4:00 in the afternoon Moscow time. He did not need the clocks to tell him that he was ready for dinner and bed. But he waited dutifully for his aide to buzz him with word that his afternoon appointment had arrived in the walled Kremlin, at the surviving core of the Commonwealth of Independent States.

"He's here, Sir," the desk intercom crackled.

"Thanks, Tasha. I'll be out."

"Yes, Sir."

The Russian rose, reset the cufflinks in his French cuffs, climbed into his pin-striped suit jacket, and walked toward the double doors. He tried not to slouch.

"Welcome, Enrique," the Russian said with strained civility.

"Thank you, Vasily Fyodorovich," Enrique Hernandez grinned rather warmly. "I owed you the pleasure of sending me out into the cold after this morning." He extended his hand.

The Russian diplomat led the cheery Cuban into the inner offices of the Ministry of Defense. He closed the heavy doors behind them.

"It doesn't look any different," the Cuban smiled as he took one of the small leather chairs in front of Golitsyn's small desk. Large chairs and large desks meant power in the new Kremlin of the second Revolution which had followed the aborted coup of August 1991.

"But it is, Enrique," the Russian nodded. He still spoke softly as he had done in the old days when the drapes were likely to be bugged. "General Shaposhnikov slowly but surely turned this ministry upside down after the coup."

The Cuban nodded. Yevgeny Shaposhnikov had taken over the position of Russian Minister of Defense immediately after the 1991 coup when former Defense Minister Dmitri Yazov destroyed his career by casting his lot with the 100-hour coup which failed. General Shaposhnikov of the Soviet Air Force assured his ascension into the New Russia when he refused to engage the Air Force on the side of the coup. He had subsequently been replaced by Pavel Grachev.

"Did you carry my government's message to these new men?" The Cuban leaned toward the Russian who had taken the other chair in front of his desk.

"I did, Enrique. The consensus is that Cuba must not engage the American submarine if indeed there is one close to Cuban waters."

The Cuban's face showed genuine surprise.

"I am deeply disappointed. Don't these people understand that Cuba is your last chance for a presence in the West?" The Cuban's face darkened and he pointed his finger at his Russian host. "If you do not support us with continuing assistance, if Moscow does not sanction our little game of cat and mouse with an American submarine with no harm intended, then you will have forfeited any say in the Western Hemisphere, the Caribbean, and Latin America for not less than a generation."

Enrique Hernandez leaned back in his chair as if winded. He was finished with his argument.

The Russian had to stand to break the tension. He walked over to the office window, small and stained with dirty Moscow snow. Everything about the little office reflected a man on the way down in his career. Vasily Golitsyn turned and faced the Cuban across the room.

"Enrique, you must advise Havana to recall your submarine. *El Tiburon* must return to Cienfuegos. At once."

The Russian looked down into the Cuban's black eyes.

The Cuban rose. His face was not angry so much as disappointed. When he stood up beside his chair, he was a head taller than his host. The Cuban's well-dressed presence and his overbearing confidence and authority belonged to a man with a future in his government.

"And if we do not recall *El Tiburon*?" he asked in Russian.

"Then, Enrique, all—*all*—Russian aid to Havana will be ended at the end of this calendar year. That's final."

The Cuban nodded with a frown on his strong face. He looked across the dismal room.

"Vasily Fyodorovich, your government has made a very serious misjudgment."

"Perhaps, Enrique. What shall I tell Minister Grachev? Will Havana recall *El Tiburon*?"

The Cuban hesitated only for a moment.
"Nyet."

By 1400 UTC, on board *Sam Houston*, 10:00 in the morning local Atlantic Time, SSN-609 continued to cruise slowly
eastward across the lip of the trench. With her single propeller
making turns for 4 knots, she made way with only 400 feet
of water between her sail tower and the surface. She stayed
shallow until hull technicians could confirm that her aft propulsion compartment could take the pressure of diving deeper
and to await the low frequency chime from the Pentagon which
would signal that a message from DCNO was on the way.

Two hours earlier, the crew had gone through the daily
ritual of muster to quarters. Section chiefs took the roll and
reported to division leaders. Divisions reported their status to
their department heads who, in turn, reported to the executive
officer. Pappy Perlmutter then compiled all of the reports into
his Eight O'Clock Report for Captain Milhaus, the first such
ship-wide report of the day.

All ship's hands were accounted for except one: Bradley
Frazier who lay disemboweled in the meat locker.

"I am satisfied that Frazier was infected, Captain, but only
moderately." Dr. Shaffer nodded gravely toward his coffee on
the wardroom table.

"What is 'moderately' infected, Stan?" the CO asked with
fatigue in his voice. He had already been awake for eight hours
and it was not yet halfway through the forenoon watch which
would end in two hours at local noon.

"Well, Sir, Dr. Dugan and I concluded that he definitely had
self-mutilated. He did bite off the fingertips on his right hand.
The stumps were barely clotted. Although the salt water from
the fire hoses dissolved some of the clotting, there was enough
left for microscope analysis to suggest that the remaining clots
were quite fresh. He must have self-amputated within minutes
of the fire."

"What about the fire, Stan? Engineering doesn't buy the
accident theory."

During the six hours since the fire had erupted in the upper
compartment of the engineering spaces, a repair party had
examined every inch of the wire bundles which ran to and
from the electrical box which had burned. Everything was

normal, except for black chunks of charred skin found inside the blackened, electrical cabinet.

"I'm not surprised, Commander. When Dr. Dugan and I did a preliminary enzyme work-up on Frazier, we found him completely devoid of HPRT. Zero, Sir. We'll be doing more detailed tests on the basal ganglia removed from his brain later. That's where HPRT concentration is the highest in the body normally. There is no doubt that Frazier was suffering from Lesch-Nyhan. But we did not find much damage from uric acid over production. The autopsy confirmed that he was certainly gouty, but kidney damage was just minimal. We had to do microscopic examination to find any nephritis at all. In a nutshell: he simply was not all that far gone."

"Just gone enough to eat his damned hand off?" The CO was showing the strain.

"Yes, Captain," the medical officer nodded. His voice was firm as it tended to be when he felt an invasion of his field of expertise by the uninitiated.

"Sorry, Stan. Didn't mean to sound disrespectful to you and Commander Dugan. It's just that I don't feel that we have much of a handle on all this yet."

"I know, Captain." The physician's voice softened. He looked into his CO's tired eyes. "Dr. Dugan and I don't really understand Frazier's case. Limited gouty symptoms, self-mutilation, zero HPRT. Electrician Hendrix was far more advanced when he died. But with Frazier, it's like he was normal 48 hours ago and just went over the edge. Strange, to say the least. But we are certain of one thing, Sir . . ."

The CO's eyebrows lifted toward his crewcut hairline.

" . . . Frazier deliberately electrocuted himself. His left hand was badly burned and we found skin inside the breaker box. He must have reached inside and was electrocuted. The short started the fire."

"No way it could have been an accident, Stan?"

"Not according to engineering, Captain. The electrician confirmed to me that there are simply no exposed wires inside that box. Frazier had to deliberately wedge his hand inside to make contact. There is utterly no other way a man could electrocute himself by accident. Besides, he was a radioman. His knowledge of marine electricals was superior to mine by a long shot. I glanced at his records, too. He was in the top of his class at both intermediate and advanced electronics school. Accident? No way, Captain. Frazier chewed off one hand and shoved the other into a hot wire bundle."

Captain Kurt Milhaus rubbed his face with both hands. Then he stood up. With his right hand, he gestured to his ship's physician to remain seated. Otherwise the medical officer would have extended the courtesy of standing with his superior officer.

"Stan, my ship is in jeopardy. I can really feel it now."

The CO spoke with his back toward the physician. Captain Milhaus spoke toward the shelves of books and manuals which made up *Sam Houston*'s official library.

"Thurston killed himself 36 hours ago. Hendrix almost two weeks ago. Now Frazier. I am fighting an enemy which has invaded my boat and I can't even see him."

The CO turned to face Lt. Shaffer.

"With respect, Stan, Jessica Dugan has not made an iota of difference yet. She means well; I know that. But she has found nothing concrete."

"Captain," the physician tried to interrupt.

"Hear me out, Lieutenant. My ship is under attack—by wild genes or rogue viruses, for God's sake. I am at a loss. I need to know, I need to know right now: Do you recommend that we abort the mission?"

The medic looked up at his frustrated commanding officer.

"Not yet, Captain. Besides, DCNO might make that decision for us, when he calls. Otherwise, we may make some headway with inoculations."

"To what end, Stan?"

"I can't say, Sir. To begin with, we can't just administer the drugs indiscriminately. Too many risks. We'll have to do a uric acid test on everyone first. Anyone registering higher than normal concentrations will go on allopurinol if DCNO agrees. It's still not a raging epidemic down here or I could give the go-ahead on my own authority. But with only two confirmed cases of Lesch-Nyhan on board—I can't quite call Thurston confirmed without his body—I don't feel justified in medicating the crew without DCNO authority."

"I agree, Stan." The CO took two steps to stand beside

the long table. "What will you and Dr. Dugan do in the meantime?"

"Take her down to BL-4," the physician shrugged. "She still hasn't been through the laboratory. If there is a containment breach down there, she'll find it. I have confidence in her."

"Me too, Doctor. But we must have results soon or I'll have no choice but to return to port, or," the CO hesitated, "or even abandon ship and ask for an underway rescue."

"I just feel that those options are still premature."

"Hope you're right, Stan."

A knock at the wardroom door broke the tension.

"Come," the CO said softly.

"Good morning, Sir. Doctor Shaffer."

"Chief," the physician nodded, still sitting.

"Come in, Chief."

Robert Wilcox, Command Chief Petty Officer and official Chief of the Boat entered the wardroom. Although a noncom and not normally privy to the officers' mess, Chief Wilcox was accustomed to going where he pleased when he pleased. Next to the executive officer, the chief of the boat in the submarine service is the most vital link in the chain of command.

"Coffee, Chief?" the CO smiled.

"No thanks, Sir. Just came up to report that engineering has advised that they've given the green light to diving. They did a complete magneflux of the welds in the damaged compartment. Everything appears sound, Sir. You can go deeper whenever you wish."

"Good. Thanks. Now," the CO sat down at the table beside the MCPO. "What else brings you up, Chief?"

The COB smiled.

"My men are uneasy, Captain. They know that Frazier was killed. They're putting two and two together, Sir. What shall I tell them?"

The CO glanced across the table toward the physician.

"Tell them that the medical department is working around the clock to solve this riddle and that no unnecessary risks will be taken with this crew. I'll pass that word myself when I go back to CIC."

"That would go a long way, Captain."

The chief stood up.

"By your leave, Captain," he said pleasantly.

"Carry on, Chief."

"Thank you, Sir. Doctor."

The chief left and closed the door silently behind him.

"No unnecessary risks to this crew, Stan."

"Understood, Captain."

The bulkhead speaker crackled softly.

"Wardroom, CIC for the captain."

Kurt Milhaus stood and walked to the telephone.

"Conn, this is the captain. Go ahead."

"Radio has a bell, Captain."

"Very well. Have the XO meet me below."

"Aye, aye, Sir. CIC out."

The CO turned to the physician.

"Radio has the ELF beacon, Stan. Have time to lay below with me?"

"You bet, Captain."

The extremely low frequency bellringer beacon penetrated 400 feet beneath the mid-morning Caribbean. Nothing more than an alert, the electromagnetic beacon tripped SSN-609's unique transponder code. Only *Sam Houston* would come up to receive a forthcoming message.

Captain Milhaus and Lt. Shaffer walked aft through the red-lit passageway. The junior officer walked to the CO's left.

"Captain on the bridge," a petty officer announced to the control room.

"Good morning, Sir," the officer of the deck saluted from his standing position behind the seated diving officer of the watch. "Steering 0-9-0, Captain, making turns for 4 knots at 400 feet."

"Very well," the CO nodded. "Take her up to periscope depth, Mister Gentry. Doc will join me in crypto."

"Yes, Sir. Commander Perlmutter is already below."

"Thank you. Carry on."

"Aye, Sir."

The CO led his medical officer aft toward the companion way ladder down to Two Deck and the radio compartment. Walking forward on Two Deck, the CO and the physician heard the groan of high-pressure air rushing into the forward and aft trim tanks. Air bottles stowed in the auxiliary spaces blew air at 4,000 pounds per square inch into the small internal tanks used for precision depth control.

Sam Houston stopped her ascent with her outside deck still awash 40 feet under water. In the control room, the OOD carefully monitored the passive sonar sweep of the surface to confirm that no ships were near. Once satisfied that SSN-609 would not ram anyone or be rammed herself, a radar mast was raised to break the surface. A radar man in the control room watched the television screen of his radar repeater as microwave energy swept the deserted surface. The scope's plan position indicator also confirmed no radar returns in the vicinity of the mast's feather of white water. The mast carved a wide wake in the Caribbean's green water.

The submarine rolled slightly so close to the surface. The CO below in the radio compartment had to hold onto a vertical stanchion to maintain his balance. At periscope depth, seakeeping is maintained by careful attention to the ship's internal trim tanks. Near the surface, depth is controlled mainly by the fairwater planes, the wings on the sail tower. The stern planes maintain the ship's pitch attitude. The combination of control surfaces and trim tanks kept the ship running slightly bow high through the water. This "up bubble" trim kept the stern and its precious control fins from accidentally "broaching" or breaking through the nearby surface. Broaching would deprive the tail surfaces of the sea they need to maintain trim and would cause momentary instability, a common trait of U.S. submarines when operating near the surface.

U.S. boats have their fairwater planes mounted high on the sail. The horizontal planes are thus close to the surface where they are buffetted by surface turbulence in rough seas. The next generation of American attack submarines, the *Seawolf* class, will have their fairwater planes mounted low on the bow for better seakeeping at periscope depth.

"Sea must be up, Sir," the radioman said dryly as he felt the ship skid sideways through a rising sea. "Maybe some weather."

The CO said nothing.

"CIC, radio, go ahead . . . Radio mast deployed, Captain," the radio compartment's telephone talker said after taking the message in his earphones from the control room one deck above.

"Anything?" The CO leaned over the seated radioman.

"Negative contact, Sir."

The seamen wedged into the narrow compartment waited impatiently. The executive officer stood beside his captain.

"Got a burst now, Sir." The radioman did not hear anything at all. But his array of electronic sensors sucked in a compressed burst of coded beeps from the gray, mid-morning sky overhead. "That's it, Sir."

The message to SSN-609 had come across the hemisphere by very low frequency radio. The signal had originated in the VLF antenna farm at Annapolis, Maryland. Submarines can monitor the digital signals sent by VLF, but they cannot receive voice over the band nor can they transmit back in this radio spectrum.

"Take her back down to 800 feet, Pappy."

"Aye, Sir."

The XO picked up another telephone connected to CIC, the 22MC circuit.

"Rig for dive, Mister Gentry. Eight hundred feet. Maintain present course and speed."

The ship groaned softly as *Sam Houston* became progressively more stable as she settled lower in the sea en route to her cruise depth.

The radioman printed out a sheet of digital gibberish and handed it to the cryptographic officer.

"After you, Captain," the crypto man said softly. He then followed the CO, the XO, and Dr. Shaffer into the adjacent decoding compartment. Inside, he fed the coded message into another bank of computers. As fast as he input the raw data from the sky, the teletype quietly cranked out a message in Pentagonese:

CD. CD.
DCNO/SSN-609. 0315/1330.
REFURDIS CASCOR. QUAR IMDT. INP AUTHGR TRT. RPFW
EXREP. ADSTADIS SESCO NLT 0315/2000. WEAX TRW 0317.
CARBASORD UFN. GLASS. EOM. EOM.

The crypto man handed the transcribed cable to Captain Milhaus who read it out loud to the other three men in the cramped compartment: crypto, the XO, and the physician.

Confidential document. Confidential document. Deputy Chief of Naval Operations to SSN-609, March 15th, 1330 UTC. Reference your dispatch on casualty correction: quarantine immediately. If not possible, authority granted for treatment.

The CO looked up at the physician.

"Good, Sir. At least we can do something positive down here."

The captain continued to recite the dispatch.

"Make expeditious repair of reactor plant fresh water. Advise status and disposition by secure submarine communications not later than March 15th, 2000 UTC. Route weather forecast: thunderstorms by March 17th. Carry out remainder of basic orders until further notice."

"Well," the CO smiled weakly, looking up again. "At least we can stay out here a while longer. Strange to see storms in the spring." Then he chuckled softly as he translated "GLASS."

"Good luck and smooth sailing. End of message."

"Hope so," Pappy interrupted without much cheer in his voice.

Captain Milhaus looked at his wristwatch.

"That gives us another six hours before they expect to hear from us again. Pappy, what about the reactor repairs?"

"Don't know yet, Captain. Six hours will cut it pretty tight. Engineering has eight men on it right now. They're doing all that can be done, Sir."

"Very well. Stan, brief Dr. Dugan and let me know when you plan to start testing the crew for uric acid and whatever. Use the fore and aft BDS to set up shop."

"Yes, Sir."

The CO's tired voice was animated by relief. At least for the moment he could remain on station continuing to carry out his orders.

"Captain?" Dr. Shaffer continued, "I still would like to walk Commander Dugan through BL-4. That is her specialty after all."

"Yes, yes. Go ahead. But I want the blood work done just as soon as you can."

"Will do, Captain."

"Very well, Stan. Pappy and I will be in CIC if you need us."

The three officers left the cryptographer alone with his computers and code books. The CO and XO headed toward the hatchway leading up to the control room. The medical officer continued down the Deck Two passageway toward the deep freeze where Jessica Dugan was putting Bradley Frazier back together before stuffing him into a zippered body bag so he could repose on the deck beside electrician's mate Richard Hendrix and several tons of frozen beef, pork and chicken.

The clocks on the control room bulkhead on board *El Tiburon* indicated 1030 Atlantic Time; 1430 UTC.

She made 15 knots at periscope depth. Her periscope led her radar mast through six-foot waves. The snorkel mast also cut through the ocean. Although the sea broke roughly over the three iron pipes which cut long green wakes through the water, the Cuban boat rode rather smoothly. With her diving planes located on her bow quarters instead of along her conning tower, plenty of water rushed over the control surfaces to ensure stable seakeeping.

Captain Barcena stood quietly at the periscope pedestal. Every few moments the ship lurched as a wave breaking over the snorkel automatically shut down the diesels to prevent them from sucking air from the boat. The snorkel's valves slammed shut to stop the induction side of the snorkel from flooding.

The captain moved to the navigator's maneuvering board. He studied the lines of position where each intersection marked the ship's course made good. By 1430 UTC, *El Tiburon* still ran eastward, parallel to Hispaniola's northern coastline. She had crossed from Haitian into Dominican Republic waters three hours earlier. Forty nautical miles to the southeast was the international airport at Puerto Plata. Seventy miles due north of *El Tiburon* was England's Grand Turk Island.

El Tiburon cruised only 25 nautical miles north of Hispaniola and in 3,000 feet of water.

Martinez Barcena returned to the periscope. He took another look through the optics. The sea was green, with white foam.

"Any messages?" the captain asked his radioman for the third time in one hour.

"Nothing, Capitan."

"Very well. Rig for dive. Take her down to 70 meters."

"Yes, Capitan," the executive officer responded.

On the XO's orders, the diesels were shut down and the batteries were engaged to run the electric motors.

The captain turned to the quartermaster who stood beside the navigator.

"What is your last barometer reading?"

"Ten eleven, Capitan. Down one millibar in six hours, Sir. No wonder it's gray this morning."

The barometer had dropped from 29.88 inches at 0800 UTC to 29.85 at 1430.

"Very well, Lieutenant," the captain nodded. "Must be a low out there somewhere. Not too close yet."

The old boat creaked as the sea pressure outside slowly increased to 6 atmospheres as she sank to 210 feet.

"I'll be in my cabin," El Viejo said softly. "You have the conn, Pepe."

"Yes, Sir."

The Old Man was tired. He had been awake for six hours. His four-hour nap had not been enough. But he could sleep only in fits and starts on his first operational command.

"We'll go back up this afternoon," the captain said over his shoulder. "I want to monitor the barometer closely. If it goes down to ten eight, the sea will certainly be too rough to use the snorkel."

"Yes, Capitan . . . El Capitan off the bridge."

At 1,008 millibars, the barometer at 29.75 inches would signify a full-fledged blow across the surface: too turbulent a sea for the snorkel to be used. A hurricane begins a 1,000 millibars atmospheric pressure, 29.53 inches, with winds exceeding 64 knots.

Captain Barcena opened the door to his narrow cabin and sat down in a metal chair. His bunk was retracted against the bulkhead to make room. With his head bowed, the CO raised a faded red and black piece of cloth to his mouth. With the July 26th Movement armband under his nose, El Viejo closed his eyes tightly.

El Tiburon returned to an even keel and leveled off at 210 feet. The deck did not vibrate at all as the ship ran on her electric motors in the stern. An electric boat with her diesel engines off in deep water is the quietest predator in the sea. Not even the fish can hear her coming.

TEN

15 MARCH; 1500 UTC

THE CARIBBEAN sun shown brilliantly red through the oval windows of the Soviet-built Mil Mi-8 helicopter. In its Hip-K version bristling with antennae, the 30-year-old chopper is used by the Cuban military to jam enemy communications.

High patches of vertical cumulus clouds filtered the long rays of the sun into slanting orange columns more like a tropical sunset than mid-morning.

The twin Isotov TV2-117 turbojets each pounded out 1,700 horsepower. The large cabin can carry 4 tons of cargo or seats for 28 troops. Vice Admiral Perez vibrated inside the spacious cabin for three hours until even his eyeballs hurt from the high-frequency buzz radiating through his body.

Making 150 knots through the Cuban morning, the old copter needed two hours to vibrate westward on the first leg of the flight from the People's Navy, Eastern Naval Flotilla headquarters at Nicaro on the island's northeast coastline. Admiral Perez was grateful for the fuel stop at the Cienfuegos airfield at the HQ for the Central Naval Flotilla and the Submarine Flotilla.

From Cienfuegos on the island's middle southern coastline, the helicopter chugged and whined westward for another hour across 140 nautical miles of Cuban countryside. At Cienfuegos, the chopper picked up Admiral Esquino, commandant of the antisubmarine warfare forces there. The two officers could communicate in the noisy cabin only by the electronic intercom wired into their heavy helmets.

The Hip-K arrived at the Mariel Naval Air Station at 1500 UTC, 10:00 in the morning, Havana time. The 6,000 feet of concrete at Mariel looked delicious to the two passengers after bouncing through their final approach. The morning air was bumpy as a stiff westerly wind burbled over the Sierra del Rosario mountains just west of Mariel.

The Mariel field sat under broken gray clouds midway between La Habana to the east and Cabanas 12 nautical miles to the west. Cabanas is the Western Naval Flotilla headquarters.

Vice Admiral Perez was bone tired from his three hours in the helicopter. It seemed longer than only nineteen hours since he had looked out the window at Nicaro and had ordered the submarine *El Tiburon* to hunt for Buddy Thurston's submarine.

Standing on the tarmac, Admiral Perez looked skyward at the overcast. The wind on the ground was as brisk as it had been in the air. Instead of the usual southerly winds blowing in from the island's northern coastline, the breeze was humid and came from the west. The air mass was blowing eastward into some unseen depression in the barometric pressure out over the Caribbean.

"Gonna blow somewhere," Admiral Esquino said with fatigue in his voice.

"Yes. Maybe more of the storm over the Dominican Republic yesterday." Vice Admiral Perez shrugged.

A high-ranking Cuban naval officer greeted the two admirals on the airport's concrete ramp. He led them to a waiting car.

Inside the old limousine, Admiral Perez pulled a brown Cuban cigar from his uniform.

"Mind?" the superior officer asked Admiral Esquino.

"Not a bit."

The vice admiral began to unwrap the metal foil. The driver glanced into his rear-view mirror.

"Sure wish we could still get those," the driver smiled.

Admiral Perez hesitated. When the slow strangulation of Russian aid to Cuba accelerated after the August 1991 "second revolution," Havana went so far as to begin rationing Cuban tobacco to its own citizens within two weeks of the failed coup in Moscow. The admiral quietly put the unlit cigar back into his breast pocket.

The two officers said nothing for the half-hour drive westward to the naval base at Cabanas. Both were in desperate need of quiet after their helicopter ferry across the island.

The car stopped at the colorless building which housed the Eastern Flotilla operations command. When an orderly opened the door guarded by armed sentries, the two admirals were met by Raul Castro himself, the island bastion's Vice President and Defense Minister.

The Vice President shook hands with his admirals and ushered them into a large conference room. No one joined the three men who sat at a massive conference table. The room smelled delightfully of ocean air and rich, black Cuban coffee.

"Gentlemen, El Commandante sends his respects," the Vice President said cheerfully. Both admirals nodded with mutual deference to their chief.

"I am glad that both of you could come up here on such short notice. I wanted to brief you in person on the *El Tiburon* mission. Our man in Moscow reported in while you were still airborne, just about two hours ago." Raul paused and dramatically sipped his coffee.

The two admirals glanced sideways at each other for an instant before the Defense Minister continued.

"Consul Hernandez met twice with that Golitsyn squirrel; once at 11:00 our time last night and then again this morning. To get right to the point, the Russians have demanded that we recall Capitan Barcena immediately or they will cut off what's left of our civilian and military assistance. I am authorized to ask both of you for your opinions. I don't know what else those revisionist cowards can do to us after Black Wednesday."

On Wednesday, August 11, 1991, Moscow had announced that the Russians were pulling the last 11,000 of their ground support troops out of Cuba to placate the Americans into providing food aid for the upcoming, post-coup Russian winter.

Each admiral lowered his face toward his coffee cup. Vice Admiral Perez spoke first.

"I ordered *El Tiburon* to sail on the basis of two assumptions: First, that there was indeed an American submarine operating in local waters somewhere near the Dominican Republic or Puerto Rico; and, second, that we had an opportunity to attempt to find that boat and perhaps harass it. I was aware of our precarious position with the Russians, of course. I thought the operation might inspire Moscow to increase or at least continue the aid."

"My sentiments, too," the Minister of Defense nodded. "Admiral Esquino?"

"Frankly, Mr. Minister, and with the admiral's leave, I would have opposed sending out *El Tiburon*. Let me say that I am admittedly prejudiced by my own experience: my specialty is antisubmarine warfare. Being in ASW all my life, my confidence will remain with our airborne and surface ASW capabilities. Aircraft, helicopters, and perhaps a frigate would be far more likely to find that submarine than *El Tiburon* would be.

"I mean no disrespect to Capitan Barcena. I served with him in the ASW division when he was between commands. It was I who recommended him for his first command on a Koni frigate. He's a good man. But his submarine experience is limited. And worse, the capabilities of his Foxtrot class boat are even more limited. In a line, Mr. Minister, if the mission is right politically, the equipment is wrong." Rear Admiral Esquino looked directly at Vice Admiral Perez. "Sorry, Sir."

"No objection," Admiral Perez nodded graciously.

"You agree with Admiral Esquino then?" Raul Castro leaned forward and rested his elbows on the table.

"No, Mr. Minister. I simply can agree with my colleague on the broad points that *El Tiburon* has no chance of sinking the American boat even if she finds it. I should say, even if the American submarine is really out there. We were not totally certain of that, as you know." The admiral paused.

"Go on, Admiral," the minister prodded.

"Well, Sir, I frankly believe that an air and sea operation would be too provocative. After Iraq and the collapse of the Soviet government, the United States has little need to exercise restraint. I fear that a task force pursuit of their submarine might result in a repeat of the 1962 embargo and quarantine of the entire island. But a single, diesel-powered submarine would hardly be taken too seriously by Washington. We could still prove our point by letting the American captain know that we can find him and can shadow him for a day or two.

"If the Americans acknowledge privately or publicly that we succeeded in that much, Moscow will certainly have proof positive that we are capable and essential allies well worth their commitment of financial support."

"Then you do support the operation in concept?"

Vice Admiral Perez nodded.

"Admiral Esquino, can you agree with Admiral Perez' assessment?"

"Let's just say that I do not disagree. I repeat that I speak from my ASW expertise, not from any real evaluation of the diplomacy of the situation. I would fear, however, that a complete failure by *El Tiburon* to find the Americans could seriously damage our credibility. The Americans will surely know that we are looking for their boat: their underwater listening posts in the Caribbean and the electronic support measures equipment on board their submarine will have no trouble locating *El Tiburon*. If they know we are patrolling for them and then fail to find them, the loss of face with Moscow could convince the Russians that we are not worthy of further help at all. I am more willing to risk success than I am to risk total failure."

"Well said," Raul Castro nodded. "Now, given Moscow's overall objections to our operation, I need your recommendation: continue or abort?"

"Continue, Mr. Minister," Admiral Esquino said without hesitation. He and the Defense Minister looked hard at Vice Admiral Perez.

"Continue, Mr. Minister," the senior admiral said firmly. "With either approach, but continue."

Raul Castro stood up and the admirals followed.

"Very well then, gentlemen. I shall convey your views to El Commandante this morning."

"Mr. Minister?" the vice admiral asked gently. "What is *your* recommendation."

"The same, Admiral. We'll press on for the moment. Thank you both, again. I recommend that you return to Cienfuegos and manage the operation from there unless ordered to recall

El Tiburon." Raul Castro smiled warmly. "I'm sure that both of you would welcome another helicopter ride."

"I wouldn't do that unless you really want to lose a breast."

Jessica Dugan turned to see Dr. Shaffer standing behind her. He was not smiling.

"Yes, I guess I forgot."

Dr. Dugan stepped back from the narrow bunk in sick bay where the stuporous planesman struggled against his restraining straps.

"It's common, you know," Lieutenant Shaffer said softly as he stepped forward, "for nurses of Lesch-Nyhan patients to have their breasts bitten when they try to feed them. Let me do that."

The medical officer leaned over the planesman as the doctor stepped aside. Dr. Schaffer leaned against the patient's arm, put all his weight on the forearm, and quickly loosened the restraint strap one notch.

"There," the GMO said as he stepped back. The patient continued to twitch against the straps but he never opened his eyes. A nasal-gastric tube fed the planesman through a nostril. Weak, barbiturate-laced glucose water dripped into the planesman's other arm and kept him semi-conscious for the 21 hours since he had tried to drive *Sam Houston* to the bottom.

"I stopped by to look in on him," Dr. Dugan said as if apologizing. "I noticed that his nails were slightly blue so I wanted to release a little pressure on the strap."

"I know, Jessica. I'm going to try one more time to make it into BL-4. Wanna go?"

"Sure—unless you think it brings us bad luck every time I try?" She tried to chuckle.

"Don't know. Let's try." The GMO smiled.

The last time they had tried to enter the maximum containment laboratory eight hours earlier, a man had fried himself to death after biting off his own fingers.

On the way out of sick bay on Two Deck, Jessica Dugan glanced at the bulkhead clock which read 1600 UTC. In her mind, she imagined the Caribbean sunshine glistening on the green water at noon, 800 feet above her. After exactly 24 hours on board *Sam Houston*, the thought of working under water did not seem quite so terrifying. The GMO saw her hesitate at the clock.

"Congratulations, Jessica. One whole day of being a submariner. How do you like it so far?"

She looked over her shoulder at the drugged but struggling planesman.

"I'm too old for all this excitement." The 38-year-old doctor smiled as she followed the general medical officer into the passageway.

They made their way down the hatchway to the cramped confines of Deck Three and the entrance to BL-4. They had to shoulder their way past a dozen seamen who were coming or going from their positions. At noon local Atlantic Time, the men of the forenoon watch were giving up their duty stations to the men of the afternoon watch which would end in four hours with the first of the two-hour "dog watches."

"Shaffer and Dugan," the officer said into the intercom on the BL-4 bulkhead next to the sealed hatch.

"One minute, Sir," a voice crackled. "Have to change and shower first."

"Take your time," the physician answered.

The two officers milled about in the red-lit passageway.

"Just came from briefing the captain for the Noon Report," Dr. Shaffer said. "I told the CO that, as far as we could tell, Frazier was definitely infected. While you were finishing up with him, I ran a quick serum assay. He was full of uric acid all right. The HPRT test on the brain specimen is still cooking in BL-2."

"I don't think there's really much doubt that you won't find any HPRT." The doctor frowned.

"Not likely," Dr. Schaffer agreed.

"So we'll start running hair follicle tests on the crew for HPRT?"

"Yes," the GMO nodded. "Ordinarily we wouldn't do that in a clinical setting, unless uric acid excretion exceeded 1,000 milligrams daily. But we don't have that much time to monitor 55 crewmen."

The two physicians faced the heavy bulkhead hatch when it opened with a whoosh of air. Jessica's hair immediately flowed with the compartment air toward the opened door. Positive pressure toward the BL-4 lab was designed to prevent the spread of airborne contaminants from the maximum containment facility.

"Sorry, Sir, but I had to scrub and change."

"No problem, Mister McGraw. Can we go in now?"

"Yes, Sir. Ma'am. After you."

The officers stepped over the lower sill of the watertight hatch. When the physicians were inside the inner compartment, the seaman reached for the door, pulled the hatch closed, and dogged it tightly locked. Their six ears popped with the sudden change of air pressure inside the suit-up space.

"Lieutenant Shaffer, if you would change in number one. Number two is for you, Commander. I put your overalls in the change rooms for you: a medium for you, Lieutenant, and a small for the commander."

"Thanks, Mister McGraw," Jessica Dugan smiled. She stepped into the changing stall and closed the flimsy door behind her.

"Everything, Doctor," the sailor called toward the closed door.

"I read the manual, Mister McGraw," the female voice replied from behind the door.

The first class petty officer glanced at Dr. Shaffer.

"No problem, Mister McGraw. She's fine. I'll be right with you."

"Yes, Sir."

With both officers in separate stalls, the noncom Biohazards Control Officer found himself starring at Dr. Dugan's closed stall. The young seaman in his mid-twenties could not stop thinking of the woman with the black eye undressing ten feet away.

Jessica Dugan felt strangely warm. She stood barefoot and naked. She could not shake her awareness of being surrounded by more than four dozen men and boys 800 feet under water inside a steel tube. She looked down at her white jumpsuit folded neatly on a metal chair. On top of the chair was a white T-shirt and undershorts—men's jockey shorts. BL-4 regulations require laboratory clothing down to one's underwear. She hurried to dress.

Dr. Shaffer was already in the outer compartment when Lt. Commander Dugan came out of the dressing room. She was still adjusting her head cover which was a surgical-style cap which came down over her ears. Latex gloves were wrapped tightly around the sleeve cuffs of her overalls. Lieutenant Shaffer noticed that her unbruised cheek was slightly flushed.

"Doing okay, Jessica?" He regarded her closely. The cap hiding her hair seemed to accentuate the black and blue welt on her left cheek and the black eye above.

"Just fine," she said rather hoarsely. She wondered if the GMO could see the sudden warmth on the good side of her face.

"Great."

"Guess we're ready, Mister McGraw."

"Okay, Sir." The Biohazards Control Officer required in all BL-4 facilities pushed the intercom button with his elbow. He wore a fresh set of overalls, gloves, and a head covering. "Three to enter, Sir," the petty officer said softly into the speaker.

"Permission granted," a voice called by wire.

The Laboratory Director authorized the locked inner door to open with a pop as the outer compartment's pressurized air rushed into the lab proper. Air flowed quickly into the outer space through ducts lined with HEPA filters, high-efficiency particulate air filters.

Once the officers entered the brightly lit lab ahead of their guide, the hazards officer dogged the hatch closed.

"The log, please," PO McGraw gestured toward a small open book. Both officers quickly signed in and logged 1620 UTC in the time-in column. The next blank column was headed "Time-exit."

Dr. Dugan noticed a large sign with red letters on the back side of the airtight hatch. The NIH-mandated sign said "RECOMBINANT DNA . . . RNA TRANSFERASE . . . HAZARDOUS REAGENTS."

"These are the decontamination materials reception ports," Lt. Shaffer said calmly. He pointed to three breadbox sized containers bolted into the hatchway bulkhead. "This one's the autoclave, and these are the fumigation chamber and airlock."

National Institutes of Health guidelines for DNA labs require BL-4 facilities to have special ports for transferring materials into or out of the lab. Materials must pass through an autoclave for decontamination by broiling, or a fumigation bath, or an airlock sealed at both ends.

"Welcome to the zoo, Jessica. All of the animals live down here. You'll notice all of the cabinets. Depending upon what the experiments are, we have Class I, II, and III safety cabinets for all living specimens, including culture dishes. We use ultraviolet irradiation lamps on the holding racks."

The doctor leaned sideways to scan down the 150-foot compartment, past the 16 empty missile silos rising from floor to ceiling. Lab benches and equipment surrounded the old silos. Four technicians appeared to be simulating a moon walk at the compartment's far end. They wore space suits.

"Those guys are in positive pressure suits at Class III cabinets."

The sealed suits with air hoses attached protect the men from contamination.

"The suits are worn when working with some of the hamsters in advance stages of chromosome mutation experiments."

"Oh," Jessica said softly.

"Let's walk through. Thank you, Mister McGraw."

"My pleasure, Sir. Ma'am." The noncom did not salute his superiors per submarine protocol.

"This is where we actually do the inoculaton tests with Lesch-Nyhan at the nucleus level. We also do quite a bit of related research while we're at it. Since Lesch-Nyhan is a defect in the X-chromosome, we generally limit our work to the X where at least sixteen hereditary diseases and fetal defects have been located.

"We do a little work on cystic fibrosis recombinant DNA. We're pursuing the University of Michigan regimen performed there in the fall of 1990 when U of M people were first able to insert a correcting gene into CF-damaged cells. They used a virus vector to inject the genetic material just like we do here.

"Those two guys are working on beta thalassemia, one of the very few ethnic-specific genetic diseases." The physician pointed to middle-aged scientists hunched over culture dishes. "It's like Sickle Cell in blacks, but causes fatally fragile red blood cells in Mediterranean people. After the Saddam Hussein party in the sand, this part of our research was given top priority by the Dugway and Fort Detrick people."

The doctor followed the GMO down the missile compartment aisle.

"We do our genetic screening down here when we want

to actually direct the Lesch-Nyhan enzyme shutdown. This is the meat and potatoes of the whole experiment. In theory, Lesch-Nyhan patients have a normal gene for HPRT production. But actual expression of the gene for production of the HPRT enzyme fails. We think this is due to instability during cellular reproduction when the DNA is converted into messenger RNA."

Protein production from genes inside every living cell, plant or animal, only involves a few distinct steps. Inside the mother cell's nucleus (its command center), natural DNA needs messenger RNA (m-RNA) to grow a copy of itself with opposite base pairs. "Sense" DNA builds an "antisense" DNA complement. The two DNA strands fit together perfectly like a left and right hand (the same, but opposite). The coil of double DNA then unwinds.

The GMO continued his discourse.

"It's really a matter of how much precision a genetic engineer can wring out of his equipment. The gene for HPRT production may have 34,000 bases. The messenger RNA has a critical zone of perhaps as few as 1,600 bases. The m-RNA has 654 nucleotides which code for a polypeptide of 217 amino acids in the actual, HPRT protein.

"The HPRT amino acid sequence for the protein wasn't even discovered until about 1982. In the States, HPRT genes really have been cultured from only one patient. Four other tissue samples have been cultured from patients who almost have Lesch-Nyhan, but these four are really just serious gout cases. The Kingston, Jamaica, tissue sample is still the only real sample being passed from laboratory to laboratory. The actual site of the mismatch of genetic material is the 193rd amino acid position where asparagrine is substituted for aspartic acid. That substitution is enough to render the HPRT enzyme useless for uric acid regulation in the body.

"We have seen some substitution of arginine for glycine in the gouty, near Lesch-Nyhan cases at position 71 and substitution of glycine for cytosine, too. All told, we've seen seven sites of mutations in the gene which codes for the HPRT enzyme."

The doctor nodded as if the lecture had suddenly sunken in. Her questions confirmed her new awareness of the terrible science all around her.

"So what this whole project is about would be simply inducing the gene mutation at one of those sites along the DNA strand? Switch the gene on or off and you either have Lesch or you don't."

"Exactly, Jessica. We've tried several protocols down here for getting a fragment of RNA into the host's cells. That RNA is a probe designed to latch onto the healthy gene at just the site where the mutations can occur naturally. The RNA more or less interferes with the mother cell's DNA trying to reproduce an exact duplicate DNA in the offspring cell. The RNA probe is exactly the opposite nucleotide base sequence of the healthy DNA in the gene. It prevents the offspring DNA from copying the parent DNA perfectly."

"Antisense RNA?" the doctor asked with excitement in her voice.

"Precisely. The trick is getting the antisense RNA frags into the host cell. Look over here."

The two officers stepped to a work bench with electronic equipment.

"We do electroporation here. We send an 8,000-volt electrical shock into a cell culture. This blasts microscopic holes in the cell's membranes. Our magic RNA bullets can then enter the cell to block HPRT enzyme activation down at the gene level. It works in a lab dish, but we can't hardly electrocute an entire enemy army in the field." The GMO smiled.

"Guess not, Stan. All I really know is that genetics is mind-boggling to me."

"I know, Jessica. It's hard not to be overwhelmed by the simplicity and the unspeakable complexity of the process. Keep in mind that in a human being, to go from the moment of fertilization to a finished fetus only requires that the fertilized egg cell of the mother divide 47 times. It even overwhelms me!"

The doctor nodded.

"Anyway, back to introducing the magic bullet into the host cell: we can do the electrical shock in a dish, but hardly in a whole animal. So that leaves two other primary means of getting our bugs inside the target cells. We can inject the RNA by transfection: a chemical or physical insertion such as micro injection. Or, transduction: a viral vector. Transduction is our aim down here.

"Once we can insert our antisense RNA into the host cell, that opposite RNA will baffle the host DNA by blocking duplication of the host DNA. It's like a jigsaw puzzle: the antisense RNA fills in a row of pieces before the DNA can duplicate at that row."

Jessica shook her head.

"Baffling is the word here all right."

"Well, it's not just new to you, you know. The first gene map wasn't done until 1920, and that was for fruit flies. No one knew that bacteria and viruses could exchange genetic material until 1951. And no one knew that humans have 46 chromosomes until 1956. Messenger RNA wasn't discovered until 1960 and the first recombinant DNA transfer from animals into bacteria wasn't performed until 1973. It's still new to everyone. Believe me."

Jessica nodded and then listened carefully as she followed the GMO from station to station in BL-4.

"The whole key to our research into a biological weapon is antisense RNA: get that molecule into a host cell and it is literally an artificial on-off switch for whatever gene it fits. Our objective is to produce antisense oligonucleotides. It binds to messenger-RNA, behaves like antisense RNA, and prevents the RNA from building the corresponding piece of the offspring's DNA strand. Oligos are really nothing more than DNA scraps.

"This whole line of stations builds the oligos. We can grow the fragments with a sulphur atom substituting for an oxygen in the sugar-phosphate core. These have particular affinity for passing through cell membranes.

"Over here, we're duplicating the NIH experiments with ADA deficiency. Adenosine deaminase deficiency strikes about ten babies every year in the country. Most die within three years from Severe Combined Immunodeficiency. An ADA deficient child is ten thousand times more likely to develop leukemia than a normal child.

"In the fall of '90, gene therapy for ADA deficiency was approved by the NIH for testing. The human gene for the ADA enzyme is artificially inserted into the patient's blood cells outside the patient. Then the blood is transfused back to the patient. We're running our own similar protocols down here since the NIH used a retrovirus as the vector for getting the genetic fragment into the cells. That's exactly what our research is all about."

Dr. Shaffer led Lt. Commander Dugan to the aft end of the missile bay on Deck Three of *Sam Houston*.

"Colonel Epson," Dr. Shaffer smiled at the only Army officer on SSN-609: the Principal Investigator for the Lesch-Nyhan induction program.

"Commander," the colonel nodded. The officer was gowned in smock, latex gloves, and surgical cap.

Jessica Dugan looked into a row of specimen cabinets where brown mice and hamsters played.

"Most Lesch-Nyhan research is done on wild mice and Chinese hamsters," Dr. Shaffer pointed toward the maximum containment, Class III cabinets. "Humans, wild mice, and Chinese hamsters have greater than 90% similarity in their DNA coding for the HPRT enzyme. Although the human gene is about 42,000 bases long compared to 33,000 for the mouse, seven out of nine DNA segments—'exons'—within the gene are identical. The HPRT enzyme with its 217-amino-acid protein only shows seven differences between the human protein and the mouse. We got on the trail of the Tiger mosquito as our delivery system when we realized that the HPRT gene in the malaria parasite is also very similar to the human HPRT protein."

"Where do you do the actual mosquito work?" Dr. Dugan asked.

"Down there, inside the sealed glass chamber."

Colonel Epson followed Drs. Shaffer and Dugan to the end of the old missile bay.

"The mosquitos are kept inside reduced pressure cabinets. They cannot fly out against the pressure gradient. And the whole compartment has positive airflow inward from the BL-4 lab which has directional air flow inward from the rest of the ship. No one goes into the mosquito chamber without a positive pressure suit."

Three technicians looked like they were on a moon walk in the mosquito cubical.

"Colonel," Jessica Dugan asked gravely, "do you see any way those flies could have migrated into the ship or the duct work?"

"No way in hell, Commander. Every air duct and plumbing

fixture in BL-4 has HEPA filters and disinfectant traps. There must be half a dozen barriers to the mosquitos between BL-4 and this boat. Can't be done, Doctor."

"But it *has* been done, Colonel."

"I just don't think so. Besides, Doctor, as far as I know, no one has been infected with Lesch-Nyhan who actually works with it down here. All four of your possible cases were crewmen who never stepped into BL-4. At best, they went through BL-2 on Deck One to get back to engineering. But all three of our labs are completely isolated from each other by filters, atmospheric pressure barriers, bulkheads, disinfectant traps, and . . . the most rigid monitoring and antisepsis procedures anywhere in the world." The colonel was adamant.

The two Navy physicians shook their heads.

"I don't mean to question your protocols, Colonel," the woman said gently.

"I know that, Commander. I didn't mean to be short with you. But these outbreaks of Lesch reflect on me, mainly. I have to take it a little personally. Sorry."

"I know," the doctor continued. "But we're all in the same boat."

Colonel Epson had to laugh out loud.

"Well said, Doctor," the Army scientist chuckled. "The same boat, indeed."

"Can you show me the actual transfection of the Lesch-Nyhan RNA into the virus which is delivered by your Tiger mosquitos?"

"You're looking at it, Commander." The colonel pointed to the glassed-in chamber where men in pressure suits worked with sterile glassware and deadly flies.

Jessica looked down the starboard side of the rounded lower level of the three-deck-high missile bay and its sixteen silos filled with concrete ballast instead of Polaris A3, SLBM nuclear missiles. None of the five *Ethan Allen* class subs had their A3 submarine-launched ballistic missiles converted to Poseidon missiles when the fleet was modernized.

Sandwiched between the thick silos were glass bubbles from deck to overhead, completely self-contained. Each bubble contained a double electric door.

"The final stage of manufacturing the m-RNA plasmid fragments is done in the bubbles. We then inject the plasmids into LaCrosse or dengue viruses down the line here. At the end in the last two bubbles, the mosquitos are actually fed a solution of hamster blood laced with the virus. We call it 'loading' the mosquitos. The virus will survive in the mosquito like the malaria parasite until it is injected by the fly when it bites its target."

"Yuk," Jessica Dugan smiled.

Colonel Epson looked closely at the woman with the bruised face. Lieutenant Shaffer stood quietly at her side.

"Not very professional," he smiled down at her, "but close enough to the truth, I suppose."

"Could you follow the process through for me? I need to know the viral flow and the air and waste circulation if I'm to find the containment breach."

Colonel Epson, Principal Investigator, bristled.

"I know that's your job, Commander. And I intend to help you in every possible way. My staff has been instructed to do likewise. But," his eyes narrowed, "you'll find no containment breach in my laboratory."

Dr. Dugan said nothing. She noted that the colonel had said "my" laboratory with precisely the same icy tone that Captain Milhaus had used to describe his submarine.

"Well, Commander, we culture LaCrosse in this bubble. Viruses are a whole separate life-form on our planet. They live in their own world. They are Nature's ultimate and perfect parasite. They must live inside a host's cells. Bacteria, as you know, can damn near live anywhere: in the air, on our food, in our blood, on an eyelash if they want. But viruses can only live inside someone else's cells."

The colonel paused.

"Sorry, Doctor. Didn't mean to bore you with philosophy."

"No, Colonel. Don't stop. I'm very interested in your thoughts. I do want to know what moves you down here."

The tone in the woman's voice inspired the scientist to continue.

"All right. Viruses, you know, have no enzymes at all for producing their own energy. They can't even reproduce on their own. Outside a host cell, they are completely inert, almost dead really. Their outer coat, the 'capsomere,' gives each virus its unique shape. There are only about 20 shapes which viruses tend to assume. A group of capsomeres form their characteristic capsid shell. The inner, living segment is pure DNA or RNA. Viruses have nothing inside except pure genetic material. They have to invade the host cell to inject their viral DNA or RNA into the host. They literally turn the host cell into a virus factory.

"The key to our work down here is the retrovirus. Normal viruses kill the host cell when they fill it with their viral, DNA or RNA, genetic material. But retroviruses do not kill the host cell. They just sort of borrow it for viral reproduction. But you know all that . . ."

"Yes, Colonel. But keep talking."

"Well, we handle pretty nasty stuff down here. Those two bubbles are just for storage. We carry for study eight of the Class Five viruses."

The National Institutes of Health classify viruses into groups. Class V viruses are forbidden entry into the United States. *Sam Houston* had a sterile jug of each.

"Those two bubbles are storage for African horse sickness virus, camel pox, hog cholera, Nairobi sheep disease, Asian Newcastle disease, Rift Valley fever, sheep pox, and swine vesicular disease. You'll never see that stuff anywhere."

Colonel Epson sounded proud.

The doctor's skin felt suddenly prickly.

"Why would I want to?" she shuddered.

"Right. But we use these specimens to study basic virus structures and reproduction. Couldn't get along without them . . . That bubble is devoted exclusively to LaCrosse. The virus is one of the Bunyaviridae family: spherical capsomeres no more than 120 nanometers in diameter."

Jessica forced her weary mind to convert the metric dimension: three billion viruses to the inch.

"Once we elected to use the Tiger mosquito as our delivery vector, we had to zero in on the viruses which can live in the fly's salivary glands. We only came up with LaCrosse and dengue. We prefer LaCrosse since its RNA nucleocapsid has a lipid envelope with glycoprotein spikes around the circumference. The spikes facilitate binding with the target's cell membrane.

"We lean toward loading the mosquito with LaCrosse since the capsomere contains three strands of RNA coils. We insert our RNA probe targeted for the locus of the HPRT enzyme into all of their coils. When the LaCrosse is injected by the Tiger mosquito into a target, the virus coat dissolves and our cloned RNA is absorbed into the host's bloodstream. It then migrates to the blood-brain barrier, crosses into the basal ganglia, and takes part in cell division there. The RNA probe latches onto the host's DNA, prevents the offspring DNA from duplicating at the HPRT gene location, and . . ."

The colonel snapped his fingers.

"And the host cannot produce HPRT enzyme."

"How much time is required for the host to absorb the virus vector?" The doctor was completely captivated by the science going on quietly all around her 800 feet beneath the mid-afternoon Caribbean.

"About 48 hours total; it takes about eight hours for the virus coat to dissolve and the viral DNA or RNA to migrate to the nucleus of the host's cells. Then, within four hours, the new messenger-RNA is created and the host's DNA production increases to make more viral, genetic material. Another 36 hours is required for complete reproduction of the viral DNA and viral replication. Then it's a self-sustaining chain reaction: The new viral DNA migrates to ever more cells in the host until the host-target is a viral factory."

Jessica could only exhale with a little whistle.

"The next to the last bubble aft is where we work on the dengue fever virus. As you know, it's a Flaviviridae. Used to be classified with Togaviridae. At 50 nanometers in diameter, it's half the size of LaCrosse which makes it a little harder to work with for us, but that also makes it easier to absorb in the host. Dengue fever has only a single strand of RNA within the virus capsule which makes it easier than LaCrosse to inject the antisense RNA probe for disabling the HPRT gene locus."

The Army biochemist took a breath.

"Dengue is really voracious: a single host cell infected with a single virus will reproduce and eject 100,000 new virus units into the host." The colonel had to smile. "We like that here."

"I guess you would," Jessica nodded with a sour tone of voice.

The Principal Investigator stepped toward the doctor. Towering over her, he spoke in the hoarsely whispered anger of a submariner.

"My job, Lieutenant Commander Dugan, is to carry out

the directives of my government. Just like you. Right now, down here, my duty is to perfect a biological weapon which will incapacitate the enemies of my country. I did not pick that biological agent. The disease process and pathology were chosen for us. I merely am charged with making the damned thing work. I do not require your approval. Or, for that matter, your assistance."

The colonel did not blink until he had unloaded on the startled woman.

"Colonel, I'm sorry. Please believe me. I am just tired. My left eye is swollen shut. My whole face hurts. And I don't really know why they sent me down here. Please. Please excuse me."

The Army scientist took a deep breath of the lab's sanitized, twice-filtered, pressurized air.

"All right, Dr. Dugan. All right. Let's just all concentrate on our respective responsibilities. If that's okay."

"Yes, yes, Colonel. Please be kind enough to continue with your explanation of this facility."

Jessica struggled to sound both cheerful and confident. But the truth of the matter was that her superior's rebuke stung her to the core. She had earned it and she knew it.

"Very well, Doctor." The colonel calmed himself. "These last few bubbles are for processing retroviruses. LaCrosse and dengue fever are both basic viruses. But what we would prefer are *retro*viruses. They turn their host into a continuous supply of virus products. Retroviruses contain two copies of viral RNA, genetic material.

"We are working to turn LaCrosse and dengue into retroviruses; in effect, taking a lethal virus and making it even more deadly. If we need to, we can make the retrovirus unable to reproduce at all by cloning retroviruses which lack the gene for replication. But for now, a retrovirus hybrid would make our viral vector for Lesch-Nyhan damn near invincible."

"But what about the risks to indigenous populations, Colonel?" The doctor forced her voice to sound clinical and detached.

"Keep in mind, Dr. Dugan, that our bug bomb would be a substitute for thermonuclear weapons, if perfected. It would never ever be used unless total annihilation of an enemy were required. It would be the most unconventional of unconventional weapons. And it only attacks males."

"Yes, of course," Jessica nodded. "Tell me about the ultimate delivery mechanism."

"The whole process takes place down here in BL-4," the colonel continued. "We use routine restriction enzymes to cleave the necessary DNA fragment. Type II restriction endonuclease can crack a DNA strand at specific sites. The result is the oligonucleotide DNA probe we need to turn off the HPRT enzyme production gene in the host. Then we implant the frag into the LaCrosse or dengue virus. We store the oligos down here in desalted, lyophilized powders activated by deionized water. We can store it for about a year if we keep it frozen.

"We toyed with using liposome encapsulation to carry the DNA or m-RNA fragments."

"Fat?" Jessica had to smile.

"Liposomes: microscopic spheres of cationic lipid which tend to fuse with the host's plasma membrane. When the lipid dissolves, the transferred DNA or RNA is absorbed into the host. But manufacture of liposomes is difficult and expensive. So we went down the virus vector track instead.

"We went through the entire animal kingdom for the right vector and we kept coming up with the Asian Tiger mosquito. Our injected and cloned virus is put into a solution of blood—blood soup we call it. The mosquito drinks his fill and the viral agent lives in the mosquitos until we need them."

"Need them?" the doctor said softly.

"Yes," the colonel nodded. "A thousand infected mosquitos would spread Lesch-Nyhan to a division of infantry."

The woman shuddered.

"Well," Lt. Shaffer looked at Jessica, "now you've seen BL-4 at last. What do you think?"

"About what?" Dr. Dugan was still trying to absorb the science all around her.

"About a containment breach, Jessica."

She looked carefully at the white smocked technicians, the stainless steel sinks whose handles were labeled in red with DO NOT TOUCH WITH HANDS placards, and the men in space suits working with the mosquitos, mice, hamsters and monkeys.

"It looks even tighter than this ship," she had to conclude.

Colonel Epson nodded.

"Dr. Dugan?" the colonel said cordially. "What do you smell?"

"Smell?"

"Yes, what do you smell in here?"

"Me, mainly," she frowned.

"Commander, look around you." The Principal Investigator's voice was cold. "You see hamsters, wild mice, half a dozen Rhesus monkeys and ten chimps. It's a zoo down here. But," he looked hard at her bruised face and black eye, "what do you smell?"

She sniffed the BL-4 laboratory.

"Nothing. Maybe a whiff of aromatics of some kind. Organic solvents, probably. But that's all."

"That's right." The tall colonel looked over the woman's head at his laboratory. "You don't smell animals because my laboratory is just that tight. Not even the smell of monkey shit escapes the Class III cabinets. Do you really think I have a containment leak in here?" He waved his arm across his missile compartment. "Anywhere?"

"No, Colonel. I don't think you have a containment breach in BL-4." Jessica Dugan felt suddenly angry. "But I do know that three men are dead with acute HPRT deficiency symptoms and that the planesman went mad with Lesch-Nyhan. The compromise is somewhere inside this vessel. My job is to find it, Colonel."

Her voice was as chilly as her inquisitor's.

"I know that, Jessica."

Colonel Epson had never used her first name.

"But, Jessica, the breach is not within my jurisdiction. I simply would not permit it!"

"Well enough," Jessica argued softly. "Where does the air vent from down here?"

"By NIH protocols, the air we breathe and the animals' exhaust air vents through HEPA filters. The animal cabinets have two such HEPA filters connected in series. Even the equipment with vacuum lines passes through HEPA filters. Floor and sink drains have disinfectant traps as does the shower in the personnel changing compartment. All air ducts are maintained with differential pressure and directional air flow from areas of low contamination risk to areas of high risk. Manometers for sensing pressure variations are posted everywhere with alarms.

"The air, after it is filtered and refiltered, then exhausts directly into the boat's reactor compartment."

"Reactor compartment?" the woman asked with surprise.

"You weren't briefed on lab ventilation?"

"Briefed? They didn't give me time to collect my toothbrush."

"Oh. Well, the air lines leave here and enter special radiators in the reactor's steam line. The air is literally baked by a twice-through heat sink in the reactor's steam generator loop. The steam heats the lab air circuit to 600° Fahrenheit before it is cooled in one of the condenser loops for recirculation back to the lab. That air line is a dedicated line: completely isolated from the rest of the ship's environmental systems. The air is either in BL-4 or being boiled back in engineering. Period. There cannot be a breach in that line without a reactor alarm. Never happened yet."

Jessica sighed. She was tired and hungry.

"I suppose I should go aft to take a look at the lab air line in the reactor spaces."

"Whatever," the colonel said dryly. "You won't find any containment compromise back there. But I wish you well, Doctor."

"Sure. And I do appreciate your time." She glanced at Dr. Shaffer. "We both do. Really." She tried to smile but her face hurt too much.

"Good. Let me know if you learn anything back there. Believe it or not, I am always open to ways to improve my shop."

"All right. Thanks."

Jessica Dugan and Stan Shaffer walked the length of the missile compartment to the forward bulkhead. They walked nearly half a football field.

The biohazards officer retraced their steps out of the lab through the electric door into the outer suit-up compartment. Before leaving, both physicians signed the EXIT column in the personnel logbook. They clocked out of BL-4 at 1740 UTC.

"You can shower first, Jessica," Lt. Shaffer nodded.

"Okay. What do I do?"

"You shower in there. Dump all of your clothes in the disinfectant bin. You'll find robes in there for getting back to the changing room on the other."

"All right. I'll be quick." She was anxious for her first shower in nearly three days.

"Don't even try," the physician laughed. "A Navy shower takes longer than the real thing. Don't forget to turn the water off after you soap up. Then on again to rinse."

"No real showers on this cruise?" Her one good eye twinkled.

"Gotta earn it, Jessica . . . Find the containment compromise!"

"Sure."

Jessica stepped into the private shower area where she stripped and piled her lab clothing into the hamper for chemical decontamination later. She stood under the hot water for only fifteen seconds to wet down. Then she shut the comfortable water off. She tried not to think about the water being heated in a nuclear reactor 250 feet behind her. As she lathered the disinfectant soap between her legs, she felt more naked than she could remember. Lieutenant Shaffer was right, she thought. She did not hurry at all.

ELEVEN

15 MARCH; 1800 UTC

EL TIBURON made way at 15 knots, flank bell, with 25 feet of water above her weather deck and 6,000 feet of black water under her keel. Only 10 miles north of the Dominican Republic's village of Abreu, 35 nautical miles east of Puerto Plata, her thin periscope, thick snorkel, and radar mast cut a wide foamy feather through rough seas. The sun at 2:00 on a humid Caribbean afternoon sparkled on the snorkel's wake of white water. The sea was green where the sun directly overhead burned brightly. Great patches of ocean were dark gray under billowing clouds. Alternating crests of bright water and cloud shadows gave the surface a mottled appearance.

El Tiburon pitched slightly as westerly winds churned the surface close to her conning tower below.

"How's the barometer now?" Captain Barcena asked his chief quartermaster for the fifth time during his four-hour watch.

"Ten-oh-nine, Capitan," the QMC replied from his instruments beside the maneuvering table and chart case.

"Hmm. Down another 1.7 millibars in three and a half hours, QMC."

"Yes, Capitan. It's certainly not getting any better outside this afternoon."

The 2:00 barometer reading of 29.80 inches had fallen 5/100 inch since 10:30 in the morning, Atlantic Standard Time.

The captain picked up the engine room telephone.

"Engineering, how is your snorkel?"

"Adequate, Capitan," the division leader called from the submarine's aft spaces. "It shut down twice in the last 30 minutes but it's open for the moment, Sir."

"Very well."

The rising sea had caused the snorkel's automatic dampers to close twice when sea water splashed into the tube.

"What about your batteries?"

"Just fine, Sir. We have a full charge on all cells."

"Thank you, Engineering. Disengage diesels and rig for quiet running."

"Yes, Capitan."

Captain Barcena looked into the twin binocular eyepieces of his periscope again. He squinted into dazzling daylight with occasional dark shadows cast by broken clouds. He looked southward toward Hispaniola's coast. The great island was over the horizon, twelve nautical miles away. The captain imagined the coastal light flashing near Abreu at Cape Viejo Frances. All he saw were splashes of water and rolling waves of green surf.

The middle-aged captain was growing tired and his eyes burned slightly. He had been awake for 14 hours since his last four-hour nap. He had spent the day mustering and personally inspecting each of *El Tiburon*'s divisions.

"Sonar, how are your soundings now?" The captain straddled the hole in the deck from which the periscope had risen.

"Two thousand meters, Capitan."

"All right. We'll run at periscope depth unless sonar picks up anything. Mind your keel soundings."

The captain was keenly aware of skirting shallow water. Although 6,000 feet of water flowed under *El Tiburon*'s keel, dangerous shoals only 450 feet deep were ten miles to the northeast. The submarine ran between the shallow Silver Bank to the north and the Dominican Republic's coastline to the south. The shoals were just off the port bow. With his dark eyes closed to concentrate, a young sonar man listened to the sound of deep water.

"Good water, Capitan."

"Very well, Sonar. Maintain passive watch. We're within 150 miles now of the possible position of the Yanquis."

"Yes, Capitan."

"Pass the word, quiet in the boat."

"This is the control room," a seaman said into the vessel's ship-wide intercom, "rig for quiet."

The captain nodded his approval. The deck radiated no vibration through El Viejo's soft-soled shoes.

"I'm going to lay forward. Call me immediately if the sea state worsens or compromises the snorkel, or if sonar gets any returns. Otherwise, maintain this depth, course, and speed, and mind your helm in this sea."

"Yes, Capitan. One Two Zero magnetic and 15 knots."

El Tiburon steered southeast to follow the Dominican coastline.

"Carry on, gentlemen."

El Viejo hesitated at the control room hatchway. He looked once around the entire compartment and then disappeared through the hatch in the bulkhead. The watertight door was dogged behind him.

"El Capitan off the bridge."

By 1830 UTC, Captain Kurt Milhaus had been on duty for twelve hours. Good Navy coffee injections and work he loved kept him alert. But his frustration showed in his voice.

"Well, Lieutenant? I have to report to the DCNO in 90 minutes."

"Let's walk through, Captain," the engineering officer of the watch said with fatigue in his voice.

Three shifts of seamen had been troubleshooting the condenser failure for exactly 23 hours since *Sam Houston* had been driven toward the bottom of the Puerto Rico Trench by a crazed planesman. EOOW Richard Stone led the Reactor Department's second shift of technicians and nuclear engineers who labored to correct the malfunction. Men from the feedwater section of the Engineering Department assisted the watch's 3M Coordinator. On all U.S. Navy vessels, a 3M specialist coordinates the three M's of Maintenance, Materials, and Management.

The CO walked aft in the red-lit passageway with his EOOW. Their soft-soled shoes made no sound on the deck's G.I. linoleum tiles.

The commanding officer of SSN-609 felt at home in the aft,

engineering and propulsion spaces. All submarine officers in the U.S. Navy are engineers by education. They come to the Silent Service from Annapolis, college ROTC, or the collegiate Nuclear Propulsion Officer Candidate Program. All officer candidates pass through Nuclear Power School at Orlando. Every submarine officer except the ship's supply officer has a background in nuclear propulsion.

Commander Milhaus did his post-graduate nuclear internship at the civilian nuclear reactor at Ballston Spa, New York. Twenty years before *Sam Houston*, he stood his first submarine watch as a nuclear safety officer. He advanced to Reactor Officer, the head of the reactor department, on a *Permit* class nuclear attack submarine. The class had been originally named the *Thresher* class in 1957, but was renamed when the *Thresher*, SSN-593, was lost with all hands on a test dive in April 1963. (*Thresher* and the attack sub *Scorpion*, SSN-589, lost at sea in 1968, are America's only nuclear sub disasters.)

Kurt Milhaus always felt at home in the reactor spaces. He had cut his submariner's teeth back there. Walking beside Lt. Stone was always like a homecoming.

To their left on the far side of the lead-lined bulkhead was the seething reactor. The nuclear reaction is contained within the reactor vessel's 8-inch thick inner shell of magmolly steel. The whole vessel is covered with insulating "cladding." The bottom of the vessel (the hot end and nuclear "core") is clad in Inconel, an alloy of nickel, chromium, and iron. The top two-thirds is clad in stainless steel. Carbon steel pipes carry coolant water into the top of the reactor vessel. The steam generator which powers the turbine is housed within the shielded reactor compartment near the reactor vessel.

The inside of the reactor vessel has another thermal shield of stainless steel to protect the vessel's walls from the 650°F maximum temperature and operating pressure of 2,500 pounds per square inch (psi). The vessel can take up to 3,125 psi. Radioactive coolant water enters the vessel at 557°F and leaves the vessel at 607°F. This inner shield of type 340, SA-240 stainless steel prevents gamma radiation and stray neutrons from leaking out of the reactor.

In the CO's mind, he knew like the back of his hand the layout of the reactor core where atomic fission simmered. The nuclear fire is stoked and controlled by the control rods which are raised and lowered in the reactor vessel core by highly trained, nuclear technicians.

The heart of the reactor core is the fuel assemblies: dozens of hollow rods packed with fuel pellets of powdered and enriched uranium-235 manufactured as uranium oxide. Each pellet is wrapped in a ceramic coat the size of a sugar cube. The pellets can stand over 5,000°F before melting. The fuel rods are tubes made of Zircaloy-4, an alloy of zirconium, tin, iron, and chromium. Each rod is pressurized with helium at 400 psi. When the nuclear chain reaction in the core is "critical" and running normally, the fuel rods' helium pressure increases to 2,000 psi. The rod temperatures hover at 700°F.

The nuclear fire is managed by the Control Rod Assembly. The CRA has one control rod for every three fuel rods. The control rods absorb neutrons to slow down the chain reaction by taking neutrons out of circulation before they can slam into each other to produce nuclear fission. Each rod is type 304 stainless steel, packed with 80% silver, 15% indium, and 5% cadmium.

Among the control rods are other rods of the Axial Power-Shaping Rod Assembly. These APSRA rods, one for each fuel rod, are clad with Inconel and stainless steel. They absorb neutrons but do so less vigorously than the control rods. The power-shaping rods are lowered into the core to "shape" the fission to prevent hot or cool spots within the nuclear fire, like putting three or four bricks inside the oven of an Amish wood-burning stove to even out the heat around a Dutch apple pie.

Inside the core are permanent Burnable Poison Rod Assemblies. These rods are Zircaloy-4 tubes filled with aluminum oxide and boron carbide. They absorb the overflow of neutrons in a freshly fueled reactor. As the marine reactor cools off slightly from prolonged use over its 8-year lifetime, the poison is slowly dissolved. Most of it is consumed when a new load of nuclear fuel is allowed to go critical for the first time after refueling. The poison rods are not replaced until the reactor is refueled with fresh fuel rods.

"God, I love it," the CO said absentmindedly, walking down the passageway.

"I heard that, Captain," Lt. Stone smiled. "Sure does beat stoking coal into boilers."

"What would you know about coal?" the captain grinned. "I don't think we had a coal-fired ship still on the line when your daddy was a swabby."

"Guess not, Sir," the EOOW nodded. "Captain?"

"Lieutenant."

"Forgive me for asking, but I'm curious about something."

"Yes?"

The two officers paused in the narrow passageway which smelled faintly of the rubber fittings within the ventilation ducts.

"Is it true that your father was a submariner?"

Kurt Milhaus looked away from his youthful junior for an instant. Then he turned to look him squarely in the face.

"He was indeed. He's still on board."

Lieutenant Stone blinked as his captain turned and pressed aft through the passageway.

They crouched through the bulkhead leading into the maneuvering room space. The engineering officer paused to dog the watertight hatch behind them. Hatches in the propulsion compartments are never left open when submerged.

From the maneuvering room where the reactor and throttle controls are manned, the CO and the lieutenant descended through the hole in the deck down to Deck Two and the diesel generator room. The captain led the way down another square hole in the floor to the bottom deck and the turbo generator room. On Deck Three, they stood among the condenser equipment. Two watertight bulkheads enclosed the compartment at each of its rounded ends. One space forward was the reactor; one compartment aft was the main machinery room where air conditioning plants hummed softly.

"Good afternoon, Sir," each seaman said in turn as they spotted Captain Milhaus. The men crawled around the maze of condenser pipes. The CO acknowledged the courtesy. The tight compartment smelled of lube oil and sweat. The processed air carried the faintest scent of rubber from the insulation mats placed under all of the submarine's electrical, electronic, and communications equipment and propulsion machinery.

"Where are we, Chief?" the CO asked the section leader.

"Just can't isolate the casualty, Captain. There are no malfunctions anywhere. Just the damned water hammer in the main steam lines. We've run every possible failure mode.

But nothing shows a failure and we can't dry the steam. I am sorry, Sir."

"Okay, Chief. Stay with it."

"Aye, Sir."

"Captain, I would recommend running the coolant pumps," the lieutenant said softly.

"Yes. I'll advise sonar."

Ordinarily, the condenser's coolant pumps are not run on nuclear submarines due to the noise. At cruise speeds, convection alone circulates sea water through the lines. Captain Milhaus picked up the telephone.

"CIC, captain here. We're going to the coolant pumps back here."

The sonar man would monitor the ship's passive sonar to listen to the telltale hum of the pumps. If the hydrophones towed behind *Sam Houston* could hear the pumps, so could enemy submarines within hundreds of miles.

"Navigation," the CO continued, "I'll need a recommendation for optimum depth with the pumps running."

The ship's sensors monitor the sea's temperature and salinity. There would be a unique depth which would allow 609 to mask its noise behind the ocean's different layers of moving water.

"Very well." The CO hung up the telephone on the bulkhead.

The seaman and petty officers waited anxiously for the CO to finish his business.

"Let's go, Rick. Carry on, Chief. Let me know."

"Yes, Captain."

Lieutenant Stone followed the captain forward. They climbed two levels to Deck One and the maneuvering room.

"Captain."

"Chief. We'll run with the coolant pumps for a while."

"Yes, Captain."

The CO lingered at the reactor throttles called the steam chest. His career in the nuclear Navy had begun here.

"Captain. Lieutenant Stone."

The officers turned to the hatch filled with Jessica Dugan. The executive officer followed her.

"Dr. Dugan," Kurt Milhaus nodded gravely.

The woman led Pappy Perlmutter into the maneuvering

room compartment. A faint pinging sound echoed through the ductwork.

"Captain?" the XO said.

"Water hammer, Pappy. Can't seem to get a handle on it down below."

The XO nodded. The captain looked at the woman with the black eye.

"Just wanted to follow the steam and air lines from the labs, Sir."

"Good, Doctor. Learn anything?"

"BL-4 looked really tight, Captain. I've spoken with the crew some. Thurston and Hendrix were both seen in the engineering spaces off and on. I want to follow the ventilation and steam lines. Never know what I might find."

"Okay." Kurt Milhaus seemed distracted. His voice was as cold as the colonel's voice down in the maximum containment laboratory. "Maybe something will turn up."

"It has to, Sir," she said firmly.

"Yes. Keep her company, Pappy. I'll lay forward if you need me. Thank you, Mr. Stone."

"Yes, Sir."

The captain's voice sounded tired.

"I'll stop by radio to get the 2000 report off to DCNO. Then we'll go down."

Captain Milhaus eased through the hatchway. He would report to the Pentagon that no progress had been made on the runaway virus and that his nuclear reactor was pounding its vitals with a faint but steady rhythm which could be heard for miles unless the ocean masked the muffled tapping sound. *Sam Houston* would ascend closer to the surface for the coded transmission. Then she would submerge further into the permanent darkness to seek cover among the clicking of the fish and whatever temperature inversion layers she could find.

"I hate to see the old man so stressed out," Lt. Commander Perlmutter said softly to Jessica.

"Yes. He really feels for this boat and crew."

"We all do, Jessica. Every submarine is a family, you know. Any man here can kill us all if he loses his edge or save us all if it comes to that." Pappy Perlmutter's voice was grim. The physician had to shrug off her sudden claustrophobia.

The XO led Dr. Dugan through the aft propulsion compartments where fans hummed softly and turbines whirred. The massive shock-absorbing struts in the floor raft absorbed the rattle of powerplants before the sound could penetrate the steel hull of *Sam Houston*.

"The first subs didn't put to sea until 1914," the XO continued softly. "Not until nuclear boats did we really become true submersibles. During World War II, the subs only went down to evade the enemy. They didn't live down here. A day or two submerged was their limit. We could stay under for eight years if we could carry the food. We could surface once per decade if we reduced the electrical load."

"Commander. Doctor," a petty officer nodded when he passed the XO and the physician in the passageway. Pappy and Jessica woman had to flatten their backs against the passageway wall so the seaman could slither past them with his backside pressed against the opposite bulkhead.

"That's what it's all about down here, Jessica. The closeness of everything and everybody. My grandfather was on a boat in World War I. They would pee in buckets filled with oil. Our facilities are a little more comfortable, it's true. But the fundamental reality of submarine living hasn't changed in 80 years. What granddad said is still true down here: 'In a submarine, you breathe in what the man next to you breathes out.' He was right. That's why the CO talks about this ship as if he were in love with it. He probably is. I suppose we don't call ships 'she' for nothing."

"No, Pappy, I suppose not. I'm a test tube jockey in the world. My life has nothing to do with this place. I have to remind myself what you people feel down here. I have to remember that."

Lt. Commander Phillip Perlmutter, a third-generation submariner, looked down into Jessica Dugan's swollen face. A suddenly lovely face, he thought. When she exhaled up into his face, the executive officer sucked her vapors into his lungs.

"You're doing fine, Jessica. Just fine." The XO paused and smiled. He dared not touch her. "We just have to find what's ailing the skipper's baby."

"Lead on, Pappy." She gestured toward the engine room through the closed hatchway.

The XO nodded and gave the wheel on the watertight door

a series of turns. He pushed the heavy hatch inward toward the compartment. A hot and oily breeze blew through Jessica's frazzled hair. To her, the warm air smelled like a locker room where athletes rinse their jocks in lube oil.

"After you, Jessica."

The physician bent down to ease through the hatchway. Pappy Perlmutter followed and pushed the hatch closed behind them. He spun the wheel latch to dog the hatch tight.

"Good afternoon, Commander," a first class petty officer smiled to the XO. Jessica's wristwatch told her that it was 3:00 in the afternoon in the Caribbean 800 feet above her. The bulkhead clock indicated 1900 UTC.

Standing on the engine room deck, Jessica Dugan could feel the vibration humming through her feet. High-pressure steam from the steam generator next to the nuclear reactor drove the turbine like a massive tea kettle. The compound condensing turbine radiated no heat.

"The turbine has a high-pressure section and two low-pressure sections," the XO pointed. "Steam enters the high-pressure stage from the main steam line. It exhausts the HP section, passes through the moisture-separator reheater here, and then enters the low-pressure stage. The main governor valve controls turbine speed and power. From the low-pressure side, steam passes into the main condensers. The propeller shaft runs off the turbine. When the turbine is off-line, we can also turn the propeller with an electric motor.

"The condensers are cooled by sea water. The cold water condenses the used-up steam back into water. Low-pressure feedwater heaters reheat the condensate before it is recirculated to the main feedwater pumps. Hot steam is bled off the high-pressure turbine to preheat the condensed steam. This prevents thermal shock when the condensate recycles through the steam generator. The condensate is 'polished,' as we say. Ion exchangers remove dissolved salts from the water and resin beds remove solids. When the condensed feedwater is polished, deaerated, deionized, and heated, it goes back through the steam generator in the reactor compartment."

The doctor nodded. Her ears buzzed with the turbine whine which was absorbed on the floating deck raft. None of the vibration or noise touched the submarine's hull. None radiated into the sea.

"Colonel Epson mentioned that air from the labs is heated in the steam cycle. Where does that take place?"

"In the reactor compartment. The steam generator is within the nuclear compartment. At our last refitting, they built a bypass loop into main steam where lab air lines are boiled before returning to the closed lab environment."

"That would be in the steam line itself?"

"Yes. Let's go forward."

"Okay."

The XO led the doctor up one level to an overhanging platform deck. They crouched through the hatch which had been opened for them by the engineering duty officer.

Dr. Dugan followed Pappy Perlmutter forward through the turbo-generator room where a diesel engine could generate electricity when the turbines are not running. Continuing forward, the two officers stopped at the closed vault of the reactor compartment.

"It's right in there," the XO said. He nodded toward the sealed hatch. "The steam which runs the turbines is really the coolant system for the reactor. Coolant water flows into the top of the reactor and flows down the reactor vessel wall toward the core. From the core, hot water heated in the nuclear pile flows upward through control rod guide tubes. The coolant water enters the reactor vessel at 557°F and exits at 607°F. The systems maintain pressure of 2,185 pounds per square inch."

Jessica Dugan stared at the bulkhead which protected her from the three-deck high reactor compartment.

"The water coming out of the reactor is the primary loop called the high-pressure side. After three passes through the S5W reactor, the high-pressure coolant passes through the pressurizer which keeps the 600-degree water from boiling into steam. It must stay liquid even though it's three times hotter than the boiling temperature at sea level. High pressure keeps it liquid. The high-pressure side is radioactive. It enters the steam generator through thousands of Inconel tubes. Each tube can withstand 2,500 psi.

"The line between the reactor and the top of the steam generator is called the hot leg. The line carries saturated steam. That means that the liquid and gaseous phases exist together in equilibrium. The pipes are carbon steel with austenitic stainless lining. The pipes in the hot leg are almost three inches thick. The lines are tested to over 3,000 psi.

"The pressurizer is between the reactor and the hot leg running to the steam generator. A series of heaters keep the pressurizer circuit hot. Steam at the top of the pressurizer makes up for changes in volume in the liquid system as coolant temperatures change. We must maintain the steam bubble above the liquid phase of hot water. Collapse of the bubble could allow the water to boil and fill the pipes with bubbles: a potential disaster if the coolant pumps cavitate.

"The line connecting the steam generator to the turbines is the feedwater line. Steam running through engineering and propulsion is not radioactive. Feedwater enters the steam generator at the bottom. It flows upward over the tubes through which radioactive heated water is flowing downward. Clean, pre-heated feedwater enters the steam generator at 470°F and exits at 570°F under 925 psi pressure. The clean steam from the generator running to the turbines is the secondary loop, called the cold leg."

"And it all fits into this little compartment?"

"You bet. A ground-based reactor is the size of a small city with its cooling towers and control room. Down here, we do it in a space the size of a three-car garage. Amazing, even to me."

"This is where that water hammer business starts?"

"Probably not, Jessica. More likely it's below in the condenser compartment where the steam is cooled back to high-pressure water. The boys back there will isolate the problem and fix it. They always have."

"Nuclear propulsion baffles me, Pappy. When you get right down to the bottom line, we're just a steam ship after all."

"That's right. But we can run about eight years on the nuclear propellant on the other side of this bulkhead. Complete fission of one pound of uranium-235 creates the same thermal energy as burning 6,000 barrels of oil or burning 1,000 tons of coal. It still amazes me after twenty years. And water runs everything. Can't get much simpler than that.

"Water in the reactor is the moderator. It slows down the uranium neutrons so they can collide with each other to produce the heat which turns the water to steam. Everything sort of works in reverse in the reactor: When the throttle man in the maneuvering room closes his throttles to slow the turbine, less heat is drawn off the reactor into the steam generator. This makes the reactor water heat up. But when it heats, it become less dense which decreases the nuclear collision rate. When we want to speed up the turbine to generate more power, the throttles are opened. This draws more hot water into the steam generator. When that cools the water in the reactor vessel, the neutrons slow down and hit each other more often. More neutron collisions produce more heat which produces more steam."

"Oh." Dr. Dugan shook her head.

The executive officer of *Sam Houston* smiled. Like his captain, the XO loved the maze of pipes and humming machinery.

"So it's as tight as the proverbial drum, just like Colonel Epson said?"

"Better be, Jessica. A break in the radioactive hot leg would be a major crisis. The reactor shielding is designed to contain it, of course. And we have multiple safety and emergency systems to prevent a core meltdown. In the last resort, the sea itself would cover a ruptured reactor vessel to prevent meltdown. Of course, we'd all be blowing salt bubbles."

The doctor looked deeply troubled.

"Three men are dead, Pappy. Two with confirmed infection. The planesman in sick bay is infected. But Colonel Epson tells me that his bugs cannot escape from any of the labs. You tell me that the steam line is fail-safe where the lab air is sterilized. I'm at a loss."

"Look on the bright side," the XO smiled, "we've given you the challenge of a lifetime. Be thankful. Crack this case and you'll get your third stripe."

"Or—what do they say in the sub service?—learn to take my coffee green?"

It was Pappy's turn to frown.

"That's what we say all right." The XO turned away from the reactor compartment hatchway to look down into Jessica's face. "So where do you go from here?"

"Back to the wardroom. I'll go back through all the logs and bills again. It's in there. It's in the records somewhere and I'm going to find it."

The exec nodded.

"For some reason, Jessica, I believe that. I'll lay aft to see to the condenser problem. I'd like to have an answer when I make the Eight O'clock Report to the CO in four and a half hours."

The weary woman leaned against Lt. Commander Perlmutter when the deck under her feet pitched slightly. Instantly getting her bearings, she could tell that the ship's bow was rising. She stepped back from the XO who looked at his wristwatch before he spoke softly.

"Going up to send the CO's 2000 message to Washington."

"Wish I could help him," the physician sighed. The captain's despair was beginning to soak into her own bones.

"Me too, Jessica. Only you can."

Nodding without a word, the doctor walked up the slanted deck toward the BL-3 laboratory on the far side of the bulkhead. From the other side of the lab, she would climb up to Deck One and the wardroom where piles of documents waited where she had left them. After 27 hours on board SSN-609, Jessica Dugan knew her way around.

Skirting the northern coastline of the Dominican Republic, El Tiburon pitched below the surface of a rising sea. Westerly wind blew white foam from the wave crests which rolled twenty-five feet above the submarine's weather deck. Her thick snorkel and radar mast exploded in frothy plumes when they slammed into each wave front at 15 knots.

El Tiburon's seakeeping was unsteady as a distant low pressure area in the east drew a wave train of ocean against the prevailing set of the current. The rising wind out of the west drove the sea toward the snorkel from behind. The submarine made way toward the southeast. The damper valves closed when overtaken by each wave. When the wave passed the mast, the snorkel opened to suck air into the three diesels working hard beneath the churning surface.

As the snorkel's dampers opened after a large wave had passed, a wind eddy pounded the mast with two quick crests which ran perpendicular to the parallel wave fronts. The snorkel closed for the primary wave but opened in time to suck the second and third waves into the snorkel mast. Water poured in past the head valves, through the water trap in the double hull, and through the induction drain valve. The surge of green water rushed through the engine room induction valves which entered the center of three diesel engines. The tiny flood breached the snorkel's safeties in seconds.

The diesel gurgled as eight cylinders flooded in succession as sixteen air induction valves drew sea water through the snorkel piping.

Throughout the submarine, 75 Cuban seamen instinctively grabbed their ears as the engine sucked air from the ship's compartments. Bulkheads and hull plates creaked as the sudden vacuum pulled air from the submarine's cramped spaces toward the suffocating diesel engine in the stern.

With a clatter of soon-to-corrode metal, the diesel pounded to a stop. The grinding metal vibrated through the engine and into the engine room deck. The metallic clatter travelled into the inner hull and clanged through the outer hull and into the sea. The center engine stopped within three seconds of the induction failure. Within another two seconds, backup electric motors engaged the thrust blocks connected to *El Tiburon*'s three propeller shafts.

By the time the sailors had yawned to clear their ears, the vessel was driving through the sea under full battery power without skipping a beat.

"Better call El Capitan," a sonar man said over his shoulder toward the startled officer of the deck. In the narrow control room, the seamen had heard the huge diesel strangle as it gulped sea water. The young sonar man felt the engine grind to a stop when his ears popped. He saw the engine gag on the video monitor of his passive sonar.

When the diesel drowned, a pulsating pressure wave radiated from the submarine's aft spaces into the ocean. The sudden noise dissipated quickly in the sticky salt water 12,000 feet beneath the submarine between the shallows of Silver Bank and the Dominican Republic.

Before Captain Barcena could sit up with clogged ears in his narrow bunk after a 90-minute nap, the hull of his boat had radiated the tiniest ripple of a pressure pulse into the warm ocean.

The Cuban captain on his first real war patrol swallowed to clear his ears. He knew that the diesels had sucked air from the ship. His experience in antisubmarine warfare on the surface told him not to worry about the noise which had clanked from *El Tiburon* into the sea. Running at periscope depth, the submarine cruised in one of the sea's safest noise zones. The "surface layer" was naturally noisy from wave and current motion. The rising sea would further mask the sound pressure pulse. When El Viejo swung his legs to the deck, he was tired; but he was not worried about giving his position away.

The surface layer is about 150 feet deep. Beneath it for another 600 feet is the seasonal thermocline where water temperature and the speed of sound decrease as water depth increases. That deep sound waves bend downward toward the bottom.

The sound of *El Tiburon*'s engine shutting down radiated through the sea at 4,500 feet per second, nearly four times faster than the speed of sound in air. The sound pressure pulse quickly attenuated and became muffled. Isotropic noise from the water and its jungle of fish further diluted the mechanical noise from the engine room.

The short noise pulse travelled northwestward through the channel between Hispaniola and the shallow sand banks to the north of *El Tiburon*. From the submarine's position just under the surface off the northern coast of Hispaniola, the noise from the diesel rippled astern. It travelled northwestward with the prevailing current.

The ripple from the submarine's engine room accident radiated 250 nautical miles to Great Inagua Island north of the Windward Passage which separates Cuba from Haiti.

Hardly anything but wave and fish noise was left when the noise pulse rolled up the shoals on Great Inagua's southern coast. The water molecules on the beach barely twitched when the faintest ripple bounced off the island and radiated 60 miles southwest toward Cuba's northeastern coast.

Not many molecules at all were upset by *El Tiburon*'s pressure pulse rolling over them. The infinitesimal disturbance gently tapped the ship's homeland before bouncing back into the sea.

From Cuba, the last whisper of the submarine's engine failure reverberated back into open water toward the northwest. For another 240 nautical miles, the pressure pulse nudged the green water one molecule at a time.

By the time *El Tiburon*'s noise broke on the shallows of Great Bahama Bank, the clatter of one diesel engine was softer than cat's breath. The beating hearts of the fish made more noise thes final sigh which disappeared against Andros Island.

The ripple of pressure from *El Tiburon*'s metal hull had travelled 550 nautical miles. It took 13 minutes.

TWELVE

15 MARCH; 2000 UTC

LIKE A sunken oil rig, the spindly steel legs of an antenna cluster rested on the sandy bottom of the Great Bahama Bank. Near the Andros Island coast, the latticework of corrosion- and crustacean-resistant metal resembled an underwater NASA tracking station. Two Navy antenna dishes, each ten feet across, nestled within the forty-foot tall structure. Supersensitive FFQ-10(V) hydrophones listened to the eternal gurgling and roar of the Atlantic Ocean.

The Sound Surveillance System—SOSUS—scanned the sea depths for the telltale signatures of far-off ships and submarines. SOSUS listened to the underwater babble in the Atlantic with the CAESAR listening posts. COLLOSSUS units monitored the Pacific.

Underwater hydrophones were first deployed for ocean defense in 1915 by the English. By the last year of World War I, 21 underwater hydrophone sites surrounded Great Britain. Modern CAESAR and COLLOSSUS outposts stand their corroding watches beneath the sea around North America.

SOSUS and its highly trained technicians separate manmade acoustic "signals" from natural background "noise." Wideband, passive sonar in the SOSUS arrays listen to ambient sound. Computers filter out the flow noise generated by water breaking over the hulls of fast-moving submarines and the unnatural sound of propellers cavitating under water.

Narrow-band sonar tracks slow moving acoustic targets and low-frequency (1 hertz range) machinery noise.

Low-frequency noise under water travels much further than high-frequency signals.

The low-frequency clank of a 6,000 horsepower diesel engine drowning in a gush of salt water was virtually invisible among the sea's living sounds after travelling 550 nautical miles.

The SOSUS antenna dishes scanned the afternoon ocean for the faintest whispers of mechanical noise. The sunken hydrophones do not hear sound. Instead, they feel acoustic pressure measured in micropascal units. One micropascal equals the pressure of one-millionth Newton per square meter in metric units. It is equal to one ten-billionth of normal atmospheric pressure.

By the time the sound pressure from *El Tiburon*'s engine room pressed against the Andros Island SOSUS antenna, the acoustic pressure wave was less than fifty micropascals. But CAESAR's computers sucked it in and separated its low-frequency rumble from the swirling sea around it.

Computers running equations called Fast Fourier Transforms analyzed the signal and filtered out the background noise of waves, soprano whales, and clicking shrimp. Microprocessors did the work of applying sonar equations to Wenz Curve graphs of signal pressure plotted against noise frequency.

When the computers had filtered out the background noise of the Caribbean, nothing remained except the momentary sound of *El Tiburon*'s diesel grinding to a stop.

Intense young men and women wearing U.S. Navy winterblues passed the word quickly through Naval Facilities (NAVFACS) which passed it on to the regional Ocean Surveillance Information System which passed it to the Naval Ocean Surveillance Information Center in Maryland. The Information Center then relayed the contact report to Deputy Chief of Naval Operations, Submarine Warfare. A copy went into the secret Dugway Wet file at N-8, Deputy Chief of Naval Operations for Resources, Warfare Requirements and Assessments.

The cylinders in *El Tiburon*'s drowned engine were still wet and were slowly turning to white corrosion when the Deputy Chief of Naval Operations received the decoded cable from Andros Island. "PROSUB" was the only operative word: probable submarine contact. The next level of contact classification is CERTSUB. Since all American submarines are nuclear powered, the sound of a disabled diesel underwater had to fly a foreign flag.

The Deputy Chief laid the SOSUS dispatch beside the last report decoded from SSN-609:

DCNO 0315/2010. SSN-609. ROV FTR. RPMS NOR(M). RDT 0315/2200. MEDCON LTLCG. WP UABHA. EOM.

The officer, two other admirals, and one civilian unscrambled the message beamed into the sky from the Puerto Rico Trench:

To the Deputy Chief of Naval Operations. March 15th; 2010 UTC [4:10 pm, Washington time]. From SSN-609: Repair of vessel fails to respond. Reactor plant main steam not operationally ready due to maintenance. Reliability determination test will be initiated at 2200 UTC. Medical condition little changed. Will proceed until advised by higher authority. End of Message.

"What do you think, gentleman," the DCNO asked his two-star colleague from Research and Development.

"Possible submarine contact somewhere west of 609? No progress on the viral contamination? Still a mechanical in the feedwater or main steam system? I think it's time we brought him in if we have secondary confirmation of submarine activity in the area."

"I believe that we do." The only civilian among three admirals shuffled his manila folders. The CIA man represented the National Photographic Interpretation Center managed by the Central Intelligence Agency for the Defense Intelligence Agency. The CIA's Committee on Imagery Requirements and Exploitation maintains overall supervision of satellite photographs used for spying. The analyst in business suit had driven up from the Satellite Data System HQ at Fort Belvoir, Virginia.

"These shots represent 36 hours of raw data from the Cuba desk." The CIA man passed a pile of photographs around the large table. "We've been keeping an eye on the Cuban submarine pens at Cienfuegos. Fidel has remained adamant about flexing his muscle in this hemisphere ever since the U.S.S.R. dissolved into the C.I.S. in December '91. You'll notice a clear wake profile there in a KH-11 image. The Keyhole satellite series, the first of which was deployed by the Space Shuttle in 1989, gives us real-time, digital imagery. It can read the proverbial newspaper from its polar orbit. We highlighted what we believe to be a submarine in the bay ahead of the wake."

The three admirals squinted at the 8x10 glossy prints.

"Problem is the weather. We got these shots on the 13th through a hole in the cloud deck caused by the weather over the Caribbean. We had to wait until this morning to shoot through the clouds when our newest, all-weather AFP-658 satellite moved into position. It was launched in November '90 by the shuttle *Atlantis* on STS-38. It replaced the AFP-731 which disintegrated a few days after its February 1990 launch on board STS-36. The 658 was sent up to monitor the Gulf War in visual and electronic spectra. Look there."

The CIA specialist pointed to a false-color photograph of black water and blue clouds.

"This is digital far-infrared imagery highlighted by radar imagery which can penetrate cloud decks. The false yellow line there just north of the Dominican Republic is believed to be the heat wake signature of a snorkelling diesel submarine. We got this LACROSSE satellite image of the Cienfuegos sub pens six hours ago. LACROSSE can also penetrate clouds.

"The LACROSSE imaging satellite went up on the second shuttle to fly after the *Challenger* disaster. She went up on Mission 27 in December '88. That hole is one of the pens empty. Our people believe that a Foxtrot class sub left Cienfuegos sometime within the last two days. There's a high probability it's one of the Foxtrots manned by an all-Cuban crew. The Russians would never run on the surface in daylight. It is probable that the boat is the SOSUS contact you Navy people picked up this afternoon. If I were to vote, I'd change your PROSUB to a CERTSUB."

"Thanks." The DCNO turned to his two-star colleague. "I think it's time to bring 609 in. Opinions?"

"Reluctantly agreed, Admiral. What kind of hardware do we have out there?"

The DCNO looked across the table to an unrestricted rear admiral from the office of the DCNO, Surface Warfare, N-86.

The rear admiral, upper-half, unrolled two large charts upon the table. Defense Mapping Agency, chart number 400, showed the Caribbean from western Cuba all the way southeast to Venezuela. Chart number 25700 was a finer scale chart of just the Mona Passage ocean between Puerto Rico and the Dominican Republic.

"I checked the board on my way down here. We have the destroyer *Hayler*, DD-997, in the Caribbean down here, 80 miles north of the island of Aruba off Venezuela. She's down there patrolling the Aruba Gap for drug traffickers going out of Colombia by sea. If we order 609 to proceed south through Mona Passage en route to Roosevelt Roads, she can rendezvous with *Hayler* here in ten to twelve hours if both ships make flank bell, 30 knots. Should rendezvous about 0700 UTC tomorrow morning, two hours before daybreak. *Hayler* is our newest, *Spruance* class destroyer. She'd put a Russian nuclear boat down for the count, let alone a 35-year-old Foxtrot submarine, if 609 needs assistance."

The admiral pointed on the Mona Passage chart to the silver-dollar size Isla de Mona.

"The island is U.S. territory," the admiral continued. "It's also relatively shallow water, averaging 1,500 feet. If we rendezvous with *Sam Houston* there, we're 30 miles west of this sand bar just off Puerto Rico's west coast. The bar is only 250 feet deep, just in case we have to scuttle the sub or effect an underwater evacuation to maintain quarantine of their viral products and infection."

"Good. I'll order 609 to Roosevelt Roads. Do we have adequate quarantine facilities at Roosevelt Roads if we need it?"

"Yes, Admiral. And the sub tender *Frank Cable*, AS-40, is already at Roosevelt Roads for routine maintenance. She'll be able to service 609, no problem."

"Very well. I'll get word to Captain Milhaus. Let me know immediately if we get any intelligence on the possible sub contact."

The two officers and CIA man left the DCNO alone. He typed a message on the keyboard of his desktop computer.

Other computers would compress his dispatch to *Sam Houston* into Pentagonese and code which would travel at the speed of light to the Puerto Rico Trench.

Sam Houston had cruised at a depth of 400 feet for nearly an hour since the CO's last report was beamed into the sky. Had the ELF tone not bounced across the surface during the hour, the submarine would have gone deeper, out of range, for another four-hour watch.

"Radio room to the Captain," the intercom crackled throughout the vessel.

"Radio room; Captain," Captain Milhaus answered from his cabin. The CO had been lying awake on his narrow bunk for fifteen minutes. After fifteen hours on his feet, he needed to rest his lower back which throbbed from fatigue. Still on his back, the CO listened to the petty officer in the ship's mid-section.

"ELF, Captain."

Kurt Milhaus glanced at the red-lit clock on the bulkhead wall. It was 2045 UTC, almost 5:00 in the afternoon 400 feet above.

"Thank you." The captain pushed a button on the phone. "Captain to CIC."

The officer of the deck answered quickly.

"Control room, aye."

"Periscope depth, Lieutenant. Have the XO meet me there in ten."

"Aye, Sir."

Captain Milhaus swung his feet to the deck. His back ached when he stood beside his bunk. By the time he splashed cold water onto his dry eyeballs in his private lavatory, the floor of the metal head tipped slightly as 609 pointed her round bow toward the surface.

Jessica Dugan felt the wardroom pitch up as the ship ascended. The black surface of her coffee changed from a perfect circle to an ellipse as the sub inclined. The pile of logs and watch bills on the table did not move. SSN-609 climbed at only a ten-degree angle "up bubble." Almost a veteran, she ignored the unexpected motion. The rounded sides of the hull which formed the wardroom walls creaked softly as the water pressure decreased as the ship rose. She lowered her face to the documents in her hands.

Pappy Perlmutter greeted the captain in the control room.

"Periscope depth, Captain," the executive officer confirmed.

"Very well. Alert radio."

The CIC's telephone man called the radio room. In the next compartment aft, the petty officer's teletype sucked in the message being repeated continuously.

"RATT has it," the radioman telephoned the combat information center.

"Rig in the antenna mast," the XO ordered and the black pipe disappeared beneath the green surface.

Sam Houston pitched slightly in the churning water close to the surface. Her seakeeping was not stable at only 4 knots running speed.

"How's the barometer topside?" the CO asked a lieutenant junior grade in brown.

The antenna mast had taken a quick reading of surface conditions thirty feet above the rolling submarine.

"Twenty-eight point seven seven, Captain. And falling," the quartermaster replied from his maneuvering board.

"Gonna be a crummy day tomorrow upstairs," the captain smiled weakly.

"Seems so," the XO nodded.

A petty officer third-class crouched through the aft watertight hatchway. Without saluting, he handed the CO a folded piece of paper.

"Thank you, Mister Hill. If you would wait a moment, please."

"Aye, Sir."

Captain Milhaus led the XO to the chart table's maneuvering board. The quartermaster and navigator stepped aside so the two officers could huddle privately. The captain opened the dispatch and squinted at it for half a minute before he handed it to Lt. Commander Perlmutter.

"Well, Pappy," the CO frowned.

The XO studied the decoded cable from the Pentagon.

CONFBUL. SSN-609. DCNO 0315/2030. EAM. EAM. ASWCCS
ALNOT. ACINT PROSUB VCNTY. OPA UKN. ORMOD.
PWOD RSVLT RDS. A/H 270 W/P MNA PSG. RX MONA CYN

NLT 0316/0400. COMPRESECTASWU ADVD ASP. DD-997
UNW TAC/R. EXPC SAREX. TTI 10H. WEAX TRW. EOM.
ACK.

He read slowly as his tired mind translated the dispatch from the sky.

Confidential bulletin to SSN-609 from the Deputy Chief of Naval Operations. March 15th, 2030 UTC. Emergency Action Message. Antisubmarine Warfare Centers Command and Control Systems Alert Notice: Acoustic intelligence probable submarine contact your vicinity. Overall probability of attack unknown. Your orders are modified. Proceed without delay to Roosevelt Roads. Alter heading to 270. Way-point Mona Passage. Report crossing Mona Canyon not later than March 16th at 0400 UTC [11:00 pm, March 15th, Eastern Standard Time]. Commander, Puerto Rico Sector, Antisubmarine Warfare Unit advised [for] antisubmarine patrol. DD-997 underway [for] tactical reconnaissance. Expect search and rescue exercise. Time to intercept 10 hours. Route weather forecast: thunder storm. End of message. Acknowledge.

When the XO handed the message back to his captain, the CO turned to the loitering radioman. "Send and log-in, 609 to DCNO: 'Will comply.' "

"Aye, Sir. Six oh nine to DCNO, wilco."

"Very well, Mister Hill. Carry on," the captain nodded to the teenager.

The young seaman retraced his rubber-soled steps aft toward the radio room.

"QMC," Pappy said to the Chief Quartermaster. "Come about to two seven zero. When radio confirms that we've acknowledged, we're going to Roosevelt Roads."

"Aye, Sir," the QMC nodded. A dozen faces in the control room turned from their consoles to study their captain, who looked tired. The skin on the CO's face was tight and gray.

"We're leaving the trench," Captain Milhaus said softly. "Commander, make flank bell at 800 feet when the radio room reports."

"Thirty knots at 800 feet, Captain."

The petty officer manning the telephone in the port side, forward corner of the CIC turned to the CO.

"Radio room, Captain. Message transmitted, Sir."

"Very well," the CO nodded. "Take her down, Pappy."

The executive officer took the few steps to stand beside the officer of the deck who stood above the three seated sailors at the front of the compartment. The OOD spoke to the diving officer of the watch sitting in front of him. And the diving officer spoke softly over the shoulders of the helmsman and planesman sitting just ahead of the diving officer. As the stern planes pitched *Sam Houston*'s bow downward, the ship left the rough green surface behind.

When the bow of SSN-609 dipped downward, Jessica Dugan watched her cold coffee climb an inch closer to the rim of the half-full cup. The high side of the coffee's surface rose toward the low side of the compartment as the ship banked into an easy turn. The submarine turned 180 degrees to come about from her eastward heading until she faced west. In the control room behind her, the planesman pointed the ship toward the bottom while the helmsman steered the descending turn. The sloping gray walls of the wardroom creaked as the ship descended. With each 100 feet, outside water pressure increased by 3 atmospheres. When the vessel trimmed for level cruise at 800 feet, 24 atmospheres compressed *Sam Houston* with 25 tons of pressure on every square foot of black hull.

In the darkness where sunlight never penetrated, the submarine slowly accelerated to flank speed of 30 knots. The physician could feel the back of her uncomfortable metal chair as the speed increased. She was surprised at the acceleration rate of 8,000 tons of steel driven by a nuclear reactor turning a single propeller 400 feet away.

Just as she glanced at the bulkhead clock which read 2130 UTC (5:30 pm, Atlantic Time), the wardroom's door of plastic wood opened. The XO entered.

Dr. Dugan remained seated. The executive officer quickly sat down beside her.

"We're going faster, Pappy?"

"Yes. DCNO has ordered us out of here—back to Roosevelt Roads. We're making turns for flank speed."

Jessica furrowed her brow.

"Aborting the mission?"

"Yes, Jessica. Washington seems to think that an old Cuban submarine might be lurking about out here."

Lt. Commander Perlmutter paused to watch the color drain from her tired face. Her pale cheeks made her left eye seem even blacker. His words drove into her mind and her adjustment to submarine living evaporated. She was embarrassed when she felt perspiration leak from her forehead. She drew her clammy fingers across her eyebrows.

"Another sub? In the trench? Can they go this deep? This fast? Can they find us?"

Although she did not raise her voice, her words tumbled out in a single terrified breath. She remembered the U.S. nuclear attack submarine *Baton Rouge*, SSN-689. On February 11, 1992, the fifteen-year-old *Los Angeles* class boat collided under water with a Russian, Sierra class, nuclear submarine under the Barents Sea. The collision occurred some twelve miles off Murmansk above the Arctic Circle. No casualties were reported to the public. The back of Jessica's chair stuck to the sweat erupting along her spine. The physician imagined that she could smell herself again.

"Easy, Jessica."

Pappy Perlmutter laid his hand gently upon hers. Before she drew her next breath, he pulled his hand back.

"Washington isn't certain. They're just being careful. They're recalling us only because we haven't gotten a handle on the feedwater problem or the disease situation yet. I suppose they would leave us out here if we could crack either problem. Otherwise, we'll steam westward for about the next five hours, then south through Mona Passage, then up around Puerto Rico to the base. Don't worry."

The XO smiled warmly toward the tense woman.

"If their boat is what DCNO thinks it is—a retired Soviet sub in Cuban service—there's no match at all. We can stay deep for years. He can only submerge at full speed for a day on diesel-electric power. His maximum endurance under water is seven days—if he makes only 2 knots. We're making 30. Once we turn south tomorrow morning, the Cubans will only see our wake, if that. Besides, our people have a *Spruance* class destroyer coming hard for our position. *Hayler* will shadow us eight hours from now. She was commissioned in '83 and is the best we have for ASW. We're as safe as we can be, if our own mosquitos don't get us."

"Antisubmarine warfare?" Jessica shuddered. Pappy smiled.

"Relax, Jessica. You're in good hands." He looked down at her pile of handwritten rough logs and printed battle bills of crew assignments. "What have you and Doc Shaffer learned?"

"I'm not sure, Pappy. But I just might be on to something here." She laid her hand atop the stack of documents. "I went through the ship's logs and bills since you sailed. Seems that Torpedoman Thurston and Electrician's Mate Hendrix were both in the same DCC fire drill five weeks ago. Still can't find any concrete overlap in assignments for the sick planesman or radioman Frazier. But I'm working on it."

Dr. Dugan momentarily forgot about submarines duelling in the salty blackness as she concentrated on her work.

"Well, stay on it, Jessica." The XO glanced at the clock. "Almost 2200. I have to lay aft for the feedwater reliability determination test. That'll tell us if we got the water hammer licked in the condenser loop."

The executive officer stood up and pushed his chair toward the wardroom table.

"I can defend this ship against all comers from the outside, Jessica. But you have to save us on the inside." He smiled above the seated physician.

She laid both of her hands upon the documents.

"If it's here, I'll find it."

"Good."

The XO paused for a breath before he turned to leave the wardroom. In that instant, Jessica Dugan was seized by the need to reach up if only to return the XO's kindness. But all she did was nod.

"Good luck with the power plant, Pappy."

"Thanks. We'll need it."

The flimsy joiner door closed silently behind him.

Jessica Dugan, M.D., lowered her gaze back to her paperwork. Her brow furrowed as she worked hard to push from her mind the thought of another warship on the far side of the wardroom which now headed westward across the rim of the Puerto Rico Trench. As she squinted down at the Watch, Quarter and Station Bill, all she could think about was the four miles of black ocean underneath her hard steel chair.

At 2200 UTC, 6:00 in the evening 30 feet above, *El Tiburon* cruised close to the choppy surface. All three model 2D42 diesels were back on line and were sucking air through the snorkel two hours after the induction accident. The mast's dampers were working well to keep out the green water which exploded over the metal tube with each passing swell. *El Tiburon* sailed eastward, 25 nautical miles north of Cape Cabron on the Dominican Republic's coastline. The submarine chugged fifteen miles south of the Navidad Bank's shallow sand bar. Between the bar and the Dominican Republic, the Cubans plowed through water 12,000 feet deep.

"Barometer now, Quartermaster?" Captain Barcena asked wearily.

"Ten-oh-seven point three, Capitan."

"Thank you, QM." The captain turned to the officer of the deck who braced himself on a corner of the navigator's maneuvering table. "Take her down to 100 meters. Engineering can service the diesel and the crew will get a smoother ride."

"One hundred meters, 085 heading, 15 knots flank bell, Capitan."

"Very well," the captain nodded. "Sonar, report if you get any contact at all, no matter how distant. The Americans could be anywhere now."

"Yes, Capitan."

"I'm going to lay forward. Carry on."

El Viejo slouched as he walked toward the forward bulkhead. His last 90-minute nap had been interrupted by the diesel failure. He had slept for six hours in fits and starts during the last 30 hours at sea. They had left Cienfuegos harbor 50 hours earlier. As the captain left the boat's control room illuminated in red standing lights, *Sam Houston* and *El Tiburon* were closing on each other from opposite directions. Two hundred twenty-five nautical miles of rough seas under heavy, gray clouds separated them.

The American destroyer steamed north through calm seas at 2230 UTC. At 6:30 in the evening local time, *Hayler*, DD-997, made turns for 30 knots. Four General Electric LM-2500 gas turbine engines drove two propellers. Eight thousand tons of steel rode her 529-foot length. Fifty-five feet wide, she carried 30 feet of hull beneath the green water. Large enough to hangar two Seahawk LAMPS helicopters, *Hayler* bristled with weapons and electronic equipment.

Hayler's SPS-49 radar scanned the empty horizon for aircraft while her SPS-55 radar probed the darkening horizon for ships. SQS-53A sonar mounted within her submerged and bulbous bow listened for *Sam Houston* and a possible Foxtrot class Cuban submarine coming down through Mona Passage 225 nautical miles to the north. With the destroyer 150 miles north of the island of Aruba off the Venezuelan coast, any traffic cruising the Passage remained well out of range.

The gas turbines put out 80,000 horsepower and drove *Hayler* through 4-foot waves in water 12,000 feet deep.

The 315 seamen and 19 officers had been unusually chatty earlier in the balmy Caribbean day. They had thought they were homeward bound. The homeward leg of any voyage induces a strange euphoria among men of the sea. Old salts call it Channel Fever and its giddiness is prime time for careless mistakes on board any vessel. So watch officers and division leaders had been particularly vigilant for the last two days.

Then the captain had passed the word that DD-997 was under new orders to cover an American mystery submarine somewhere to the north. Channel Fever was quickly cured as officers and men returned to the mindset of a tactical evolution at sea. Apprentice seamen put their shoulders to polishing the brass brightwork and to faking firehoses for the new mission at hand. Talk of home and easy women became careful attention to checklists. *Hayler* was a man-of-war again. Although everyone assumed the operation to be a drill following the collapse of the Soviet Union, the drill was taken seriously in every department, division, and section of the ship.

Material condition yoke and readiness Condition III for possible threat alert were set throughout the ship. The newest *Spruance* class destroyer made way northward with disciplined dispatch.

An hour before midnight UTC, Captain Milhaus stood anxiously in 609's maneuvering room. The CO was an hour behind schedule for the feedwater test. Executive officer Perlmutter stood by his captain's side.

"Chief?"

"We're making turns for 25 knots, Captain."

"Very well. Bend on turns for thirty."

"Aye, Sir. Turns for 30 knots. Throttle to 95 percent."

The CO only nodded. He fidgetted with the DT-60 dosimeter secured to his belt for recording the day's dose of gamma radiation. Every crewman's dosimeter is read regularly by the ship's CP-95/PD computer.

The engineering officer of the watch instructed the throttle man to rev up the steam turbine which turned the submarine's single propeller. The control console operator opened the nuclear throttle which in turn commanded the turbine in the engine room behind them to increase its speed.

"Positive EHC, Captain."

"Very well."

The steam turbine's electro-hydraulic control system, EHC, drove the turbine's governor valves. The throttle man controlled feedwater flow rates which affected the rate of steam being generated in the steam generator within the reactor compartment forward of the maneuvering room. The engineering officer carefully monitored his throttle man who ran the propulsion system in its integrated control mode. Advancing the throttle to send more high-pressure, non-radioactive steam into the turbine told the integrated control system, ICS, circuits to ask the nuclear reactor and the feedwater system for more power. The ICS "stole" energy from the steam generator by momentarily changing the setpoint on the turbine governor valve. This allowed the turbine to spin faster and to allow lower than normal pressures in the steam line until the reactor could catch up with the sudden steam shortage. Without changing the pressure setpoint, the system would have thought that the steam generator was failing when the line pressure decreased.

As the engineers under the captain's eye put the propulsion system through its paces, petty officers monitored the health of the reactor. Excore nuclear instrumentation counted the neutron level within the reactor core. Eight channels of electronic data were fed into the Safety Parameter Display System, the Reactor Protection System, the ICS, and the Control Rod Drive Control System. Four power range channels used ion chambers to monitor the top and bottom halves of the reactor core.

A neutron flux signal generated by the ion chamber instruments carried reactor health information to the linear amplifier and on through the compensated ion chamber, then the logarithmic amplifier, and finally to the neutron level indicator on the instrument consoles. Four channels of data converged on the Reactor Protection System from the excore instrumentation, the Non-nuclear Instrumentation System, the Turbine Autostop Oil System, and the Main Feed Pump Control Oil Systems. Two of the sensor circuits must sense an out-of-limits error to induce an automatic shutdown of the nuclear chain reaction.

A lieutenant junior grade who looked like a teenager monitored chain reaction information coming into the maneuvering room compartment. The data arrived from neutron detection cylinders filled with argon and nitrogen gases within lead armor just outside the reactor but within the primary shielding of the reactor compartment. The young officer had come out of a Navy ROTC program on the prairie. From college, he went to Nuclear Power School for 687 hours of classroom study in 26 weeks. From there, he had interned for another 24 weeks at a nuclear power plant at Idaho Falls, Idaho, before heading to Sub School at New London for 13 weeks.

The young officer had not yet taken his nuclear oral examination which would qualify him to wear dolphin insignia on his khaki shirt. The engineering officer of the watch studied him carefully.

"Stable one, Captain," the lieutenant "non-qual" said confidently.

"Very well."

One deck below, on Two Deck, seamen observed the steam pipes running from the reactor aft toward the main turbine. The Navy's double-check protocols put two men at each critical valve or switch box. As in all U.S. Navy vessels, the M Division of the engineering department manned the turbine in the aftmost compartment while the A Division monitored auxiliary equipment, the E Division manned electrical systems, and the R Division stood by to make required repairs.

"ECCS idle, Captain, A and B trains."

"Very well."

Two separate Emergency Core Cooling Systems were ready to flood the reactor core with borated water should a leak develop in the superheated water lines running into the reactor. Emergency flooding of the reactor core is designed to keep the control rods from exceeding 2,200°F.

"Main Steam, report," the engineering officer of the watch said softly. Down below, men listened carefully for the clang of high-speed water droplets slamming into the steel sides of the steam pipes leading to the turbine. Drain traps along the line are designed to recover loose water within the 570°F steam. The EOOW faced his telephone man who spoke by intercom to the engine room further aft and one deck down.

The EOOW shook his weary head.

"We have water hammer, Captain." The officer looked his CO in the eyes. "Sorry, Sir. We start again at the low-pressure condenser. Feedwater read-outs are all normal. Problem has to be in the steam drains or condensers."

"Keep on it," Captain Milhaus sighed.

"I'll go below, Captain." The XO looked tired, too.

"All right. I'll be in CIC. Is Dr. Dugan still in the wardroom?"

"Yes, Sir."

"Okay. I'll stop there first."

"Maintain 30 knots, Lieutenant. Advise sonar to monitor the hammer."

"Thirty knots, Captain. And advise sonar."

The ping jockeys forward would listen for the water hammer reverberating against the long cable of the towed array passive hydrophones.

Captain Milhaus and his XO left the maneuvering room for the passageway. The XO went first. Four quiet sailors walked slowly toward them.

"Gangway," an enlisted man called. The seamen pressed against the passageway bulkhead so the officers could pass. Navy courtesy reserves the "gangway" call for officers passing. Enlisted men making a path through other men only rate a "coming through."

"They told me to expect days like this when I signed my 339, Pappy." The CO wanted to smile, but he could not.

U.S. Navy officers sign their Naval Military Personnel Command, Form 339, to accept their commissions.

Walking forward with 800 feet of black water above him, Kurt Milhaus imagined that he could hear droplets of water pounding the inside of his ship's scalding steam lines. He knew that if the hydrophones dragged behind *Sam Houston* could hear it, so could sonar on board any enemy submarine within listening range.

THIRTEEN

15 MARCH; 2330 UTC

JESSICA DUGAN'S head ached and her bones ached. Her swollen left eye throbbed in time with the pounding behind her eyebrows. She had not slept for 19 hours. Although she had showered in the BL-4 lab's decontamination compartment six hours earlier, the armpits of her khaki shirt begged for soap and powder. It did not help that Lieutenant Shaffer smelled worse after wrestling with the drugged planesman in sick bay.

"Did you hurl your midrats, Stan?" the weary woman smiled broadly in the narrow infirmary.

In submarines where crewmen are on watch around the clock, the mess serves a full-course meal every six hours. The midnight meal is known as midrats. In half an hour it would be midnight UTC.

"No, Jessica. My patient here lost his dinner in my lap twenty minutes ago. The allopurinol caused GI distress, to put it mildly. So I put him on a colchicine I.V. drip for the acute gouty arthritis. He should tolerate that all right."

The planesman dozed fitfully in his restraint straps.

Dr. Dugan noticed that the officer whose ear had been chewed off by the planesman 28 hours earlier was gone.

"Where's the lieutenant?"

"I sent him back to his stateroom with orders to stay put for the duration. He'll be more comfortable up there."

216

The ship's physician read the concern in the woman's face.

"I examined the planesman's mouth minutely. He has no lesions of any kind. I'm as confident as I can be that he didn't lose any blood when he bit the lieutenant. And I did a serum assay on the lieutenant first: his uric acid level is normal. He's showing zero signs of Lesch-Nyhan. I'll monitor him closely, of course."

The doctor nodded.

"You look tired, Jessica."

"Yes. I've been up to my eyeballs in ship's logs and bills all evening. Found some possible infection modes, I think. But the old man just paid me a visit in the wardroom." She shook her head.

The GMO chuckled softly toward the woman standing on the far side of the dopey planesman's bunk.

"Sounds like you got The Treatment."

"That what you call it? The captain grilled me for fifteen minutes. You would think that I had questioned his parentage."

The sleeping seaman moaned softly.

"Sit down, Jessica."

The GMO motioned toward two chairs along the sick bay bulkhead. After she sat down, the lieutenant sat next to her. The backs of their heads touched the cold metal wall.

"Captain Milhaus means no harm. It's just his way when the boat's in jeopardy. I've seen it before."

"You served with the CO before this cruise?"

"Yes. I was GMO in *Pollack* with him. Old 603 was a *Permit* class hunter-killer based out of San Diego. She was the first of her class decommissioned in March of '89. There were thirteen in her class. The first was *Thresher*. The CO was exec in 603. *Sam Houston* was his first command on two cruises before this one. He brought me with him. Chief Wilcox, too, and a couple of men in the engineering department. Pappy Perlmutter was already on board."

In Navy English, seamen serve "in" a ship. Only pilots serve "on" an aircraft carrier.

"So why the riot act, Stan? I think I'm finally making headway tracking the infection. But the captain wants it done yesterday."

The GMO paused and sat thoughtfully.

"This boat is the CO's life. The Navy is too. He's a mustang, you know."

"Not Annapolis?"

"No. Couldn't get in. So he started as an electrician's mate before he made it to officer candidate school."

"Why couldn't he get into the Academy?"

"You don't know?"

"No."

"His father. His father was in the German Navy during the war. Went down in '42 on U-85."

"The captain's father was a Nazi, for God's sake?"

"Not hardly. His father was a teenager who got drafted in '39. Captain Milhaus' mother was an American. She came home in '39 after the invasion of Poland, but her husband stayed in Germany. The captain was born in 1940 after his mother got back to the States. His father was in one of the dozen or so U-boats sent to raid the U.S. coastal waters in Hitler's Operation Drumbeat. Ever hear of that?"

"No, don't think so."

"Well, I did some research after I met the skipper. Seems the Germans sent about a dozen subs to the east coast between January and June 1942. They sank about 400 ships. Our destroyer *Roper* sent U-85 to the bottom with the captain's father in the engine room. The odds weren't exactly with them half a century ago. The Germans lost 784 submarines and 32,000 sailors. The Brits lost 75 boats and nearly 3,500 men. In the Pacific, our people lost 52 subs: a quarter of the submarine fleet."

Jessica shuddered. She felt the sea crushing her from all sides 800 feet under the Caribbean. And she thought of her grandfather still on board *Yorktown*, sunk at the Battle of Midway, June 4th, 1942 . . . two months after Captain Milhaus lost his father to the cruel sea.

"So that would explain why the captain is a little old to be wearing three stripes?"

"Yes, Jessica. He spent ten years becoming chief. Then he got on the officers' track, a decade behind everyone else. He graduated first in his class at PCO. Even though he was born in the States of an American mother, the Navy punished him for his father, it would seem."

PCO is the Navy's Prospective Commanding Officer school.

"Oh." The woman nodded sleepily.

"After all this time, it still eats at him. Don't read me wrong, Jessica. The CO is a good officer and a good man for that matter. But losing his father in a sub and having to come up the hard way left its mark. He has a personal relationship with his subs that goes beyond his duty. When I shipped with him in *Pollack*, he never left the boat. When we had shore leave, he always stayed on board."

"If I left late or came back early, I usually found him taking periscope liberty."

"Periscope liberty?"

"Yes: looking through the periscope at the shore but never quite getting there."

"God." Jessica shook her head. Dark ringlets were loose from her hair knot at the back of her head. Her hair fell toward her khaki collar. Lieutenant Shaffer tried not to notice how smooth the sides of her neck looked where perspiration glistened faintly.

"Anyway, that's the old man's life history. No family other than whatever boat he serves. Now tell me what you found upstairs."

"Well, I combed the operational bills, emergency bills, and all of the rough logs for each division down to the section level since you left the States. It seems that Buddy Thurston and Hendrix were both in the same DCC fire drill right after you reached the trench area. Were there any injuries during the drill that would appear in your records?"

"We had one casualty: Senior Chief Randy Morrow, a hull maintenance technician. That's an HTCS rating. I already reviewed the whole company's records so many times that I have the charts damn near memorized. He slashed his forearm on a piece of loose equipment. I gave him the usual tetanus booster and the routine serum assay for dengue and LaCrosse. He was negative all around so I sent him back to duty. He has no laboratory assignment. The HT's are always on call and cannot have other billets."

"Okay. For the moment I have no other commonality of infection. And even if Thurston and Hendrix did pass blood between them somehow, that might give us the route of transmission but not the vector itself. Worth a look though."

"All right. My patient will be out for a few hours. I can start after the next watch cycles through for their allopurinol."

Jessica Dugan glanced at the bulkhead clock which showed midnight, UTC: eight o'clock at night 800 feet above. At 8:00, the second two-hour "dog watch" would change positions with the men of the first watch whose 4-hour watch would end at midnight, Atlantic Standard Time. One by one, the tired seamen would trickle through sick bay for their prophylactic dose of the drug which controls excess uric acid. Their blood levels of the acid would be tested first.

"Wanna help, Jessica?"

"Sure." She yawned which made her bruised face hurt. "Let me run forward to put on a fresh shirt first. I'll be back . . . unless the CO claps me in irons."

Both physicians stood. Lieutenant Shaffer smiled toward the lieutenant commander who smelled of female sweat and baby powder.

Captain Martinez Barcena crouched through the frame of the watertight door into *El Tiburon*'s red-lighted control room. The Cuban submarine heaved with the rough seas 30 feet above her weather deck.

"El Capitan on the bridge," the officer of the deck announced softly. "Ten meters as ordered, Capitan. Periscope depth."

The CO had ordered the ascent toward the surface from his cabin. He wanted to recharge the batteries with the diesel generators breathing through the snorkel.

"Very well," the captain smiled. Although his two-hour catnap had revived him, the CO's eyes remained dark with fatigue. He had slept for a total of eight hours during four such naps, but each interrupted nap had robbed the middle-aged officer of the deep sleep which flushes the brain of yesterday's care. When *El Tiburon* rolled steeply, coffee sloshed from the captain's thick mug onto the deck and dripped into the hole in the floor which housed the periscope. The optical tube remained stowed below deck.

"Do you have a barometer reading, QM?"

"Yes, Capitan. Ten-oh-six point three millibars, Sir. Down another one point seven in the last three hours. And the snorkel has closed about every two minutes in this sea."

The submarine's seakeeping was unstable so close to the churning surface. The barometer had fallen outside to 29.72 inches. A decrease of another two-tenths inch would classify the brewing storm above as a full-blown hurricane with winds in excess of 60 knots.

Captain Barcena looked around the narrow control room. A dozen young faces in red standing lights looked up at him. Their moist faces were tense. Each time the snorkel automatically slammed shut to keep another flood of water out of the diesels, the crew's ears popped as the engines sucked air from the boat. When snorkels were first used on German U-boats half a century earlier, at least two complete crews were suffocated by their own engines.

"All right, Quartermaster," the CO nodded as he wiped warm coffee off of his forearm. "Lieutenant Collado, take her down to two hundred meters and make turns for 15 knots. Maintain your present course."

"Two hundred meters, 15 knots, zero-one-zero, Capitan."

"Very well. Battery status?"

Lieutenant Collado, officer of the deck, leaned over a console of instruments.

"Full charge, Capitan."

"Good. We should get a better ride down below."

The snorkel mast retracted along with the Snoop class, surface-to-air radar mast which had been scanning the sky for aircraft out to 25 nautical miles.

As the deck pitched down by the bow, a collective sigh rose from the control room. Above them, thick gray sky in the last wisps of daylight touched the horizon in the darkening west. The eastern sky was already dark. Forty knot winds drove eight-foot and rising swells toward the low pressure cell further east over Puerto Rico.

At 550 feet, the OOD gave orders to level off. The ship would stabilize as she settled through another 50 feet and be on an even keel by 600 feet. Once level, more commands and a flurry of activity trimmed the submarine for level cruise. High-pressure air blew water out of the port and starboard compensating tanks to perfectly match the sub's buoyancy with the weight of the water it displaced in the black ocean. Her three propellers were driven silently by electric motors as the quiet diesels cooled in the engine room.

Running on the electric motors fed 5,300 horsepower to the three shafts and would conserve what was left of *El Tiburon*'s 360 tons of diesel fuel.

Each compartment called the control room by intercom to confirm the ship's watertight integrity. A telephone man relayed the reports to Captain Barcena. The old boat was still tight over 30 years after rolling down the Sudomekh shipyard ways at St. Petersburg (then Leningrad).

"Sonar, report," the CO ordered.

"All clear, Capitan."

Well forward of the control room, a flat Trout Cheek antenna wrapped completely around the stubby bow. The passive array listened to the ocean roaring over the ship. The hydrophones heard only water which hummed softly where it became turbulent along the row of limber holes on each side of the double hull's ballast tanks.

The sub's ride was smooth at 600 feet and the crewmen relaxed at their watch stations in the control room.

She made way eastward at full speed parallel to the north coast of the Dominican Republic. *El Tiburon*'s narrow bow pointed toward *Sam Houston*'s rounded bow which approached from 130 nautical miles further east. Between them lay the rising surf in the treacherous waters of Mona Passage between the Dominican Republic and Puerto Rico.

Hayler drove headlong into ten-foot waves which exploded over DD-997's sharp bow. At 8:30 in the evening local time, March 15th, the pounding ocean and overcast sky were dark. The ship's clocks read 30 minutes into March 16th, Coordinated Universal Time. Captain Robert Webster strapped himself into his high-backed seat on the bridge. Two hundred ten nautical miles south of Mona Passage, the CO glanced at the barometer which fell slowly through 29.74 inches. The ship's two propellers made turns for flank bell at 32 knots. The petty officer standing his trick at the helm struggled to maintain the northbound course toward the passage.

Heavy seas had slowed the midnight change of watch throughout the ship as extra care was taken to assure the destroyer's condition of readiness. Normally, the new officer of the deck would take an hour to interrogate his department heads before assuming the watch. Tonight, the inspection took 90 minutes with an extra 20 minutes spent below with the engineering officer of the watch.

Two lieutenants stood stiffly on the pitching bridge fifteen feet from Captain Webster. The new OOD saluted the retiring OOD.

"I am ready to relieve you, Sir."

"I am ready to be relieved," the retiring OOD returned the salute after four hours on the bridge.

For five minutes, the two officers reviewed the ship's status beside the chart table and maneuvering board. Then they separated to stand toe-to-toe.

"I relieve you, Sir."

"I stand relieved."

With another exchange of courtesy, the weary officer requested and received Captain Webster's permission to leave the bridge.

The new OOD faced the officers and enlisted petty officers on the bridge to formally announce, "I have the deck."

"Aye, aye, Sir," the helmsman at the wheel replied. "Making zero-one-zero, 32 knots, flank bell, Sir."

"Very well," the OOD nodded in the humid and comfortable evening. With the skipper on the bridge, the new OOD assumed only the deck. Had the CO been off the bridge, the OOD would have announced his assumption of both the deck and the conn.

"Two hundred ten miles to rendezvous point, Lieutenant." The quartermaster of the watch addressed the new OOD. The QMOW is the link between the ship's navigator and the officer of the deck.

"Thank you."

The northbound *Hayler* dove beneath a southbound wave front. Spray slapped against the bridge windows.

"Taking it green tonight, Sir," the lieutenant smiled toward Captain Webster.

"For the last two hours, and getting worse. Barometer is still dropping and the ceiling is coming down. Don't think it will improve much in the morning when we range along *Sam Houston*."

"No, Sir. Any contact yet, Captain?"

"None, Mr. Collins. But if a Cuban sub is out there, we'll hear him. *Hayler* isn't about to be any flaming datum. Not on my watch anyway."

"No, Captain." The young OOD smiled in the red standing lights of the bridge. The surrounding windows were black and dripping with rain and salt water splashing over the bow with each new wave. A flaming datum is the best place on the ocean to begin an antisubmarine search: the last spot where a sub sank a target.

"The towed array is still quiet except for our own noise," the CO said softly. He squinted into the nighttime gloom.

Hayler towed a hydrophone cable which trailed out a full mile behind the destroyer. The SQR-19 listened to the ocean for the sound of submarines. Normally, the cable is towed through the water slowly at 8 to 12 knots. But DD-997 was in a hurry to close the distance to Mona Passage. Driving on at over 30 knots, the cable tended to whip under water in large arcs generated by the ship's two propellers and their 80,000 horsepower. The motion generated its own noise which interferred with the passive sonar's ability to listen to man-made sound.

"Air contacts, Captain?"

"Yes, just before you came up. Should be on us momentarily to sweep on ahead of us."

The destroyer's SPS-49 air-search radar had picked up its low-flying target ten minutes earlier. *Hayler* is the only *Spruance* class destroyer to carry the SPS-49. The other 30 ships in its class carry SPS-40 series radar.

"Mister Morgan?" the CO spoke over his shoulder to a two-stripe petty officer second class who manned the telephone.

"Three miles and closing, Captain. Bearing three-three-zero."

"Very well."

The CO and his OOD looked out the forward window into the blackness to the left of the pitching bow.

"Contact," the OOD pointed. A single red light blinked through the mist low on the portside horizon.

A shiny new version of the 30-year-old Orion sub hunter growled across the destroyer's bow. The P-3G aircraft drowned out everyone's voice on the bridge for five seconds when she passed low overhead before banking to her left to track a northbound heading toward Mona Passage.

The Orion rode four turboprop engines on the old Lockheed Electra airliner body. The huge engines pulled the surveillance aircraft through the night sky at 400 knots. The aircraft had slowed considerably before dropping down to 500 feet above the rising black seascape.

The bridge was quiet again when the Orion turned her nose toward the north.

"She's making her first run, Captain."

"Very well."

The P-3 droned above the rough surface. Her belly-mounted tubes carried banks of sonobuoy cannisters. Electronic sensors and hydrophones would splash into the sea to gather intelligence data about the ocean itself and to listen for the predicted approach of *Sam Houston* and a PROSUB speaking Spanish. The buoys would relay data back into the sky where the Orion's U.S. Navy crew of twelve would feed the raw data into their Proteus digital computer.

"Bathythermograph buoy away, Captain," the telephone man said after his headphones crackled.

Five miles ahead of *Hayler*, an SSQ-36 sensor buoy hit the water beneath the Orion. The cannister would sink to 1,000 feet and relay back sea state information for twelve minutes. The P-3 computer would reduce the telemetry to soundings of the ocean's temperature. Water temperature has an impact on underwater sound propagation. Real-time knowledge of water conditions would enable *Hayler*'s sonar men to better calibrate their on board sonar equipment.

"Two and three away, Sir," the petty officer reported.

Ten miles to the north, the Orion jettisoned a Spartan SSQ-41B sonobuoy. A small parachute eased the device into the water. Sea water would activate the SSQ-41B's battery so its passive sonar could listen carefully for noise in the 10 hertz to 2.4 kilohertz range. The hydrophones would hover at a depth of 65 feet for nearly 90 minutes.

An SSQ-77A went into the water nearby to listen to deeper water.

"She's getting good feed on all three drops, Captain." The telephone man looked toward the CO whose breath fogged the wet window.

"Thank you."

Lieutenant Collins stood close to the CO.

"Think there's really a Cuban sub out there, Sir?" The OOD's voice was soft but firm. He could not conceal his hope that the answer would be yes.

"I can't believe the Cubans would do such a thing. Not now

with their sugar daddy in Moscow in shambles. But . . . ," the captain looked over his shoulder at the youthful and intense face studying his own. "Might just be something in the air when the sea is up, but yes, I think she's out there." Captain Webster squinted into the darkness. "And I think she's going to have a really bad day tomorrow." The CO frowned and nodded as if stating an immutable fact.

At 1:00 in the morning, UTC, on March 16th and 9:00 at night, local time, on the 15th in Mona Passage, a hard winter still gripped Moscow, C.I.S., two hours before dawn.

Vasily Golitsyn paced anxiously in the admiralty building of the defunct Soviet Union. Exactly twelve hours earlier, the Russian had spent an infuriating hour with Cuban Consul Enrique Hernandez, who still burned with revolutionary fervor years after Vasily Fyodorovich's fire had gone out.

"The admiral will see you now," the round woman smiled from behind her desk. She sounded cheery in spite of drawing the night watch in the Kremlin.

"Thank you," Golitsyn nodded. He moaned out loud when he rose from the comfortable chair in the outer room. He could not remember when he had last slept between sheets and with his shoes off.

The 35-year-old diplomat was surprised to see Rear Admiral Vyacheslav Shcherbakov fill the archway under the open double doors.

"Good morning, Vasily."

"Admiral, Sir."

"Come in, please." With a sweep of his arm, the officer gestured toward his inner office. "Two glasses of tea, Mrs. Simyonova."

"Yes, Admiral." The woman left the two men in the door-way.

The diplomat took a seat in front of the admiral's desk. To his surprise, Rear Admiral Shcherbakov sat down next to him instead of behind the imposing desk.

"Since we don't have time to enjoy pleasantries, Vasily Fyodorovich, I'll get to the point. Your formal objection to the Cuban effort to harass an American submarine was routed to me." The admiral spoke with open cordiality to compensate for his bluntness.

"To you, Sir?"

"Yes. Does that surprise you?"

"Yes, Sir. My memoranda seem to move in the opposite direction of late."

"I would suggest," the admiral smiled, "that your present journey in the desert might be over, my friend."

"Oh?"

"Times are changing faster than I can keep up with them. We're in the desert one day, and here the next." The officer swept the stately room with his hand. "Or in front of a wall," he added seriously. "It would seem that we were both on the right side in the August Revolution after all." He nodded with a hard smile. The admiral had also chosen the correct faction when he sided with Boris Yeltsin in the fall of 1993 instead of with former general Vice President Alexander Rutskoi, who had seized the White House parliament building at gunpoint.

Rear Admiral Shcherbakov had made an impromptu decision during the August 1991 coup which had propelled him to the political stratosphere. At the time Mikhail Gorbachev was ousted by the coup, the admiral was chairman of the submarine department at the Leningrad Kuznetsov Naval Academy. The admiral was also Leningrad's Vice Mayor after retiring from a submarine career which culminated with the command of a nuclear boat. Immediately upon the coup's seizure of power, Professor Shcherbakov announced that he would take no part in the attempt to overthrow Gorbachev.

The admiral then began intense negotiations with local military commanders who were surrounding Leningrad with intentions of seizing the city in the name of the coup. The discussions resulted in the city remaining free and open. When the city reverted to its former name of St. Petersburg after the coup collapsed, Admiral Shcherbakov was given a political commission by Russian President Boris Yeltsin. Since then, his political future in the new Russia of the Commonwealth of Independent States shone brightly. He had been the right man at the right place at the right time—and he was a life-long submariner.

"I miss the smell of an old submarine, Vasily."

"Yes, Admiral." The diplomat had no idea what the admiral was talking about.

The woman from the outer office knocked at the closed door before bringing in two glasses of tea on a silver tray.

"Thank you, Mrs. Simyonova," the admiral said warmly.

"Forgive me, Sir, but I can't keep my eyes open. Might you tell me why I'm here at 4:00 in the morning?"

"Simple: I agree with your assessment of the situation in the Caribbean. Challenging an American boat in international waters would be a disaster for us. We need Washington's assistance right now more than their disapproval of misguided political adventures." The admiral paused to reach for a file on his desk. "What did you tell Hernandez?"

"I told him that I would recommend a cutoff of all economic aid to Havana if their submarine sailed to intercept the Americans—assuming that an American submarine is out there."

"It's out there, Vasily."

"Oh?"

The admiral opened his file folder and handed it to the exhausted bureaucrat.

Golitsyn squinted at a color photograph of the sea north of Puerto Rico. His weary mind stumbled over the colors: black land masses and orange ocean.

"It's a false color radarmetric scan. The yellow line running east and west just north of Puerto Rico is a submerged submarine. Our crew on board the Mir space station has experimented with new sensors for detecting the very small swell on the surface which follows a large submarine, even a deep one. The Americans' SEASAT satellite can pick up a swell only ten centimeters higher than the surrounding ocean. We're not quite that refined yet; but we're getting there. The Cubans are quite correct in their sub sighting."

The diplomat blinked at the classified image in his moist hands. He gave the photo back to his host.

"It's out there, Vasily. And the Cuban's Foxtrot sub is heading right for it. This we cannot allow. I want you to deliver one final message to Hernandez immediately."

"Yes, Admiral?"

"Tell him that Havana will dispatch a surface ship to the area to recall their submarine. The issue is not negotiable. If they refuse, we will do more than terminate all aid to them: Russia will give the Americans through appropriate channels..."

—The admiral paused without smiling—" . . . the complete KGB file on the assassination of President Kennedy. Ask Hernandez how the brothers Castro would like that."

"My God, Admiral."

"N'da," the submariner nodded.

"I can meet Consul Hernandez for breakfast."

"Do that."

The admiral rose. The diplomat staggered to his feet.

"You may sleep after you speak with Hernandez. I imagine the issue will be settled quickly in Havana. And, Vasily," the admiral laid his hand on the pale man's rumpled shoulder, "your time has come again. The President is mindful of your opposition to deploying troops in the Baltics before the coup. Your time will come soon."

Vasily Golitsyn straightened his sagging shoulders before he spoke to the Vice Mayor of St. Petersburg.

"I only did what I thought was right, Admiral. Like you at the Academy."

The middle-aged admiral smiled broadly.

"Precisely like me, Vasily Fyodorovich."

The submariner-turned-politician led the diplomat through the double doors. While waiting for the woman to bring his heavy topcoat, Vasily Golitsyn toyed with the coins in his pocket. Admiral Shcherbakov heard the copeck pieces jingling dully.

"The Metro doesn't open for another 90 minutes," the officer smiled. "You won't need the pocket change, Vasily Fyodorovich. The Foreign Ministry will be providing you with a car and driver from now on."

The diplomat who had plummetted from grace directed his nervous smile toward the colorless carpet. He only looked up when Mrs. Simyonova approached with his coat. Vasily Golitsyn felt reborn.

By 0130 UTC March 16th, still the 15th at 9:30 pm Atlantic Time, Dr. Shaffer completed his medical logs in sick bay. As the seamen and officers of the second dog watch shuffled in for their uric acid tests, the medical officer handed out in tiny paper cups a minimal dosage of oral allopurinol. No one showed elevated uric acid, the first sign of Lesch-Nyhan Syndrome. But the drug was given anyway to ward off the discomfort of gouty arthritis. The physician doubted the efficacy of allopurinol prophylaxis, but orders from DCNO were obeyed.

Lieutenant Shaffer neatly stacked his medical records and inserted the paperwork into a folder. Then he rose from the small metal desk bolted to the deck. He carried a carton of allopurinol vials. With a glance at the sleeping and drugged planesman strapped to his bunk, SSN-609's GMO opened the metal joiner door to the ship's pharmacy.

On his knees, Dr. Shaffer opened a metal cabinet close to the deck. He shoved the box of pills into a far corner to await the next change of watch at midnight, local time, when the first watch would give up their positions to the midnight-to-4:00 A.M. midwatch. The tired officer quietly cursed the cramped conditions of submarine living as he knelt on his hands and knees to stow the medication in the deep cabinet.

To make room for the half-used box of allopurinol, he shoved two unopened cartons to the side. One sealed box read ALLOPURINOL and the other COLCHICINE (I.V.). The allopurinol box skooted across the stainless steel shelf and thudded to the deck.

The squatting physician blinked down at the box resting on its side. The carton hit the linoleum floor with a dull hollow sound. Lieutenant Shaffer picked up the carton, the size of a half loaf of bread. It felt light.

The box sounded strange, with something rattling around inside. He tore off the tape from the box seam. The tape had thick lettering across it: DO NOT USE IF SAFETY SEAL BROKEN. Inside the box was a single small vial of pills. There should have been a dozen little bottles. Several boxes of the drug were issued to *Sam Houston* before she left her Virginia refitting nearly two months earlier.

With his tired face creased around his dark eyes, the physician reached in for the sealed box of injectable colchicine. He held the feather-light box to his ear and shook it.

The colchicine carton was empty.

FOURTEEN

16 MARCH; 0200 UTC

LIKE NEON tubes arcing between thick clouds, lightning illuminated the ocean. Between electrical bursts, the heavy sky was coal-mine black. The sea churned with walls of towering green beneath the white flashes.

A massive low pressure area spun counter-clockwise with its center over Puerto Rico where clapboard shutters were closed tightly. Five hours of storm warnings had been broadcast across the island. The rising wind rotated from north to west and around to the south, as the atmosphere sucked at towering cumulus clouds billowing above the Dominican Republic. Tropical humidity from the sea fed the swirling air mass. It pulled thunderheads across Hispaniola's eastern plains toward Mona Passage.

Torrents of rain pounded the Dominican Republic and the runoff drove rising streams and rivers toward the sea. Cool and unsalted rain water surged into the ocean where it sank invisibly beneath warmer salt water. A great freshwater river plowed into the sea from the Dominican Republic.

New riverlets of rain water rushed down the steep mountain sides of the Cordillera Central Mountains, ten thousand feet high in the central Dominican Republic. It washed eastward across the marshy lowlands and into the Bay of Samana. The surge of fresh water picked up the rotting remains of Buddy Thurston which stank on the gritty beach. With a smile on his face, the seaman had blown himself out of *Sam Houston* exactly 48 hours earlier.

In the darkness at 10:00 Atlantic Standard Time, the little flood carried Buddy Thurston, Torpedoman's Mate, back into the crashing surf. Rolling waves beat his bloated body upon the sandy bottom in the shallows. The grains of sand like ground glass shredded his pealing skin. A storm-driven riptide dragged the slimy gray lump toward the deep water of Mona Passage where the sailor would become a banquet for shrimp and plankton.

Sam Houston made way 800 feet deep on her westerly course 70 miles north of Plata Borinquen, Puerto Rico's northwest corner. With 24,000 feet of water under her keel, SSN-609 approached the western rim of the Puerto Rico Trench which straddles Mona Passage.

The officer of the deck, half way through the midwatch, spoke softly to the boatswain's mate of the watch.

"Inform the captain that we're crossing Point Borinquen by inertial." The submarine navigated by her Sperry Marine ring laser inertial navigation system. The MK-49 MARLIN translated every minute change of course and speed into a computerized most probable position. The young officer assumed that Captain Milhaus was resting in his cabin. The CO had not slept for almost 20 hours. "The captain should be in quarters. We can head south after clearing the point."

"Aye, Sir."

Running so deep, the submarine was well below the surface turbulence and she enjoyed smooth seakeeping although the sea boiled above her.

When the petty officer did not find the CO in the captain's narrow cabin, he knocked softly on the wardroom door.

"Come," a tired voice said on the other side. The seaman entered officers' country slowly. He found the CO sitting with Dr. Dugan whose brown shirt looked freshly pressed. It was hard for the seaman to take his eyes off the woman with the black eye.

"With Mr. McMillan's respects, Sir. We're passing Point Borinquen."

"Very well," the CO said firmly. "At the OOD's discretion, alter course to one-eight-zero. Continue to make turns for 30 knots at 800 feet."

"One-eight-zero, 30 knots and 800 feet, Captain. Thank you, Sir. Ma'am."

"Carry on," the weary CO nodded. He had not dragged himself out of his metal chair.

The seaman closed the wardroom door behind him when he headed aft to the control room.

"That's all I know so far, Captain." The doctor shuffled her logs and watch bills. "Thurston and Hendrix were both in the same DCC party. There were seven other men with them. I left Dr. Shaffer half an hour ago. After he tests the last watch for uric acid, he's going to review the medical reports, if any, for that DCC evolution. Maybe something will turn up to link the planesman and Frazier with that drill."

"You've been on board my ship for how long, Commander Dugan? Thirty-four hours, give or take? And you're still looking for coincidences?"

Captain Milhaus could not conceal his impatience. He rose, walked to the coffee pot, and started to refill his mug. When he realized that his cup was still full, he poured the cold liquid down the small sink before he filled the cup with fresh. Then he set the hot cup on the sink ledge. He laid a hand on either side of the steaming cup, bowed his head, and did not turn to face the physician.

"I haven't aborted a mission in twenty years at sea. Now we're ready to change course to leave our assigned station to beat a retreat back to Roosevelt Roads." He turned, stooped with fatigue, and glared down into the woman's smooth face.

"I'm retreating from an enemy I cannot see but which has invaded my ship. Three men are dead. My planesman is now a slobbering lunatic. And you have discovered that two of the casualties were on a fire drill together? A damned fire drill? None of the other men on that drill are symptomatic yet. Is that the best you and Dr. Shaffer can give me?"

Jessica stopped her thoughts before they could flow intemperately from her face.

"That's all we have, Captain."

Before the CO could respond to the color rising in her face, another knock on the wardroom door interrupted them.

"Come," the CO sighed. Lieutenant Shaffer entered.

"Captain; Dr. Dugan."

"Coffee, Stan?"

"No thank you, Sir. Has Dr. Dugan briefed you on Hendrix and Thurston?"

"She has. What did you learn about the last watch?"

"Nothing, Captain. Everyone checked out fine: no sign of elevated uric acid levels."

"Good. What about your patients?"

"Seaman Richards is resting. I released Lieutenant Wright but ordered him to remain in quarters for a day or two. His uric acid levels are normal and his HPRT serum levels are normal. No sign of Lesch-Nyhan contamination at all. But I'll continue to watch him."

"All right. I'll drop by to see Mr. Wright tomorrow. We'll be leaving the trench any time now. You people keep on this thing." Captain Milhaus looked down at Dr. Dugan. "If you can crack this contamination and resolve it, we still have time to return to our position and continue this mission."

"Yes, Captain," Jessica Dugan nodded. Her voice was cold and dry.

"Yes, well, I'll be in engineering if you need me. Mister MacMillan has the night order book."

"Captain," Dr. Shaffer said gently, "when did you sleep last?"

The CO paused and grinned weakly.

"I'm fine, Stan. We all need to drive on just now."

The standing physician frowned and said nothing. The captain stepped into the passageway and closed the door softly. Lieutenant Shaffer joined Jessica at the table.

"What's up, Stan?" Jessica read the distraction on the GMO's face.

"When I went through the pharmacy, I found that substantial quantities of allopurinol and colchicine were . . . missing. Someone is pilfering the drugs."

Jessica rocked back in her chair. Her forehead creased as the words sunk in.

"Who has the key, Stan?"

"There is no key except for the narcotics locker. This isn't exactly a prison, you know. Besides, we have half a dozen pharmacist's mates on board who are trained to give medication and dress wounds when I'm not available or during real casualties at sea. We can't lock up routine pharmaceuticals. The pharmacist's mates all have keys to the Schedule III drugs. But the allopurinol and colchicine have never been secured."

"Oh. What do you recommend?"

"For starters, I'll post security personnel in the pharmacy. Maybe whoever is helping himself will come back. He may be able to provide some information on who else is taking prophylactic doses of medication. May be some connection to the contamination."

"Yes. But those drugs wouldn't inhibit Lesch-Nyhan if someone were infected."

"I know. But the crew might not understand that."

"Maybe not. But none of the infected people—Hendrix, Frazier, Seaman Richards—showed any symptoms of LaCrosse or dengue fever."

"They wouldn't, Jessica. We are using retroviruses to carry the Lesch-Nyhan HPRT inhibitor gene. The viral vectors have been denatured; they no longer infect their host. They're just the messenger. Anyone bitten by the mosquito vector would not show symptoms of anything except Lesch-Nyhan."

"Clever," Jessica Dugan sighed into her coffee.

"Someone thought so at Fort Detrick," Lt. Shaffer nodded.

When the wardroom creaked and tipped slightly to the side, Dr. Dugan looked hard into her associate's tired eyes. She gripped the sides of the table bolted to the deck.

"It's all right, Jessica. We're turning south. The sail makes us bank to the outside of a turn. She'll level out in a moment."

As *Sam Houston* entered a turn to her port side and southward, water hit her tall sail structure and pushed it north. The sail tipped back toward the outside of the turn's arc. After ten seconds, the tabletop and the deck rolled level.

"The helm must be making the course change in increments. That reduces flow noise over the hull in case the Cubans are really out there listening for us. Flow noise is a serious risk when we're ripping through the water this fast. Any turbulence creates pressure pulses that passive sonar can hear."

Jessica nodded. She recovered her cheer and confidence quickly.

SSN-609 had made a five-degree heading change as she eased out of the trench to round Puerto Rico. Gradual course changes would bring her about to a southward heading over half an hour.

"Why don't you continue to check your sick bay records, Stan. I want to take a look at the BL-2 personnel records here." She laid a hand atop a pile of files.

"The laboratory? I can't imagine how we would get a contamination leak from BL-2. After all, it's the least restricted of the three labs. Nothing goes to BL-2 unless it's sterile and denatured."

"I know. But it also has the least rigid quarantine regimen. Can't hurt to take a look. Are the lab people AMRIID or Navy?"

"Both. All three labs have Army and Navy technicians. The Army boys received a crash course in basic submarine science, emergency drills, damage control, and escape procedures, while *Sam Houston* was laid up for her two-month refit before she was decommissioned and sent out here. About a fourth of the laboratory crewmen are from the Army Medical Research Institute of Infectious Diseases, Fort Detrick, Maryland. The rest are from the Naval Biosciences Lab at Oakland. They all seem to get along pretty well for an interservice crew."

"Okay. I'll just browse the lab bills and then lay aft to walk through one more time."

"Fine." Lt. Shaffer rose and dumped his cold coffee into the sink. He spoke through a yawn. "I'll look in on Lieutenant Wright and then go below to sick bay." He stifled another yawn. "Sorry, Jessica. Wonder what the weather's doing upstairs? It's real easy to forget that there's wind and water somewhere above us."

He smiled down at the dark-haired woman.

Jessica Dugan did not smile. She lowered her face toward the station bill describing every laboratory assignment and position.

"I never forget," she said softly.

At 0230 UTC, *El Tiburon* cruised 300 feet deep down the northeast coast of the Dominican Republic. *El Tiburon* made way on a southeast heading where the coast curves southward toward Mona Passage. The Cuban ship made 15 knots, 55 nautical miles due north of Cabo Engano, the easternmost tip of Hispaniola. She headed over the western rim of the Puerto Rico Trench.

"No return on the fathometer, Capitan."

"Very well," Captain Barcena nodded to his diving officer. "Quartermaster?"

"MPP here, Capitan." The quartermaster pointed to his chart on the maneuvering board. "Nineteen degrees fifty minutes north by sixty-eight degrees fifteen minutes west. We're over the trench with about 8,900 meters under the keel. Too deep for the fathometer to get a reading on the bottom."

"Very well, QM."

The ship's dead-reckoning most probable position placed *El Tiburon* 50 nautical miles west of *Sam Houston* which was cruising 500 feet deeper.

Martinez Barcena nursed his third cup of black coffee in the two and a half hours since his last two-hour nap. He felt refreshed but vaguely uneasy. He knew that every mile that passed without contact with the American submarine increased the odds that contact would be made during the next mile.

"Sonar?" the CO said softly across the narrow control room.

"Negative contact, Capitan."

"Very well. Self-monitor status?"

"All quiet, Sir. Very slight flow noise."

The captain kept a careful sonar watch on his own ship's noise. If he could hear it through his passive sonar, so could the Americans if they were there at all.

"Wait one, Sir," the teenager at the sonar screen said tensely. His right hand pressed his headphones closer to his head. The television screen looked like a vertical row of video hourglasses where sand trickled quickly from the top to the bottom of the monitor.

"Distant signal, Sir. Very weak. Brief contact, dissipating now."

Captain Barcena walked over to the seated sonar man and he leaned over his shoulder to study the screen.

"Impression?"

The seaman squinted at the monitor.

"Low frequency contact, Sir. Two or three seconds only. Definitely not background noise."

"A ship?"

"Don't think so. Maybe a bird hitting the surface. The weather could cause that. Or maybe . . ." the sailor hesitated.

"Maybe a sonobuoy?"

"Possibly, Capitan."

The gray-haired CO stood up straight. He closed both hands around his warm coffee mug.

"So. Do you think they can hear us?"

"Not likely, Sir. Our signature is very quiet. I'm monitoring our noise very closely." The young man sounded uncomfortable. His captain gently touched his shoulder.

"Yes, I know you're listening to us. Just keep me posted."

"Yes, Capitan."

The CO walked toward his executive officer who stood beside the officer of the deck.

"Deeper, Capitan?" the XO was calm. He had been a submariner for two years—four times his captain's experience under water.

"Battery report?"

"Eighty-five percent, Sir," the diving officer answered over his shoulder.

"Very well. Take her down to 200 meters. Mind your ambient sensors."

"Yes, Capitan. We'll generate a print-out once we stabilize."

"All right. Take her down. Maintain present course and speed."

El Tiburon's bow dropped slightly as the diving planes drove the ship deeper. The diving officer kept close watch on the ballast and trimming tanks. A low pitched vibration rumbled through the submarine for ten seconds as she descended. Then the ship steadied at 600 feet as the bow rose back to level cruise.

"Temperature inversion, Capitan," the XO said softly as the ship shuddered. *El Tiburon* broke through a layer of turbulent water where a mass of warm Caribbean water sat on top of colder, deep water.

A rush of air could be heard just beyond the control room inner hull. High-pressure air blew into the compensating tank on each side of the submarine to trim her depth-keeping. The CO grimaced visibly as the sound filled the compartment for five seconds.

The sonar man could feel his captain's dark eyes on the back of his perspiring neck.

"All quiet now, Sir."

"Very well."

*   *   *

"Better call the CO, Mr. McMillan." The sonar man blinked at his video monitor as he spoke softly into his intercom microphone over the 27MC sonar/radar circuit. He spoke to SSN-609's control room in the next compartment.

The pattern of drifting video pixels on the screen had disrupted for seven seconds and then returned to smooth bands of normal, ambient ocean noise.

Kurt Milhaus needed three minutes to work his way forward from the after engineering spaces. He cut through the BL-2 laboratory in Deck One's empty missile bay.

"Good evening, Captain," the bleary-eyed technician said from his sonar console. It was almost 11:00 above in a Caribbean night.

"What do you have, Chief?"

"Maybe a contact, Sir. Here."

The master chief sonar technician, STCM rating, replayed the perpetual video tape record of his sighting. *Sam Houston*'s passive sonar fed its data into the ship's computer which memorized the last hour's contacts: mostly fish sounds, reverberation off temperature and salinity layers, and the sub's own flow noise of disturbed water. Captain Milhaus squinted at the screen where the columns of static dissolved for five seconds before reforming neatly.

"I cleaned it up as best I could, Sir. Must be sheet cavitation. Two screws, maybe three. Range maxed out at over 60 miles off the scope. Don't think it's *Hayler*."

The CO glanced at his wristwatch: 0245 UTC.

"No. *Hayler* can't be closer than 150 miles by this time." Kurt Milhaus sighed deeply. "The Cubans, Chief?"

"Well, Sir, it was definitely sheet cavitation. No beat but maybe ten seconds of blade rate. If it's a sub, she must have transited an inversion. Here's the sea condition feed."

The STCM displayed sea chemistry readouts.

"Hmm. Down to 30 PPT, Captain. Must be raining up top. That would explain it. I have to call it a probable submarine." Sensors along the lines where sea water entered the submarine on the way to the condensers monitored salinity: salt concentration in the water, measured in parts-per-thousand.

"Very well, Chief. I'll alert CIC. You keep me posted. I

want to go back to engineering to watch the next condenser test."

"Aye, Sir."

Captain Milhaus crouched through a non-watertight hatchway into the control room which had just become the combat information center.

"Blue room has a probable sub contact, Lieutenant. Rig for quiet in the boat and general quarters. Make turns for 20 knots."

"Slow to 20, Captain. GQ and condition zebra."

On the OOD's command via the ship's IMC public address system, SSN-609 went to wartime conditions. Throughout the ship, all watertight doors were tightly dogged. All seamen not on watch made their way to their bunks to observe quiet conditions.

With all watertight doors closed, SSN-609 functioned as a half-dozen completely isolated compartments cruising in tight formation. Only hatches and fittings painted with a "Z" inside a circle, condition circle-zebra, could be opened for a moment to allow food to pass or crewmen to use the head. Guards were posted at all hatches to assure their closure. *Sam Houston* was now a warship.

Slowing to 20 knots would improve the sensitivity of the half-mile length of hydrophone cable towed behind the submarine. Half that speed would have been better, but 609 had a rendezvous to make in less than five hours.

Ship propellers work on the same principles as airplane propellers: each blade is a small wing which cuts through a fluid. The blade motion generates an area of low pressure on the back edge of the blade. Since the boiling point of a fluid goes down as the pressure goes down (a cup of boiling water at sea level is hotter than boiling water in Denver), sea water "boils" in the very low pressure of the propeller's sharp edges.

On the low pressure side of the prop, dissolved gas can bubble out of the water. These microscopic bubbles collapse under the pressure of the sea near the tips of the blades. The crushing bubbles make a hissing sound heard for miles by sensitive, passive sonar hydrophones. The faster the blades are rotating, the louder the hiss. When the cavitation bubbles cover the entire blade, it is called sheet cavitation which increases as the blade speed increases.

At low speeds, the cavitation bubbles collapse with a beat sound like a heartbeat under water. Since cavitation beat rides the blade's natural frequency of vibration, it is as unique as a fingerprint. A good ping jockey can name a ship by its beat signature. When the wake behind a propeller is disturbed by other currents or eddies in the water, it creates blade-rate noise.

Cavitation decreases as a submarine submerges into water with greater and greater pressure.

Normal sea water has 32 to 38 parts per thousand (PPT) of dissolved salt. A change in salt concentration by only one PPT will change the speed of sound by about four feet per second, a factor critical to sonar interpretation. Fresh water falling as rain or land run-off alters ocean salinity. A good sonar man knows the chemistry of his surrounding ocean—salinity, pressure and temperature—better than he knows his own body temperature and blood pressure. Of the three variables, water temperature has the greatest effect on underwater sound waves.

Back in BL-2, Jessica Dugan's circulation stopped for an instant when the general quarters alarm sounded in the laboratory. The color drained even from her black eye and from the dark blue bruise on her face. She was suddenly quite aware of a distant flutter at her anus. She swallowed hard and licked new perspiration from her upper lip and a downy mustache.

"You all right, Commander?" a technician asked gently beside the sweating woman.

"Yes, thank you." Her face was pale where it was not bruised.

"Wouldn't worry, Ma'am. Probably just another drill." The seaman's voice betrayed a hint of nerves.

The physician noticed that the seaman was so young, he still had pimples.

"I'm getting ready to run the TEM, if you want to watch." The youthful technician was uncomfortable so close to the woman. Even through her laboratory coat, the boy could smell her fresh dose of powder under her clean brown shirt.

When the technician with the teenage face inhaled deeply, Lt. Commander Dugan blinked.

"Are you feeling okay," she asked with a squint.

"Yes, Ma'am. Sometimes the disinfectants in here plug up

my nose. No problem. Really." He turned abruptly and walked forward to a huge instrument resembling the control room's periscope pedestal. He spoke nervously over his shoulder. "Do you have a TEM at your facility?"

"Four. But nothing this compact."

Dr. Dugan followed the third-class petty officer to the instrument, a transmission electron microscope. He sat down in front of the television monitor with Jessica standing at his side.

"It was built especially for us. It's about half the size of normal TEM equipment, but has no deficit in resolution or magnification. We just have to watch the coolant more carefully down here."

"Oh. You using negative stain?"

"Yes, Ma'am. I just finished with the specimen. We use routine 4% PTA and 1/2% UA. The UA works really well with ribonucleoproteins."

"You can work when the ship is at general quarters?" The woman was fascinated by the sailor's calm.

"Sure. Round the clock, three shifts per day. We only close up down here when real shooting starts." He had to smile when he saw the woman shudder. He tried not to look up at her breasts.

The potassium phosphotungstate (PTA) and uranyl acetate (UA) stain virus specimens. The background is made opaque to the electron beam. The stain is absorbed by the virus body and the electron beam is absorbed by the stained areas and photographed. Viral fragments are magnified tens of thousands of times.

Jessica Dugan noticed a small vial near the instrument.

"Glutaraldehyde?"

"Yes," the youth mumbled as he fiddled with the electronic controls. "We have to use it with these specimens after we apply the 1/2% Formvar to the dried, viral suspension to form the membrane layer."

The doctor creased her forehead as she looked down at the technician.

"But glutaraldehyde is used with a Bunyaviridae sample."

"That's right, Commander." He looked up, trying to keep his eyes on her face.

"That's LaCrosse, isn't it?"

"Yes, Doctor. But don't worry. It's stone cold dead. We don't have any live or unfixed tissue cultures up here in BL-2. The nasty stuff stays below in BL-3."

She noted the speed and skill with which he worked the electron microscope's controls.

"You do that like you've done it for years," she smiled.

"Not hardly. Took a crash course before this cruise in Minneapolis and at MIT for two months."

"IHG and Whitehead?"

"Yep. I really enjoyed it, actually. Most of my advanced work at sub school was electronics. Guess that's why they gave me the TEM."

The University of Minnesota is the home of the Institute of Human Genetics. The Whitehead Institute for Biomedical Research is based at Massachusetts Institute of Technology.

"Once I got into this bug stuff, I wanted to visit Pitt, but there wasn't time. But I guess they taught me all I need to know." The technician smiled with his face pressed against the double stereo eyepieces of the aiming optics.

The University of Pittsburgh's Technology Center for Biotechnology has received research grants from the Army Chemical Research and Development Command.

"You certainly know how to fly this equipment."

"Thank you, Commander."

He worked his console for half a minute without looking up.

"There. Seventy thousand magnification."

When he heard nothing, he looked up. Jessica Dugan was gone. The sailor shrugged and leaned toward the eye pieces. He imagined that he could still smell the woman in air sickly sweet with disinfectant vapors.

Dr. Dugan stood at the end of the laboratory where the bulkhead was covered deck to overhead with books and manuals. In her concentration, she forgot that she was 800 feet under the Caribbean in a ship at battle stations. The bulkhead clock showed 3:00 in the morning UTC, 11:00 at night on the surface.

She leafed through a National Institutes of Health manual titled *Laboratory Safety Monograph*. The document known as the LSM lists chemicals handled by the BL-2 crew and procedures for monitoring crew health through blood samples.

She carefully studied the handwritten appendix detailing crew injuries and illnesses since leaving Newport News nearly two months earlier. There were only two entries: a bruised forehead from bouncing off a microscope when the ship had lurched near the surface and one head cold which Dr. Shaffer had treated with decongestants and a one-day holiday off duty. She returned the manual and walked aft, stopping at another intense young technician.

"Commander," the man blinked from his lab stool bolted to the deck.

"Good morning, Mister. Running the HPLC?"

"Just finished." He looked up from the high-pressure liquid chromatography instrument. "Don't think I'll start another until we stand down from general quarters. No use cranking up if I have to interrupt the cycle if it's not a drill."

"No. You're quite right. Just looked over the LSM. Pretty healthy crew."

The petty officer leaned back and looked up at the woman. Half a dozen heads turned to watch them. Ten men manned the night watch in BL-2.

"Yeh. Once old Magnet Butt went down to BL-3."

"What?"

"Sorry. I mean Mister Walsh—Jack Walsh. He kind of tends to bump into things. Used to say the equipment liked to bump into him; so we started calling him Magnet Butt."

"Did he ever get hurt in the lab?"

"Nothing more than bruised once or twice, Commander."

"Good. Well, do whatever you're doing. I'm just passing through."

"Yes, Ma'am."

Dr. Dugan hesitated.

"BL-3 you said?"

"For what?"

"Old Magnet Ass."

The sailor looked up and smiled.

"Yes, Commander. BL-3. But he should be off duty by now, most likely racked out when we're at GQ."

"He can sleep through general quarters?"

"Oh yeh. Keeps an even strain better than anyone else I know."

"Thanks."

"Yes, Ma'am."

Dr. Dugan walked forward toward the bulkhead separating the laboratory from the control room. After removing her lab coat and dumping it in the decontamination bin, she asked the Laboratory Director for permission to leave, which was granted. When the watertight door swung open slowly, she entered the muted red glow of the CIC. XO Pappy Perlmutter held the conn beside the standing officer of the deck.

Lt. Commander Perlmutter walked over to the physician.

"Mister Perlmutter," the doctor said stiffly in the sudden gravity of the control room.

"Doctor," the XO nodded. "We have a sonar contact which may be that Cuban submarine." He had not waited for her question. Her tense face was enough. "We can outrun her if we have to. Our flank speed is twice that of old Russian boats. Not to worry." He smiled warmly.

"Thanks. Am I still free to roam about?"

"For the moment." The XO tried to sound cheerful. "We will maintain quiet conditions for the time being. That means even quieter than usual. All non-essential personnel are confined to quarters under a GQ evolution. Seamen are also posted at all watertight hatches to maintain our integrity. Other than that, you are welcome to carry on."

"Thanks. Where's the captain?"

"Engineering. Scoping out the condenser test being run. Still have that damned water hammer in main steam. Seems to be pretty well dried out for now; but the old man's watching the test to put his mind at ease, I guess." The XO smiled. "It's the skipper's boat, you know."

The woman nodded.

"I'll be down in sick bay if you need me."

"All right. You on to something?"

"Don't know. Just want to touch base with Stan on his medical logs."

"Okay. Drive on, Jessica."

The XO turned his back on her before she could reply. Jessica Dugan noticed that the young sailors were not interested in her as they hunched over consoles, environmental control displays, and fire control systems. The tenseness around her nudged the sense of claustrophobia which she had managed to ignore for her 35 hours on board SSN-609. She wiped her forehead with the palm of her hand as she stepped down the companionway and held the railings down to Two Deck. She continued forward to sick bay's cold walls of regulation haze gray paint.

"Good morning, Jessica," Lieutenant Shaffer smiled. His tired face was as gray as his little hospital.

"What's up?" she asked toward the busy GMO who wore green scrubs.

"Just going through the drill, Jessica. Sick bay is the primary BDA. All battle dressing areas are made ready for casualties during GQ."

The physician was stacking trays of instruments and bandages as dictated by the ship's Battle Bill of GQ assignments and duties.

"We do triage throughout the ship at the BDA stations. Only critical cases are brought directly to sick bay if the way is clear."

"Clear?"

"Yes. Should compartments flood between here and a BDA, the corpsmen and pharmacist's mates are trained to do minor surgical procedures in the battle dressing areas."

"Oh." Jessica felt suddenly cold all over. She crossed her arms to hide her trembling.

The GMO paused.

"Don't worry, Jessica. We may have only a half-complement skeleton crew down here, but they're the cream of the crop."

"Sure, Stan. I just came down from BL-2. You have the medical log from that space?"

"On the wall rack, there. What you looking for?"

"Not sure. One of the lab techs mentioned a petty officer Walsh who is prone to accidents."

"Magnet Ass?" the GMO grinned. "Best electron microscope driver I ever saw. His feet are just too big."

"You know him by name?"

"I know everyone here by name. Hell, I've probably dressed every man's hemorrhoids or palpated everyone's prostate at least once on this cruise—except maybe for the captain. He doesn't much care for medics, I guess."

Dr. Dugan smiled as she pulled the BL-2 and BL-3 medical files from the bulkhead. Each bound volume was an inch thick. Leafing through revealed mainly empty pages.

"Pretty clean, Stan."

"Of course. Between their training and the tight ship run by Colonel Epson in the labs, we just don't have many casualties. Check the BL-3 records for five weeks ago. That rings a bell with Walsh."

The doctor thumbed through the manual.

"How long was Walsh in BL-2?"

"Not more than two weeks before he was transferred down to BL-3."

"Why was he transferred?"

"The colonel's request. He wanted the best when they started the microscopy of the RNA splicing."

"Oh. Here's one. 'Walsh: bruised left wrist.' What's this all about?"

The GMO stepped over to the file in the doctor's moist hands.

"He rammed the corner of a lab bench. Since it broke the skin, I wrote it up. Ran serum tests daily for ten days looking for infection, uric acid levels, and the like. Nothing turned up."

"Hmm." She looked up from the records. "Anything on the missing allopurinol?"

"Nothing. But it's definitely missing. I cross-checked every dose administered since Newport News. We're missing enough to treat half a dozen men for gouty arthritis for a month."

"A month? That would go back even before Hendrix was killed."

"Yes, by about two weeks."

"Okay. Mind if I take these with me to the wardroom?"

"Help yourself. What do you expect to find?"

"I don't know. I don't know where else to look for the contamination leak. Has to be transfection between crewmen somehow."

"Maybe. But I went through every record down here when Buddy was killed. Found zip. Maybe I'm just too close to it to see the key. Hope you do better."

"Stan, I don't mean to second-guess you on this."

"I want you to, Commander. This is my watch, too, you know. I hope you find whatever I might have missed."

"Thanks. I'll let you know."

"Good. And Jessica, walk softly."

She smiled.

"Pappy already told me that."

The GMO nodded and continued to unpack his instrument trays.

Cuban admirals Esquino and Perez waited impatiently outside the office of Defense Minister Raul Castro. Outside the darkened window it was a quarter past 10:00 on a warm spring night. Rain pounded the black windowpane. Admiral Esquino paced while Vice Admiral Perez, Chief of Naval Operations, sucked hard on his second cigar.

"The Vice President will see you now," a senior grade lieutenant nodded as he laid the telephone receiver down.

"Thank you." Admiral Perez deposited his cigar in the ashtray beside the last inch of his first smoke.

The admirals were greeted at the doorway by the Minister of Defense.

"Sorry to keep you waiting, gentlemen. Do come in."

The two tired sailors took seats opposite Minister Castro's desk. The politician seemed equally fatigued and distracted. His right ear was remarkably red as if he had pressed a telephone receiver against it for a long time.

"Admiral Perez. Admiral Esquino. Thanks for flying back here so late. But I wanted to brief both of you personally."

The two sailors with their drooping, tired eyes nodded. They had arrived in La Habana exactly twelve hours earlier, were dispatched to the naval base at Cienfuegos, and were then summoned back to the capital 90 minutes ago. Neither flag officer had slept or changed his shirt in 20 hours. Both seamen were wet with perspiration borne of a helicopter ride through driving rain which hit the chopper's sides like steel shot.

"I just spent fifteen minutes on the phone with my brother. El Commandante has been briefed again by Consul Hernandez in Moscow." The defense minister sighed deeply. "It would seem that your reservations on *El Tiburon*'s mission, Admiral Esquino, have carried the day after all."

The two seamen glanced at each other and then back at Raul Castro.

"Based upon the last word out of Russia, my brother has reluctantly agreed to recall Capitan Barcena. Unfortunately, we cannot raise him by radio at the moment."

"Has any action been reported, Mr. Minister?"

"No, Admiral. However, our elint post at Lourdes has monitored quite a bit of low frequency traffic in the Caribbean throughout the day. I believe more than ever that the Americans are operating a submarine in this region."

Lourdes, near Havana, is the home of Cuba's center for electronic intelligence ("elint" to the intelligence community)—the most sophisticated Communist listening post outside the former Soviet Union's borders.

"Be that as it may, we must recall *El Tiburon* as soon as possible. If communications fail from here, what's the fastest vessel you can dispatch from the Eastern Flotilla at Nicaro, Admiral Perez? We need something we can reposition immediately to the Puerto Rico waters."

"Sounds to me like a job for the Air Force." Vice Admiral Perez shifted his weight which felt doubled by the wearisome pounding of his recent helicopter flight. "If *El Tiburon* is on schedule, she's nearly 500 miles east of Nicaro. One of our aircraft could be on station within an hour. Finding him by ship would take some 16 to 24 hours. That might very well be a full day too late to prevent a contact with the Americans."

Admiral Esquino nodded his assent.

"We thought of that," the Vice President sighed. "Here."

The minister handed a limp sheet of facsimile paper to his Vice Admiral. The officer took it and held it between himself and Admiral Esquino. The two seamen studied a faxed weather map generated by the military's atmospheric bureau.

The map depicted the Caribbean Sea with a thick black line printed across the Dominican Republic. The line cutting across the entire map was a weather front lying over central Hispaniola. Under the weather depiction map was another map showing surface weather reports from observers at the major airports scattered across Haiti and the Dominican Republic. Each station in western Hispaniola behind the weather front showed low clouds, hard rain, and strong winds. East of the front line across the Dominican Republic eastward to Puerto Rico, the airports were reporting 40-knot gusts of wind driving unseasonal hail.

"I see what you mean, Mr. Minister," Vice Admiral Perez frowned. "Can't send an aircraft into that if she has to fly on the deck to drop a messenger buoy to communicate with El Tiburon. The aircraft would be skimming the surface in

40-knot winds gusting to 50 knots and slamming into hail at 300 knots. She'd be pulverized."

Admiral Esquino released his grip on a corner of the long sheet and his colleague handed it back to the defense minister.

The weary vice admiral blinked dully. He gathered his wits slowly.

"Well, Mr. Minister, we do have one of our nine hydrofoil fast attack ships in harbor. The Turya class vessel can make 35 knots. But you're talking 480 nautical miles one way. Her range is only 600 miles. She could get there, but could not get home. Two of our Konis are standing off Nicaro tonight. One could get out within two hours. The frigate can make 27 knots at flank speed. But her best range of 1,800 miles requires a max speed of only 14 knots. We could dispatch her at flank bell and bring her home more slowly, of course."

Both the Koni class frigates and the hydrofoils were gifts from the Soviets. The last hydrofoil patrol boat arrived in 1983 and carries a crew of 30 in her 250-ton hull. The 1,900-ton frigates arrived in Cuba between 1981 and 1988. Their 110-man complement has massed batteries of surface-to-air SA-N4 missiles, four 3-inch guns, two RBU-6000 antisubmarine mortars, and a sonar suite making Cuba's three Koni class ships a formidable force.

Admiral Esquino leaned forward and spoke thoughtfully.

"Mr. Minister, shouldn't we be concerned that a fully outfitted frigate might be seen as far more provocative to Washington than a small patrol boat?"

"Indeed, Admiral. Quite true. But we can't have a patrol craft run out of fuel on the return leg, 200 miles from home. And this weather would be too dangerous for the smaller patrol boat. You gentlemen know that better than I."

The defense minister spoke softly.

"Admiral Perez, dispatch the Koni immediately. Have her steam eastward as far as Puerto Rico. She is to use all communications means at her disposal to recall Capitan Barcena. I don't care about security. I don't care if we tip our hand to the Americans. If they are cruising those waters, then we have just as much right to patrol international waters. Just get him to come about and return to Cienfuegos."

"Understood, Mr. Minister," Admiral Perez nodded more

wakefully. "Might I suggest that we wait for the weather to break, however? There's a full gale blowing off the Dominican Republic right now." He looked sideways at Admiral Esquino. "We just flew through it, Sir. And that was on the back side of the front where the storm was dissipating. I wouldn't want to fly through the leading edge of the system tonight."

It was 10:30—half an hour before midnight, Puerto Rico time, 0330 UTC.

The minister nodded with sympathy on his tired face.

"I must rely upon our ship and your crewmen, Admiral Perez. We don't have time to wait."

The admiral's back stiffened.

"Very well, Mr. Minister. The ship will sail within two hours."

Vice President Castro stood up, sighing as he rose.

"Good. Thank you both. I'll remain here at the ministry until you confirm contact with *El Tiburon*. Admiral Esquino, you can monitor the situation from the submarine base down at Cienfuegos."

Admiral Esquino's face seemed to grow more pale at the thought of going back up into the furious sky.

"Yes, Mr. Minister," the sailor said softly. "We also need to know about our rules of engagement. What if the frigate is fired upon?"

"She will defend herself, Admiral," the minister said firmly.

Fidel Castro's brother led his officers to the closed doorway.

Vice Admiral Perez could contain his curiosity no longer. "The Russians must have really leaned on Hernandez. With respect, Mr. Minister."

The Minister of Defense for the Revolutionary Armed Forces shrugged his sagging shoulders.

"*Leaned* would be the operative word, Admiral. Good night, gentlemen."

"Contact, Capitan."

"Submarine?"

"Seventy-five percent probability, Sir. Dead ahead, I'd say. Faint pressure pulse, but definitely man-made."

"Surface shipping?"

"Not likely, Capitan."

"Very well."

Martinez Barcena straightened after hunching over his sonar man's console.

"Our position, QM?"

"We've rounded Hispaniola, Sir. Heading one-seven-five, making turns for 15 knots."

"Thank you."

"Battle stations, Sir?"

The officer of the deck tried to restrain the excitement borne of his youth and his inexperience.

The silver-haired CO hesitated. He glanced around his quiet control room.

"Not yet, Lieutenant. The target is still moving away from us. We can ride his wake for a while. Our mission is not to provoke him. He shouldn't hear us at this range."

"Yes, Capitan." The OOD turned to face his men who sat in the forward section of the compartment where they steered *El Tiburon* southward into Mona Passage. The ride was smooth 600 feet beneath the turbulent surface. At the northern end of the passage, she sailed across Mona Canyon just south of the Puerto Rico Trench. The canyon's black water was 23,000 feet deep, nearly one mile shallower than the trench.

The Cuban vessel's passive sonar could get an approximate bearing on the source of the pressure pulse ahead. But passive sonar cannot produce range estimates.

The CO looked up at the bulkhead clock which showed 3:30 in the morning, UTC.

"Capitan?" the sonar man spoke softly over his shoulder.

"Ensign?"

"There it goes again, Sir. Must be a plumbing noise of some sort. He either can't hear it himself or he has no idea we're out here with him. He would be more careful otherwise."

The CO nodded as he looked down into his empty coffee mug.

"Maybe, Ensign."

FIFTEEN

16 MARCH; 0345 UTC

"SONAR, THIS is the Captain."

"Sonar, aye," a petty officer second class said softly into his microphone and headset over the 27MC intercom circuit used for communications to sonar or radar operations.

"Did you hear that?"

"Affirmative, Captain. Loud and clear, I'm afraid."

"Understood, Sonar." The sonar man heard Captain Milhaus click off the line 300 feet behind him in *Sam Houston*'s aft auxiliary spaces.

"CIC, aye," the telephone talker said where he stood beside Pappy Perlmutter. He listened to the CO over the 42MC circuit dedicated to coordinating tactical functions in the combat information center. "Aye aye, Captain. Right to two-seven-zero, turns for eight knots. Maintain five minutes."

The executive officer beside the officer of the deck faced the telephone man. Both men had winced at each other two minutes earlier when the control room was filled with what sounded like a light hammer beating against a distant steam line. The ping-ping-ping of the water hammer tormenting the reactor's coolant circulation was audible through the dull-sounding steel hull.

"Commander, the CO orders 2-7-0 with turns for 8 knots for a five-minute sonar sweep."

253

"Very well," the XO nodded. "Make it so, Lieutenant." Lieutenant Commander Perlmutter turned toward the telephone talker. "Advise the blue room to execute a passive sweep."

"Aye, Sir."

The control room banked slightly to the outside of the turn as SSN-609 entered her 90-degree heading change from southward to westward. Changing course to run perpendicular to Mona Passage would also drag across the passage the half mile of hydrophone cable trailing out along the hull. This would enable the BQR-15 passive sonar to listen to the submarine's own wake and to hear any noise radiating from the northern end of the passage. The turbulent water just behind the submarine's single propeller prevented accurate listening directly behind the ship, her sonar blind spot. By running at 8 knots—optimum, passive sonar speed—the sonar technicians could listen to sounds running up and down the passage.

The OOD stood behind the seated diving officer of the watch who closely monitored the third-class petty officers manning the stern planes and fairwater planes (the "conning tower" wings) to maintain depth and the rudder to make the turn.

"Have sonar confirm when the cable has settled down." The XO spoke to the telephone man.

"Aye, Sir."

The cable would whip through the sea in a corkscrew arc as SSN-609 banked into her turn.

Sam Houston had slowed as she made her gradual change of heading. Back in the aft maneuvering room, the throttle man had commanded the nuclear reactor's control rods to descend into the atomic caldron. The rods absorbed most of the careening neutrons which reduced the number of subatomic collisions. The hot leg water cooled and the steam generator cooled enough to reduce the torrent of steam rushing into the turbine. The single propeller turned slower than during the ship's high-speed sprint out of the trench.

The BQR-15, digital, multi-beam passive sonar listened to the ocean through 2,624 feet of 3.7-inch thick cable towing three dozen hydrophones. The whole affair had been borrowed from an early *Los Angeles* class attack submarine to bring SSN-609 up to date.

"Sonar reports negative flow noise, Commander," the telephone man reported.

"Thank you," the XO nodded.

The cuprous oxide paint on the submarine reduced the amount of marine life which clings to steel hulls. Tiny crustaceans can make a submarine sound like a submerged dumpster when they disturb the smooth flow of water over the ship.

Lt. Commander Perlmutter walked through a thin joiner door into the blue-lit sonar room where half a dozen seamen crouched over their consoles.

The sonar men listened to the 1 kilohertz, very low frequency end of the noise spectrum.

"No one is snorkeling, Commander."

"All right."

The passive sonar which can only listen and cannot "ping" can hear another sub's snorkel machinery and the flow noise of a snorkel tube slicing the surface from 125 statute miles away (108 nautical miles).

SSN-609 cruised slowly westward across the width of Mona Passage. The passive sonar trailing behind *Sam Houston* had hydrophones spaced in equal increments for the length of the cable. When the pressure pulse of a sound wave strikes the cable at an angle, the pulse moves like a sonic wall across the long cable. The sound-wave front will bang into each individual hydrophone at slightly different instants of time as it moves along the cable. Shipboard computers then reduce the succession of impulses into two possible bearings to the source of the sound wave. Computers work with the Directivity Index which equates the intensity of the incoming sound wave to a relationship between the length of towed cable and the wave length of the sound waves.

Even though the computer can sense the probable direction from which the sound wave is coming, passive sonar cannot tell whether the glancing passage of a sound wave is coming in from the left or from the right. The only way a listening submarine can resolve this "bearing ambiguity" is to change course again and take a reading from a different angle.

"Sounds like we're just under a transient halocline, Sir. Must be from rain on the surface. I noticed a change in salinity readings over the last hour, too."

Just as the sea has temperature layers or thermoclines which distort underwater sound, there are also layers of different salt concentrations which bend sound waves and confuse sonar systems.

The sonar man studied the video display which cast its eerie blue glow onto his face, the pale face peculiar to all submariners who work for 70 days at a time without the comfort of a single ray of sunlight. The display of grainy patterns resembling drifting sand dunes had ragged edges and open holes.

"Quite a bit of attenuation this morning," the XO frowned. He leaned over the young seaman's shoulder and the staleness of their mutual sweat made for uncomfortable intimacy.

"Yes, Sir. Scattering, mainly. Must be a lot of particulate disturbance outside. Surface must be cooling too quickly from the rain."

The XO only nodded and squinted.

The underwater scattering of sound is caused by reflection of sound off marine life and particles suspended in the ocean.

"Wouldn't want to bet the farm on the FOM just now, Sir."

"No." The executive officer straightened his back, which felt stiff.

The best measure of sonar performance is the equipment's Figure of Merit. The FOM is the maximum allowable degradation of sound or equipment which would still allow at least a 50-50 probability of detecting a sonar contact. The FOM equation relates the strength of a sound wave to natural, outside ocean noise and a factor known as receiving directivity (all values in decibels). Sonar, whether active or passive, is an extremely complex science and a good sonar man has years of experience under his belt. When he's home on leave, his ear instinctively counts the revolutions of the family washing machine and he can tell if it wobbles to the left or to the right. Sonar men acquire an opera diva's perfect pitch.

"What do you have on temperature?" The XO rubbed his eyes. His eyeballs felt dry in the cold blue light.

"I've monitored an inversion on the way down, Commander. It got warmer as we descended. Surface was cooled by the rain."

"Hmm." Pappy Perlmutter labored to focus on the television screens in the sonar compartment. "Potential for a shadow zone?"

"Have to say excellent. Even though I have no contacts out there, I would predict a shadow zone for sure. Only question is whether or not the Cubans can find it, if they're really out there."

"Thank you. I'll advise the captain. Carry on."

"Aye, Sir." The seaman had never taken his eyes from the screen.

The XO returned to the slightly brighter, red-lit CIC. He picked up one of the control room microphones and selected the 2MC, one-way PA link connecting the bridge to the propulsion spaces.

"XO for the captain," Pappy said softly.

He laid the mic down and turned toward the communications man.

"Captain on the horn, Commander."

"Thank you."

The XO picked up the phone.

"Captain, sonar confirms negative contact this heading. Recommend resuming course. Sonar feels that conditions are good for a shadow zone . . . Yes, Sir. . . . Will do, Captain, back to one-seven-five and thirty knots . . . Aye, Sir."

"Resume one-seven-zero, Lieutenant, making turns for thirty."

"Aye, Sir," the OOD said firmly. "One-seven-zero and turns for thirty."

SSN-609 banked to starboard away from the turn as she came about to her southerly heading. The XO and his officer of the deck held their collective breath as word went back to maneuvering for the throttle man to stoke up the reactor. The two officers listened hard for the faraway tapping of water hammer in the steam lines of the reactor's pipeline to the engine room. They did not have to wait long after the throttle man withdrew the control rods from his atomic pile in the shielded reactor compartment.

Pappy Perlmutter shook his head. He said nothing.

Before the OOD could acknowledge the telltale but faint clanking, the forward watertight door to the control room swung open without a sound. Jessica Dugan crouched through quickly. Then a seaman from the other side heaved the door closed. The bridge watch-standers could see the steel hatch dogs all round the door frame turn to clamp the massive hatch closed.

"Commander," she exhaled into the XO's stubbled face. The back of his neck tingled when her warm breath blew into his nostrils and mouth.

It was almost 4:00 in the morning, UTC: midnight in the storm-swept Caribbean 800 feet above them. Throughout the ship, men of the first watch were being relieved by the men assigned to the midwatch which would last until 4:00 in the morning, Atlantic Standard Time.

When 609 shuddered, Dr. Dugan bounced off Pappy Perlmutter's chest. He gently touched her shoulders as she regained her soft-soled footing on the deck.

"What was . . . ?"

"Easy, Jessica. Just a layer of rough water. Probably a temperature change in the sea as we head south through the passage. Water is just like flying: there is always a boundary layer of turbulence between masses of fluid with differing temperatures or pressure gradients." The busy XO steered the terrified woman toward the navigator's maneuvering board. The quartermaster stood close to the navigator.

"What do you have, QM?"

"We're here, Commander, by inertial. Looked like a temp eddie all right."

The quartermaster pointed to his chart of the waters between the Dominican Republic and Puerto Rico. His index finger lay at the northern tip of a triangle which had one point on the Dominican Republic's easternmost point at Punta Cana and one point on Puerto Rico's northwestern corner at Aguadilla. SSN-609 cruised southward some 60 nautical miles north of the line joining the Dominican Republic with Puerto Rico. Just barely into the mouth of Mona Passage, Sam Houston had 18,000 feet of water under her and 800 feet above.

Within only 30 miles, the sea bottom of Mona Canyon had risen nearly two miles closer to SSN-609. The water shallowed out quickly south of the Puerto Rico Trench. By the middle of Mona Passage 60 miles further south, the water would only be 3,000 feet deep with isolated bars and ridges almost breaking the surface. Currents rushing through the passage drift faster and faster as the water becomes progressively shallower. The mutual change in water depth and current makes Mona Passage turbulent and treacherous.

Dr. Dugan caught her breath. Slightly more than an hour at general quarters, the ship changing course, and the watertight doors closed all around her had wet the doctor's khaki shirt from her armpits to her beltline.

"You all right, Doctor?"

"Okay. Thanks, Commander," the doctor smiled gamely. "I'm sorry to be such a nuisance all the time."

Pappy smiled down into her upturned face. He quickly studied the tiny lines around her gray eyes. Her blackened left eye was now more red than purple after 33 hours. Her moist forehead glistened in the red standing lights of the CIC.

"No problem, Doctor. It does get a little close on board when we're buttoned up at GQ. You'll get used to it. Everyone else has."

"Right." She exhaled and Pappy Perlmutter inhaled her warm breath. "Any contact with the Cuban boat?"

"None. But that doesn't mean much. She's diesel-electric if our intelligence people are correct. If she's running submerged on electric motors, she'd be dead quiet, especially in this noisy passage. As the sea gets shallower, sound bounces off the bottom. That reverberation attenuates the sound and masks it from our sonar. So does the generally noisy background of the turbulence."

In Mona Passage, sound energy is scattered and disrupted by volume reverberation and bottom reverberation. Volume reverberation is caused by marine life, solid particulates churned up in the stiff current, and temperature layers now aggravated by cool rain falling in sheets into the warmer Caribbean. Sound waves also deflect off the rising bottom to further confuse submarine sonar.

"Oh. Well. I need to get to sick bay."

"Found something new?" Pappy squinted down at her furrowed forehead.

"Dr. Shaffer and I could just be getting somewhere." She paused. "I'll let you know. Where's the CO?"

"Engineering. We're still clanging and banging back there."

"Great. I'll be below."

"Carry on, Doctor." The XO smiled. So did the young OOD at his side.

"Commander. Lieutenant." The physician smiled nervously and walked softly toward the companionway and the hole in the deck.

As she descended through the square opening, she could sense the OOD's eyes focused on her backside. On Two Deck, she hurried forward into sick bay where she found the ship's general medical officer sitting wide awake in the dark. Only one, small red light burned in a corner to faintly illuminate the sleeping planesman strapped to his bunk. The ship's clock on the bulkhead glowed an eerie green where irridium stained hands pointed to 0415 UTC.

"That's five contacts, Capitan. Shall I ping him?"

"Not yet."

Captain Barcena stepped from his senior sonar man toward his executive officer. The XO waited patiently in the center of the cramped control room.

"I don't understand it, Geraldo. He is either damaged or careless."

"Or confident of his capabilities, Capitan."

"Not unjustified, I suppose. He can certainly outrun us at twice our flank speed. But he can hardly outrun a torpedo." The weary XO spoke freely. His time in Cuba's fledgling submarine service was far greater than his captain's. But El Viejo was gracious about deferring to subordinates with superior experience. "Besides, Sir, we have no reason to believe that he knows we're here."

"Then why would he be making flank bell to the south? And where did he come from?"

"Maybe going around Puerto Rico to Roosevelt Roads? Maybe a training cruise for torpedo practice? They do practice out here."

"Yes, Geraldo. But if his plumbing noise were a failure of some kind, I would think he would run on the surface so he would not be challenged by a round of cat and mouse with us or a Russian boat."

"True, Capitan, but the sea state in this storm would keep anyone under. Mona Passage is rough enough in clear weather."

The CO walked to the maneuvering board.

"MPP, Lieutenant?"

"Here, Capitan." A dead-reckoning line of position intersected an LOP reduced from the navigator's sighting on the setting sun. The sun sight was shot through the periscope and the LOP had been advanced through the last four hours since the observation. The old submarine did not have inertial navigation equipment and navigating was done the ancient way with a sextant fitted to the periscope optics.

The LOPs crossed on the north-south center line bisecting Mona Passage. *El Tiburon*'s most probable position at the LOP intersection was 55 nautical miles north of a line joining the northern coastline of Puerto Rico with the middle of Hispaniola.

The Cubans were 25 miles astern of *Sam Houston* and the distance was widening as SSN-609 pulled out ahead.

El Viejo turned back to his sonar man.

"Anything more?"

"Negative, Capitan."

The young seaman squinted at his video monitor. He closed his eyes when he pressed his earphone tightly to his cheek. *El Tiburon*'s Trout Cheek passive sonar listened hard to the noisy gurgling of the ocean running roughly through the passage. The shiny antenna wrapped around her bow like a thick metallic smile. The ambient noise reverberated down from the towering whitecaps which were driven across the surface 600 feet above by 50-knot winds—only 14 knots below hurricane force.

"I may have lost him in the background noise, Capitan." The seaman opened his eyes to blink over his shoulder at the CO.

Captain Barcena quickly looked around his control room. Ten youthful faces looked back at him.

"Geraldo? Recommendation."

"I'd ping him, Sir. That's our mission, after all."

The gray-haired captain nodded. His cheeks seemed to sag with the weight of command.

"Lieutenant, rig for general quarters."

"Yes, Sir!" the ebullient XO saluted smartly—an unrequired but heartfelt courtesy.

The exec pushed a thick round button which sounded the GQ alarm throughout *El Tiburon*. Her crew quickly sealed half a dozen watertight hatches. Damage control parties assembled at fire mains and first aid compartments. One by one, division heads called in over the intercom to confirm that each compartment was sealed and that each battle station was manned and ready.

"All spaces reporting, Capitan," a telephone man confirmed.

"Very well," the CO nodded. His voice was disciplined and calm. The dark eyes watching him carefully were all filled with anxious respect. Confidence in their El Viejo shone brightly in all of the sweating faces. The captain turned to the sonar station.

"Can you put us inside the shadow zone?"

"Yes, Sir. Ambient sensors suggest that we need to come up to 175 meters."

"Trim the boat for 175 meters, Geraldo."

"One hundred seventy-five meters, Capitan."

On the XO's command, compressed air blew water from the ship's small compensating tanks inside the double hull to stabilize the submarine. No water was blown out of her main ballast tanks. Her three propellers and the "up bubble" of pointing the bow toward the surface drove *El Tiburon* up to a depth of 350 feet.

"Sonar?"

The sailor worked his consoles quickly and expertly.

"I think we're masked now, Sir. The surface must really be boiling tonight. Lucky for us, Capitan, that it is pouring up there. The temperature layer is as predicted here. Perfect salinity fluctuations, too."

"Thank you. Stand by with the active sonar."

"Yes, Sir." The boy's voice rose slightly in pitch.

The upper ocean had cooled when sunset came four hours earlier. Heavy rain was still pounding the surface, cooling it even more. Normally, the sea gets progressively cooler as depth increases. But the effects of nighttime and rain caused the sea to be cool near the surface and warmer further down: a temperature inversion or "negative gradient."

Where the cooler surface water met warmer deep water 350 feet down, one layer rode on top of the other. Sound generated by *El Tiburon*'s engines and the flow noise of the sea rushing over her hull produced a horizontal "critical ray" of pressure which travelled parallel to the zone where the two layers of water came together. The speed of sound is highest just where the two layers meet. *El Tiburon*'s noise signature, her critical ray of sound, split where the cool upper layer of water met the warmer, deeper layer. Half of the sound wave front refracted upward toward the surface and the other half bent toward the bottom 3 1/2 miles down.

The ocean just ahead of the point where the sound wave split is a "shadow zone." No sound waves will penetrate a shadow zone where two layers of water meet and split the critical ray. *El Tiburon*'s own wake of mechanical and water-flow noise would not escape the shadow zone so long as she could track the "critical angle" of the upward branch of the divided critical ray. Only a hard ping from her active sonar could break out of the sonar shadow.

The deadly quiet, electric submarine instantly became even more quiet. She was virtually invisible to nearby sonar listening for her.

Captain Barcena looked down into the sonar man's sweating face. The seaman's hand pressing the earphone to his moist cheek dissolved in the captain's mind into another face. The CO blinked. Before him flashed another teenager's face dripping with jungle humidity. The hand held a radio headphone tuned to Radio Rebelde set up by the revolutionaries in the Sierra Maestra ridges in February 1958. The Fidelistas broadcast anti-Batista messages and coded orders to rebel troops throughout Cuba. For a terrifying instant, the captain's face went blank.

"Capitan?"

The CO sighed as he came back.

"Can you find him with one ping, Ensign?"

"I think so, Sir."

El Viejo could feel his heart in his temples.

"Then make one ping, Ensign. Make it a good one." The CO smiled with a father's pride.

"Yes, Capitan."

The sailor carefully worked his console. The Herkules medium-frequency active sonar shot a burst of sound southward into Mona Passage. The single ping would radiate through the passage until it either hit another vessel and bounced back to *El Tiburon* or until it slowly dissipated somewhere between Mona Passage and Antarctica.

The young seaman closed his moist eyelids. He pressed his headphones tightly to his cheek.

Jessica Dugan took a seat in the shadow beside Dr. Shaffer. John Richards, the planesman, slept soundly. He no longer fought the restraint straps secured to his arms.

Lt. Commander Dugan sensed the disquiet in her colleague. The GMO showed no trace of his usual good cheer. Even in the Christmas glow of the single red standing light, Jessica Dugan could see that Lt. Shaffer's right eye and cheek twitched slightly with a nervous tic which she had not noticed during their day and a half beneath the waves.

"You all right?" Her voice was genuinely concerned.

"A little tired maybe," the man whispered. He spoke more softly than the sound of air rushing into sick bay from the ventilation duct. The atmosphere was so well scrubbed through biological filtration devices that the air conditioning had no smell at all. Jessica could smell only sick bay's disinfectant scent and the humid aroma of her own shirt.

"Were you resting in the dark, Stan?" Jessica sat close to the lieutenant. They appeared to hide just within the shadows of a corner. Sam Houston's rounded hull curved above them where their chairs touched the bulkhead ten feet from the sleeping planesman.

"No, Jessica. I've been waiting. Whoever took my allopurinol must come back here eventually." He looked down at the dark deck. "He has to."

"Maybe. I went through your medical logs for the BL-2 and BL-3 labs."

"Zip, right?"

"Yes. The few injuries were all routine cuts and scrapes. And all your antisepsis protocols followed NIH guidelines and good medical practice to the letter."

"Yep, Jessica. A regular living breathing Merck Manual. That's me."

Dr. Dugan could see the GMO's face twitch slightly when he forced a smile.

"Stan, did you ever correlate your medical logs from the labs with the 3M records?"

The tone of her voice clearly suggested what the answer should have been.

"No, Jessica. I don't get into materials and maintenance. What are you driving at?"

Stan Shaffer faced Jessica Dugan. They sat close enough to smell each other in the small compartment.

"You should have checked the material logs, Stan. I just did in the wardroom." There was not a trace of condescension in her voice and the GMO felt no irritation at her suggestion of negligence.

"Oh?"

"Yes. I found an incident of broken glassware. Seems that a technician in BL-3 broke a slide five weeks ago. He was preparing to run a protein assay on a tissue sample."

The GMO perked up.

"Was he cut?"

"There is no record of medical intervention of any kind."

"Well?"

"I just found the broken glass event within the last half hour. You show no injury anywhere in any of the three laboratories for that entire week. But I spoke to another technician who remembered a cut finger on the technician who picked up the slide from the deck."

"Bloodshed without a report in my logs? Impossible, Jessica."

"I have an eyewitness."

"Why would a crewman not come to me and then speak to you: a total stranger—and an officer?" The lieutenant's voice was icy.

"Perhaps because I'm a woman. The man is scared to death about the repercussions of talking to me. But he admitted to bandaging the cut hand of a first-class petty officer cut in BL-3 twelve hours before the fire drill in which Thurston and Hendrix participated. It's the closeness in time of the injury and the drill that we need to investigate. The injured man may have been in the drill party. We need to interview everyone who participated. I have the emergency bill for that damage control unit."

"Good," the GMO nodded. "But I can't believe that anyone in this ship would gundeck the medical record on which everyone depends for his own safety."

"I'm not suggesting that anyone falsified medical records, Stan. Perhaps they just left out an incident too minor to really get their attention at the time. It's likely that the DCC fire alert made them forget about a wound so small."

The GMO's face softened at her charitable conclusion.

"All right. All right. Who was the injured lab tech?" The GMO's tired eyes narrowed. "He may be our 'Typhoid Mary.'"

"Sorry. The man who confided in me wouldn't give me the name of the wounded technician. He was frightened enough as it was."

"Then I want the son of a bitch who spoke to you. I want him now, Commander."

"I know. I told him that the physician-patient privilege would not prevent me from discussing this with you. But I had to give my word that he would not be hauled before a captain's mast for talking to me."

"Okay." The GMO looked down at the deck. "Tell him it will go no further than this compartment. Will that do?"

"Yes."

Lieutenant Shaffer stood up in the gloom. Dr. Dugan followed him. She squinted in the near darkness as the general medical officer began to pace beside the bunk where their patient slept as peacefully as in his own bed at home a thousand miles from blue water.

"A wound without my knowledge," the GMO raved in a hoarse whisper. "That violates everyone's most basic training on this mission." He paused and turned toward Jessica. "We need a roster of everyone on that fire drill. Where was it anyway?"

She reached into her pocket and retrieved a crumpled piece of paper filled with names scribbled in longhand. She handed it to the GMO.

"Auxiliary control room."

Dr. Shaffer smiled at the paper which trembled with his hand. He looked over the top of the sheet to the woman an arm's length away.

"Thurston and Hendrix." He spoke gravely as if stating a certainty like the laws of gravity. "And someone on this list may have been cut in a laboratory."

"Maybe, Stan. Buddy Thurston was on the repair party and Hendrix was the nozzle man. Any one of the other dozen men could be our carrier."

The GMO was suddenly alert and revived. He spoke firmly.

"We need to examine the records of the supply department."

"For what?"

"Equipment breakdowns. Perhaps the injured crewman worked on some piece of equipment touched by Hendrix or Thurston. We need a common link of transfection."

"Yes, yes. You're right."

Before the GMO could respond, sick bay rang with a single high-pitched rumble. The hull clanged as if hit once by a sledgehammer outside in the cold, black water.

Jessica Dugan's eyes showed white all around. She reflexively clutched both hands to her heart.

"Stan!" She began to tremble, first her knees and then her hands across her chest. She blinked at the sudden perspiration running into her eyes. She took a step to keep from falling. The dark deck was rock solid beneath her.

When Stanley Shaffer quickly grabbed her shoulders and pulled her close, he could feel her heart pounding against him. She shook with a small convulsion of clammy terror.

"Did something hit us?" she whimpered into his neck. The oak leaf Medical Corps insignia on his collar scratched her nose.

"No, Jessica." He inhaled deeply the scent of her hair. "Not yet."

Captain Milhaus barely heard the high-frequency twang of ultrasonic pressure which slammed into *Sam Houston*. The pulse lasted one-third of a second. Active sonar pings can be pulses as fast as 12 milliseconds or as long as 700 milliseconds. In the ship's auxiliary machinery spaces behind the reactor compartment, the captain had been concentrating on listening to his ship's steam lines. With the deck "floating" on its shock- and vibration-absorbing raft, the sonar ping did not radiate from the aft hull into the insulated deck. But the CO did look up when the sonar pulse struck.

Captain Milhaus picked up a telephone and activated the 42MC communications circuit.

"Captain to CIC."

In the control room, Pappy Perlmutter had recognized the sonar assault before the blue-lighted sonar suite could confirm it. He heard the beam ricochet off the hull.

"What do you have, Pappy?" the weary CO demanded nearly 200 feet aft of his executive officer. He closed his eyes briefly as he listened to Lt. Commander Perlmutter.

"Understood. Any chance that contact was generated by Hayler?" The CO thought of the destroyer pounding up Mona Passage. "Very well. Then we'll assume it's hostile." His face was tight under darkly brooding eyes.

"Do you have a best range estimate?" Captain Milhaus was perspiring although the engineering spaces were comfortably cool. "All right. Make turns for 10 knots. We'll slow her down to maneuver. Keep me advised, Pappy, if you can get a range and CPA on him."

The CO returned the telephone to the bulkhead. The vessel slowed from 30 to 10 knots as the governor on the main turbine reduced the high-pressure steam surging into the powerplant.

At high speeds, American submarines are unstable. Even the modern *Los Angeles* class hunter-killers tend to pitch dangerously at flank speed. This longitudinal instability can cause dangerous loss of depth control. The subs are also prone to roll violently at high speed, creating the risk of a deep-water snap-roll.

Active sonar beams in the 5 to 20 kilohertz frequency band are susceptible to transmission loss: a reduction in acoustic intensity over long distances. As range increases between the sonar source and its reflected sonar pulse, the transmission loss increases. SSN-609's sonar technicians would use their computer to enhance the record of the single pulse out of the darkness. Then they would ask the computer to follow the pulse wave back to its origin based upon the degree of transmission loss. If the technicians could retrace the pulse, they could estimate a closest point of approach (CPA) by *El Tiburon*.

By 0435 UTC, five minutes after the active sonar ping had found SSN-609, Kurt Milhaus crouched through the aft watertight door into the control room. Since his ship was still rigged for general quarters alert, the captain had to wait for four heavy doors to be cranked open before he could pass through to the Deck One bridge. The doors were then dogged as he passed.

"Commander," the CO said to his XO. Both officers looked tired but fully alert.

"Captain, sonar advises that the deep scatter layer is interfering with locating the source of the contact. But at least it works in both directions."

"Yes."

At night, especially in tropical waters like Mona Passage, marine life rises toward the surface. It scatters sound waves which would mask any noise generated by SSN-609 and would cause some reverberation confusion in the sonar reflection which had bounced off the hull.

"Any word from medical?" The CO had not forgotten his other enemy while he was aft nursing the water hammer in the steam trunk.

"Dr. Dugan is down with Stan. They may be on to something."

"I need more than wild guesses. But Colonel Epson's mosquitos aren't our biggest concern just now."

"No, Sir," Pappy Perlmutter shrugged.

"We're still generating wet steam back there," the CO continued with a sigh. "Damnedest thing I ever saw in engineering. No casualty that we can isolate. Just water hammer throughout main steam."

"But it doesn't really matter now, does it, Captain?"

Kurt Milhaus' face was hard. He felt the eyes of his control room crew upon him.

"Guess not, Pappy." The CO smiled, almost against his will. He spoke over the XO's shoulder to the entire CIC watch-standers. "Now, we will all do what we are trained to do and sworn to do. We've all taken the Queen's shilling."

Taking the Queen's shilling is an old British idiom for accepting the risks of soldiering.

Captain Milhaus let his eyes pause upon each seaman's up-turned face. One by one, each sailor blinked before turning back to his console or instruments. The men were visibly calmed.

"Captain on the bridge," a young sailor called. The boy smiled with relief. So did the other submariners throughout the compartment.

The CO picked up the telephone instead of dictating his command to a subordinate.

"Sonar, this is the captain." The CO waited. "I want a tactical report the second you can resolve a range, bearing, and CPA. Captain out."

Pappy Perlmutter looked at the bulkhead clock. It was 0445 UTC, a little more than two hours until *Sam Houston* should have completed her rendezvous with *Hayler*. But after slowing to 10 knots from 30, the destroyer's protective wing would be nearly six hours further south down Mona Passage.

Captain Milhaus faced his executive officer.

"Torpedo room status, Commander?"

"Loaded, armed and ready, Captain."

"Very well."

SIXTEEN

16 MARCH; 0445 UTC

"ANYTHING BY echo ranging?"

Captain Barcena's upper lip perspired as he leaned over the sonar man hunched at a console and monitor.

Inside *El Tiburon*'s antiquated black boxes, her echo ranging sonar listened for the reflection of acoustic energy bouncing off nearby targets. The sonar's receiver would amplify the return, filter out ocean background noise, and demodulate the returning wall of ultrasonic energy.

"Possible MTI, Capitan. Very faint. Might be a scatter layer or an MTI at extreme range."

"All right." Captain Barcena straightened.

The reflection off *Sam Houston* fifteen miles away was barely audible to *El Tiburon*'s 20-year-old sensors. After scrubbing the contact to filter out the noise of the sea, only a possibility of a credible MTI—moving target indication—could be detected.

"Sorry, Capitan. I'm reading the slightest trace of down-Doppler. Too faint to be conclusive. But I have to speculate that it was a contact. Probably the Americans, Sir."

"Bearing?"

"Judging by the faint return, I estimate we scored a stern reflection. He must be dead ahead, Sir."

"So," the CO shrugged toward his executive officer. "Havana wanted cat and mouse. It would seem that we've carried out our orders."

"Yes, Capitan."

Active sonar senses minute changes in frequency between the strong outgoing ping and the weak incoming reflection. This frequency difference or Doppler Shift indicates whether the target is approaching or pulling away. Down Doppler means that the incoming signal is of lower frequency than the outgoing ping—the target is moving away.

"Do you have orders, Capitan?" The XO still sounded giddy.

"Make turns for 15 knots. Maintain present heading. And I want ultra quiet in the boat. Continue general quarters."

"Yes, Sir. Flank speed and one-seven-five. Ultra quiet. Maintain GQ. I'll pass the word."

The CO nodded and turned back to his sweating sonar man.

"Continue the passive sweep. Let me know instantly if you hear anything."

"Yes, Sir."

The captain spoke very softly to his exec.

"The Americans now know we're here. Think they can get a bearing?"

"Not likely, Capitan. If a scatter layer caused the serious signal degradation, it will work both ways. His attenuation and transmission loss working the solution backwards should be as great as ours, even with his superior sensor suite."

"Good. We can hope so, anyway."

"Yes, Capitan."

The submarines *El Tiburon* and *Sam Houston* ran submerged and 20 nautical miles apart through the northern entrance to Mona Passage. Ninety nautical miles away, the destroyer *Hayler* steamed hard toward the southern approaches of the passage.

Hayler made way northward through towering seas which exploded over her bow. She heeled toward her leeward side when waves setting toward the southwest slammed against her haze-gray hull on the windward side. The 60-knot wind drove the sea under a midnight sky heavy with thunderclouds. The barometer fell through 29.62 inches, having dropped another tenth of an inch in the 4 hours and 45 minutes since midnight, UTC. Now at 15 minutes before 1:00 in the morning Atlantic

Time, the falling barometer was only .09 inches from the hurricane level.

Captain Robert Webster labored to maintain his footing in the CIC of DD-997. Seamen sitting at consoles had to wear their seatbelts to stay at their posts.

"No question, Captain," a queasy, first-class petty officer said toward his television screen.

"What do you have?" the swaying CO asked impatiently.

"One of the Orion's sonobuoys definitely picked up an active sonar pulse fifteen minutes ago. Fairly strong ping with a very weak return. Quite a bit of diffusion from these seas tonight."

"Ours or theirs?"

"Well, Captain, I have to guess that the pulse came from a foreign vessel, probably submerged. The return could be off anything from 609 to a whale."

"Reverberation?"

"No, Sir. Definitely a return off some object down there."

"Can you run a passive sweep?"

"Trying, Sir. But the sea is just too rough for accurate returns. I may have just a barely audible skip coming through a convergence zone. Sounds like plumbing noise in the 15 kilohertz band. Could be 609's feedwater problem. The Cubans' electric propulsion is too quiet for a return at this range."

"Very well. Keep on it."

Sound under water travels at its slowest velocity through what sonar men call the deep sound channel usually about 4,000 feet deep. Sound pulses bounce off the submerged sound channel and form massive sine waves of noise. The pressure waves bend up toward the surface about every 30 miles until they are absorbed in the normal chatter of the ocean. Each peak in the moving wave of sound is a convergence zone. If a passive sonar hydrophone is located at such a zone, it can hear the sound generated 30, 60, or 90 miles away. In 1960, a test depth charge was detonated under water. Its pressure pulse traveled inside the deep sound channel and was heard 10,800 miles away 3 1/2 hours later.

Captain Webster staggered toward a telephone.

"Engineering, CO here. Can you get any more revs out of her, Chief?"

The CO frowned.

"Very well. Make maximum turns and do the best you can to crank up the turbines. I want to get on station at best speed. Thanks, Chief."

Robert Webster swayed toward his midwatch navigator who held onto the waist-high table of charts and plastic plotters. Although 997's modern inertial navigation and high-speed computers could resolve surface evolutions at the speed of light, a warm body with a #2 pencil backed up the integrated circuitry.

"Where are we, Lieutenant?"

"Here, by inertial, Captain. Predicted rendezvous with 609 in another three hours if she's still running at flank bell."

The navigator's finger pointed to a chart of the open Caribbean south of Mona Passage. His captain nodded. A tiny red triangle was drawn near the northern mouth of the passage.

"That the sonar contact?"

"Yes, Sir. It's sonar's best estimate of the origin of the pulse. Pretty iffy though in this sea state."

"Okay. Thanks."

The CO turned to a master chief petty officer whose moist face was red in the muted glow of the standing lights within CIC.

"Chief, have crypto advise COMPRESECT-ASWU of the sonobuoy return. Give 'em our position and confirm ETA with Dugway Wet by 0800."

"Aye aye, Sir. Commander Puerto Rico Section, Antisubmarine Warfare Unit, position and contact report. Rendezvous at 0800 UTC."

"Carry on, Chief."

"Yes, Sir."

By 0500 UTC, physicians Shaffer and Dugan stood tensely in the pharmacy space of sick bay on Deck Two. On the far side of the thin joiner door, planesman John Richards struggled fitfully against the restraints binding his ankles and wrists. The single sonar ping which had reverberated through the compartment half an hour earlier had pierced his drug-induced stupor. With his eyes closed, he moaned softly while his limbs twitched with each spasm of fearful disorientation.

The two officers faced three weary seamen. Two had been pulled off their battle billets and the third had been roused from his bunk. Each was a three-stripe, petty officer first class.

Lt. Shaffer spoke over the clipboard in his hands.

"You three men were on a DCC fire drill in auxiliary machinery last month. Do you remember?"

"Yes, Sir," the men answered in a single nervous chorus.

"And all three of you are assigned to BL-2, is that correct?"

"Yes, Sir."

"Sanders, you're rated on the high-pressure liquid chromatography equipment?"

"Yes, Sir." The petty officer in his early twenties blinked sweat from his weary eyes.

"Petty Officer Clark, you're assigned to the protein fractionators?"

"Yes, Sir."

"And, Petty Officer Collins, you're checked out on the electron microscope?"

"I am, Sir."

"Were any of you ever cut in the lab?" Dr. Dugan stepped forward and spoke impatiently.

The three men glanced sideways at each other.

"No, Ma'am," they answered in unison.

"Let me see your hands, please."

Lt. Commander Dugan stepped to the first man who held out his moist hands. She put both of her hands on first his left hand and then his right. When she lowered her head to study the palms for scars, the seaman took short whiffs of her hair.

Then she stepped to the second man and the third. When she looked up at the youngest of the men, 20 years old at most, she could see the artery in his neck pounding hard as she held his sweating hand. She let go gently and turned toward Dr. Shaffer.

"Nothing, Lieutenant." She observed formal courtesies in the company of the noncoms.

Dr. Shaffer laid the clipboard down and spoke firmly to the three men.

"Do all of you remember Thurston and Hendrix from that drill?"

"Yes, Sir."

"Yes, Sir."

"Yes, Sir."

"Do you remember anything unusual about them?"

Two men said no and the third shrugged.

"Nothing at all?" His eyes narrowed. "Your lives and every-one else's in this vessel may depend on your answer."

The three men hesitated. They blinked as they tried to remember a non-event and routine drill six weeks ago.

One of the men wiped perspiration from his chin.

"Maybe the air masks?" His answer was a question.

"What about?" Dr. Dugan stepped between the petty officer and the GMO.

"Thurston's air mask was dirty or broken or maybe the inlet valve was stuck. But he couldn't breathe. So Hendrix gave Thurston his and then Hendrix went out into the passageway. That was the drill: a toxic fumes exercise along with the fire simulation."

In fire or fumes emergencies, submariners wear air masks resembling goggled gas masks. Each is connected to a pres-surized air main by a thin hose. The lines carry air but not pure oxygen. Surface ships carry them too along with OBAs: oxygen breathing apparatus masks which are self-contained oxygen generators. But submarines do not carry OBAs. Oxy-gen gas within the confines of a submarine would be too explosive since submarines tend to generate free hydrogen gas into the atmosphere from their backup batteries.

Shaffer and Dugan looked at each other for an instant.

"They shared an air mask?"

"Yes, Ma'am."

"Do you men remember Randy Morrow getting hurt? Cut on some equipment? It's in the med logs."

The three petty officers looked at each other.

"Sure," the oldest man said nervously. "It wasn't too bad. He came down to sick bay when the section chief relieved him."

"All right," the GMO sighed. "You're dismissed. Return to your stations."

"Sir. Ma'am." Each seaman nodded without saluting and then headed quickly toward the passageway.

"Well, Jessica?"

"I don't know, Stan. Seven more men to question, scattered all over the ship. Can we track down the mask that Hendrix gave to Thurston?"

"I can try. I'll give 3M a call while we're waiting for the next bunch. You can tell Pappy to send down three or four more."

"Okay."

Jessica Dugan followed the three sailors into the passageway. When she stepped through the hatchway, she saw her shadow disappear as Dr. Shaffer extinguished the bright lights inside sick bay. He again sat alone in the compartment's red glow.

She climbed through the companionway ladder and entered the Deck One control center from the aft corner.

"The CO and exec are in the sonar suite, Ma'am," a seaman said softly before she could inquire.

"Thank you."

Dr. Dugan stepped into the blue light of a small sonar space adjacent to CIC. The captain and XO Perlmutter huddled near a bank of video monitors. The two officers frowned every time a wiggly disturbance traveled down the screens.

"No letup, Sir." The sonar man shook his head.

"I just don't understand it, Pappy. We've done everything except tear the condensers apart back there. I'm starting to think the water hammer is coming from the reactor plumbing itself."

Just hearing the word "reactor" made Jessica Dugan shudder. Captain Milhaus turned around.

"Doctor."

"Captain. Commander Perlmutter."

Pappy's tired face nodded wearily.

"You and Doc making any headway?"

"Some, Captain. It's looking more and more like a lab tech was contaminated but didn't report it. May be some link to the missing allopurinol medication. We need another group of men from that fire drill to report to sick bay."

Captain Milhaus glanced at his exec.

"I'm going to delay that for the moment, Commander. I don't want to take anyone else off station just now. If the Cuban boat made us on his last active sonar sweep 45 minutes ago, I won't be able to spare anyone from battle stations."

"Do you think he found us, Sir?" She spoke to the captain, but she looked at Pappy.

"Impossible to say," the CO shrugged. "But SOP requires that we assume a positive contact."

"Oh. You were mentioning the reactor?" Her voice was no longer confident.

"Yes," Pappy answered for his captain. "If the noise is not coming from a condenser failure, then we must troubleshoot the reactor circulation. We can fine-tune the steam generator circulation without any problem. I wouldn't worry." He smiled with absolute conviction. "It's all computer driven. We can tune her to a gnat's eyelash. Not to worry. The only question really is where to make the adjustment: the hot leg and pressurizer, or the cold leg and feedwater? We'll find it."

"Yes. Good."

"In the meantime, Doctor," the CO interrupted. He turned his back to her and squinted down at the sonar screen. "I suggest you lay forward to the wardroom and secure your paperwork. The ride will be getting a little rough here shortly." He turned around to look down into her pale face with the purple eye. "I'm taking her up closer to the surface. It's pretty nasty topside tonight. So you may want to pop a scopolamine on your way forward."

"Ah, okay. If you recommend it." Her shaky voice was a question. The CO looked into her tired gray eyes. He did not labor to sound cheerful like his XO.

"I recommend it. You're new to green water, Doctor."

Pappy Perlmutter laid his hand upon her shoulder. He nodded with kindness in his eyes. He said nothing as his hand returned to his side.

"I'll be in the wardroom, Sir, if you need me. Please let me know when I can resume questioning the crew. I feel like Stan and I are really getting close."

"Sure. I'm glad you're cracking this thing." The CO turned away again. "Too bad you couldn't have done it yesterday. We would still be safe in the trench."

Dr. Dugan turned and stepped back into CIC.

"Sorry, Captain. But we're really radiating noise."

"All right, Chief." The CO spoke across the sitting sonar man's shoulder. "I'm going to take her up. What depth do you recommend to mask our steam line noise with surface reverb?"

"In this sea with a gale up top? One hundred feet should do it. I can refine that once we go up and I can take a few

"Well, I'm going over the ship's duty bills one last time, looking for common watch assignments and such. I think we're on top of it."

The CO leaned forward. When he looked into her eyes, he did not steal a glance at the open folders identifying suspect seamen.

"Can you assure me that none of the potentially infected men are in my CIC watch or down in weapons or propulsion?"

"I was just reviewing those station bills. I'm very confident as to the weapons people, CIC, damage control central, and electronic support and countermeasures. I haven't gotten through propulsion yet."

"What about nuclear engineering?"

"Can't say, Sir. I'm sorry. But it's just a matter of maybe another hour."

"An hour, Jessica? We're less than an hour from rendezvous with *Hayler* and the Cuban boat is close astern. I wish you would share your present list of exposed men."

"I gave my word, Captain. Lieutenant Shaffer, too."

"Okay. Okay. I'll give you thirty minutes. Then I shall order you to reveal your source of information. I'll note your formal protest in the CIC rough log."

"Thank you for that courtesy, Captain. But I really think I can get through the records in time to secure the ship and still protect our patients."

"Good. Wish to hell we had a lazaret on board."

"Me too, Sir. Then we could quarantine the lot of them."

"Yes. Don't know why the NIH people didn't think of that when they had this ship renovated for this mission."

A lazaret is an isolation ward for infectious diseases on hospital ships.

"Captain? Did we change course? I thought I felt us come about."

"Yes. We're steaming southwest to meet 997 near Isla de Mona, a spec of rock in the middle of Mona Passage. We're about 15 miles off the rendezvous point right now. And we're mustering four hours early just to be cautious that all duty hands are alert."

"Yes, Captain, I heard on the PA. What about the Cubans? Do you expect trouble?"

"Trouble?" The CO laughed in a way which made her shudder. "His trouble not ours. I can assure you of that. I can't imagine he'll do anything stupid. Not with *Hayler* coming hard up the channel. The Cubans must have heard 997's screws by now. He knows we're getting shadowed by our own flag."

"Good."

"Well." Kurt Milhaus stood up and Dr. Dugan followed. The CO touched her shoulder to keep her from rising. "As you were, Doctor." The captain pulled his hand back as if her shirt were on fire. "Carry on, Jessica, and keep me posted. Otherwise, Pappy or I will be back at—" he glanced at his wristwatch "—at 0815. We'll be taking names if you can't assure us absolutely that the contamination is confined to men not essential to general quarters."

"Right, Sir."

"All right, Jessica. Quarters for muster right now. Officers' call probably in 15 or 20 minutes. Commander Perlmutter should be dropping by for your results before he briefs me in his Eight O'clock Report."

"I'll have something for him, Sir." She blinked her dry eyes, one still black and blue. Her face sagged with fatigue.

"Very well."

The CO nodded and walked into the passageway through the door he had left wide open. He softly closed the door behind him, leaving the woman alone with her files.

Jessica Dugan fought sleep. She had been on duty for 25 hours. At least her seasick stomach was pacified by the scopolamine in her system for two and a half hours. Her bowels were also calmed by the smooth ride 600 feet beneath the hurricane blowing across the black surface. Her joints were beginning to ache, especially her hands and feet. Her shoes felt a size too small as her feet were filled with fluid from not reclining for so long.

She had not showered for fourteen hours and had last changed her shirt eight hours ago. The stuffiness and rising humidity of the submarine shut down tightly at general quarters only made matters worse. Without thinking, she scratched her wet armpit.

She pushed back her chair, rubbed her bloodshot eyes hard, and stood up. Her swollen knees cracked like an old man's.

She shuffled to her metal closet and pulled a fresh shirt off a hanger. From a formica bureau, she pulled clean underwear. In the small head, she scrubbed her armpits with warm, soapy water and splashed cold water into her bruised face. Then she frowned at herself in the mirror. Naked to her belt, she studied her body. A rash was erupting under her arms from perspiration.

"Gag me," she sighed to herself. She was startled by the sound of her whisper in the all-steel bathroom which amplified her voice. With the basin full of water, she dropped her khaki trousers and lowered a warm washcloth between her thighs.

By 0800 UTC, Randy Morrow and Mitchell Jackson had passed through the mid-deck laboratory. A dozen biologists did not look up from protein stew pots and optical equipment when the two seamen calmly walked between the concrete-filled missile tubes rising from the deck and up through the overhead. No one but the Laboratory Director spoke to them when he granted them permission to transit the BL-3 facility.

Just on the aft side of the laboratory's stern bulkhead, the two men stopped in the red glow of the passageway standing lights. Most of the compartment was filled with the bank-vault steel doors leading to the nuclear reactor compartment where the S5W pressurized water reactor boiled silently. The seaman who guarded the watertight hatch to the laboratory wore a sidearm. His M-9, Beretta 92 SB-F 9-millimeter pistol hung low on the sailor's thigh in a nylon holster. The holster flap completely concealed the 15-shot semiautomatic weapon.

"Jackson and Morrow," Randall Morrow smiled cordially. "Just passing through to propulsion."

"All right," the guard nodded. He held a warm coffee mug in his left hand. The coffee was sent through the hatch minutes earlier when Captain Milhaus had ordered rations distributed to the general quarters watch-standers. Some men in particularly vulnerable spaces were not permitted by submarine protocols to open the entire watertight hatch for a snack. So they opened small watertight tubes within the larger hatch. Their coffee and doughnuts were then shoved through this passing scuttle and the port was quickly resealed. The guard's right hand rested on his sidearm.

"Any Cubans get past yet?" Mitchell Jackson said cheerfully. His voice sounded strained.

"Not on my watch," the weary sentry said firmly.

The guard did double duty; he was the man posted to make certain that the watertight hatch between compartments remained closed during material condition zebra or general quarters. The hatch had a red "Z" painted within a black "D." The "dog-zebra" hatch was closed during flooding or fire alerts or when at GQ. But the guard was armed because his assignment in the general quarters battle bill also had him stand watch beside SSN-609's armory: the small arms lockup where sidearms and Navy-issue M-14 rifles were kept. The 20-round 7.62 millimeter M-14 is standard issue on all ships of the fleet. (The 5.56mm M-16 rifle is government issue ashore.)

"Good," Morrow said softly.

"Are you a relief detail?" the guard asked casually while blowing into his steaming cup. "I thought the midwatch already changed back there."

"It did," Morrow answered quickly. "The XO wanted us to take Chief Wilcox's report up to the wardroom."

"Oh."

As Chief of the Boat, Senior Chief Petty Office Robert Wilcox's word was gold throughout the ship.

"I hope you don't mind if I give the chief a call? At GQ, I really have to play it by the SSORN." The *Submarine Standard Organization and Regulations of the Navy* manual is The Bible underway. He raised the hot mug to his stubbled lips.

"We'll be glad to wait," Morrow smiled warmly.

When Randall Morrow's fist impacted the guard's middle just below his breast bone, the sentry's face exploded in a black mist of coffee which warmly covered Morrow and Jackson's faces. The teenager dropped his cup, exhaled mightily, and dropped quickly into a denim heap outside the armory's locked door. He fell with his mouth wide open and gasping for air, but his chest was paralyzed by the blow. His eyeballs rolled back white and his limp body lay perfectly still.

"Jesus Christ, Randy!" Mitchell Jackson's face was whiter than the drooling guard's.

"Last contact twenty minutes ago, El Capitan." The sonar man spoke over his shoulder toward Captain Barcena.

"Nothing since the buoy jettison?"

"No, Capitan. And I'm only guessing on that. Ambient noise is quite intense from the storm. If the Americans did send up a buoy of some kind, they are equipped to arrest the bubbles of the ejection air. It was just barely a contact, Sir. More flow noise than anything. Still picking up double screws approaching from the south. Estimated range twelve nautical miles."

"One of ours?" The captain studied the video monitor.

"I think not, Sir. Screws are deep draft and slow. A heavy destroyer or light cruiser would be my guess. I don't think he's coming straight up the passage."

"American?"

"Probably, Capitan." The sonar man looked over his shoulder.

"Nothing from the American submarine." Captain Barcena was thinking out loud. He walked to the maneuvering table where a chart of Mona Passage was spread open.

The XO approached his captain.

"Emillio, no contact with the Americans. We should still hear his wake if nothing else when we're this close. Last hard contact was only two miles."

The CO tapped the chart with his finger tips. His index finger pecked at the only island in Mona Passage.

"Look here, Emillio. The Isla de Mona: shallow water to increase bottom bounce on the active sonar. Rough shoals to add ambient noise to confuse passive sonar. If I were the Yanquis, that's where I would steam."

"I suppose, Capitan."

El Viejo squinted at the chart. He could not take his eyes off Mona Island.

"That's where I would go if I were them. Sonar?"

"Yes, Capitan?"

"Could the surface contact be steaming northwest?"

"Yes, Capitan. It's very possible."

"Very well." The CO turned to his exec. "Take her down to 250 meters and come to course two-one-five for Isla de Mona."

"Two hundred fifty meters, aye. Turns for 15 knots and two-one-five."

"Let's back down to 8 knots. Better passive sonar reception if we reduce our flow noise."

El Tiburon's planesman pointed the submarine's boxy bow toward the bottom which had come up to 1,500 feet in depth.

As she leveled off at 750 feet, the boat blew high-pressure air into her forward trim tank to balance the ship. Her seakeeping was quite stable so far below the churning storm.

"Two hundred fifty meters, 8 knots, Capitan."

"Thank you. Sonar?"

"Negative contact, Sir, on hydrophones."

"Thank you."

The CO turned back to his XO.

"Torpedoes armed and ready?"

"Aye, Sir."

"Very well."

Captain Barcena saw the color fading from his young executive officer's face. The CO laid his hand on the officer's shoulder.

"It's just another drill, Lieutenant."

"Yes, Sir," the XO nodded weakly. He took comfort from the calm and kind confidence in El Viejo's tired eyes.

Running on electric power only, ultra-quiet *El Tiburon* remained astern of *Sam Houston*. The distance between them had opened to five miles as SSN-609 had veered to the west.

Hayler had reduced her twin propellers' revolutions to match the thundering ocean. Five miles east of Punta Este on Isla de Mona, DD-997 kept station by maintaining 20 knots directly into the wave fronts. Since the sea surged westward at the same speed, the current kept the destroyer dead in the water. The ship rose fifteen feet as each wave crest passed under her keel. Then her rounded bow plunged over the top and slid down into the black valley of the trough leading the next rising crest. The tiny island was barely visible on the western horizon when *Hayler* was atop a frothy crest and lightning struck the rocky landscape. Daybreak was a little more than an hour to the east.

"Anything?"

"Nothing yet, Captain. Still too much noise from the storm. The surf on the island is just overpowering the passive sonar."

"All right."

Captain Webster leaned heavily against the back of his command chair on the bridge. Rain swept the windows illuminated by bursts of lightning.

The CO struggled to maintain his balance as he spoke into the telephone. He spoke loudly over the din of the storm.

"Let me know the minute you pick up his screw."

"Aye, Sir," the sonar man in CIC said softly. He swallowed hard to keep from throwing up as DD-997 dove down the back side of a wave.

Captain Webster squinted into the darkness toward where he knew Mona Island to be. He saw only flashes of lightning followed two seconds later by thunder which rattled the bridge windows.

Jessica Dugan blinked at her computer monitor. The screen's data blurred in a brain numbed by lack of sleep and by seasickness medication. She rubbed her eyes. She looked up at the closed door to her stateroom.

"Come."

Lieutenant Shaffer entered and closed the door.

"Jessica. What do you have from the watch and station bills?"

"Just about nothing. I've run every sort I can think of. There are no other crewmen who billetted together on other submarines. Just the few we know to be exposed from the needle stash here. I even ran their surface ship and shore-based school records. No one on this ship has served with anyone else before. I also ran damage control billets, battle dressing station assignments, damage control details, everything. The computer can't find any common link which would suggest a sufficiently close relationship among 609 crewmen to make a conspiracy likely."

The GMO sat down heavily in the second chair. Since her stateroom had accommodated two junior officers, there were two bunks, two small writing tables, and two sets of drawers for personals. He pulled his chair close to the woman's so he could see the screen. Jessica Dugan could smell the GMO's two-day-old sweat.

"Doesn't mean, though, that a conspiracy didn't grow among men thrown together from unrelated billets when they feared for their safety."

"I know, Stan. You're still zip on the medical records?"

"Yes. I can't find anyone else in my files who presented with symptoms suggesting allopurinol contraindications."

Dr. Dugan turned to face the officer she could smell.

"Maybe we already found them all."

"Maybe. How's the old man?"

"Captain Milhaus was here ten minutes ago. Said he'd be back at 0815—any minute, I guess—to demand that we name names."

Lt. Shaffer rubbed his forehead. He closed his eyes for a moment.

"I think we have to reveal the names we know."

"What about privilege, Stan?"

"The ship is at risk. The CO has no choice . . . and we don't either. You could order me not to say anything, I suppose."

The lieutenant looked closely at the lieutenant commander who looked and smelled freshly scrubbed.

"I could. Do you want me to, Stan?"

The general medical officer looked down at the deck. He realized that she had removed her shoes and socks. For three months he had not seen feet and ankles without hair. He could not take his eyes off her bare feet.

"No."

"I understand, Stan. Okay, we talk to the CO."

"Sonar, aye."

"CO here. Any contact?"

The sonar man on board *Hayler* wanted to say "Nothing since you asked me five minutes ago."

"Negative, Captain."

Captain Webster checked the bulkhead clock set to Atlantic Time: 0420, half an hour to first light.

"Very well. Make one active sweep. At least 609 will know we're on station."

"One sweep, Sir. Stand by."

While Randy Morrow stuffed an M-9 pistol into his denim shirt, Mitchell Jackson carefully propped the unconscious sentry against the bulkhead. Morrow had forced the armory door. Since an M-14 rifle would be impossible to conceal, he took a semiautomatic pistol from the small arms rack. Morrow rammed a full magazine of 15 rounds of NATO hardball into the grip and racked the slide to load the chamber. He knew that taking the M-9 from the sentry's hip would immediately alert the next watch-stander that Morrow was armed. It would take longer for an inventory of the armory to confirm the stolen weapon. Jackson was as gentle as a woman as he eased the sentry's head into the corner where he would be able to sit upright.

"Sure you don't want a piece?"

"Positive."

"Okay. Let's go forward to the pharmacy. The kid will be fine; don't worry. I barely touched him."

"Right. I just don't want him to choke." Jackson checked again to make certain that the boy would not fall sideways to the deck.

As the two seamen walked nervously through the narrow passageway, they stopped suddenly in the reddish glare when they heard a far-off rumble. Instinctively, they each glanced toward the submarine's curved side. The sound of a fast freight train seemed to approach through the jet-black ocean 600 feet beneath a hurricane.

Jackson and Morrow clasped their palms to their ears when the ultrasonic shock wave slammed broadside into *Sam Houston*.

Twenty paces away from them behind the locked armory door, the unconscious sentry was jolted by the vibration moaning through the bulkhead. The teenager slid forward across the smooth deck. He stopped when his back hit the slippery linoleum. When the back of his head slammed against the deck, he vomited and inhaled the foul soup with his next breath, his last.

NINETEEN

16 MARCH; 0825 UTC

"REPORT, PAPPY."

Captain Milhaus rubbed his forehead where a purple welt was rising quickly. The CO banged his head when he crouched at a trot through the CIC watertight door which a sentry had sealed behind him.

"One active sweep, Captain, with a solid ghost echo." The XO spoke over his shoulder. He squinted at the sonar equipment.

"Narrow band active from the Cubans with bottom bounce so close to the island?"

The sonar man looked up from his console and spoke for the executive officer.

"Not likely, Captain. The sweep came from well above us, Sir. Judging by the power and frequency, it had to be from *Hayler*. She must be three to six miles east of the island and maybe five miles west-southwest of us. The echo came from astern. Must have bounced off us and then reverberated off the Cubans."

Kurt Milhaus straightened his back from leaning over the sonar monitor screen. The XO stood wearily at his side.

"Can you resolve a range to the Cubans?"

"Four to seven miles, relative bearing one-six-zero. I can only guess at the transmission frequency so I can't determine the intensity of the up-Doppler to get his CPA."

"Best guess, Chief?"

The CO had not removed his hand from his forehead where a lump like half a golf ball was swelling above the moist bridge of his nose.

"Guessing rather widely, Captain, I'd have to say closest point of approach 1500 yards in twenty minutes."

"Very well. Thanks, Chief."

The CO stepped toward Pappy Perlmutter.

"We went back to full GQ when the sonar hit us, Captain."

"Good. Did the crew get rations and coffee in time?"

"Not every compartment. Probably not the reactor crew or fire control."

"Okay. We'll feed 'em as soon as we can."

"Maybe Doc should look at your forehead, Captain."

The XO spoke softly when he made suggestions to the CO. He expected a quiet rebuke.

"Yes, Pappy. I was on my way to Commander Dugan anyway."

"Good, Sir."

"Your conn, Pappy. TAO is still yours."

"Aye, Sir."

The CO carefully walked back through the CIC forward bulkhead hatch. He lowered his throbbing head well below the level of the upper rounded frame of the doorway. In the control room behind him, the executive officer, as Tactical Action Officer, had full and independent authority to launch weapons if necessary.

Doctors Dugan and Shaffer were still standing and quietly wondering whose sonar had struck them when Captain Milhaus knocked on the stateroom door. The CO entered after Jessica's invitation.

"Who pinged us?" the woman asked without waiting for the pleasantries.

"*Hayler*, but the Cubans are running up our wake."

"Oh." Dr. Dugan squinted at the captain's forehead. "How'd you do that, Sir?"

"The bulkhead bit me, I'm afraid." He smiled lamely.

"Let me see, please."

The doctor lifted the CO's hand from the bump. The swelling was deeply purple and looked very much like her fading black eye.

"You'll live, Sir. No blurred vision? Headache?"

"Just from lack of sleep, I guess. I'll slap some ice on it when I can."

"Yes. My prescription, too. Some ASA will help the inflammation."

"Say again, Commander."

"Aspirin, Sir. Sorry."

"Yes, yes. Aspirin and ice. Pretty high tech treatment for a floating laboratory."

All three officers chuckled softly. The CO pulled a metal chair across the deck.

"Sit down, Commander."

Dr. Dugan resumed her seat at the small desk. Without a third chair in the cramped compartment, Lieutenant Shaffer stood with his arms crossed. He looked ill at ease standing behind the sitting CO.

"Well?" The captain looked closely into the woman's dark eyes.

"Captain, I've run every conceivable computer sort of the crew: billets, past ships, shore training, everything. There are no other combinations of crewmen who shared common assignments. If anyone else is pilfering drugs or needles down here, they had to join the little conspiracy here and on their own."

"Fine. Go on."

"I reviewed my findings with Stan. We are in agreement," she glanced past the captain toward the uncomfortable GMO, " . . . that we must reveal the names of the men we know to have stolen allopurinol or colchicine. Our list is limited to Randall Morrow and Mitchell Jackson so far. They seem to be tied in with Thurston, Hendrix, Frazier, and Richards. But neither Morrow nor Jackson is showing any symptoms at all of Lesch-Nyhan. Stan did a preliminary serum scan and found no genetic abnormalities. He's running more detailed genetic mapping on them now, but that won't be done perking for six to ten hours. But I'm as confident as I can be that they're clean. In the meantime, they're both confined to quarters."

"Fine. But that doesn't answer the real question: Who else has been stealing drugs and may have used contaminated needles used by the dead men?"

"I know that, Captain. Stan and I have agreed to withhold the prophylactic allopurinol from the entire crew. If anyone is masking symptoms of Lesch-Nyhan, at least the uric acid over-production, that'll show up in urine and blood samples within twenty-four hours, before we get back to Puerto Rico. We can at least isolate anyone testing positive before we dock at Roosevelt Roads."

The CO nodded.

"All right, Doctor. Thank you."

Captain Milhaus stood up and Jessica Dugan followed. Lieutenant Shaffer uncrossed his arms and looked pensive. His tired eyes met the captain's.

At the stateroom doorway, the CO turned and faced both physicians.

"I know that naming names pains you both. I want to thank you. These are good men on this boat, hand-picked men. No harm will come to Morrow and Jackson or to anyone else who turns up taking unauthorized medication. They did what they had to do, I suppose."

The medics looked quickly at each other.

"Thank you, Captain," Stan Shaffer mumbled.

"Sure," the CO nodded as he stepped into the red-lit passageway. He rubbed his throbbing forehead.

"It wasn't the American submarine, Capitan. It came from the surface maybe ten miles south of us. He had to get a return off us, even in this sea state."

"Thank you."

Captain Barcena stood close to his exec.

"So, Lieutenant. We seem to have found more than La Habana bargained for."

The young XO was stunned by the peculiar smile lighting his captain's haggard face.

"It would seem that our mission is accomplished then? We found the Yanqui boat and one of his surface combatants can confirm that we found him. The admiral will be pleased."

The executive officer barely concealed his hope that El Tiburon would quickly come about and turn its three screws toward the American submarine's stern.

The CO silently nodded. He looked so intensely into the XO's sweating face that the sailor had to blink and glance away toward the bulkhead.

"Helm, report," Captain Barcena called forward.

"Two-one-five compass, 250 meters, 8 knots, Capitan."

The CO frowned and quickly looked around the crowded control room of *El Tiburon* where dark-faced boys sweated in the stuffy air with the watertight doors and ventilators dogged for general quarters.

In the air hard with sweaty fear, El Viejo could smell the jungle in the rainy season before Christmas 1958. In the Revolution's last week before victory, Che Guevara with 249 men and one woman was marching toward Santa Clara, the capital of Las Villas Province. The Castro brothers, Fidel and Raul, led their columns against Palma Sorino on the road to Santiago and Caimanera across the bay from Guantanamo and the U.S. Navy base.

Che captured Sancti Spiritus on Christmas Eve and was laying siege to Santa Clara by New Year's Eve. The young rebel Martinez Barcena and the dark-eyed girl marched with Guevara. At dawn on New Year's Day and only 20 hours before Batista and his family fled the island forever, a bullet from a government Regular's rifle ripped into the girl's chest. Within minutes, Amalia was dead in her rebel lover's bloodied arms. She never made a sound.

El Tiburon's captain could not shake the haunting memory that his Amalia had been the real soldier. He had only followed her. She had July 26th branded hotly upon her heart and soul. He had slept under her blanket on the wet mountain earth. But he had hungered for the Vedado neighborhood of Havana where the rich Spaniards lived along Malecon Boulevard and for El Carmelo Restaurant where they dined on white table cloths. Amalia had been the real soldier.

The captain's eyes looked into each face for a heartbeat.

"Helm, make turns for 15 knots."

"Ahead flank bell, Capitan."

The XO swallowed twice as the CO turned back toward his sonar man.

"One burst active."

"One burst, aye." The technician's voice was a question.

El Viejo laid his hand firmly upon the sitting sailor's sweaty shoulder.

"One sweep, Pepe."

A huddle of enlisted men on Two Deck spread out in the passageway so petty officers Morrow and Jackson could pass.

The men were whispering about the sonar blast which had rattled their nerves as they made their way from the mess compartment to their box-like racks in the crew quarters amidships. The men had taken their midrats when their watches changed at 0800.

A seaman who was not mingling stood watch at the closed watertight door which he opened to allow Morrow and Jackson to pass. He pushed the door closed and cranked the handle when the two men crouched through.

Morrow and Jackson walked beside their red shadows in the aft end of the long passage. Sickbay was at the forward end. Twenty paces astern of the medical unit and its adjacent pharmacy, they heard muted voices.

Randy Morrow pulled Mitchell Jackson into the shadows of an open compartment, a space stuffed with cloth firehose segments faked tightly along three walls. They stood silently in the darkness of a damage control repair station which was unmanned since SSN-609's reduced crew complement could not assign a watch-stander to every compartment.

Listening intently, Morrow and Jackson heard the subdued voices of the two physicians.

"Damn," Jackson whispered. "Randy, I can't do this."

"Shut up, Mitch! They'll hear us."

"I can't go in there when the medics are there. Someone might get hurt." The seaman's eyes were wide in the gray shadows.

"They've already hurt us." Randy Morrow's whisper was raspy with rage. "Killed us most likely. Drove us insane for sure."

"We don't know that. For God's sake, Randy. We can still go to the skipper and tell him about the armory. The old man's got to understand."

"And go to prison for ten years? We struck a man and stole firearms at GQ. They'll throw away the key. Just stay cool, all right?"

Morrow glanced past the bulkhead into the passageway. The corridor of red light was silent.

"They went inside. No one will get hurt. Just stay behind me."

When Morrow stepped into the passageway, he felt Jackson grab the back of his belt and pull him back into the dark hole.

"No, Randy. No. I'm going to sick bay. The woman will understand. I just know it. You come too. Leave the gun here. It'll be okay."

Jackson's voice was pleading.

"You're a coward," Morrow whispered acidly. "You go to prison. Not me."

Morrow pushed Jackson hard into the rolls of firehose. Then he turned and walked quickly aft.

Gathering his wits, Mitchell Jackson sniffed hard, tucked in his shirt tails, and walked slowly forward toward sick bay.

Behind him, Randy Morrow clutched the M-9 pistol to his belly under his denim shirt as he approached the watertight door which he heaved open with his free hand.

Mitchell Jackson shuffled into sick bay as Randy Morrow disappeared through the hatch at the aft end of the passageway. Doctors Dugan and Shaffer did not look up from a small unit of bioelectronic equipment.

"My God," the woman sighed.

"I can't believe it only took two and a half hours to migrate." Lt. Shaffer spoke softly so he would not wake the dozing planesman who snorted breakfast through a tube in one nostril.

"Both readouts?"

"Identical, Jessica."

The physicians leaned over two complex devices: an AnCon Genetics automatic gene analyzer from Melville, New York, and a similar chromosome mapper from the California Institute of Technology. The AnCon machine uses microscopic probes to zero in on specific genetic sequences of hereditary code. The Georgetown Medical Center had developed the technique for locating genetic defects at the amino acid level.

The Caltech machine uses dyes and a laser scanner to map genetic code. It can "read" 15,000 nucleotide pairs within chromosomes per day.

"Who's going to tell the captain?"

"You outrank me, Commander," Dr. Shaffer grinned feebly.

"But you're General Medical Officer," Jessica Dugan nodded. She squinted her still black eye.

Mitchell Jackson cleared his throat to announce his presence.

"Mitchell?" Dr. Shaffer blinked as he looked up from his expensive toys.

"Ma'am. Sir. I think we need to talk. I think I know the consequences now."

"Sit down, Mitch," the GMO said softly. He pointed to a metal chair with rubber feet to prevent noise on the deck.

The disheveled seaman sat down. His face was grim.

"Are you talking about us, Sir? Me and Randy?"

The physicians looked briefly at each other.

"I see, Sir. Do we both have it? The bug, I mean."

The lieutenant sat down beside the sailor. Jessica Dugan hovered over them both.

"No, Mitch. Just Randy. These machines sort out gene fragments. I'm running blood samples from both of you that I drew at 6:00. Randy's sample is showing a defect in his genetic material where we would expect to see the disease that took Richards over there."

The GMO looked past Jackson's shoulder toward the sleeping planesman.

"And Hendrix, Frazier, and Buddy?"

Stan Shaffer gently touched the seaman's knee.

"Yes, Mitch. I'm afraid so. But you're fine. Do you understand me? Your sample is perfectly normal."

Mitchell Jackson looked down at the deck. His voice was a whisper.

"For now, Sir."

"I think permanently, Mitch."

"Sure, Doc. I came down here to talk about Randy."

The GMO looked up at the woman.

"He's in quarters, right Mitch?"

"No, Sir." The seaman rubbed his hands together nervously. He looked at the deck between his soft shoes. "He has an M-9."

"What!" Dr. Dugan stepped forward and laid her hand firmly upon Jackson's shoulder. She squeezed hard, he thought.

"Yes, Commander. Took it off the sentry in the armory. Hit him, too. Maybe you should send a corpsman back there."

"God," the woman whispered. She reached for the telephone and called CIC. She asked for Lt. Commander Perlmutter and spoke too softly for Jackson or the GMO to hear her. Then she returned to stand above Jackson.

The lieutenant leaned toward Jackson.

"Names, Mitch. Who else shared needles for the colchicine?"

Jackson rubbed his knees. He closed his eyes and began speaking toward his shoes.

"Folley the assistant 3M coordinator, O'Brien the nuclear handling supervisor, Lieutenant Foster the nuclear safety officer, Chief Pitmann the top secret control officer, Master Chief Lyon the crypto technician, Walden the DSI data systems technician first class, GSCS Thorp senior chief gas turbine systems technician, ICC Buford chief interior comm electrician, and STILO Milford the scientific and technical intelligence liaison officer."

"Jesus!" Jessica rolled her eyes and blinked at the overhead.

"I don't know how many men in the labs, Commander. They pretty much keep to themselves off duty."

"All sharing the same batch of hypodermic needles?"

"Guess so, Sir. We hid them in the hot wells in the turbine steam lines. Thought the heat would sterilize everything."

"Well, the heat would work on bacteria—germs. But probably not on the viruses they're using in the labs."

"Oh. Nobody knew that, Sir."

"All right. You know that Dr. Dugan and I have to brief the CO."

"Yes, Sir." Mitchell Jackson looked up. His face was twisted with a terrible pain. "I just didn't want to go insane. But I didn't want to hurt nobody. That's the God's honest truth, Lieutenant. I swear to God!"

"I know, Mitch. Can you go forward on your own?"

"Aye, Sir." The seaman stood up between the two physicians. "Don't let them hurt Randy. He's not himself." Jackson looked hard into Stan Shaffer's tired eyes. "He didn't do this to himself."

The GMO laid his hand upon the grieving man's shoulder.

"We know that, Mitch. Go on to your quarters. We'll explain everything to the skipper."

The seaman nodded and took a step toward the doorway. He paused and turned to face Jessica Dugan. When his eyes met the woman's, his face cracked and tears rolled quickly down his young face. She stepped toward him. His shoulders trembled as he wept with his hands clenched into fists at his sides.

"We'll help you," Dr. Dugan said weakly.

"I have a wife and babies," Mitchell Jackson whimpered.

Jessica reached out and wrapped her arms around the weeping seaman. Jackson forced one eye to open and he looked over the woman's shoulder toward Lieutenant Shaffer. The sailor had never touched an officer. Stan Shaffer nodded slowly with his face brimming with his own tears and with bone-deep sympathy.

Mitchell Jackson raised his arms and embraced Jessica Dugan lightly. He lowered his face into her khaki collar and he wept uncontrollably.

"I don't want to go insane," Jackson sobbed.

Jessica Dugan patted his back between his shoulder blades as if he were a child. She longed to assure him that he would not go insane, that he would not gnaw his own fingers off, that he would not slowly lose his mind and become an idiot.

Dr. Dugan could say nothing.

The sonar man fiddled with his console. He shook his head.

"Ready yet?"

"Sorry, Capitan. Still can't seem to isolate the failure. I'm going back through the checklist."

"Very well. Let me know when you have the Herkules on line."

"Yes, Sir."

The technician had failed to generate an active sweep of *El Tiburon*'s sonar, called Herkules by the Russians and codenamed Wolf Paw by their NATO adversaries.

The XO stood close to Captain Barcena.

"Sorry about the sonar, Capitan." The executive officer remained uneasy about steaming down the wake of the American submarine.

"No problem," El Viejo said softly. "She's an old boat with a young crew." He smiled as he scanned his cramped control room. "Sometimes their great hearts just cannot make up for tired electronics. If we can't get a sweep, we'll come about and go home." The CO closely studied the exec's reaction.

"Yes, Sir." The officer's face brightened instantly.

"Capitan?"

"Yes, Ensign."

"I think I found it. A circuit breaker popped only half way: just enough to open the connection to the transducer, but not enough to see it on my panel."

"Excellent. Well done. Make ready and transmit at will. One sweep."

The captain heard his XO exhale audibly close behind him.

"I don't understand it, Stan. How could half a dozen men, maybe more, share the hypos and still be asymptomatic when you've run genetic serum scans at least every two weeks and urinalysis for uric acid weekly? It doesn't make any sense."

The two physicians walked slowly through the passageway toward the hole in the overhead which would take them up to One Deck and SSN-609's CIC to report to Captain Milhaus.

"I can't answer that, Jessica. It's probably a matter of vector concentration. The Tiger Mosquito in BL-4 would inject dengue or LaCrosse viruses by the tens of millions. Who knows how few of the contaminating retroviruses would have survived in the hot wells of the steam turbine line. The wells remove condensation from the pipe. Might be 200 degrees down there. Maybe only a few viruses would survive long enough to be injected with IV colchicine: not enough to cause overt symptoms in most healthy men. But they were injecting the drug intravenously.

"Randy Morrow might be the only one of the group who absorbed enough live virus to respond. Maybe he had some other low-grade infection—a common cold, perhaps—that compromised his immune system enough for the virus to get a hold on him. Enough of a hold to start replicating in his system until Lesch-Nyhan secondary effects became serious. He might not have had enough viral agents to test positive when I last ran his blood in the gene analyzer ten days ago. I just don't know."

Randy Morrow said little to the sailors-turned-scientists and the NIH biologists-turned-submariners when he walked quickly through the BL-3 laboratory on Two Deck. None of the dozen men looked up from their protein fractionators or HPLC gene separators when he passed. Hull technicians are everywhere on a nuclear submarine. Having them underfoot is a comfort when their job is to keep out the crushing pressure of the sea. ·

So HTSC Morrow walked between the sixteen empty missile silos toward the aft bulkhead of BL-3, signed out in the logbook, and threw his smock into the decontamination hamper in the outer dressing compartment.

Crouching through the last positive pressure bulkhead, Morrow eased the heavy hatch closed.

He stood alone in the dim red lights of the passageway which skirted the nuclear reactor compartment and its walls of lead shielding. He only paused long enough to pull his M-9 pistol from under his shirt to inspect the chamber-loaded indicator once more. He flicked the thumb lever to engage the safety.

"In his cabin probably. I thought the CO was with you two in the wardroom." The XO perspired heavily. "I sent two HT's to the armory."

Hospital technicians are skilled in first aid.

"Thanks, Commander," Dr. Dugan nodded. She quickly followed the GMO through the forward, watertight door.

The physicians walked past the closed wardroom door and knocked softly on the captain's cabin.

"Come."

Lt. Shaffer opened the fake wood door and let Dr. Dugan enter first. Then he stepped inside and closed the door.

Captain Kurt Milhaus was drying his sagging face on a towel which he tossed through the door open to his private head.

"Sit down please," the CO gestured. The physicians pulled two chairs close to the one by the captain's small desk.

When the CO sat down and the medics followed, Jessica Dugan noticed a small needlepoint design in a frame just above the desk on the bulkhead. During her 40 sleepless hours on board 609, she had not been to the captain's narrow quarters.

Stitched into the blue background was the ensign of submariners' crossed dolphins. A paragraph of text was neatly inscribed with gold thread beneath the dolphins. She recognized Article 1102 of the Regulations of the United States

Navy: "All commanding officers and others in authority in the naval service are required to show in themselves a good example of virtue, honor, and patriotism."

Captain Milhaus followed her eyes.

"My mother made that for me when I was exec in *Henry Jackson*, ballistic missile boat 730."

"It's beautiful, Captain."

"Yes, Doctor. But I need to get back to CIC. What do you people have to report."

Before the physicians could answer, the telephone buzzed. The CO picked it up quickly as he rubbed the blue knot on his forehead.

"Captain . . . Jesus, Pappy! . . . Alert the MAC."

Kurt Milhaus hung up the telephone and swivelled in his chair to face Dr. Shaffer.

"The HTs found the sentry in the armory. . . . The boy's dead. Suffocated in his own puke. You heard me ask for the master sergeant-at-arms." The CO closed his eyes and rubbed his forehead hard. "Pappy reports that the damned water hammer is back in the cold leg of main steam. We might as well be dropping bread crumbs for the Cubans to follow us. Now, what do you have to report from sick bay?"

The weariness in the captain's eyes was too painful to look at. The woman had to look away toward Dr. Shaffer. She waited for him to start. The general medical officer shrugged his shoulders and spoke in a whisper of anguish.

"We think it might be everywhere, Sir. . . ."

Six hundred feet beneath the stormy surface, *Sam Houston* sped toward the southwest. She glided directly under *Hayler* which remained stationary where her propellers drove her northward into the swift current rolling south down Mona Passage. DD-997's sonar men did not hear 609 pass below nor the silent electric submarine pursuing her.

The all-night downpour had dropped tons of cool rain into the warm Caribbean. The cold, fresh water sank into the sea and formed a thick submerged blanket of temperature and salinity gradient. The throbbing of *Hayler*'s twin screws bounced off the freshet layer and reflected back to the turbulent surface. The destroyer's noise could not penetrate down to the hydrophones of either *Sam Houston* or *El Tiburon*. The destroyer was acoustically invisible to the two vessels far below which plowed through black water toward the shallows off Mona Island.

At 0845 UTC—0445 Atlantic Time—sunrise was half an hour away, delayed by the thick canopy of thunderstorms.

"Belay the sonar sweep," Captain Barcena said firmly. For the first time on this hastily ordered cruise, he sounded impatient. "What do you have?"

"A passive contact through the Fenik, Capitan."

The teenager pressed his earphones closer to his head. With a flick of a switch, he replayed the audio tape for the third time.

"It's that same mechanical noise I heard before, Sir. But much closer. Much closer. If it's the American boat, it might be some kind of anomaly in his reactor system. Coolant loop maybe."

Captain Barcena squinted at the boy.

"There's never been a reported breakdown of an American nuclear reactor at sea."

"No, Capitan. But that's my guess, Sir."

Not until October 1993 did the U.S. Navy finally announce that the submarine *Thresher* had sunk in 1963 from bad welds in her plumbing and that *Scorpion* had gone down in 1968 after being struck by her own runaway torpedo.

"Could it be ambient noise from the storm? Whales or dolphins?"

"It's just not quite right for that, Capitan. Too high a frequency. And the amplifier analysis shows it almost identical to what we heard earlier."

"All right," the captain sighed. "Sweep him once."

"Yes, Capitan."

An ultrasonic pulse erupted from *El Tiburon*'s bow-mounted Herkules transducer.

The executive officer grimaced when he heard the echo powerful enough to vibrate back through *El Tiburon*'s hull. The active sonar return banged into the Cuban submarine only two seconds after its transmission.

The sonar man looked up with his eyes wide. He looked stunned.

"Fifteen hundred meters, Capitan."

TWENTY

EL TIBURON'S sonar beam bounced off *Sam Houston*, reflected back to *El Tiburon*, and split when it glanced off the Cuban boat. The deeper half of the ray sped toward the bottom of Mona Passage to seek out the deep sound channel. The upper reflection struck the sinking freshet layer of cold rain water and deflected downward to become a rumbling of bottom reverberation. None of the acoustic radiation pierced the watery inversion layer beneath the angry surface.

The destroyer *Hayler* heard nothing: not the sonar noise and not the hum of powerplants or hull flow turbulence of *El Tiburon* and SSN-609 which passed underneath DD-997. *Hayler*'s nauseated crewmen heard only the steel shot rain against the bridge windows and the creaking of the hull.

SSN-609 led the Cuban submarine into the shallows of the Isla de Mona where the eastern coast descended toward the sandy bottom only 1,200 feet deep two miles from shore.

Doctors Dugan and Shaffer gathered stacks of personnel files and watch bills in her stateroom at 0855. Captain Milhaus returned to CIC. The two physicians said nothing to each other when the PA system crackled with Pappy Perlmutter's fourth call for Hull Maintenance Technician Randall Morrow to report to CIC.

The body of the dead sentry was still warm when sailors laid him gently onto the deck in *Sam Houston*'s frozen meat locker.

The chief master-at-arms was the last man out of the armory. The MAC and his two assistants each carried an M-14 rifle loaded with NATO hardball ammunition.

"One hundred fifty meters under the keel, Capitan."

"Thank you, Quartermaster."

Captain Barcena leaned over his sonar man who was exhausted from his cat and mouse game in the black water.

"Hydrophones?"

"Two more spikes of mechanical noise, Sir. Definitely below us and definitely from his plumbing. But with nearly a mile between us and with the sea state so rough, it's getting harder to filter his noise from the storm echoing off the bottom."

"Did you get a trend?"

"Yes, Capitan. He seems to be making for the island. Maybe he's going to go around it from the south to hide from us."

El Viejo smiled and patted the boy's moist shoulder.

"Yanqui boats hide in deep water. Not in shoals. He's probably trying to rendezvous with other American ships behind the island. Maybe another submarine; maybe a surface vessel. But he's not hiding. Just keep advising the quartermaster of his estimated position so we can steer into his wake. Inside his wake, with his own plumbing noise, and the sea state, I don't think his trailing hydrophone array will hear us. Electric boats are too quiet. All will be well."

The CO spoke loud enough so his tense XO could hear him.

"How close and how long, Sir?" the executive officer inquired.

"Oh, just till he rounds the island. Then we'll give him one final sweep to say goodbye before we come about for home."

The XO could not conceal his relief.

Randy Morrow made his way aft on Two Deck toward the propulsion spaces. He planned to enter the main condenser compartment and descend there to the bottom deck. Once on Three Deck, he would make his way forward through the BL-4 maximum containment laboratory. Forward of the lab, he could then go up a companionway back to Two Deck and sick bay's pharmacy where the drugs were stored. Getting there from below would keep him from having to pass through the One Deck control room where the XO or the captain were waiting for him. Cutting straight through Two Deck would have exposed him to whatever mischief Mitchell Jackson had caused in sick bay. No one would stop him in the lab since hull technicians have the run of the ship.

Petty Officer Morrow climbed down the steel ladder beside the main condenser heat exchangers. He stepped onto the deck just as three armed men entered the space from the watertight hatch on Three Deck.

Captain Webster on the rolling bridge squinted through the rain-swept window on *Hayler*'s starboard side. To the east where Puerto Rico's southwest corner lay 30 nautical miles beyond the horizon, the faintest visible shade of pink separated the hazy ocean from the ragged clouds. The bulkhead clock showed a few minutes past 0900 UTC, 5:00 in the morning Atlantic Standard Time in Mona Passage.

The CO picked up the telephone.

"Sonar, bridge. Anything from 609 or the Cubans? . . . Very well. Keep trying and advise immediately if you have contact."

Five miles east of the Isla de Mona, the destroyer heaved upward as each 15-foot wave rolled under her keel. Then she slid down the windward side of the swell. The dawn barely illuminated the canyon of green which towered above *Hayler* on all sides when she pitched into the trough between waves. White water blown from the crest of the next approaching wave pounded 997's single forward cannon.

Captain Webster and his pale officer of the deck gripped chairs bolted to the deck when their ship pitched steeply to drive up the slope of the oncoming wave front.

"Make turns for 10 knots," Captain Webster called to his OOD.

"Ten knots, aye, Sir."

The CO swayed over to the bridge chart table. He consulted the ship's performance graphs of surge (distance traveled while changing speed) and tactical diameter (distance traversed right or left when a 180-degree turn is executed).

"I hate to do it in 15-foot seas, but we have no choice but to come about to one-eight-zero," Captain Webster ordered. "We can't stay out of the troughs station-keeping on a northerly heading."

"Aye, Sir," the OOD replied as his shoulder pounded a navigation console with each passing wave.

Steaming at a velocity equal to the speed of the current causes a ship's rudder to become inefficient or ineffective altogether. Especially in rough seas, a ship must keep her speed different from that of the current to guarantee that water flows over the rudder surface. So Captain Webster called for *Hayler* to make turns to steam 10 knots slower than the ocean current. He also ordered a risky turn back to a southerly heading.

Steaming downwind with the southerly current would increase the time between the rising crests of the waves. Ships tend to skid down the back side and then twist parallel to the waves in the trough between crests. This motion exposes the vessel to being slammed broadside by waves which can capsize the ship. More controllable sailing with current and wind, *Hayler* would have more rudder authority for steering out of the dangerous troughs. DD-997 would slowly pull away from Isla de Mona— a decision necessary to prevent the ship from swamping. Over the years, the U.S. Navy has lost four destroyers in hurricanes. Robert Webster was not about to become the fifth.

Randy Morrow took two steps backward as his right hand reached for the M-9 inside his sweat-soaked shirt. Five seamen on watch in the condenser compartment dove for cover behind tons of cooling and distillation machinery.

Without a word, Morrow raised his pistol toward the three armed men standing at the open watertight hatch. The master-at-arms stood between two younger men. The seaman on the MAC's left raised his M-14 until the plastic stock touched his cheek.

"Don't, Randy!" the master-at-arms called forcefully.

Morrow trained the pistol on the older man's chest.

"I'm no monkey," the hull technician said softly. His voice did not carry past the humming of the condenser equipment mounted on the floating raft deck. The sailors hiding behind steel heat exchangers had been troubleshooting the water hammer in the steam lines.

The M-9 Beretta made no sound when Randy Morrow flicked the safety on the left side of the black slide.

The pistol jerked when the slide cycled and slammed back into battery after a 9mm bullet exploded from the muzzle. The round caught the MAC just below his left collarbone. The bullet entered his upper chest, ricocheted off the inside of his shoulder blade and pierced his heart. The jacketed bullet stopped in the big man's breastbone before he fell backward against the bulkhead, dead.

When an M-14 rifle cracked with a deafening report, Morrow was lifted off the deck. Airborne, he fired one more pistol round into the steel overhead.

While Morrow was still rising, the rifle bullet which entered his breast pocket splintered his spine like fresh wood. In the instant he stopped motionless in midair, the spinning projectile exploded out of his back in a cloud of yellow bone fragments and shreds of shiny white spinal cord. The bullet's metal jacket kept the soft lead from mushrooming and slowing the bullet as it passed through the already dead sailor.

Before Morrow fell to the deck, the rifle bullet thumped into the feedwater line running through the compartment. The pipe carried non-radioactive, high-pressure steam from the steam generator to the turbine driving 609's single propeller.

Steam roared out of a half-inch hole in the stainless steel pipe. A white surge of 500°F vapor under 750 pounds of pressure covered Randy Morrow's corpse as he hit the deck in a motionless heap. White billows of cloud shot from the pipe with a force six times greater than a firehose—a boiling firehose.

Within three seconds, the steam peeled Morrow's face and hair cleanly off his skull. His entire head above his collar was glistening, pink bone. As his brain boiled and expanded, the tiny bones and membranes of his inner ear were pushed out of the skull's ear holes like cooked snails.

All five crewmen who had huddled behind the main condenser plant ran for the open watertight door. They stomped through waist-high steam clouds and jumped over the dead MAC.

One of the two riflemen stepped backwards and tripped over the master-at-arms. The guard held his ears against the roaring steam. The other sentry fell to his knees, covered his ears, and vomited.

In *Sam Houston*'s maneuvering room, crewmen sat quietly monitoring 609's nuclear fire. Aft of the steam-filled condenser compartment, the watch-standers sipped hot coffee an hour into the morning watch.

Two seconds after the main feedwater line was penetrated, red lights flashed. The maneuvering room petty officers and the engineering officer of the watch were stunned by the sudden noise of alarm bells and warning buzzers.

The Feedwater Control Subsystem of the once-through steam generator responded automatically to the sudden loss of steam pressure in the thick pipe leading from the steam generator to the turbine further aft in the engine room.

"EFIC engaged!" the EOOW shouted, nearly choking on a swig of coffee.

"AFW commit!" a petty officer replied as he sat wide-eyed while lights and meters confirmed that the ship's plumbing was responding automatically.

The nuclear powerplant's Emergency Feedwater Initiation and Control system had kicked in the Auxiliary Feedwater System to plug the loss of steam pressure.

When the pressure fell in the pipe, the temperature decreased too. When the temperature dropped, steam quickly began to condense within the line. Water droplets rode the steam down the pipe toward the turbine. The drops gelled into globules of boiling water within the steam which is designed to flow "dry."

Within five seconds of the line's penetration, a mass of wet steam and water slammed into the blades of the humming main turbine attached to 609's propeller shaft. Balls of water hammered the turbine blades like bullets. Instantaneous vibrations triggered alarms in the engine room as the turbine blades deformed. Now out of balance, the massive main turbine vibrated on its floating raft. Engineers squinted at their monitors and consoles to isolate the cause of the imbalance. The main turbine sounded as if it would tear itself apart.

Wet steam and water droplets careened through the bending blades of the jet-like steam engine. The high water concentration set off alarms in the moisture separator reheaters where steam exits the turbine between the high-pressure and low-pressure sections of the turbine.

Watery exhaust from the low-pressure side of the turbine made the loop back toward the main condenser where steam continued to erupt from the hole in the main feedwater pipe. Making the circuit through the condensers, the water separation equipment was overwhelmed within half a minute.

The engine room steam chest shook violently where the throttle equipment controlled from the maneuvering room meets the turbine's governor valve.

"IMCS has taken the conn!" the engineering officer shouted in the maneuvering room.

The Integrated Master Control Subsystem had taken over regulating feedwater flow, steam generator heat, and the nuclear reactor itself.

Feedwater steam and growing puddles of flying water slammed into the steam generator in the reactor compartment. The steam and water were driven upward through the steam generator. Water globules bounced off the tubes inside the steam generator where boiling water was flowing downward from the nuclear reactor coolant loop. Within two minutes of Randy Morrow's execution, 750 of 15,000 Inconel tubes shattered from the water hammer inside the steam generator. The twisting pipes carried water circulated through the nuclear core. Each broken tube released water pressure from the reactor cooling loop.

Sensors felt the pressure drop in the high-pressure side of the Reactor Coolant System when the hot water tubes collapsed.

"Jesus!" the engineering officer whispered when a red light on the center of his console illuminated with a wail. "SFAS activation!" he shouted into the telephone connected to CIC.

The automatic Safety Features Actuation System was compensating for the sudden drop in the coolant flow which connected the steam generator to the nuclear core. The steam generator sucks heat from the reactor's hot water loop. That heat boils water in the generator for transfer to the turbine. But that steam was blowing into the main condenser compartment. When the tubes within the generator failed and let the pressure drop within the reactor's coolant loop, automatic systems took over to manage the nuclear plumbing crisis before the reactor suffered a catastrophic meltdown.

In CIC, Kurt Milhaus anxiously waited for details on his

ship's nuclear plumbing seizure. Pappy Perlmutter held the telephone and listened to the abrupt status reports coming in from the maneuvering room well aft of the missile compartments behind the sealed CIC bulkhead.

The SFAS had taken command of the propulsion crisis. Computers drove the automatic procedure for cooling the reactor now that the steam generator was unable to carry heat out of the nuclear furnace.

SFAS electronics initiated a series of emergency routines which were loud enough to reverberate through the hull and into the black ocean. Any passive sonar within ten miles would hear the torrents of emergency coolant water flooding the reactor.

The safety system turned on the high-pressure injection which powered up two water pumps to keep the reactor core flooded. Borated water from emergency tanks kept the seething core covered with 300 gallons per minute. Backing up the high-pressure system was the low-pressure injection system. It can pump borated water into the core without electricity to run its pumps. Nitrogen gas would drive the water into the reactor containment vessel.

"Captain! We have a scram and trip," The XO called breathlessly.

SSN-609's nuclear reactor was automatically disconnecting from *Sam Houston*'s electrical systems. The reactor was being shut down and emergency batteries were kicking in without even blinking the red standing lights in CIC.

"Can maneuvering initiate a battle short?" the CO demanded hoarsely.

A battle short is an emergency manual override of a nuclear power interruption.

The XO spoke into the phone.

"Negative, Captain. We have a scram condition alert."

"Very well."

The captain pounded his fist into his open palm. Sweat beaded on the welt above his eyes. He turned toward his executive officer.

"Pappy, emergency surface. Sound radiation alert."

"Aye, Sir! Emergency blow and radiation alert!"

The surfacing klaxon and the radiation alarm sounded together in painful discordance.

The XO stepped toward his captain. Both men were wet with perspiration.

"We won't get rooms in Carl Vinson Hall this way, Pappy." Captain Milhaus smiled lamely. His face sagged from exhaustion and from controlled terror.

"No, Captain," the exec nodded thoughtfully.

Carl Vinson Hall is the U.S. Navy's home for service widows. Navy couples are allowed to retire there when accommodations are available.

The flood of boron-flavored water surging into the nuclear reactor was joined by the roar of high-pressure air exploding into *Sam Houston*'s main ballast tanks. The planesman in the front of the control room pulled back on his aircraft-style yoke to jerk 609 into a 30-degree emergency ascent. The steep up-bubble forced everyone standing to grab onto the nearest console or seat back to keep from falling backward. The ship's single propeller drove the boat toward the stormy surface southeast of Mona Island.

The CO shouted over the disharmony of the warning sirens toward the front of CIC where a teenage seaman wrestled with the control wheel. Beside him, another seaman sat his trick at the helm and tried to keep the 8,000-ton vessel from rolling over in the uncomfortable ascent angle.

"Planesman!" the CO called, "don't let her broach!"

"No, Sir!" the boy shouted over his shoulder without taking his eyes from his gyro horizon. If the ship's stern broaches—jumps clear of the water—all control of the 410-foot long submarine would be lost as stern planes and rudder lose contact with the sea.

"Turns for 5 knots after you trim, Pappy!"

"Aye, Sir."

On emergency batteries, a nuclear submarine can go no faster.

At 0906 UTC, not more than seven minutes after Randy Morrow was gunned down, the passageway outside Jessica Dugan's stateroom erupted with the high-pitched horns.

"Stan!"

The GMO blinked and his jaw fell. Both officers stood up quickly.

"Emergency surface and radiation alert, Jessica!"

The woman dropped her stack of personnel files. Her mouth

moved but only air came out. Lieutenant Shaffer could read her trembling lips when she breathed, "Hail Mary! Have mercy on us now and at the moment of our death."

When the deck suddenly gave way toward the stern, the woman stumbled into the GMO's arms. The brown files on the floor slid against the bulkhead across the slanting deck pitching upward.

Jessica Dugan was seized by blind panic. She fought to release the GMO's grip around her shoulders. He held her with one hand. His other hand grabbed the metal frame of the double bunk. He held onto the bed with a death grip to keep from crashing to the deck which inclined steeply.

"I have to go, Stan! I have to go!" she stuttered. Tears rolled down her face under her black eye.

"Easy now, easy, Jessie. You're safe here. The radiation drill is SOP. Stay calm! There's never been a nuclear accident on a U.S. boat."

She continued to struggle. Her hot breath blew into his face in short, wild pants. He could feel her body convulsing.

"Jessica, I have you! I have you!" He gripped her harder with his free arm.

When she looked up terrified, her head fell forward until her mouth touched his. The lieutenant opened his lips to suck in her breath.

"My God, Capitan!"

The sonar man in *El Tiburon* reflexively pulled both earphones away from his wet cheeks. He let the heavy headset flop back around his ears as Captain Barcena hunched over his shoulder.

"What is it, son?"

"I don't know, Capitan. The enemy submarine is blowing everything. Even through the ambient noise from the storm, I can hear him blowing ballast. And there's some kind of additional noise: high frequency narrow band. He could be flooding, Sir!"

"Easy now." The CO and his nervous XO both leaned over the boy. "Did you hear bulkheads collapse?"

"No, Sir."

"Can you hear air bubbles?"

"No, Sir."

The CO straightened.

"All right then. It's not a fatal casualty. Must be an emergency surface though." The captain picked up a telephone. "Engineering, bridge. Are you monitoring any outside radiation? . . . That's correct, Chief, radiation . . . Very well."

Captain Barcena returned the telephone to its bulkhead cradle close to the brass clock which showed 0908, UTC. He laid a hand on the sonar man's shoulder. The cotton cloth stuck to the CO's palm.

"No radiation being monitored outside. His reactor is intact at least. When you hear him break the surface, give him a moment to trim and then sweep him once with active. I want a Doppler on him."

"Aye, Sir," the boy's voice quivered.

The CO turned to his exec.

"Confirm torpedoes armed and loaded all tubes."

The color drained from the lieutenant's moist face as he picked up the telephone to hail fire control. When he laid the phone down, his voice sounded as weak as the sonar technician's.

"Armed and loaded, Capitan, all tubes."

"Very well. Bring her up to 50 meters. We won't need the periscope at this close range."

"Fifty meters, aye, Sir." The XO repeated the order to the diving officer.

Seven hundred fifty feet down, *El Tiburon*'s planesman pulled back on his control wheel and the deck pitched upward toward the bow. Three propellers drove the ship upward.

Rising slowly through 450 feet, the Cuban boat shuddered mildly. She was passing through the cold freshet layer. The temperature gradient across the fresh water pool sinking slowly toward the bottom of Mona Passage caused turbulence. Within the freshet layer, *El Tiburon*'s ascent slowed markedly since she was less buoyant in fresh water than in salt water. Since submarines came of age in 1914, more than one has been sunk by sailing from the open sea into fresh coastal waters. Open deck hatches allowed the less buoyant, fresh water to cascade into the hull when the boat floated lower with less freeboard above the surface.

The turbulence stopped as *El Tiburon* entered the freshet blanket. The water became choppy again when she broke out above the layer.

"One hundred meters, Capitan," the diving officer called.

"Very well. Steady as you go." The CO glanced at the helmsman. "Mind your rudder when we enter the surface turbulence."

"Aye, Capitan."

Clear of the fresh water, the vessel ascended faster into smooth water. After 90 seconds of calm water, the boat began to pitch slightly as she came up beneath the wild surface.

"Seventy-five meters, Sir."

"Very well."

The deck slowly pitched down toward the bow as *El Tiburon* levelled off with 150 feet between the surface and her keel. Air could be heard hissing against the inner pressure hull as compressed gas blew water in bursts from the fore and aft trim tanks to stabilize the ship.

"Capitan?"

"Yes," the CO said as he took two steps toward his sonar man. "What do you have now?"

"High speed screws, five miles east of us."

"Torpedoes?" The captain's voice was anxious.

"No, Sir. Another ship. I hear two screws for sure, maybe three. Just one ship."

"Merchantman?" The CO leaned over the console again.

"Not likely, Sir. A light cruiser or heavy destroyer. Sounds like a gas turbine powerplant. American, Capitan."

"Hmm. Thank you." The captain turned toward his exec who was wet from his throat to his belt buckle. "So, our American friends have a support ship after all. And close."

"Yes, Capitan," the XO swallowed hard. "I recommend we break off now, Sir."

"Noted, Lieutenant." El Viejo showed his first trace of impatience. Then he turned back to sonar. "Status?"

"The submarine is surfacing, Sir."

"Then ping him one sweep. I need to know his speed. We don't want to pass him from below."

"One ping, aye."

Sam Houston exploded out of the green water which glistened white under sporadic bursts of lightning. SSN-609's round bow broke the surface between fifteen-foot waves.

Like God's own finger, the tubular hull climbed out of the

water all the way back to her black sail. When half the tower structure was clear, the bow fell forward with a terrible crash in the wave trough. The hull sank out of sight until only the sail's streamlined top broke the surging surface. A white wake trailed the sail and its closed shutters protecting periscopes, radar and radio masts, and snorkel. Slowly, the ship surfaced again and tons of water spilled over her hull.

In CIC, the diving officer and his seamen struggled to balance the air and water in the trim tanks to assure 609's level cruise. Although the computerized inertial navigation systems confirmed an even keel, she heeled wildly and the tall sail rolled well over.

Sam Houston had surfaced parallel to the wave front rushing south down Mona Passage. Each successive wave crashed into her broadside and slammed the sail over.

The men in the control room fought to stay upright where they stood or sat.

"Come left to one-eight-zero," Captain Milhaus called to the helmsman.

"One-eight-zero," the youth panted while swallowing to keep his midrats down.

SSN-609 heeled again to the left as she turned toward her portside from a westerly heading to a southerly one. As she came about, she ran perpendicular to the swift current. She stopped rolling sideways. But each new wave from the violent and following sea broke over her stern where the high rudder jutted out of the water. Tons of water forced the stern down and her bow pitched up hard. When the wave passed, the stern rose above the depressed trough which rolled under the ship's keel.

With each deep trough, 609's single propeller broached the surface and turned in nothing but misty air. When the rudder and stern planes left the water, the ship heeled slightly as she attempted to drift back parallel to the waves. Then the next wave plowed into the stern, forcing it back into the water. When the planes and propeller bit into the churning Caribbean, the boat righted herself and skidded back toward the south.

"Mind your head!" Lt. Commander Perlmutter called to his helmsman who sweated profusely at his control wheel.

"Aye, Sir!" the boy replied like a winded boxer.

The ship's bow rose and crashed down into the water with each passing wave and its trailing trough.

Captain Milhaus gripped the steel stanchions on either side of the lowered periscopes until his knuckles were white and sore on both hands.

"Bridge, aye," the telephone-talker replied above the clatter of sheets of black rain slashing across *Hayler*'s bridge windows. He repeated every word he heard from CIC several decks down.

"Radar contact, Captain. Zero-nine-zero at seven miles, Sir. Steering two-six-zero at eight knots. By the return, could be 609."

The petty officer had to shout across the bridge to be heard. The OOD turned to his CO.

"Shall I alter course, Captain?"

"Negative. Maintain one-eight-zero. All we can do is monitor and wait for the damned weather." The CO looked outside the starboard window for the radar contact off his quarter as *Hayler* steamed southward, carried along by the current.

"Aye, Sir."

"Advise fire control to look sharp."

"Yes, Captain."

DD-997 remained at general quarters. The crewmen not busy throwing up in the gale were anxious to fire their first volley in anger since *Hayler* left the shipyard with her commissioning pennant flying.

Captain Webster looked east. At 0515 Atlantic Time, the morning sun was moving quickly up toward the horizon. But dense black thunderheads obscured the line where the sky met the water. Not enough morning twilight could get through the overcast to brighten the mountains of water rolling past the destroyer. It was still nearly dark.

Lt. Shaffer finally had to push Jessica Dugan away. His arms ached from holding her upright.

"We have to get to CIC, Jessica. They'll need us below if there really was an accident in propulsion."

The woman trembled but she struggled gamely to collect her wits. She had been a submariner for 41 hours. Her left eye remained purple and tender. The scopolamine was wearing off after four hours and she was becoming seasick from the ship's violent pitching and rolling.

"Yes, yes," she sniffed. "There could be burns. You're right."

"Okay, Jessica. Go wash your face. Quickly. And watch your step. I'll pick up the files."

"All right."

Turning toward the head, she turned back to face the GMO. She had remembered pressing her mouth against his in her sudden terror.

"Stan . . . I . . ."

The GMO smiled gently.

"I know, Jessie. I'm not a member of the Tail Hook Association. You're safe here. But you know that."

"Yes."

The officers turned their moist backs to each other. He stooped to retrieve the scattered personnel records. She stepped into the bathroom.

The lieutenant felt the deck vibrate under his hand when a sonar burst slammed into 609's stern and rumbled through the hull from stern planes to the sonar dome in the bow.

"Solid contact, Capitan. Range 1,000 meters. He's definitely surfaced. Slight up-Doppler at 5 knots. We're closing quickly, Sir."

El Tiburon still made turns on her three screws for 15 knots at 150 feet depth.

"Five knots? Is he coming close aboard with another vessel?"

"No, Capitan. The other surface contact has changed course to one-eight-zero. He appears to be moving away from the island. Perhaps he is not a Yanqui ship after all. Range between him and the American submarine is increasing. It's presently 9 miles."

"All right. Well done."

Captain Barcena stepped away from the sonar man who seemed to sigh with relief when the CO stopped hovering over him.

"Well, Lieutenant?"

The officer of the deck standing close to the captain had not recovered his confidence. The enemy ship was behaving too strangely for bravado.

"I don't understand, Capitan. Either he is executing a rendezvous or he is in trouble. Running at 5 knots on the surface in a near hurricane? Nothing makes sense. Must be a very serious equipment failure—probably the plumbing noise we've been hearing off and on."

"A powerplant failure possibly," Captain Barcena nodded. "Highly unlikely. But nothing else seems more likely."

"I agree, Sir."

El Viejo stepped away from his OOD. The captain walked one quiet circuit of the narrow control room. He looked down at the deck and his brow was furrowed in thought. When he finally looked up, his eyes were shining. The glow on the CO's face made the young officer deeply uncomfortable.

"Capitan?"

"Take her up, Lieutenant."

"To what depth, Capitan?" The OOD looked hard into the old seaman's eyes.

"Surface, Lieutenant. Mind your helm in this sea."

"Capitan, forgive me, Sir, but surface? It's a hurricane up there. And we have a hostile vessel in front of us and possibly one astern."

"Take her up, Lieutenant. And make turns for 5 knots. Keep our range at 1,000 meters."

"Aye, Sir." The OOD's voice was subdued.

El Tiburon blew tanks at 0920, UTC.

Within three minutes, the ride became rougher until the Cuban submarine broke through the violent surface with a splash of white water. The two submarines ran parallel to the southern coast of Mona Island. The faintest light on the eastern horizon illuminated El Tiburon's conning tower. Water cascaded from the sail.

"Five knots, Capitan. Two-five-zero, Sir."

"Very well."

The men in the control room tightened their seatbelts if they were sitting. Standing sailors and Captain Barcena gripped seat backs or consoles to remain upright as the vessel pitched steeply.

The CO leaned over his radioman.

"Call the Americans on standard frequencies. Advise them

who we are and that we are standing by to render assistance if he is in distress."

"Yes, Sir," the radioman said weakly. His moist fingers slid off the transmitter knobs as *El Tiburon* pitched and rolled in massive swells which slammed against her stern and against the sail tower.

El Viejo spoke firmly to the OOD.

"Open outer doors all forward torpedo tubes."

The officer of the deck swallowed hard.

"All outer shutters, tubes One through Six, aye, Capitan."

TWENTY-ONE

16 MARCH; 0925 UTC

"I'M CERTAIN, Captain," the weary man at the sonar console nodded. "He surfaced no more than half a mile astern. The ambient noise from the storm is terrible, Sir, but there's just no mistaking torpedo doors opening."

In CIC's red battle lighting, tense faces looked at Captain Milhaus.

"Shall I launch nixies, Sir?"

"Not yet," Kurt Milhaus said thoughtfully toward his officer of the deck. Nixie anti-torpedo drones were loaded in the torpedo room. "He won't fire on the surface. Let me see the chart."

The CO walked to the navigator's chart table and maneuvering board.

"Here, Sir, by inertial."

The CO studied the chart. A red triangle put SSN-609 at the southeast corner of Isla de Mona. Steaming on emergency batteries toward the southwest, the ship was moving around the tiny island. She sailed two miles off the southern coastline.

Slowly, the ride on board *Sam Houston* became smoother. Although the deck pitched in the rough ocean, the interval between rising and falling with the waves increased. The island was blocking the southward surge of the current out of Mona Passage. As 609 headed westward, she aimed for the leeward side of the island where the winds and currents would be markedly less than the passage side where the hurricane moved eastward toward Puerto Rico.

Captain Milhaus turned toward sonar.

"Where's the bottom?"

"Two hundred fifty feet, Sir."

"Thank you."

Pappy Perlmutter returned the control room telephone to its cradle. He stepped to the captain.

"How long, Pappy?"

"Another fifteen minutes, Sir. DCC has two teams on rigging the jumper."

"Very well."

In the condenser machinery space, Randy Morrow's body had been removed. Damage control central parties were installing a jumper patch onto the steam line punctured by the sentry's bullet. Even when the pipe was sealed and pressure integrity confirmed, the reactor would not be brought back on line. Too much damage had been done to the inside of the steam generator. Control rods remained inserted into the reactor's core to reduce nuclear fission and the emergency flood of borated water kept the radioactive fuel rods covered and cool.

At 5:20 outside, local time, morning twilight was now able to penetrate the low, black clouds. Rain still fell in sheets blowing sideways. White water exploded from the towering wave crests.

The nuclear submarine led *El Tiburon* around the southern coastline of Mona Island. Riding low in the water, the bow of each ship plowed hard into the waves although each vessel made only 5 knots.

"Ten miles now to *Hayler*, Captain."

"Thank you."

The CO spoke to the sonar man who was getting reports from the surface search radar mast which had been extended from the sail.

"Is he still steaming south?"

"Yes, Sir."

"All right. Probably running with the current to maintain seakeeping."

The captain looked at his executive officer. Pappy Perlmutter seemed uncomfortable so close to the shallow bottom in violent weather.

"Pappy, how much speed can we get if we execute an emergency power-down?"

"Ten knots for sure, maybe fifteen."

The CO thought for a moment.

"Shut down all non-essential buses. I want 10 knots as soon as you can. Do whatever you have to do. And get a message off to *Hayler* advising her on our failure in propulsion."

"Yes, Captain." The XO hesitated. He stepped close enough to the CO that no one else could hear their conversation. "Ten knots, Sir?"

"Yes. Fifteen if you can wring it out of her."

"Water is pretty shallow, Captain."

"Yes, Pappy. Maybe our Cuban friends will make a mistake running the coastline."

The XO studied the captain closely.

"Maybe, Sir."

"Two messages, Captain, one from 609 encoded and one from the Cubans in plain language—English, in fact."

"Thank you," Captain Webster nodded.

The CO swayed with the deck in CIC, low in *Hayler*'s hull. After reading both dispatches, the captain picked up the telephone to the bridge.

"Bridge. Captain for the OOD. 609 reports a reactor casualty. She's running on the surface making 5 knots at two-seven-zero. The Cuban boat has surfaced astern 609. He's broadcasting on maritime frequencies a request to come close aboard 609 on the island's lee to render assistance. 609 is deferring to us to respond. I'll keep you posted."

After returning the phone to its bracket, Captain Webster staggered toward his fire control team.

"Can you bring the Number One 5-inch gun to bear in this sea, if we need it?"

"Yes, Captain." The young lieutenant sounded confident but his face was moist and pale from the hurricane's effect on his bowels.

"Very well."

Captain Webster turned toward his radioman.

"Acknowledge 609. Advise rendezvous in 30 minutes on the west side of the island. We'll stand off until the weather calms. Reply to the Cubans in English on their frequency. Advise them who we are. Order them to drop back five miles or we will engage. Send twice. Then send 609's report and our transmission to the Cubans to COMPRESECT-ASWU."

The radioman was scribbling notes as the ship heaved.

"Yes, Sir. Respond 609 and transmit to Cubans. Copies all to Commander, Puerto Rico Section, Antisubmarine Warfare Unit."

"Readback correct." The CO turned to his weapons officer. "Fire control, make ready all ASW munitions and stand by."

"Aye, aye, Sir."

"It's a *Spruance* class destroyer, Capitan. One of their newest. He orders us to fall back five miles or he will fire."

El Tiburon's radioman thumbed through a Russian edition of Norman Polmar's *Ships and Aircraft of the U.S. Fleet*.

"Did you pick up any transmission from the submarine?"

"Negative, Sir."

"Very well."

El Tiburon pitched uncomfortably. But she slowly became more stable as she followed 609's wake around the southern coastline of the island.

"Shall we come about, Capitan?"

The CO turned to his exec.

"Patience, Lieutenant," El Viejo smiled. "Patience. Up scope."

El Tiburon's daytime periscope rose from her sail. The instant the eyepiece jerked to a stop as it ascended from a hole in the deck, the captain leaned into it. He steered the tube until it viewed dead ahead.

In the dawn grayness, Captain Barcena saw a narrow field of the sea which still rose to ten-foot waves. The ocean ended in thick haze which climbed into a black overcast. Facing west, the captain's round image of the outside caught wallowing glimpses of 609. *Sam Houston* cut a narrow wake at 5 knots. Towering walls of following sea obscured her completely until the waves crashed upon her pointed stern which climbed almost clear of the sea when each wave passed over her. The waves slammed into the back of her sail and exploded under the fairwater planes jutting from the conning tower.

Turning the scope to look astern, the captain saw no trace of *Hayler* closing from the east where the sky was turning red. The horizon was no more than six miles away and the destroyer was five miles beyond that. Looking north, the tiny Isla de Mona was black with a canopy of low clouds. Walls of water obscured the beach only one mile away.

"Down scope. Range to the submarine?"

"Eleven hundred meters, Capitan. One mile to the shore."

"Very well. Bend on ten turns. We're falling behind. I want to maintain 1,000 meters."

"Ten more turns, aye," the OOD sighed.

"Have confidence, Lieutenant. We'll break off the chase very soon."

"Yes, Capitan."

"Fathometer?"

"Barely 90 meters, Sir."

"All right."

Captain Barcena ran his hard fingers through his short gray hair. His eyes were as dark as the morning outside from fatigue and strain. He stood for a moment and looked hard into the eyes of his anxious XO. Then he turned abruptly toward his fire control man.

"Disarm the fish in tubes One and Four."

"Disarm them, Sir?" The youth looked puzzled. "You're not going to just thump them, are you?"

"That is correct, Seaman."

"Yes, Sir. Sorry, Sir."

A junior officer stepped between the XO and Captain Barcena.

"Forgive me, Sir, but I don't understand. Is this some kind of game, Capitan?"

El Viejo nodded. He laid his hand upon the officer's sweaty shoulder.

"Of course it's just a game, Ernesto. How long have there been blackouts all over our island since the Russians stopped sending us oil in the summer of '92? Think how it will brighten El Commandante's day to know that we put a little dent in the side of a Yanqui nuclear submarine without hurting anyone? Not even Moscow can complain about that." A fierce light sparkled in the old rebel's eyes. "Just a game, my boy. Now return to fire control and give me a firing solution—in case we need it."

Before the sailor could swallow, the petty officer at the torpedo console spoke over his shoulder.

"Numbers One and Four disarmed, Capitan."

"Very well." El Viejo smiled. "Match bearings and stand by tubes One and Four."

"He's not breaking off, Sir."

"Thanks." Captain Milhaus rubbed the knot on his forehead. He stepped toward the navigator's table. He looked down at the Mona Passage chart.

"One mile from the coast, Sir. Bottom will come up fast to 250 feet. Another half mile closer and we're in the shoals with 40 feet by sounding."

"Sonar, range?"

"Wish I could ping him, Sir. But we'd only get bottom bounce in here. I retracted all but twenty feet of the towed array when we surfaced. Best estimate against the outside noise would still be about 1,000 yards astern."

"Thank you, sonar. Keep your ears on. His shutters are still open."

"Aye, Sir."

The CO turned back to the navigator.

"If he wants to play chicken, so be it. Lead him 500 yards closer to shore."

The navigator tapped the chart with his fingers.

"Captain, we'll have 100 feet under the keel."

"And we'll only be making 5 knots in there. Ride it out, Mister."

"Aye, Sir. Five hundred yards closer."

The captain stepped toward his XO.

"Electricals, Pappy?"

"Executing emergency power-down throughout, Sir. The Principal Investigator wants to know about the labs?"

The CO frowned.

"Sanitize them, Pappy. Immediately."

"Aye, Sir."

Lt. Commander Perlmutter picked up the telephone and buzzed BL-4 two decks below.

"This is the exec. On captain's orders, sanitize all biologicals." Pappy Perlmutter glanced toward Captain Milhaus. The captain waved his hand. "The CO cannot pick up the horn. Please carry out the captain's orders."

* * *

"What the hell's he doing?" Captain Webster said to the sitting radar technician in CIC. On the repeater screen, two white blips against the glowing green background inched closer to the Isla de Mona coast.

"Maybe going to beach her, Sir?"

"Never. That's a nuclear boat. He'd scuttle her first in deep water. Break the containment vessel on the rocks and all of Puerto Rico would fry from radiation contamination on these westerly winds."

"Then I haven't a clue, Captain."

Robert Webster straightened. The deck pitched under his feet as DD-997 approached the southeast corner of the island ten miles behind *El Tiburon*.

"Captain Milhaus is either a damned fool or a genius." The CO wiped his wet forehead with the back of his hand. The bulkhead clock read 0545 local time.

"How can we help, Captain?"

The CO turned to see the two physicians swaying with the deck. The ride was smoother every minute as the vessel skirted the coastline of the island speck which blocked the waves careening down the passage.

"Everything seems to be under control, Stan. Randy Morrow is dead—shot by a sentry in main condenser. The chief master-at-arms was killed by Morrow. Both bodies are in the cooler by now. DCC is working on a damaged feedwater pipe. Engineering confirms no radiation leaks yet. The reactor tripped automatically and we scrammed. It's off-line now and cooling down. Couldn't get a battle short so we're running on emergency batteries. Surfaced just in case we need to punch out. I also ordered all labs sanitized immediately."

In all three decks of the old missile bay, chlorine gas was being pumped into all cabinets and glass bubbles where viruses were stored. All inoculated mosquitos and all of the monkeys infected with dengue or LaCrosse were being gassed in a mass execution.

"What about the Cubans, Sir?" Jessica Dugan was pensive.

"In our wake for the moment. A thousand yards astern. I'm leading him into shallow water."

A faint rumble suddenly vibrated through the deck. The weak sensation felt in the crew's feet was a steady pulse beating once every two seconds.

"Squat, Lieutenant?" The CO spoke past the physicians toward the navigator.

"Yes, Captain. Three degrees and increasing slowly."

"Good." The captain looked at his exec. "Deploy the secondary propulsion motor. Bend on turns sufficient to maintain 5 knots. Stand by for diverting all available electrical power to the thrust block."

"Yes, Captain."

A strange expression deepened the lines around Lt. Commander Perlmutter's eyes for an instant. Then his whole face relaxed. He was reading his captain's mind. He understood.

"Surface screw deployed, Sir."

Sam Houston lurched very slightly as a steel door opened in the bottom of the empty aft main ballast tank. An electric motor on a long shaft with a single propeller descended into the sea from the open tank under the rear engine compartment.

"Very well, Pappy."

"Sonar, sounding now?"

"One hundred fifty feet, Sir."

"Good."

Jessica Dugan's blind terror when the reactor shut down had been nursed in the arms of the GMO. She had calmed further when the ride on the surface had become slightly smoother when 609 turned the corner to the backside of the island sheltered from the hurricane. The storm was moving in the opposite direction across Mona Passage. But the strange drumming in the deck which gently struck her soft-soled heels frightened her again. She felt her heart pounding in time with the throbbing in the deck. No sound came through the hull into the stuffy compartment. But a steady and measured bump-bump-bump vibrated against her feet like riding slowly over an old highway where tar seams crossed the pavement at regular intervals.

The exhausted woman looked into the XO's worn-out face. She imagined that she could feel the ship dipping slightly toward the stern as it heaved and settled with each passing wave generated by the storm.

"That's shallow water effect, Doctor Dugan. In shallow areas, the rate of stern squat increases. The faster a ship moves, the deeper the stern rides in the water. It's worse as the water gets shallower. And as the prop gets closer to the sea bottom, a standing-wave type of vibration reverberates back to the boat. That's the thumping you feel right now."

"Isn't that dangerous?" Dr. Dugan whispered. She did not wish to alarm anyone or to sound as terrified as she really was.

Before the XO could respond, his captain answered for him.

"We're counting on that, Doctor."

"Mind your helm and follow him in," Captain Barcena said firmly.

"We're almost 1,200 meters from shore, Capitan." The sailor's voice rose in pitch. "The Yanqui boat is 1,000 meters dead ahead and the destroyer is closing to 11,000 meters astern."

"Keep on him."

El Tiburon still pitched in rough seas, but not as badly as in the open passage. A different motion was now upsetting the submarine. Although the storm-driven ocean was slamming into her from astern, her bow began to take a pounding from ahead. A new series of waves was exploding over the ship's boxy nose.

As shallow water drove *Sam Houston*'s stern deeper, she generated a new stern wave almost ten feet high perpendicular to her white wake. The transverse wave always generated outward from a vessel's back end was higher than normal in the shallows. The Cuban boat took the lead ship's stern wave head-on. Her ride was suddenly miserable. The following sea pushed her stern down seconds before 609's high stern wave pushed the Cuban's bow downward. The men in *El Tiburon* felt like they rode a fast seesaw. The effect was nauseating.

Even Captain Barcena had to swallow hard and his palms were becoming cold and damp.

"Fire control, stand by tubes One and Four."

"Fire control, aye."

"One hundred feet under the keel, Captain!" the sweating sonar man shouted.

"Stay cool," Kurt Milhaus said gently. The CO turned toward the navigator who stood beside the quartermaster.

Doctors Shaffer and Dugan stood off to the side out of the way. The woman appeared to lean against the GMO where his arm was raised to grab a vertical stanchion for balance in the pitching control room.

"Position, QM?" the CO asked softly.

"Twelve hundred yards off the point, Captain."

The quartermaster looked down at his chart of the Isla de Mona. His index finger rested on the miniscule hamlet called Punta Caigo o'no Caigo on the south central coastline.

For an instant, the deep lines of sleepless strain evaporated from the captain's stubbled face. His middle-aged eyes glowed with a young warrior's terrible passion.

"Commander Perlmutter, divert all power to main propulsion and the secondary propulsion motor."

The XO raised his voice when he called the maneuvering room by CIC telephone. In two seconds, the red lights in the control room dimmed slightly.

When Captain Milhaus felt his ship accelerate slowly toward shore straight ahead, he called firmly to the seamen sitting tensely in CIC's forward space.

"Planesman, drive her down by the stern and don't let her broach. Helm, come left to one-eight-zero. Full deflection on the SPM and I want the rudder thrown to the stops."

"Left full rudder, aye Captain!"

"Capitan! The Yanqui boat is changing course." The radar man squinted at his screen. "He's turning south, Sir. Estimating 15 knots. Tight turn radius. Very tight."

The teenager looked up to search his captain's face.

"Left full rudder! Emergency reverse, port screw! Flank bell ahead starboard screw!"

El Tiburon's bow rose high on a stern wave generated by *Sam Houston* 1,000 yards ahead. The Cuban ship rode up the wave just as her left propeller reversed and began pulling the ship hard to the left. Her right propeller pushing full speed forward turned the submarine sharply to the left and she heeled over hard to port. Sea water poured from her two open torpedo tubes when the bow rose high out of the water in gathering daylight at 6:00 local time.

Captain Barcena pounded his clenched fist into his open palm as his vessel rolled heavily to the side in her tight turn.

"It was all a fake, Emillio," El Viejo sighed to his OOD. "He must have been faking his propulsion malfunction for two days to lure us in between him and the destroyer." Martinez Barcena frowned. "Maybe I am getting too old for this, my friend."

The young officer said nothing.

"Helm?"

"Coming about to one-eight-zero, Capitan. Yanqui submarine now making 15 knots."

El Tiburon had closed to within half a mile of the shore. Her tactical turn radius had carried her well forward even though she was turning hard to port away from Mona Island. Her propellers running at full speed—in opposite directions to crank her around quickly—generated powerful vibrations off the bottom only 40 feet under her keel. The shallow water made her stern sink low in the pounding surf, submerging her pointed stern completely. But another force peculiar to near-shore operations was upsetting her rapid turn from west to south.

Any ship is at added risk close to land, especially within narrow channels with land on both sides. Water between the closer shore and the ship travels faster than on the ship's other side. This causes bank suction which keeps sucking a vessel closer to the near shore.

El Tiburon's turn radius and the effect of bank suction pulled the ship toward Mona Island's rocky coast even though the Cuban boat was steering away from the island. The drumming of her three propellers hardly twenty feet above the bottom increased rapidly. A dull pounding vibrated through the ship, growing faster and louder with each second.

"Ahead full!" Captain Barcena shouted to be heard above the rumble of his propellers. "Rudder amidships!"

With three screws turning at full speed, she was still drawn inland.

"Ahead full!"

The deck vibrated until the crew's teeth hurt. They could not hear rivets popping in the 30-year-old hull plates and the tearing of weld seams.

Foxtrot class submarines are built no better than Russian

nuclear subs. Many have been lost to reactor accidents, inexperienced crews, and poor workmanship. At least six Soviet nuclear-powered submarines have gone to the bottom. One submarine designated K-429 sank *twice*. The last Soviet nuclear submarine to go down was *Komsomolets*, lost in April 1989 with 42 hands.

El Tiburon struggled in rough water to pull away from the island. She moved slowly southward with her stern riding deeper and deeper. The bottom fell gradually away to a depth of 100 feet. But not quickly enough.

The pounding of the vibrations from the three propellers reverberating off the rocky bottom shuddered through the submarine. Her iron seams ruptured in the engine room behind the control room.

A wall of black water burst into the compartment. The fissure in the hull opened wider under the pressure.

Cuban teenagers screamed in the darkness when the lights shorted out. In five seconds, the water swirled up from their knees to their waists and to their necks. Within ten seconds, five boys were inhaling salt water and diesel oil.

El Tiburon sank quickly by the stern. Her three propellers scraped bottom and her bow jutted upward in full morning light under a wet, gray sky.

Captain Barcena stared wide-eyed toward the stern. He nearly fell over as his ship pitched steeply downward. Water spurted around the seals of the control room's aft watertight door. The deck shuddered as the current dragged the stern planes across the sea bottom. The violent vibration ruptured the welds in the control room hull and spouts of black water erupted behind equipment consoles. Steam percolated where water pounded an electrical box.

"Fire tubes One and Four!" Martinez Barcena shouted the instant the lights went out. "Fire!" he gurgled as a narrow gush of water like a firehose struck him in the side of the face and drove him to the deck. El Viejo fell into a swirling pool of water a foot deep. He closed his eyes to dream of his Amalia and of the warm sweet wind of the Revolution blowing through the nutmeg trees. Behind the sailor's eyes, Amalia's black hair smelled like fish and lube oil.

Two 533-millimeter torpedoes popped out of *El Tiburon*'s bow with the screeching sound of dry metal scraping dry metal. Compressed air ejected the M-57 torpedoes into the air fifteen feet above the surface where the black bow pointed toward the low sky. Both fish struck the sea with a crash of white water just as *El Tiburon*'s bow slid forward, down, and out of sight 1,500 yards south of Mona Island.

The torpedoes sped southward when their engines ignited. Rolling white foam and steam bubbled wildly behind them where the rocky bottom shredded the hull of *El Tiburon*.

Sam Houston made good her turn toward the south and open water. She had but one propeller to generate enough forward way to bite into her twin vertical rudders. But the secondary propulsion motor in her stern swivelled until its single propeller added sideways thrust for the sharp turn away from the shoals.

Normally, the SPM is used only in port to ease single-screw submarines into tight berths. No ship with only one propeller can twist in her own wake like a twin-screwed vessel can do with one prop pushing while the other pulls in the opposite direction. The SPM adds the extra thrust for sharp turns in harbor. SSN-609 also executed her turn to the left with the help of the normal leftward pull of the bow generated by a single propeller's asymmetrical thrust. (Single-propeller airplanes also prefer turning left.)

"Jesus!" the young sonar man shouted above the continuing throb of the propeller's vibrations bouncing up from the sea bed 150 feet below 609. "She's breaking up! I hear bulkheads caving in even above the storm racket out there."

"Easy, son," Kurt Milhaus said as he pressed the petty officer's shoulder. "Are you sure?"

"Absolutely, Captain. I heard the tapes of *Thresher* breaking up when I was in training."

Since *Thresher* was making a test dive when she was lost, a Navy ship was on station nearby. Its hydrophones recorded the crackle of ripping steel and the screams of 129 sailors and civilian engineers when the sea poured in.

The captain's tense face darkened. He had wanted *El Tiburon* to run aground if her skipper was foolish enough, brash enough, or inexperienced enough to follow 609 into shallow water. But

suddenly, the CO was stricken by the thought of his father's
U-boat collapsing off the coast of Maine half a century earlier.
He visibly shuddered a mile south of where Cuban seamen
were holding their breath until they could hold it no longer.

Before Captain Milhaus could speak, the sonar man pressed
his earphones tightly against his cheeks. He nearly rolled out
of his chair on the pitching deck when he spun around.

"High-speed screws dead astern! Range 900 yards!"

Kurt Milhaus asked no questions before he called across
CIC's red gloom.

"Launch nixies! Fathometer?"

"Two hundred fifty feet, Sir!"

"Can you give me steam, Pappy?"

"Negative, Captain." The XO glanced for a single blink
toward Jessica Dugan huddled close to the GMO. "Negative."

"Nixies away, Captain," the telephone talker shouted from
his position near the seated diving officer of the watch.

The nixie decoys ejected from the torpedo room would
generate noise characteristic of submarines. Russian acoustic
torpedoes designed to home in on sub noise could be fooled
into going after the nixies instead of their mother ship.

"Six hundred yards, Captain." The sonar man closed his
eyes to listen to his hydrophones. "I can't tell if the decoys
might have hit bottom. Depth under the keel now 300 feet."

Sam Houston still plowed through the rough surface. Not
quite one mile south of Mona Island, she made 15 knots under
emergency battery power—three times faster than the book
recommended. CIC was humid and stuffy as all available
electricity was diverted from ventilators to the engine room.

The shelf south of Mona Island drops off quickly at the
mouth of Mona Passage. The tiny island is nothing more than
a steep mountain top barely rising out of the Caribbean. Half
a mile from the southern coast, the sea is only 90 feet deep.
One mile out, the sea bottom is a plateau 900 feet deep. There,
the bottom plunges over the shelf. Two miles out, the water is
half a mile deep.

"Five hundred yards and closing, Captain!"

"Sound collision alarm!"

A painfully loud klaxon screeched through three decks of
SSN-609. Although the watertight hatches had been securely

dogged since the general quarters alarm was sounded, 55 seamen, biologists, and one woman breathed hard and grabbed on to whatever ship fittings they could reach: stanchions, ladders, consoles, and chairs bolted to the deck.

"Bottom 800 feet! High-speed screws 300 yards!"

"Fire second round of nixies!"

"Aye, Sir!" the weapons officer called across CIC. Four more canisters were propelled by compressed gas into the wild sea. The ship climbed a wave crest as the nixies were launched. Two of them shot into the air and fell back into the water as the submarine's round bow crashed into the wave crest and the ship slid down the back side into the trough. *Sam Houston* skidded sideways down in the valley of black water as the boiling sea tried to jerk her around parallel to the waves.

"Mind your helm!" Pappy Perlmutter commanded. The petty officer sitting his trick at the control wheel was working too hard to respond.

SSN-609 rolled back to her southward heading 1,900 yards from shore. She pitched gracelessly as she crossed over the outer shelf of the coast.

"Screws two hundred yards! Fifteen hundred feet under the keel!"

Captain Milhaus steadied himself with one hand tightly gripping each shoulder of the sonar technician. He shouted over the collision alarm.

"Crash dive! Drive her to one thousand feet!"

"Crash dive, aye!" the diving officer called breathlessly. If the M-57 torpedoes were chasing 609's noise, deep water would squelch the telltale signature. Making turns for only 15 knots, the propeller would not make a cavitation hiss and flow noise would be minimal at half the ship's normal sprinting speed.

The deck dipped down by the bow. A distant roar of air exploding out of the ballast tank vent holes rumbled through CIC. Everyone lurched sideways when a wave slammed hard into the sail which was slipping deeper into the green water.

"Screws one hundred fifty yards! . . . Wait one . . . One fish is veering to starboard, Sir. She's hell-bent to the west, Captain! God bless the nixies!"

The teenager felt the painful grip of his captain tighten upon his shoulders.

"One screw closing at 100 yards! Two thousand under the keel!"

Pappy Perlmutter squeezed a steel pipe running alongside the twin periscopes still housed deep in the floor. The GMO blinked at the executive officer's hand around the tube; his fingernails oozed a fine line of blood.

When the sea closed over the suction hole in the surface which swirled where the sail had vanished, the deck stopped swaying. Quickly, the ride became smooth although the emergency 30-degree deck angle was almost too steep to keep one's footing. Stanley Shaffer leaned back against a navigation console and lowered both of his arms around Jessica Dugan. He looked down into her face which dripped with sweat running off her forehead and upper lip. The GMO was stunned by her expression.

Although the woman wrapped her arms around the lieutenant's waist when his arms fell to her shoulders, her face was perfectly calm. A terrifying peace glowed in her elegant eyes, the left one still purple.

Jessica Dugan smiled. She was thinking of her grandfather waiting at the bottom of the deep blue sea. With instantaneous clarity, she understood that it was not drowning she feared but the grinding uncertainty of not knowing when. Now, she knew. She laid her soaking wet face upon the GMO's panting chest.

The sonar man closed his eyes. Men back in the engine room heard the torpedo whining in from astern even above the sound of the collision alarm and the hum of the electric motor.

TWENTY-TWO

16 MARCH; 1005 UTC

"THE CUBANS definitely broke up, Captain. And 609 is diving through 800 feet steering one-eight-zero at 15 knots. Sounds like a crash dive. I still hear one fish. It's just too close to 609's wake noise for me to resolve the separation now."

"All right." Captain Webster spoke calmly in CIC's red glow. The situation had passed out of his control within three minutes. With *Hayler* standing five miles off the coast of Mona Island, there was nothing he could do but breathe hard down the moist neck of his sonar man and keep an even strain.

"Helm, close to one mile of 609's MPP. I don't want to risk taking blast under our keel."

"Aye, Sir. Steering two-one-zero."

"Very well."

DD-997 still rode hard in ten-foot waves. But there was now no risk of rolling dangerously on the leeward side of the island. The hurricane churned Mona Passage behind the destroyer, but the weather cell was rolling eastward at 40 knots. No breaks in the thick sky were visible yet, but full daylight illuminated the rough green ocean at 6:05 local time.

The sonar man squinted at the electronic gibberish on his video monitor and he pressed his earphones tight to his cheek.

"Lucky sonsabitches!" the petty officer shouted.

"Say again?"

"Sorry, Captain. I can't believe it. That second torpedo just bounced right off him! No detonation. Old *Sam Houston*'s skipper must just live right. Should be blowing his tanks and coming up any minute."

Captain Webster drew his palm across his forehead. He patted the sonar man's shoulder as if the young seaman had something to do with 609's escape.

"Helm, bring us in closer. Maintain 500 yards."

"Aye, Sir. Five hundred yards, maintaining course and speed."

"And comm, get a dispatch off to DCNO. 'Cuban submarine lost. Six-oh-nine safe with rendezvous imminent. Will proceed best speed Roosevelt Roads after search for Cuban survivors.' Send it coded."

"Comm, aye."

The CO looked around CIC. The deck was stable as the storm moved eastward.

"I'll be on the bridge I want to salute those people myself when 609 comes up."

All hands in *Sam Houston* heard the muted thud when the ten-foot long missile, 21 inches in diameter, struck the stern a foot past the propeller. Fifty-five hearts skipped a beat waiting for 900 pounds of warhead explosive to detonate. But all they heard was the high-pitched whine of the torpedo's engine as the fish bounced off, grazed 609's tail, and continued on at 40 knots. The Mark-57 weapon carried eleven nautical miles worth of fuel.

The entire watch in CIC exhaled together. A dozen seamen in the engine room erupted into nervous laughter where the clunk of the dud torpedo was the loudest.

"Damage control," Kurt Milhaus said with a dry mouth, "look sharp now. That fish can still blow."

"Aye, Sir."

"Pappy, level off, trim, and blow tanks." The CO released his death grip on the sonar man's painful shoulders. "*Hayler* will be waiting for us. I want to evaluate the reactor and steam generator as soon as possible. Let's try to make Puerto Rico under our own power instead of under tow."

"Yes, Captain. Planesman, level off. Diving officer, prepare to surface."

The fathometer wound down through 850 feet.

The sweating petty officer at the control wheel for the stern planes pulled back on the yoke.

The yoke did not budge.

The diving officer sitting behind the planesman and helmsman leaned forward. The junior grade lieutenant reached forward and touched the planesman's denim shoulder.

"Let's get some up bubble in there."

"She's jammed, Sir! She's jammed!"

The diving officer shouted over his shoulder toward the back of CIC.

"Planes are jammed, Captain!"

The submarine's small control surfaces were locked in the nosedown attitude of the crash dive. The wake-homing torpedo from *El Tiburon* had done its job posthumously.

Kurt Milhaus turned abruptly to the telephone talker.

"Maneuvering, emergency reverse! Blow mains! Blow trim! Emergency surface!"

The seaman shouted into the phone and repeated the engine orders while the diving officer began pumping air into the fore, aft, and trim ballast tanks.

The submarine continued down through one thousand feet as the huge single shaft ground to a stop and then spun up in the opposite direction.

"Eleven hundred feet," the diving officer called, although all eyes watched the depth gauge on the bulkhead.

Sam Houston shuddered as her descent passed through the sinking layer of cold rain water. The turbulence of the temperature change was brief.

"Twelve hundred feet."

Although high-pressure air rushed with explosive force into the three-story-tall ballast tanks, it had to work against the sea and its crushing 36 atmospheres of pressure. Ballast water in the fore and aft main tanks was forced out by the air blast slowly.

The crash dive was slowing as the propeller turned in reverse and the ballast tanks replaced water. with compressed air. But without the reactor to generate maximum revolutions, the emergency batteries could only spin the prop at twenty percent of maximum effort.

"Thirteen hundred feet."

In the shadows of a rounded corner of the control room, Jessica Dugan still held the GMO's waist and his arms lay heavily upon her shoulders. She raised her wet face and her hair touched his nose. Her words were so faint that the lieutenant could not hear them over the roar of air rushing into the tanks.

"Thank you for being kind to me."

At 1,400 feet two and a half miles south of Mona Island, the stuffing box failed which keeps the propeller shaft watertight. Streams of sea water no thicker than a pencil burst around the steel casing where the shaft leaves the hull. Water rushed into the engine room under 42 atmospheres of pressure: 14 times stronger than a fire hose.

One airborne riverlet struck a seaman squarely in the chest. It pierced his body and eviscerated his lungs like the high-speed water drills used in industry to slice steel.

At 1,500 feet, the glands sealing the main condenser inlet and outlet pipes fractured together. The thick jet of water which entered the compartment under 45 atmospheres of pressure crashed through the deck and quickly flooded an auxiliary machinery compartment.

By 1,800 feet and 54 atmospheres of pressure, the cold water squeezed SSN-609 with 58 tons of pressure on each square foot of HY-80 steel.

At 2,000 feet, Jessica Dugan's eardrums imploded into her skull as *Sam Houston*'s watertight bulkheads collapsed like a row of dominoes.

Hayler's hydrophones heard *Sam Houston* flooding half an hour before the shiny puddle of lube and diesel oil gelled on the surface. The sonar man whose eyes were wide and whose mouth hung open had to remove his headphones. He had heard the muted grinding of twisted metal as 8,000 tons of steel slammed into the sandy bottom under 3,000 feet of black water. The wreckage plummetted down across a square mile of silt as the submarine broke apart with each collapsing compartment.

The thick oil slick was first visible half a mile from DD-997 as a strangely tranquil area of gray ocean surrounded by rough sea. The wind still blew across the whitecaps at 40 knots. The heavy layer of oil subdued the waves for an hour until the weakening storm dissolved the slick. Slowly, the ocean made itself clean.

The southerly current ripping down Mona Passage whipped around Mona Island. It carried the flotsam which had surfaced from *El Tiburon* out to sea. Thick pools of diesel oil dirtied clumps of insulation and shreds of bedding. The prevailing March current in the Caribbean would carry the debris westward to wash up along the southern coast of the Dominican Republic in seven days.

Only six sailors, enlisted men all, managed to climb through *El Tiburon*'s escape trunk in the forward torpedo room. *Hayler* had to wait three hours for the storm to subside enough to put a motor launch into the water to pick them up at 0930 in the morning, local time. Four teenagers were still alive although they would suffer diesel oil diarrhea for two days from swallowing salt water while they waited and prayed.

When *Hayler*'s sonar analysis computer identified the acoustic signature of six bulkheads crumbling, no search for SSN-609 survivors was necessary.

Radio contact had been established between DD-997 and the Cuban frigate *April 17*. She would arrive south of Mona Island by 5:30 in the evening, local time. Enough daylight would remain for her to take custody of the last of Captain Barcena's crew.

Captain Webster waited for local noon when the forenoon watch was relieved by the afternoon watch. Six hours after 609 had vanished, her oil slick was gone. The storm had moved on to pummel Puerto Rico.

At precisely 1200 Atlantic Standard Time, March 16th, Robert Webster stood on *Hayler*'s quarterdeck. He wore a down jacket over his khaki uniform. His face was haggard.

Hayler's decks were still wet from the last of the rain. The low sky was gray with a few blue holes. A Caribbean sun fired blinding shafts of light down through the breaks in the clouds. The destroyer made turns for 5 knots as she approached the last resting place of the United States Ship *Sam Houston*.

Four Cuban boys stood near the rail. They were dressed in U.S. Navy denim with heavy blankets wrapped around their thin shoulders. The starboard side of *Hayler* was lined with seamen manning the rail to render passing honors.

Captain Webster nodded once to the boatswain's mate of the watch. The BMOW flipped a switch on the public address system and blew his shrill boatswain's pipe into the microphone. The ship's whistle blew one blast to signal "Attention to starboard!" Sailors came to attention on slippery decks. Then another short whistle wailed across the swells.

The men of *Hayler* saluted the empty green water.

They held the hand salute until three short whistles signaled Carry On.